WOLF MOON

HUNTERS OF THE FOREST, BOOK THREE

M.P. STARKWEATHER

PHOENIX ECLIPSE PUBLISHING

CONTENTS

I want to dedicate this book to my two biggest fans, my husband Josh and my son Thom, who will probably never read any of my books. Thanks for pushing me to chase my dream. I love you both to the moon and back.

ACKNOWLEDGMENTS

I would like to thank:

My Alpha and Beta Teams who try hard to keep me on track;

My Editing Team who does their best to make sure my books make sense and have as few typos as possible;

My Cover Artist, Lara at Wynter Designs, who's responsible for the gorgeous images on the front of this book

and My ARC Team, who catch some of the things the rest of us miss.

One

A Strange New Place

JAMES

My heart skips a beat the moment I see Garnet materialize out of nowhere. I'm both overjoyed and dismayed to see her.

Trevan claims that he's on our side, but if he has taken Garnet away from finding a way to save me, how can I believe him?

"So, where is this Fae friend of ours? I need to talk to him. He has to send me back so I can help Grammy with the potion," Garnet insists.

"Trevan?" I call, hoping that he shows up. "I don't know where he went. He was here, then suddenly, he disappeared, and you were in his place."

I step forward, not knowing if I'm corporeal enough to touch the woman I love or not. She hesitates, then falls into my arms. I hold her to me, breathing a sigh of relief that I can feel her.

This realm is vastly different than anything I've ever seen before. I don't know how to process the strangeness of it all. I'd barely begun to look around when my host vanished and my love took his place. The purple trees are disturbingly beautiful, as is the pale pink water that flows near us. Green and orange blooms cover the forest floor, and there's a faint blue haze in the air.

"His name is Trevan?" she asks, and it sounds as if she's contemplating something.

"That is what he told me. I don't know enough about him to know if he's trustworthy or not. Of course, Luca swears that you and he used to come here as kids. I can tell that he trusts this Fae man completely. Is that enough for us?" I counter.

"It's going to have to be. Otherwise, I may never get home, and you might not be saved. And I can't live with that. I'm sure the others are freaking out that I disappeared." Garnet pulls away from me and starts pacing. "Trevan! Show yourself!" she shouts.

A burst of yellow, blue, and green sparkles appears and turns into the man who saved me. "I am here, child. There is no need to raise your voice and make everyone in the realm aware of what I've done...unless you're trying to get me killed?" Trevan's voice is like honey, thick and sweet.

Garnet stares at him. It's as if she recognizes the man and has never seen him before, both at the same time. I don't know how to explain it. "Wait, I know you. How? There's no way I should feel as if I know you." He winces at her words, as if they sting him.

"I'm sure I don't know what you mean. Your little friend used to come here with you to play. That is how you know me, child. Now, if you're quite finished yelling, we can discuss why I've brought you here."

"Why did you bring her here?" I interject, not giving my girl a chance to verbally attack him again.

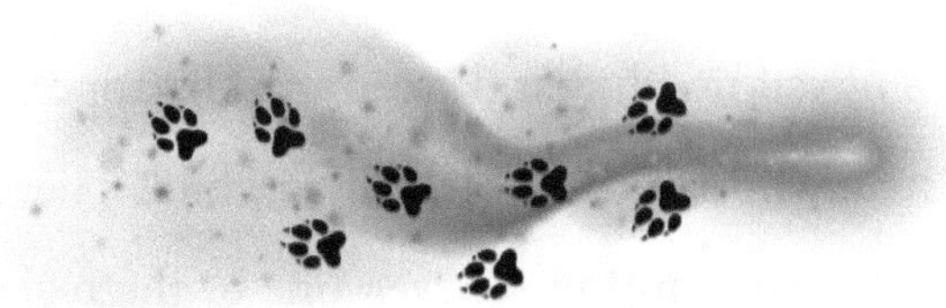

LUCA

The moment Orym comes back with the red honeysuckle and not Red herself, I start to panic. "Where is she?" I ask him, grabbing his shoulders and giving him a shake.

"I don't know. She was right behind me, then it was almost like she disappeared. I looked for her for a couple of minutes, but I knew that she would never forgive me if I didn't get this back here for Grammy to finish the brew," Orym reasoned. While I understand what he's saying, I don't necessarily agree.

"We need to go look for her. What if she's in danger?" I insist. When Orym doesn't respond, I turn to Ryland. "What aren't you telling me?"

"Feel for the bond, Luca. She's not here. Or if she is, she's being hidden by magic. It's the only reason we wouldn't be able to locate her with the bond," Ryland explains patiently, as if I'm a child who doesn't understand.

"So, either Amber has her, or she's been taken to another realm?" I ask for confirmation. I feel stupid, and hate it, but I haven't had the bond as long as the others have, and just don't understand how it works.

"That's what we're thinking," Orym finally says. I'm frustrated and annoyed, but I understand now why they aren't rushing out to search for Red. Either option means we won't be able to find her without help.

"Amber is locked up and being watched by the council, though. So, she can't be the one who has Red. Ugh. What can we do?" Panic still seizes my heart. I just completed the bond with her, I can't give up on finding her now. I waited so long to claim her as my own. I have to find her.

Ryland grabs my arm and steers me toward the chair at James' feet and gestures for me to sit. "First, we take care of James. Then we figure out exactly who has Red. Once those two things are done, we can move forward with our search." Before he can say more, his phone rings. Since he's the territory alpha, he has to answer, no matter what.

We all stare as he takes the call without leaving the room. "Are you sure?" he asks, growling. "Okay, get a team together and go see if you can figure out how. Keep me updated." He pauses, then snaps, "No. Do not go after her. She's too much of a risk to us all. Figure out how she escaped and who helped her. We'll meet and plan an attack once you have that information for me."

The moment he hangs up the phone my heart sinks. "Amber escaped. I'm sure you all figured that out from my conversation. I've sent a team to investigate. We'll have to go after her as soon as James is stable. I'll leave a protection team with you, Grammy."

She doesn't say anything in response but looks worried as she stirs the potion that's supposed to save James' life.

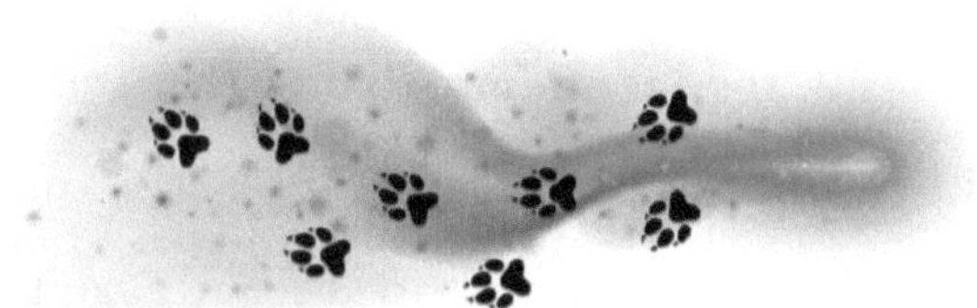

GARNET

I wait, not so patiently, for the Fae man who claims to be our friend to explain why he ripped me from my own reality to bring me here. My body shakes with rage, and I'm barely keeping my magic at bay. I know from what my guys told me that this man is probably my father, but I'm desperate for him to admit it. I just don't know how to ask yet.

"Look, I know you're pissed, child, and I understand. But this was the only way," he says.

"The only way for what?" James asks, trying to keep me from tearing this man's head off. It's working, but barely.

"This place is safe. You can learn to control your magic here without hurting anyone or being noticed by Amber. She can't see you here," Trevan explains.

"If you want me to trust you, I'm going to need some answers," I insist, snarling at him. I know that I shouldn't trust him, but part of me already does. It's as if I know him and am certain that he wouldn't hurt us. But I can't know that. Because I don't know him. I might have spent some time here as a child, but that doesn't mean I know this man, this Fae, who claims to be helping.

"I will tell you what I can," he answers carefully. "Please know that while I cannot lie to you, there are some questions I cannot answer. It's for your own safety, and that of your mates."

"Fine, whatever. Let's start with the obvious. Who the fuck are you?" I'm glad that Grammy isn't here to slap me in the back of the head for being rude. I don't care at this point. I want answers, then I want to go home and save James.

"I am Trevan Graypond, and I am the King of the Fae in this forest," he answers simply.

"Well, *Your Majesty*, what exactly is your interest in me?" His eyes go wide at my second question, and I can tell that he doesn't want to answer it. *Just admit that you're my father and we can move forward.*

"I only desire to help you, and see you succeed." The response is not the complete truth, and I know it. He's hiding something from me.

"That was a very non-specific answer. Why should I trust you?" I push further.

I watch as he fights against answering the question. It's as if the words want to come out, but he's trying to hold them inside. "I can't answer that. You shouldn't ask things like that. Those questions are dangerous." The words rush from him, and I feel like he's forced himself to speak them instead of the answer he wants to give.

I stare at him, taking in his appearance for the first time. His hair is the same red as mine, but his skin is pale and shimmers a little. His clothing is bright, covered in so many colors that it's hard to focus on any single one. If he wore different clothes, he might look normal. I get the impression that he wouldn't care for that thought, so I keep it to myself.

"It's dangerous to ask why I should trust you? That seems odd," I respond, watching his face closely. I want to dislike him, but somehow, I can't.

"I cannot lie to you, but there are some things I should not tell you. Please understand, I have good reasons for the things I do. My goal is to protect you. My desire is to see you happy. Beyond that, I cannot explain. As for trust, I believe that should be earned," he states plainly.

I continue to stare at him, trying to decipher the hidden meaning to his words. There's more to this man than meets the eye, but I can't quite figure him out. "And how do you plan to protect me and see me happy?" I can't help asking, even if he won't answer.

"I'm going to teach you how to use your Fae magic, child."

"How do you know about that?" I don't even mean to ask, but the question is out before I can stop myself.

He smiles and my heart warms. I can't understand the connection I have to this man. Maybe it's just because he's Fae and I'm half. I don't know. But something inside of me is pulling me to him. I know he's not another mate, but there is a connection.

"Oh, child. Fae can sense each other. Of course, I know your family, so I am aware of your powers." His expression changes the moment the words leave his lips. He's given me something that he didn't intend to.

"You know my family? You knew my mother? And my father is alive? Please, you have to tell me about them." I grab his arms and hold him still when he tries to flee. I will force the truth from him if I have to.

Trevan shakes his head. "I can't. You don't understand. It's not safe to have this conversation here."

"Then where is it safe? Because she deserves to know whatever you know," James says, reminding me that he's been here with me this whole time. The idea that we aren't safe is enough for me to table this conversation until later.

"There isn't a safe place here for that. I promise I will tell you what I can, but not right now. We need to move, before the guards arrive. Come to the palace with me, and I'll teach you how to use your magic."

"What about James?" I ask. I need to figure out how to heal his body and get him back into it.

"I can keep him safe in the palace until his body is healed. Please, we must go," Trevan urges. I exchange a look with James, and he nods.

"Let's go," I agree, taking James' hand and following our Fae captor. I know that it's not his intent, but Trevan is holding us against our will, which makes him our captor. It doesn't matter if he's doing it for benevolent reasons or not. Kidnapping is kidnapping.

Hopefully this time goes a little better than the last. I try to push away my worry for James and my other mates as we head to the Fae palace.

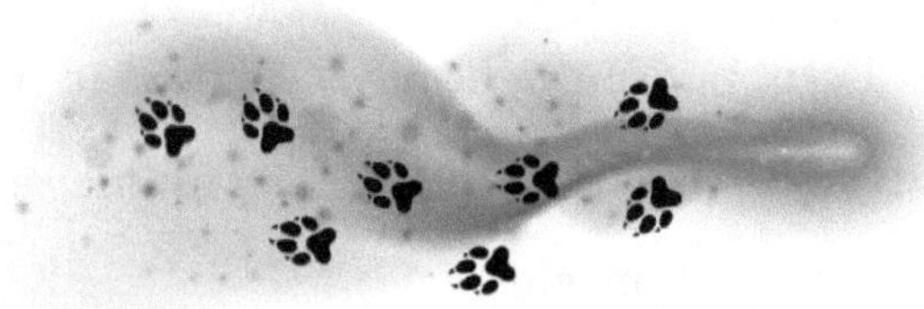

RYLAND

I don't want to leave James and Grammy, especially with Red missing. But with the call that Amber escaped, I don't have a choice. We have to find her, and hope that she isn't the one who took Red. I can't imagine what Amber has planned, but I know it's nothing good.

Once the protection team is in place, and Grammy assures us that James is as stable as possible, Orym, Luca, and I head out to meet the search teams. Just outside the door, Luca stops us.

"I have to tell you guys what Red and I realized before all of this happened. We may know what Amber has planned," he says.

"Why did you wait to tell us?" I growl. I can't believe that they didn't share their theory with us sooner.

"Because as soon as she started to say it, you made us leave to hunt Amber's people, then James got injured," he growls back. That's a good reason. I guess I should have let her finish talking before rushing them all out the door. I'll work on that.

"Well, don't keep us in suspense. What is it?" Orym asks, trying to broker peace between us.

Luca holds up his hands in defeat. "I'm not trying to fight, especially now. But something clicked and if I got the same idea that Red did, I think we've figured it out. Amber is the one who took Delilah's blood when Dec was kidnapped. She had to be. And she's been injecting supernaturals and humans with something, then getting upset when they die from it."

He pauses, and I finally understand what he's trying to tell me. "That bitch is trying to make a hybrid army," I whisper.

"Exactly. So, she's not going to stop until we stop her," he insists. I know he's right, and now there's even more urgency to find Red.

"But what does she want with Garnet?" Orym asks.

"Her power. Even if it kills her. Amber thinks that if she has Red's power, she can make the hybrid transformation work. That has to be it," I say, staring off into the woods. How can we defeat what we can't find?

"We have to find them. Maybe Amber doesn't have Garnet. But is that better or worse? We have no idea where she is or what happened to her. And with James barely hanging on, she has to be out of her mind with worry." Orym's words echo in my head.

I lead the guys to where we're meeting the search teams. Everyone is pretty organized, and they seem to be waiting for us. "We're ready to start the search, Alpha."

I don't know if I'll ever get used to being the head alpha here. It's all I ever wanted, but more responsibility than I realized. I wonder if it would have been better to take Red and leave the pack instead. But that would have left these people at Gunnar's mercy, and that's not something I could do.

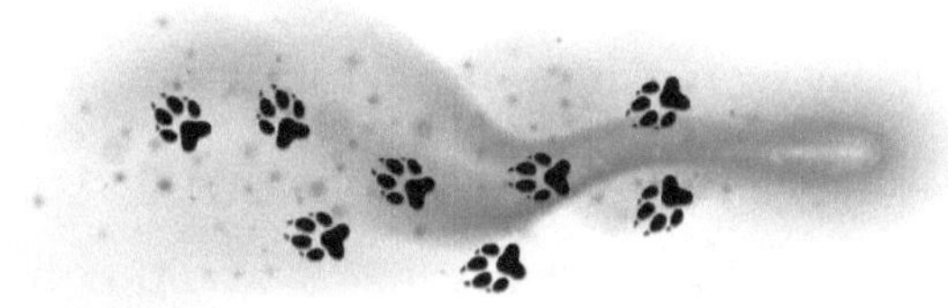

ORYM

I'm more than a little panicked that Garnet disappeared. I have no idea if Amber is involved or not, but finding out that she's escaped from where the council was holding her makes it a pretty convincing argument. I know that Garnet is worried about James, no matter where she is or who has her. She would never just abandon us, so someone must have taken her. But who? And why?

It's up to us to find out and get her back. Once we meet up with the search teams, I wait for Ryland's orders. I'm not sure if he's going to split us up or keep us together. "We should each go with a different team, since we can communicate telepathically," he decides. I nod and follow one of the teams into the woods. He and Luca can figure out which ones they'll go with. I'm too anxious to wait.

I'm not paying much attention to anything except finding Garnet. It doesn't matter which wolves are in my search team. The only thing that matters is her. I would rather start this search where she disappeared, but it's not my call to make. And I refuse to undermine Ryland's authority, even within our pack. So, I keep the thought to myself. I can always go back there later and do it myself.

Or I could sneak off now and do it. No one would know if I slipped away. I toy with the thought before making a decision that might end badly for me. With everyone else distracted, I head toward the waterfall, in the opposite direction of the search teams. I understand why Ryland thinks Amber would be on this side of the forest, but I'm not really looking for her.

I'm looking for our girl. I need to know that our mate is okay. That is the only thing I'm focused on right now. Until she's safe in my arms, I cannot search for Amber.

I work my way silently through the woods, keeping low to avoid being seen. If Ryland realizes that I've left, he can always call to me through the mate bond that we all share with Garnet. Of course, if he realizes that I'm gone, he might consider that I won't respond. That doesn't matter. I have to find her.

When I'm far enough away from the search parties, I stand straighter and pick up my pace. Desperation claws at my heart as I run to the waterfall where I last saw Garnet. I never should have let her walk behind me on the way back from gathering the red honeysuckle for James' healing potion. At the time, I had thought I was keeping her safe. Now I know it was the worst mistake I've ever made.

It doesn't matter that neither Ryland nor Luca have blamed me. I blame myself. And honestly, they should too. I have to find her and get her to safety.

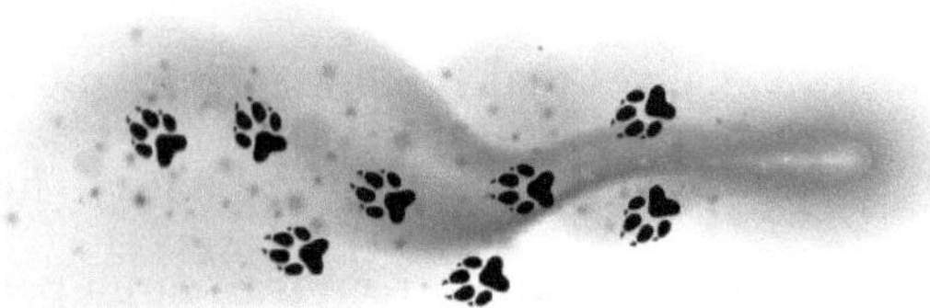

GARNET

I have no idea how long I've been in the Fae realm. Don't the stories speak of how time moves differently here? I'm certain they do. But are the stories true? I have no idea, nor do I trust my new captor to answer any of my questions.

I grip James' hand tightly as we follow Trevan through the forest. This place is like a rainbow-colored mirror version of our woods. I think I know where we're going, since I figured out how things relate to what I grew up with. We make a left turn and come to a clearing.

In the spot where Ryland's cabin sits in our reality, there's an enormous castle. It blends in with the trees, standing tall and majestic over everything. "Is this your home?" I can't stop myself from asking, though I don't expect a response.

"It is. Do you like it?" I can't see how my opinion matters, but the moment he asks, I feel compelled to tell him what I think.

"It's gorgeous. I don't understand anything in this place, but it all feels so familiar. It's like I've been here before. I know that's ridiculous, because Luca and I only played with you near the waterfall," I insist.

"The land calls to you, child. This realm is your home. The people here are your family. That's why it feels familiar." His words do little to calm the anxiety building in my chest.

Trevan leads us into a gated garden behind the castle. I'm a little surprised that there are no guards, but he seems to know that the coast is clear. I wonder how many times he's slipped away in the past.

"I need you both to be quiet. Do not speak to anyone unless I tell you that it's okay. We have to be careful getting inside. Once we are safely in the palace, you'll be able to move about freely. I just need you to trust me for now," Trevan's insistence has me agreeing without objection. I wonder if it's because he's the king and has some kind of Fae power over me.

I'll have to ask about that at some point. If I ever feel like he's actually going to answer my questions. "There are a lot of things we need to discuss, Trevan. We can go along with your request for now, but only if you promise to give us some answers."

I recoil at the harsh tone James uses with the Fae who's helping us. It's not like him to be so demanding. I'm not used to it, but it is pretty hot. My mind wanders a little and I find myself curious if we can be intimate here, since technically James' body is in another realm. I get so distracted that I miss a turn and end up running into a tree in the garden. When I turn around, Trevan and James are nowhere to be seen.

James? Where did you guys go? I call to him through our bond. My heart races and I gulp down breaths. How did I lose them? It happened so fast. Or did it? How long was I distracted? I have no idea. And James isn't answering, so I have no choice but to look for them on my own.

I wander around the garden for a little bit, looking for clues that will lead me to them. I wish I was as good at tracking as Luca. If I were a wolf like my other mates, I wouldn't be lost right now. Fuck, I miss them already. How did my life get so fucked up?

Amber. Yeah, that one is impossible to forget. It still amazes me that my own aunt is the one causing all the problems for the supernaturals. And the whole thing is just one big grab for power. I have to stop her. That has to be why the Moon Goddess blessed me with four amazing mates.

I'm distracted again, and don't see the woman following me until it's too late to hide. "Excuse me! You don't belong here. Who are you and how did you get here?" she steps toward me, and holds up a hand. I'm instantly frozen in place.

I struggle against her magic, watching the tendrils of yellow wrap around me and tighten. It takes me a moment to realize that her magic isn't as strong as mine. I shrug the yellow tendrils off and watch her eyes go wide.

"How did you do that? No one can shrug off my magic," she insists. I shrug, refusing to answer her. It was the biggest thing Trevan had asked us for. Since I'd already wrecked the rest of his request, I would at least keep that promise. The Fae woman blasts her magic at me again, but I toss up a shield and it bounces off.

Her brow furrows in concentration. As I watch her, I realize that her hair matches her magic color. That seems strange to me, since my own magic has so many hues, depending on what I'm doing with it.

Just as she lets another blast of magic go at me, I hear Trevan's voice. "Miriam! Stop now. You will not attack our guest."

The Fae woman pulls her magic back and dips her head in shame. I wait a moment, then drop the shield. "I'm sorry. I got distracted and lost." He glares at me as if he's scolding me for speaking. I shrug and drop my own head. I should be more upset about the situation than I am.

"Miriam, go inside and get the guest room prepared. I will bring our guests in," he orders. Miriam rushes away without another look at me.

"You could have killed her. What were you thinking?" he rounds on me the moment she's out of earshot.

"I didn't attack her. I wouldn't," I insist.

"But you don't even know what your magic will do yet, do you?"

TWO
TO TRUST OR NOT

LUCA

I hate the idea of splitting up, but I know that my objection will be overruled. I'm just as desperate to find Red as Ryland and Orym are. I think it's better to stick together. I'll be a good soldier and follow my alpha's instructions, though. We can have a private talk about it later, even if it won't change anything.

I'm not convinced that Amber has Red. We didn't even know that Amber had escaped when Red disappeared. I'd put my money on our Fae friend stepping in for some reason. I can't figure out why, but the important part is that Amber does not have her. We can figure the rest out. I wish I had a way to contact him.

But, like everything else lately, he's not very cooperative. The silence around me becomes oppressive, and I realize that I've lost sight of the group I headed out with. Fuck. Ryland isn't going to like this.

Ryland? Where are you? I call out through the bond, searching for hints of his location. I'm still not used to this connection and I don't really know how to work it.

Luca, are you okay? I hear his voice in my head. It still makes me jump because of how new all of this is.

I've lost my team. I don't know what happened. I wait for his response, ducking behind a tree at the next noise I hear. While I wait, I watch as a small group of witches creep past. They don't seem to see me.

I'm heading your way with my team. If they disappeared, that's a problem. Ryland's voice echoes in my head.

Wait! There's a group of witches passing by. Five of them. I'm not sure if they're responsible, but they don't see me. I strain myself to hear their hushed conversation so I can relay it to Ryland.

"There was another one. Where did he go?" one of the witches says.

"You've lost your mind, Rachel. We got them all. Let's just go home now. Amber will be happy with the six wolves we've captured for her," another responds.

"What about the other one? Doesn't she want us to search for her stupid niece, too? We haven't found her yet," Rachel counters. They bicker for a few moments more, then the second one convinces Rachel that they can go home.

I hold myself perfectly still, even my breath, until they're out of range to hear me. Once I'm certain that I'm safe from being captured by Amber's people again, I reach out to Ryland again. *The witches confirmed that they took my team. I hid while they talked. They claim to be heading back to base to give the wolves to Amber. They also said they were searching for Red. That means Amber doesn't have her.*

Fuck. I don't know if that's good or bad. Head back home. I'll meet you there. If Amber doesn't have her, this is pointless.

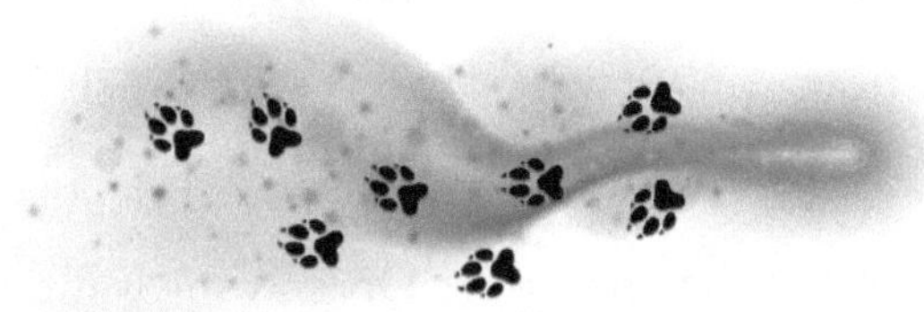

RYLAND

Luca's voice in my head makes me pause. His team disappeared and there are witches hunting us. This is not good news. I send a quick text to the team leads and let them know to bring everyone back home. I won't lose any more wolves than we already have.

Once I'm certain everyone is heading back home, I shift and race toward our cabin. If Amber and her people don't have Red, we may have bigger problems than missing wolves. I can't let my emotions get in the way of finding her. As the territory alpha, I have to remain in control. It's hard, but I know I can't lose focus.

The minute I step inside the cabin, I know that something is wrong. Grammy turns toward the door, her expression nearly unreadable. "What is it?" I ask, crossing the room to stand in front of her.

"The healing brew didn't work as well as I'd hoped it would. The infection is spreading. If it reaches his heart, that might be the end. I've never dealt with anything like this before, so I'm not certain. It could just change him," she explains.

"Change him? Into what?" I ask, my eyes searching her face for answers.

She meets my gaze before turning to look at James. "I don't know." It's not good news at all, especially since Red isn't here. If he dies, it'll break their bond, and she'll suffer. Without the rest of us near her, it could kill her. I have to keep that from happening.

"What can we do?" I hate how helpless I feel right now. I've grown to care about James too, and don't want to lose him.

We have to find Red, and we have to save James. Those are the two things I want to focus on right now. I can't defeat Amber without Red, and she won't be strong enough without James.

"I'm working on it. He's stable for now, though that can change at any moment. Have you made any progress in finding Red? I'm going to need her help." Grammy stares at me, as if I'm hiding something from her.

I shake my head. "No, but we learned that Amber doesn't have her. That's all we know."

Before she can say anything else, Luca walks in. "Where have you been? You should have beat me home."

"The witches circled back around. Amber must have sent them out to look for more wolves. Did everyone else make it back okay? Where's Orym?" Luca asks, looking around the room.

Fuck. I check my phone and see confirmation that the only group unaccounted for is the one Luca was with, but the group Orym left with hasn't seen him. "Looks like he's not with his group."

I call to him through the bond, hoping that Amber's people didn't take him, too. *Orym, where are you? We need you at home. Amber's people are taking wolves from the forest.*

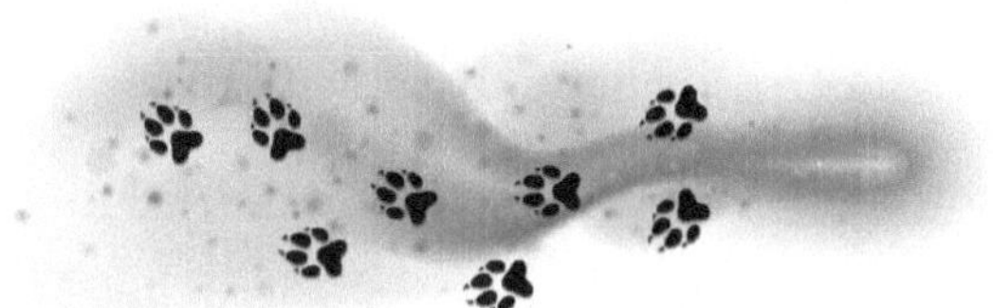

GARNET

"No, I don't know exactly what my magic will do. I didn't even know I had magic until recently. It's not like I've had help figuring it out." I look at James and wince at the hurt in his eyes. "At least not from anyone who knows about magic." His expression softens and I feel a little better. I hate that my words hurt him, but I hope he understands that I didn't mean it that way.

"Well, you have someone who knows about magic now. I will help you, but you have to listen to me. Do you understand?" Trevan seems irrationally upset by me using my magic, and I don't understand what's going on here. He's hiding things. I know it.

I nod and glare at him. I'm pissed and want him to know it. James squeezes my hand. It's surreal to me that he feels so solid here, when I know that this is just a manifestation of his soul. His body is back at home, probably dying. My heart aches because I'm here instead of there helping Grammy find a way to save him.

"It's okay, Garnet. She'll figure it out. Grammy is good at what she does, and the guys will help her," James comforts me, obviously reading my emotions through our bond. I hate this entire situation more than I could ever explain.

"How can you be so calm about the fact that you're dying?" I wail as he pulls me into his arms and holds me against his chest.

"Because I know I'm not actually going to die. It's pretty easy to stay calm when you know the people you care about won't let you go without a fight," he says against my temple. I know this isn't the time, but I melt into him and soak up his positive energy. I need this embrace as much as he does.

We stand there like that until Trevan clears his throat. "Not that this, display of emotion, bothers me," he begins, "but we have things that need to be discussed in private. So, if you don't mind, we need to get moving."

I want to punch him for being a dick. My mate is barely hanging onto his life, and this guy is worried about someone hearing our conversation. It's ridiculous. I have bigger things to worry about than his issues with privacy and affection. Who the fuck does this guy think he is, my dad? That's a ridiculous idea. Isn't it?

James and I follow Trevan into the palace. Now that one of his subjects, servants, people—hell, I never even asked who Miriam was to him—knows that we're here, I guess we don't have to worry about sneaking in. I stare at him as we walk, letting James lead me. The more I watch this Fae man, the more convinced I am that he could be my father. How crazy is that? It would explain why he claims he can help us, and why he spent time with Luca and me when we were kids.

But if he is my father, why wouldn't he just tell me? What does he have to hide? Is he ashamed of me? Questions fill my mind and I realize that if I don't stop this train of thought, I'm going to start blurting out what I'm wondering. Of course, none of it will be in order or make any sense. Then I'll be even more embarrassed than I was at being cornered by one of his people.

James, can you hear me? I wait for his response. Nothing. Fuck, why did I think that our bond communication would work here? Maybe Trevan is right, and I don't know enough about my powers yet. I'll have to talk to James after we're left alone for the night.

Our Fae host leads us to a large corridor with so many doors lining each side that I know I'll never figure out which room is ours if it's on this hallway. I can't even count how many doors we've already passed.

"Where are we going?" I ask. Trevan doesn't even pause at my question. Nor does he respond. Frustration bubbles up in me, and at the moment when I expect I'm going to explode at him, he stops in front of a door.

"Here we are," he says, throwing the ornate wooden door open and gesturing for us to enter. "This is your room, Fae child. Your gentleman will be right across the hall in his own room." He closes the door behind us, and I turn on him.

James wraps an arm around my waist to keep me from jumping on Trevan. "No, he will not. James will stay here with me. You cannot separate us. I won't allow it."

"It's okay, Garnet. I can sleep across the hall if our host requires it," James offers quietly. I shake my head and struggle in his hold.

"No. I won't stay here if he tries to separate us. And I think there's more to his offer of training me than he wants to admit. So, either James and I stay together, or I will find a way back home. Do I make myself clear, Father?" I don't mean to say it out loud, but from the look on his face, I'm right. Trevan is my father. Fuck, this just keeps getting more complicated.

"How did you know? No one here knows who you are. I've kept that secret for so long," he answers. Relief washes over him, and for some reason, that pisses me off more.

"You could have just told me, instead of trying to toss your weight around about my fated mate staying in my room, you know. It would have been a lot easier." I refuse to answer his question, since he's avoided so many of mine already.

"I never meant to hurt you, daughter. I didn't know how to tell you," he claims.

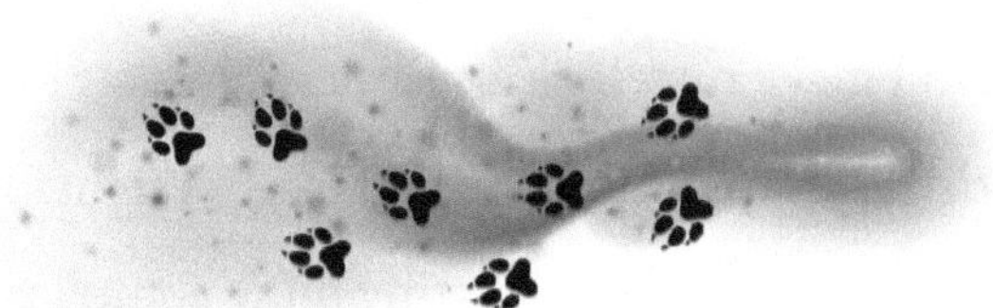

ORYM

I make it to the waterfall without anyone realizing that I'm gone. After spending a few minutes searching for Garnet, a branch cracks and I duck behind a tree. Multiple foot falls tell me that I'm no longer alone. I can't tell who it is, but they're coming up fast. I can't risk getting caught, so I climb one of the larger trees and hide in the leaves. Hopefully, whoever it is won't see me.

"I thought you said one of the wolves came this way," a voice carries to my hiding spot. Shit, that's not one of our people. I lean back further, pressing myself against the tree trunk.

"One of them did. That's why I said we needed to follow him. But you lost him already, didn't you?" another voice answers.

"Just keep looking. He has to be around here somewhere. People, or wolves, don't just disappear." This comes from a third voice. I can't see them from where I am, so I can't be sure if there are only three of them or if more are waiting silently.

"I bet he shifted and ran off once he caught our scent," the second voice insists. Which is what I would have done had I caught their scent. But the wind blows in the opposite direction, making that impossible. New information makes me happy, though. These witches don't know anything about tracking, meaning they won't be able to find me as long as I stay still and quiet.

Ryland's voice nearly messes that up when it echoes through my mind. *Orym, where are you? We need you at home. Amber's people are taking wolves from the forest.*

I'm safe, for now. Hiding from a group of witches. They don't know how to track, so I should be good. I'll get back as soon as I can. I know that Ryland will probably want to head this way and chase the witches off, but I can't let him know where I am. He'll be pissed that I didn't stay with my group. Unless he already knows and is already pissed. It never looks good when the second in command disobeys an alpha's orders.

I wait for his response, hoping that no one else realizes that I took off. *Where are you? Luca and I can get some guys and head your way.*

Don't. I'll be okay. They'll give up soon, since they can't find me. Arguments are already starting. It won't be long now. Maybe it's stupid to ignore his question twice, but I can't tell him where I am. I won't risk him or Luca getting taken. I'll wait this threat out, then head back home.

Why do I feel like you're avoiding telling me where you are because you did something stupid? The annoyance in his voice is evident. I know that I'll pay for my insubordination later. And that will be okay. For now, I have to ignore him and stay hidden to survive.

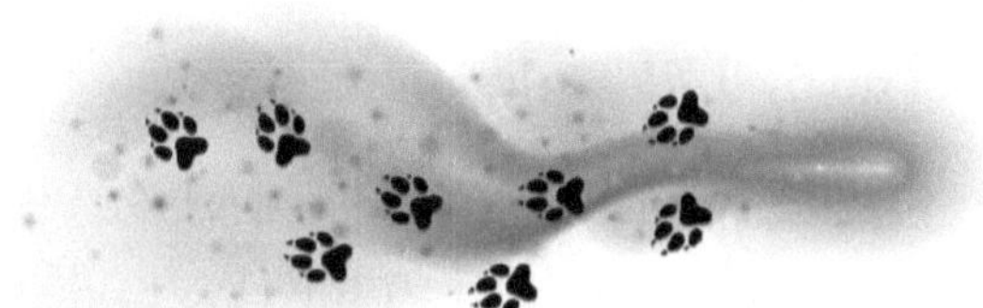

JAMES

Trevan is Garnet's father. How did I not see that coming? It explains why this Fae man intervened to save my life, and why he helped Luca escape from Amber's torture. I'm not sure how my girl is taking that revelation, though. She seems pissed and set on making him suffer for it.

"Maybe we should all take a breath and calm down," I suggest, earning dirty looks from father and daughter. "Okay, bad idea. Noted. What if the two of you just take a beat before this comes to blows?"

"I would never strike my daughter. That is a ridiculous idea," Trevan insists.

Garnet's cheeks flush. I know her well enough to know that she wants to throttle him, but she's also embarrassed by the thought of doing it. "Exactly," she claims.

"Now that we know who you are, maybe you can answer some questions for us," I offer, still trying to make peace between them.

Trevan sighs heavily and sinks into a chair. "Fine. I guess there's no point in trying to hide it any longer. I'll tell you what you want to know. Please be aware that some things may put you in danger, even here."

Satisfied with the compromise, Garnet flops onto the love seat near the chair. I take a spot next to her, positioning myself between the two. It seems safer that way, as long as neither of them tosses out any magic.

"Why did you hide who you were when I was a child?" Garnet begins.

"To keep you safe. I knew that your mother made a deal with Grammy to protect you, and part of that was me staying away. The old hybrid would kill me if she found out I'd managed to spend time with you anyway." It sounds like a valid explanation, but Garnet does not look pleased.

"What's the deal with my magic?" she asks.

Trevan stares at her for a moment before he speaks. "There was a binding spell," he begins, but she cuts him off.

"Yeah, we already dealt with that."

"The witch spell, yes. But the Fae spell is still there. It's causing your magic to react strangely and be inconsistent. If I can remove it, you'll have all of your abilities unlocked. It will make defeating Amber less of a challenge." Another reasonable explanation, but Garnet's reaction proves that she's skeptical of him.

"Look, I understand that all of this is difficult to process. For both of you...but we have to figure out a way for the two of you to trust each other. If not, Amber will win. And since she wants to kill the woman I love, I'm going to do everything I can to prevent that. I need you both to get on board," I order. I'm not usually so outspoken, but this is Garnet's life we're talking about. And I value that even more than I do my own.

"But we need to focus on saving you," she insists.

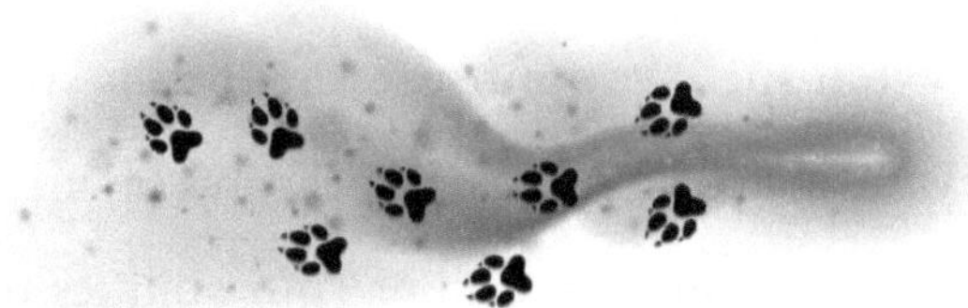

GARNET

James makes a face at my comment, while Trevan simply looks disinterested. I hate that his lack of interest bothers me, but it does. I tell myself that I don't need his approval, and I know it's true. I don't need it, but I want it. My heart aches at the thought that he doesn't care what happens to one of the men I love.

I want his help, but not at James' expense. If I have to take Amber on by myself, I will. And I'll find a way to defeat her, even if it kills me. As long as my mates survive. I don't want to leave them, but I would rather give my life than sacrifice one of theirs.

"We don't have time to debate this. Please, Garnet, let Trevan help you with your powers. Then maybe he can help us get back home and you can save me." James' plea grips my heart. I want to argue with him, but I can't. The pain in his eyes is too much for me.

"You're right. I'm sorry." I turn to my father. "It would mean a great deal to me if you would help me learn to use my powers so I can fight Amber and save James. Please." I'm not above begging, but I hope it doesn't come to that.

Trevan stares at me for a long moment. "I always planned to help you. I wanted to explain everything once you had a chance to learn more about me and this land. It was never my intent to lie to you. I kept the secrets that your mother wished me to, but only to protect you. There were forces searching for you even as a child. We had to make them believe that you were gone like your mother. It was the only way."

I don't know how to feel about his confession. Is he being honest with me? I have no way to tell. I've just met this man, and he's asking me to trust him. I'm not sure I can. There's no choice in working with him or not. I must work with him, or I'll never learn to control my magic. I can't risk the wolves, vampires, and even humans that way. It's up to me to rescue them and keep them safe. If only I knew how.

"I can't force myself to trust you. I want to, even though I don't understand that pull. But I don't know you. I hope that doesn't offend you. I will work with you. I'm smart and learn quickly. When I'm trained enough to take Amber out, I do trust that you'll send us back to deal with her. And if you can help us save James, I'll expect that as well." My words sound cold and calculated, but they aren't meant that way. I just can't express myself here, not to the father I've never known, not in a strange place that oddly feels like home.

After a few more minutes, Trevan excuses himself, leaving James and me alone for the first time since we arrived here. "Thank you, for being civil to him. I understand that you're upset. You have every right to be. But I think he's being honest. He just wants to help and doesn't really know how." James speaks softly, then pulls me into his arms.

I sink into him, enjoying how real and permanent he feels against me. I know it's only because we're in this strange reality, but I let myself believe that he's going to be okay. Here, I can pretend that we're just taking a vacation. It's easy to ignore the fact that at this very moment, people who care about us are worried that I'm never coming home and James is dying.

The thoughts come unbidden, ruining our perfect moment. I want to push them away again and focus on us, but I can't. Tears start to fall, and he wipes them away. "Garnet, it's okay. I'm sure they'll figure out how to save me. Please just focus on learning about your magic. I'm not going anywhere."

Even as he says the words, I know they're lies. I can sense it along our bond. Even though it's weak and we can't communicate with it, I can still feel his emotions. He knows that this doesn't look good for him, but he's encouraging me to stay here, with my father, and work toward our original goal. We have to defeat Amber. I understand the desperation of it.

I feel the same as he does, but I cannot sacrifice him to get there. I won't. I'm tired of fighting, so I don't say anything. Instead, I press my lips to his and kiss him, pouring my emotion into the connection between us. I can't lose him. I'll fall apart if I do.

Panic grips my heart, even as James' love nearly drowns me. I kiss him as if this is the last time I'll ever have the chance. I want more, but when I reach for him, he backs away. "Not like this. Not to say goodbye. I'm not giving up." His words cut me, and more tears fall.

I can't argue with him, because he's right. If I make love to him now, it'll be me saying goodbye. I don't want that any more than he does. "I agree. This isn't goodbye. And if I have to wait until we save you, then I will. I'm not giving up, either."

With our vows made, we sink into a comfortable silence. I fall asleep almost as soon as my head hits the pillow. My dreams are strange, but not the same as usual. I don't dream of the forest or the witches' circle. Instead, I dream of playing in a field with my mates. Where I expect darkness, all I see is light. I can't help wondering if the Moon Goddess is trying to give me a sign.

THREE
ABSENTEE FATHER

RYLAND

Orym, you need to answer me now, or I'm going to bring the entire extended pack to find you. What on Earth is he doing that he can't tell me where he is?

I'm sorry, Ryland. I'm currently hiding in a tree from the witches who are searching for me. I don't know how many of them are out there, so I would rather not tell you where I am right now. I'm trying to keep you guys safe. Orym's soft voice in my head pisses me off. I don't care that he's done something stupid and feels like he has to hide it from me.

I need to know where you are. Please, just tell me. I promise we'll wait a while before we come to get you. I'll give you a chance to get out of it yourself and come home to explain. I have no bargaining chips here. All I can do is hope he tells me.

What the hell is it with these people? Hiding things and keeping secrets seem to be the standard now for my pack. That's not going to get any of us anywhere. But how do I get them all to understand that? Maybe being the leader isn't all it's cracked up to be. Well, it's too late to change my mind now.

I, uh, took a slight detour. I'm over by the waterfall. I was going to explain when I got back. It didn't make sense to look for Garnet somewhere else. I'm sorry, Ryland. I'll be home as soon as possible. You can yell at me then. The audacity of this guy. I make him my second in command, thinking he'll be the one to uphold the hierarchy of our pack and set a good example. Then he goes and pulls this shit?

We will definitely be talking about this when you get home safely. I let my annoyance flood the bond. I want him to know that I'm pissed, and I won't soon forget that he disobeyed me like this.

With that settled, I turn my attention back to James. He looks paler, with those dark magic lines covering more of his leg. "Is there anything we can do to slow it down at least?" I ask. I'm certain that she's already explained this once, but I wasn't listening.

Grammy glares at me. "I'm working on it. I'll let you know as soon as I have something useful to offer. For now, you should figure out where Orym is and make sure he's safe."

"He's fine. I'm giving him a chance to make it back on his own." I pause at the raised eyebrow she offers me. "I've spoken with him through the mate bond. He's avoiding capture, but he isn't where he was supposed to be. I will deal with that when he gets home. Please keep working on James. We need him healed so we can find Red. We can't beat Amber without her."

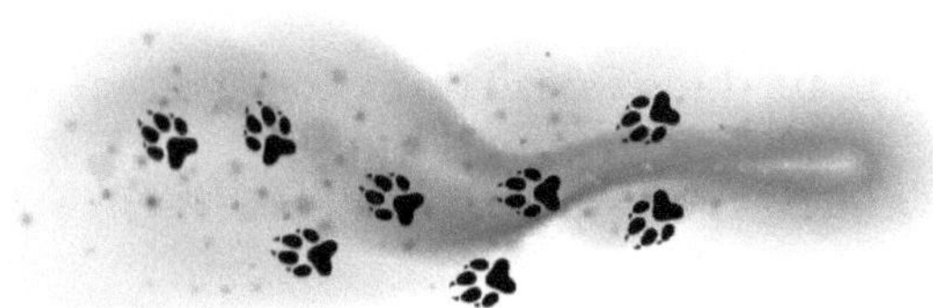

ORYM

I know that Ryland is pissed, and I can't blame him. I didn't want to have that conversation over the bond, but he kept pushing. Now, he'll be ready to fight about it as soon as I walk through the door. I deserve it, and I won't do much to defend myself, but I couldn't risk missing Garnet by looking in the wrong place. It doesn't matter now, since I didn't find her. And I'm still stuck in this tree, waiting for the witches to get bored and leave.

It's been an hour, and I know that Ryland isn't going to hold off too much longer before he sends out a rescue team. I should jump down and surprise them. That would give me an advantage and I'd be able to shift and run away. Before I can make that move, something explodes a few yards away.

"Run! Forget the wolf. We have to get out of here," one of the witches yells. I lean over and peer through the leaves in time to watch them run away. I have no idea if it's safe for me to move, but I decide to take the chance.

I drop from the tree, landing face-to-face with Ryland. "Will you at least wait to kill me until we get home?" I ask before baring my neck in submission.

He growls at me, ever the big, bad wolf. A shiver runs down my spine and my alpha fully submits to his. We may have been competitors in the past, but he is my alpha now. There is no question about it. "Only if you get back there before I catch you." The words are spoken quietly, but the fury in them is unmistakable. He will rip me apart if I don't escape.

I'm not sure that I blame him. I went against a direct order, and nearly got myself captured in the process. It would serve me right for him to punish me in any way he sees fit. My survival instinct takes over and I dash away from him. Behind me, the cracking of bone and stretching of skeleton alert me to his shift. I leap into the air and shift myself, racing away before he can tackle me.

As guilty as I feel for disobeying, I'm not ready to let Ryland take me down. I know that if I can make it back home, he'll give me a chance to fully explain myself. But if he catches me, I'm screwed. Either way, I'll have to suffer through a punishment. I, Ryland's second in command, will be the example that teaches the rest of the community what happens when they disobey our alpha. It's not the role I wanted to play in our community, but I brought it on myself.

I'll take whatever punishment he gives me with the reverence and respect that the territory alpha is due. Part of me wonders what Garnet will think about the situation, once we find her.

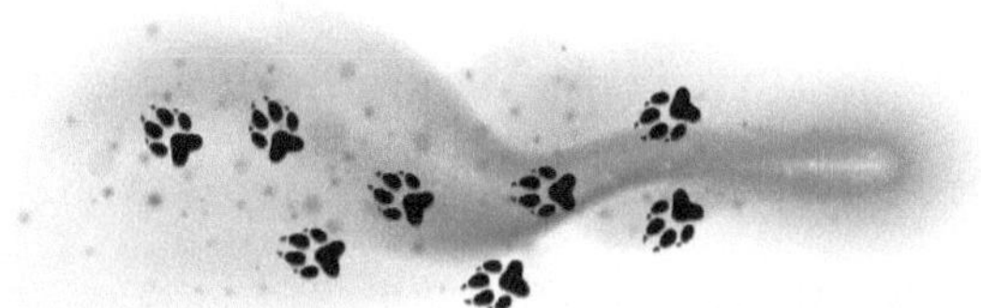

GARNET

Knowing that James won't let anything physical happen between us is supposed to be motivation for me to get this training handled. Instead, it's a major distraction. I'm not sure what his reasons are, and he doesn't want to talk about it. We've been here for a few days now, and I feel like I'm not getting anywhere with this magic.

Trevan is pushing me harder than Amber did when she wanted to unlock my witch magic. I'm tired and sore. More than anything, I want to go home. I miss my other mates, and if I'm being honest, Trevan has been annoying me.

I think he's doing it on purpose in an attempt at making me work harder to defeat him with my Fae powers. Unfortunately for me, it's having the opposite effect. As much as I want to punch him in the face, I can't seem to get my Fae magic to cooperate enough to hit him with anything. I'm cranky and on edge. Of course, orgasms would ease some of that, but I can't get James to budge on his decision.

So, I'm lying in the garden, staring at the sky. I wish I could figure out how to be good enough. I just can't do it. Gunnar was right about me. I'm not worthy of four mates, or the confidence the Moon Goddess seems to have in me. I should be training. Trevan gave me exercises to do while he takes care of some Fae business or other. And I want to learn this, I really do. But the moment he walked away, I flopped down here and started watching the clouds pass.

I know I'm being a petulant child about this whole thing. Throwing a fit isn't going to get me anywhere. Yet, here I am, doing it anyway. I could kick myself for it, but that would involve moving. And I've decided that I'm not doing that right now. I'm going to lie here and wallow in my self-pity for a while longer, then I'll get up and start training. Maybe.

If I believe everything Gunnar said about me, I should just give up. I should let Amber kill me and take my power. But if I do that, everyone I love will suffer. And I can't allow that. I just can't. The thought of my friends and family suffering urges me to leave the comfort of my self-pity.

I jump to my feet and stretch. From the corner of my eye, I see James sneaking up on my left side. I won't do anything to hurt him, but I do need to practice hitting a target. And splitting my focus. I carefully toss a shield in front of him before I shoot pink sparks directly at him. James cries out as he tries to dodge the magic blast, falling to his knees when it hits the shield.

I rush over to make sure he's okay. "I'm so sorry. Did that actually hurt you?" I ask as I pull him to his feet.

"I expected it to, but it didn't even hit me. I was more startled that it missed," he answers.

"It didn't miss. I shielded you," I smirk. "I saw you sneaking over and decided to do some target practice in a way that wouldn't hurt you."

"Well, it was very effective. What's that pink spark, anyway? I haven't seen that before." To be honest, I haven't seen it either, but I don't want to admit that to him.

"One of my Fae powers. I'm not really sure what any of them do. Trevan isn't exactly forthcoming about these things, you know." And the annoyance of my father is back. I'd almost forgotten that I'm so upset with him.

"I didn't mean to remind you that he exists. You seem happier when you can meditate and forget him for a bit," James admits with a laugh.

"I know he means well, but I am upset with him. And I'm sure I will be for a long time. It doesn't matter if he understands my reasons or not. I have every right to my feelings, and I won't apologize for them." Again, petulant child, here, and I know it. Don't judge me. Or do, whatever.

"I'm not saying you have to forgive him. Just don't shove him away so much that he can't train you. I, for one, am counting on you learning how all this works so you can go back home and save my ass," James says, pulling me into his arms and kissing me hard.

The contact makes my skin buzz with desire. I want James more than I can express. My core aches, and my panties are damp with need. I'm certain he can smell what I'm feeling, even though he isn't a shifter, but he doesn't react. I have no idea how he's able to control himself this way. I'm itching to rip his clothes off and mount him.

Sadly, I agreed that I wouldn't. And it wouldn't be fair to rape my mate, no matter how orgasm-deprived I am. I begrudgingly drag myself away from him, relishing the tiny whimper he gives me to show that he's upset. Good. You deserve to suffer a little.

My only comfort is that this will all be over soon. One way or another, I will go back home and face Amber. I'll either defeat her, or she'll kill me. I can't predict the ending, but I know that I will fight like hell to be the last woman standing.

I take a deep breath and turn toward the targets my father had set up at the other end of the garden. "Let's figure out what these do, then, shall we?" I exchange a glance with James, then focus on the targets again.

One by one, I shoot different colors of Fae magic at them. With this experiment, I learn that each stream of color does something different.

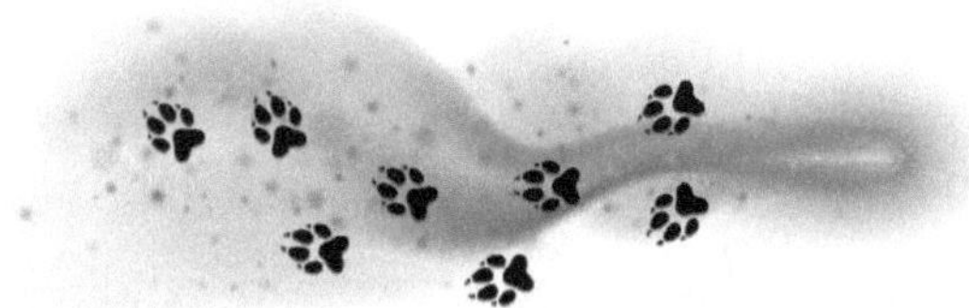

JAMES

Garnet shoots her magic at the targets, and each one lights up with a different power. The pink stream is most like lightning, crackling and sparking. Red sets the target on fire, blue freezes it, and purple soaks it as if a hard rain just fell. Green causes vines to grow, covering the target. Yellow makes the target glow, and black disintegrates it. I'm sure she has more colors to go through, but one look at her proves that she's pushing too hard.

"Garnet, love. You need to take a break. You're going to collapse from exhaustion if you keep pushing like that. Please," I beg her.

She barely glances my way before throwing more magic at the targets. If I can't make her stop, maybe Trevan can. I hate leaving her alone, but she doesn't even notice when I walk away.

It doesn't take long to find our Fae host, although I'm not sure what business he's taking care of by lounging on his throne and letting half-naked women feed him grapes, or whatever fruit here looks like grapes. I suspect that he just needed a break from his daughter's steely glare. I can't blame him for that, but hiding isn't the answer.

They need to hash it out and express their feelings. But how do I convince this man that it was his idea? Because the one thing I've noticed about father and daughter is that they would rather get their own way than admit that someone else had a good idea. Garnet is not nearly as bad about that as her father, but it's still there.

"Oh! Your Majesty, there you are. I've been searching for you," I say with over-the-top enthusiasm. Since we've been here for a few days, I know it's better to use his title in front of other Fae than to call him by his name. It's also something Garnet refuses to do.

The Fae king jumps out of his chair, swatting the fruit wielding women away. "Has something happened to the princess?" Yeah, he refused to keep her identity a secret once we were inside the palace. And that's probably why my girl won't use his title.

"Not exactly, sir. She is making progress with her training."

"That is excellent news. Did you really seek me out to tell me that?" He eyes me skeptically.

I shake my head. "No, sir. I came to ask your opinion about something." I pause, then continue. "Now that she's figured out how to produce different types of Fae magic, Garnet is set on mastering it as quickly as possible."

"Oh. That is extremely dangerous. She should take a break, especially if she's producing more than one type of magic. Most Fae can only harness one color. How many has she done?" I've piqued his interest and I'm relieved.

"So far, she's been able to produce seven different colors. When I walked away, she was working on testing more. She won't take a break."

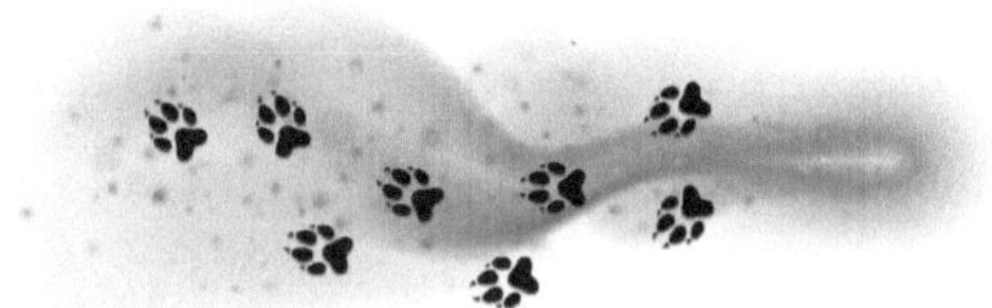

LUCA

After a few days of searching and debating what we've learned from spying on Amber's people, we settle in for a family meeting with Grammy. Eli is kind enough to loan us some of his bug-sized drones to use for listening in on the enemy, but he keeps his family away from the forest. Apparently, learning that the witch they'd all trusted wants to use his wife's blood to create a hybrid army is enough to rattle even the toughest vampires.

I don't blame them. If Red was here, I would keep her locked up, too. There is no way I would let her lead searches for Amber. It's too risky. Thinking back to when Amber and her people held me captive, I remember hearing them talk about stealing Red's power. It seems to me that Amber needs Red's abilities to get the hybrid creation to work.

And if that's true, Amber will never stop coming for her. We have to find her and kill her. I don't know how to do that, since it's become obvious nothing that we've done so far has even come close to stopping her. I'm not sure that we can defeat her without Red.

"Luca!" Ryland barks my name, and I know that I'm in trouble. I'm not paying any attention to what they're saying.

"Sorry. I missed that. What's up?" His face tells me everything I need to know. He's pissed that I wasn't listening.

"If you'd been listening, you would know. Please pay attention. This meeting isn't just for my benefit," Ryland scolds me, and I hang my head. I hate disappointing my alpha.

"Yes, alpha," I say, baring my neck in submission. I'm not usually so docile, but I've found that since Ryland took Gunnar's place, I am submitting to him more and more. It doesn't bother me, because I know that ultimately, I'm doing it for

Red. And I would do anything for her. Just to be near her, to take care of her, to prove my love to her.

To do that, I need to pay attention to what my family is discussing so that I can find Red and bring her home. "As we were saying, things are not looking good for James. If we can't find a way to stop the magic from reaching his heart, it's going to be bad. How bad? We don't know yet." Ryland holds eye contact with me while he speaks, just to be sure I'm paying attention.

"What options do we have?" I ask, hoping they haven't already discussed this.

"None that we can think of. We've tried everything that I know how to do, and a few things that were long shots. Without a witch to help, I don't know what else we can do besides say goodbye," Grammy says.

"We can't give up. If we can find Red, then she can save him," I insist.

Orym shakes his head. "But she didn't know what to do either, Luca."

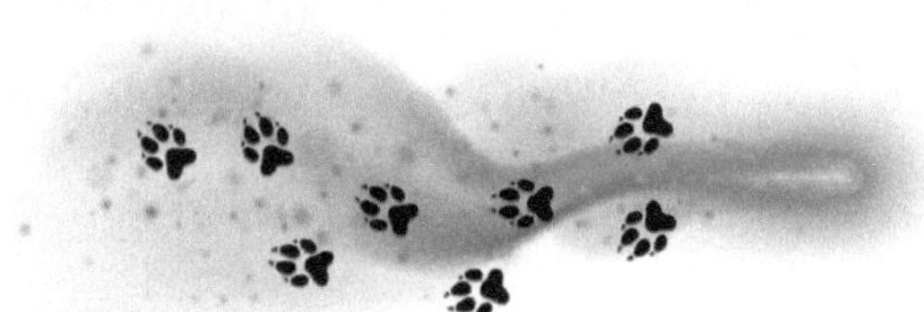

GARNET

I feel weak, and I'm barely staying on my feet. But I will not give up. I will master all of these powers, so that I can defeat Amber. I have to. The lives of everyone I love are on the line. I don't know when James walked away. Once I realize that he's gone, it's a little easier to push everything away and focus on shooting magic at the targets.

I've figured out how to use pink, red, blue, purple, green, yellow, and black. What else can I do? Closing my eyes, I reach into the magical well inside of me and shoot a beam at a target. When my eyes open, I see that the beam is brown and landed in front of the target, digging a hole. That's interesting.

I try again and make a stream of orange magic that looks like acid and melts the target into goo. I'll definitely have to try that one on Amber. If I can hit her with that, this might all be over before it gets too much worse.

One more blast at the last target, and it comes out gray. This one appears to be smoke, swirling and floating through the air. I like this one, too. It might be good for hiding people. And that could be helpful when we rescue Amber's prisoners.

At this point, I know I've used too much magic at one time without resting. I should have listened to James. But I'm trying to save him, and he doesn't seem to be too concerned about that. Dizziness washes over me and I drop to my knees. The world spins around me and I decide that laying down is better than falling.

"Garnet!" I hear voices but can't quite open my eyes to see what's wrong.

"Wait, James. Don't touch her. Just look. Her magic is making a cocoon around her for protection. She's too weak to protect herself, so it's handling the issue. If you touch her right now, you'll get zapped. And with all those colors swirling around her, I'm not sure I'd be able to save you." Trevan's voice filters through the static I didn't realize I've been hearing.

A cocoon? That's strange. But that would explain the buzzing noise I hear. This Fae magic stuff is weird. It's almost like it has a mind of its own. I like that it will protect me when I'm on the verge of passing out and can't protect myself.

I try to open my eyes but can't manage it. So, I let myself relax a little and focus on the conversation around me. "Shouldn't we try to wake her up?" James asks frantically. The panic lacing his tone nearly makes me cry.

"We should let her recover. From the look of those targets, she used too much magic at one time, and needs to rest. Normally, I would try to take her to one of the bedrooms to sleep it off. But I don't think I'll be able to touch her either. So, we'll camp out here for a bit and keep an eye on her," Trevan insists.

I wonder for a moment why they would need to watch me if my powers were in protection mode, but maybe he knows something I don't. Or maybe he's trying to keep other Fae safe. That makes more sense. His people could get hurt if they get too close to whatever this is. The idea that he's being a good leader melts my heart a little toward him. I want to stay mad, but it's hard when he's actually doing something for others.

I have no idea how long I'm out, but when I can finally open my eyes, I see James and Trevan asleep in lounge chairs on either side of me. I hate to wake them, but I need answers, and can't get them on my own. "Good morning, fellas."

James jumps at my voice, startling Trevan. Both men nearly fall out of their chairs. I can't hold back the laugh that bubbles up in my chest. "Garnet! You're okay. You are okay, right?" James asks, looking me over as if he wants to check me for injuries, but is scared to touch me.

"I think so. I don't really know what happened, though. I'm hoping you can explain that," I say to my father, who is watching me carefully. I can tell that he knows more than he's going to share. I have to figure out how to get it out of him.

"You should not have access to every type of Fae magic, but somehow you do. It's not something that has ever happened before. I don't know what it means exactly, but we need to be careful. With that much power, it will be easier for you to over use your magic and exhaust yourself," he explains.

"What do you mean, I shouldn't have access? Is it unusual for someone to be able to use all the powers?" I don't understand what he's saying. If I shouldn't have access to all the powers, then how do I?

"I mean, there has not been another Fae in our history who can wield all of the Fae powers. It's rare for one of us to be able to use more than one type. You are remarkable. Your power exceeds even mine. And I'm able to use three different types. But if you have access to all of them, in addition to your witch powers, then you have to be the most powerful being I've ever met." Trevan speaks with reverence, as if I'm someone to be respected.

"Wait, you're saying that she has all these Fae powers *and* witch powers too?" James asks in awe.

"You said that you used witch powers when Amber was training you, correct?" Trevan turns to me expectantly.

I nod. "I did. They felt different from these. I believe you're right. I have both witch and Fae powers."

Four
Going Home

ORYM

"Well, if Amber doesn't have Garnet, then who does? She couldn't have just disappeared. That's not physically possible. We need to find her so we can save James and defeat Amber,"

I insist. This meeting is going on forever, and I'm already tired of listening to Ryland berate Luca for daydreaming. I'm pretty sure he was trying to figure out how to find Garnet, which is the whole point of this conversation.

"I don't know who has her. There's no way to find her unless whoever took her lets us," Ryland replies.

"Okay, I haven't had the bond as long as either of you, but what if the reason we can't communicate with her through the bond is because she's in another realm?" Luca offers.

"What do you mean?" Ryland growls.

"I think he means their Fae friend may have stepped in. Right?" I respond. Ryland glares at me, but Luca nods.

"Exactly. And if he's the one who took her, then she's safe. We just have to figure out how to reach out to him so he can send her back. There has to be a good reason why he took her. It's the only explanation I can come up with for why we can't talk to her. You guys said the bond works anywhere." Luca's explanation is the only thing that makes sense.

"So, how do we call a Fae?" I look at Grammy and the old woman blushes. I figured that she would know the answer, even if she doesn't want to share the information.

"There are stories, but I've never tried it," she answers, her cheeks turning even more pink. Just as I thought. She knows exactly what to do to get the Fae's attention. As much as I hate the idea, if this Fae man is helping Garnet, I'll work with him or at least have a civil conversation with him.

"Tell me what you need to make it happen, and I'll take care of it." I lock eyes with Ryland, and he nods at me. I'm still trying to make up for disrespecting him by ignoring his orders. I'll do whatever it takes to bring this family back together again.

"I'll make you a list. It won't be easy to get everything. And there's no guarantee it will call the specific Fae you want it to." Grammy's warning stings, but I understand her caution. She doesn't want us to get our hopes up too much, since there's a chance that we won't be able to find Garnet this way.

"We'll find her. You'll see." Luca's confidence is contagious, making me feel more sure of this plan than I was a moment ago.

"Guys, I'm worried that this won't be as easy as the two of you think. I don't want either of you to be disappointed if we can't find her," Ryland says, staring out the window. I know he means well, but we need to be positive here.

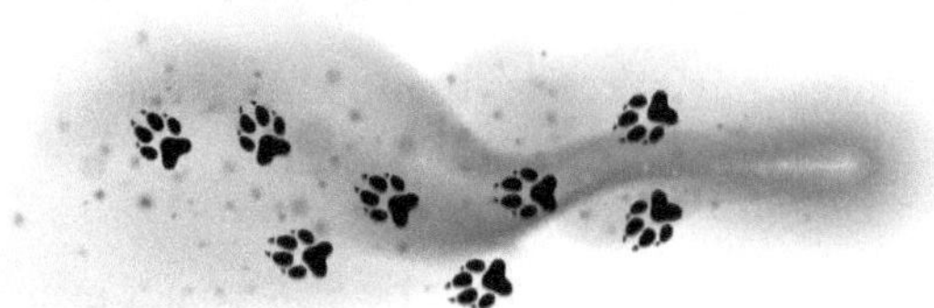

JAMES

Garnet confirming that she has two very different types of powers inside of her is a terrifying thought. I don't know if it's possible for a person to survive such a thing, especially if Trevan is right, and she's the only one to ever have this much power. "How does she control it, then?" I ask, pulling his focus from her to me.

"Practice. It's the only real way to ever learn control," he responds. I figured as much, but I know it's not what Garnet wants to hear.

"Well, if that's it, then we should go home. Because I've unlocked my powers. That was what you wanted. And you've successfully gotten me to use them. So, James and I should go home now. Then I can save him, and we can defeat Amber," Garnet says dismissively.

"Oh, you're already prepared to leave. I see. Well, I suppose I can open a portal." The hurt in his voice stabs at my heart.

"Of course, we would love for you to come with us," I offer, glaring at Garnet. She doesn't seem to notice the way I'm looking at her.

Trevan's face lights up. "You would?" He turns to Garnet and looks at her with hope shining in his eyes. He's been trying to connect with her the whole time we've been here, and she just keeps pushing him away.

"What? Why?" she asks. I elbow her in the ribs and she coughs. "Of course. Please, come with us." The glare I get from her is worth it, since Trevan's happiness is nearly palpable.

"I supposed I'll get things arranged. We'll leave in an hour," he says before darting off.

"What the fuck was that about?" she whips around to face me. "You can't be serious about bringing him home with us."

"Of course, I am. You need him to help heal me. And to help defeat Amber. Just give him a chance. For me?" I hate using guilt to get my way, but I know it's the only thing that will work right now.

She groans and rolls her eyes at me. "Fine, but you are responsible for explaining him to the others. Oh! I'm going to get to see Ry, Luca, and Orym!" I can tell that she's excited, and I realize it probably has more to do with the possibility of sex than with being tired of me.

I don't know how to explain my theory to her, but I felt like if we had sex here, it would trap me. I don't want to take the chance of being stuck here forever because of some trick her father played on us. But I also don't want to accuse him without proof, because that will turn her further away from him.

I'm walking a thin line here and trying to figure out what's best for everyone. Hopefully, I'm right, and Trevan will be able to help Garnet heal my body. My soul is growing weaker every day.

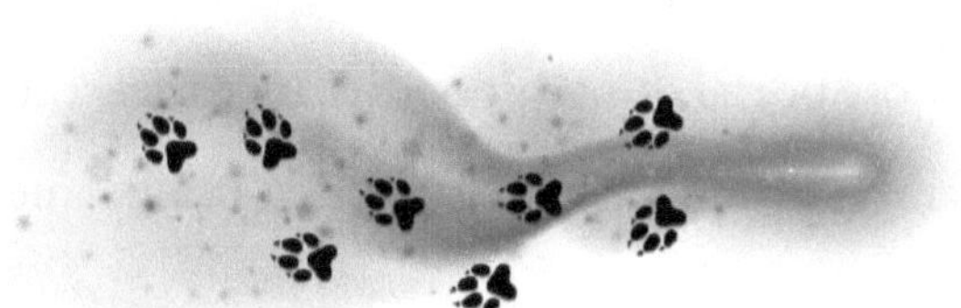

GARNET

I'm going home! I can't believe it. I was beginning to think it wasn't possible. Terror at the thought of being trapped in the Fae realm forever has started to sink into me. I've been fighting it the whole time we've been here, but I'd started to lose that battle. I can't tell James, but I've noticed that he's starting to fade.

That tells me that his body is getting weaker. I don't know how much longer Trevan can keep him away from the light. I can't lose James, though. So, I'll be nice to my father and take him home with me. We'll save James and defeat Amber. Then we'll have a conversation and set some boundaries about our relationship.

We'll start with kidnapping. There will be no more of that, because it's annoying. And he's going to teach me how to open one of those portal things, too. I refuse to get stuck anywhere ever again. If I can make a portal, then I can come and go as I please.

I hug James and dance around a little. I can't hide my excitement. I'm going home! And I'll get to see my other mates. It's going to be surreal, giving up talking to James, but being able to see the others. We have to save him. I'm desperate to find a way.

True to his word, Trevan returns an hour later. He has three backpacks with him, and they appear to be filled to capacity. "This one is for you, and this one is for you. These are loaded up with everything we could possibly need once we're on the other side. Of course, I don't know if you're spirit will be corporeal once we get there, so giving you a backpack is probably a bad idea."

He hands each of us a bag, then takes James' back. "I'll carry this for now. You just focus on staying with our girl." I've noticed that Trevan rarely uses my name. He prefers to call me *Daughter* or *Princess*. Both are annoying. And I've decided I don't like *our girl* any better.

Once the bags are organized, he motions for us to move closer. Then Trevan moves his hands in a circle in front of his abdomen. A small band of bright blue magic forms a circle in front of him, growing as he parts his hands.

"Quickly, step through. Both of you. We'll see what happens to James once we're on the other side. I'm right behind you," Trevan urges. I grip James' hand and walk through the portal, dragging him with me.

Tears fill my eyes when James evaporates as soon as he's out of the portal. "Where did he go? Is he...?" I can't bring myself to say the words, but Trevan puts a hand on my shoulder.

"He's not. It's okay. We'll figure out a way to heal him. His spirit probably just went back to his body. Give me a moment, then we'll head to your cabin," he insists.

"A moment for what?" I ask, watching as he pulls something small out of one of his bags.

"Here, put this on," he says, handing me what looks like a friendship bracelet. "It will hide us from the witches. If there are any searching the forest, they won't be able to see, hear, or smell us."

It seems odd, but I do as he requests. I slide the bracelet onto my wrist. The air around me feels warmer suddenly, as if I've become a part of it. I look around, but nothing else has changed.

"Let's go. Lead the way," he says after sliding one of the bracelets on his own wrist. Again, I do as he asks, heading toward the cabin that's been my home since Ry and I became bonded.

A noise in front of us stops me in my tracks and I almost duck behind a tree. Trevan's hand on my arm stops me. "Just watch," he says quietly. Three witches approach us, but they don't seem to see what's right in front of them.

"I swear, a portal just closed. I sensed it. But it doesn't make sense. Why would someone open a portal if they weren't going to come through it?" one of the witches asks the others.

A second one shrugs. "Maybe it was just to pick a flower or something. Fae are weird like that." I smirk at her comment, and Trevan tenses. I'm certain that she's offended him, but I can't hide my amusement.

"It doesn't matter. Amber wants us to keep an eye out for anything strange. We need to go report back to her. She'll tell us what we need to do next," the third witch states before turning and walking back the direction they came from.

I didn't know that witches could sense Fae portals. That could explain why Trevan was so hesitant to bring us back this way. I should have asked him to open it closer to the cabin. It never occurred to me that we would be stepping from one world into another and come face-to-face with danger immediately.

"Will this thing block my mate bonds?" I ask, suddenly realizing that I can feel my mates again.

"No, you should be able to talk to them, since we're in your realm again," Trevan explains.

Ry? Luca? Orym? Can you guys hear me? I call through the bond, holding my breath while I wait for their responses.

Red? Luca's voice is hesitant.

Garnet? Orym's voice is relieved.

Where are you? We're on our way. And Ry sounds pissed. I should have known that he'd be the one to blame me for disappearing.

We're coming home. Don't worry. The witches can't see or hear us. We'll be there soon. I respond carefully through the bond, not letting my annoyance go through. I don't want to fight with any of them, and I already know they're going to be hesitant to trust Trevan.

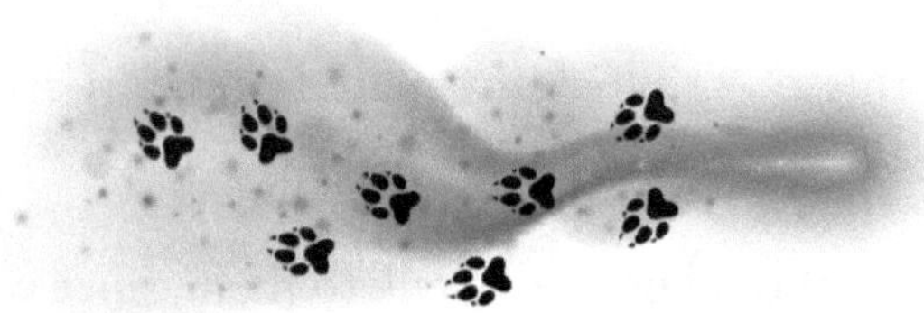

LUCA

The moment I hear Red's voice in my head, I freeze. It has to be my imagination. She can't really have magically appeared the moment we decided to summon the Fae to find her. I'm terrified to hope that it really is her.

Ryland and Orym turn to look at me and I know it was not my imagination. "Is it really her?" I whisper.

Neither of them says a word. The three of us stare at each other as we respond to our mate's call. Fear grips me again when she tells us to stay put. "Who's with her? She keeps saying *we*. It doesn't make sense," Orym wonders aloud.

Ryland shakes his head. "I have no idea, but we need to be ready in case this is an ambush." Of course, Ryland would expect the worst. I can't blame him, though. I'm not sure I believe that she's back either.

We take our places near the door to wait. I'm ready to shift at Ryland's signal. Orym stands in the kitchen, with Grammy behind him. When the door opens, everyone is on edge, but frozen in our places.

"It's okay, just come inside. Hurry up, before Ryland tackles you and pins you to the ground," Red says to whoever she's brought with her.

It's really her. She's back and it seems like she's okay. Relief washes over me. I step forward to grab her and come face-to-face with the Fae man who helped me escape from Amber. "You. What are you doing here?"

"Helping my daughter save her mate, of course. What are you doing here?" he asks me. I can tell from his tone that he's teasing, but I still hadn't expected him to be the one escorting Red.

"Wait, did you say *daughter*?" Orym steps into the room.

Red rolls her eyes as she walks in behind him. "Yes, he did. But that wasn't exactly your news to share, was it, Trevan?" Her annoyance is clear, but the Fae man does not seem fazed by it. If anything, he's amused at her irritation.

"Darling daughter, you cannot expect me to meet your men and not let them know who I am," he says with a smirk.

"Red, I'm so glad you're okay!" I pull her into my arms before either of the others can. I have to reassure myself that she's real, and this isn't a dream.

"Luca, you're squeezing too tight," she squeaks out. I let go, and Ryland drags her away from me. I watch as he kisses her deeply, then shoves her toward Orym so he can face her father.

"Why did you take our mate? Give me one reason not to tear your head off right now," Ryland growls.

Trevan holds his hands up in surrender. "I took her so she could talk to the injured one over there. His soul was moving on when I stopped it. I basically trapped it in the Fae realm so that he couldn't die.

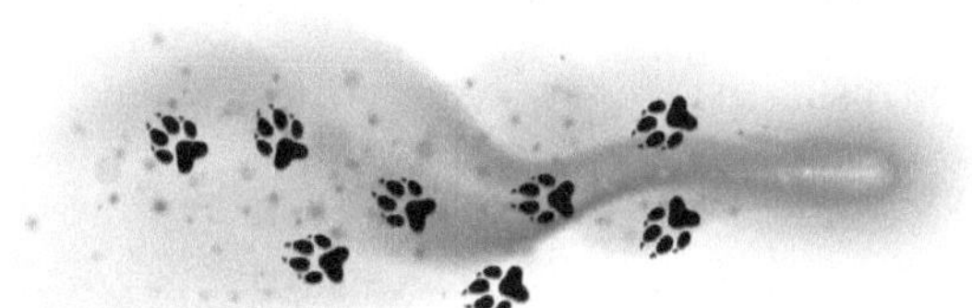

RYLAND

"You kept James alive? And that's why you took Red?" I'm astounded by this revelation. If what he's saying is true, what does that mean for James now that they're both here?

"I did, and yes, that is correct. There's a little more to it than that, but that is the basic gist of it all," Trevan says. This man is way too confident for his own good. Especially since Red is already annoyed at him.

"Then I'll welcome you into our home. But I will warn you, one wrong move, and one of us will take you out. Being Red's father won't save you here," I threaten.

I smirk at the look of fear that crosses his expression before he schools it again. Red notices it too, and we exchange a look.

"How is James?" she asks, rushing to the couch where he's been since his injury.

"It doesn't look good. We're not sure what else to do," Grammy says, walking out of the kitchen to wrap her arms around Red.

We all turn to Trevan, somehow expecting him to have the answers. "What are you looking at me for? I can't heal him. I don't have that power."

Red's face lights up. "But I do! Right? I just don't know what color that is." She turns to her father and stares at him, waiting for the answer to her unspoken question.

He sighs before he responds. "White. Please don't kill yourself saving his life. He wouldn't want that."

Dropping to her knees next to James, Red sticks her tongue out at the Fae man. Then she turns her attention back to her unconscious mate. As I'm watching, a faint white glow starts to come out of her hands.

“What is that?” Luca asks, stepping toward Red. I wrap my arm around his waist to stop him, pulling him back against my chest.

“Let her do this. The Fae is right there if things start to go wrong. If he can’t be useful, I’ll help you tear him in half,” I threaten. Luca seems satisfied with my suggestion and relaxes against me. It should be strange to hold him this way, but something about it feels right, especially with Red only a few feet away.

“It’s up to her to figure this out. Like I said, I don’t have that power, so I can’t help her. The only thing I can do is pull her away if she starts to use too much of it,” Trevan states. He doesn’t look concerned, but there’s something in his voice that makes him appear uncertain.

My chest aches, and I know it’s coming through the bond. If she’s unsure, then this won’t work. *Guys, we need to show our girl how proud we are of her and how confident we are that she can do this.* I send the command over our bond, blocking her from hearing it.

A moment later, I feel Orym and Luca pushing emotions at Red, and I join them.

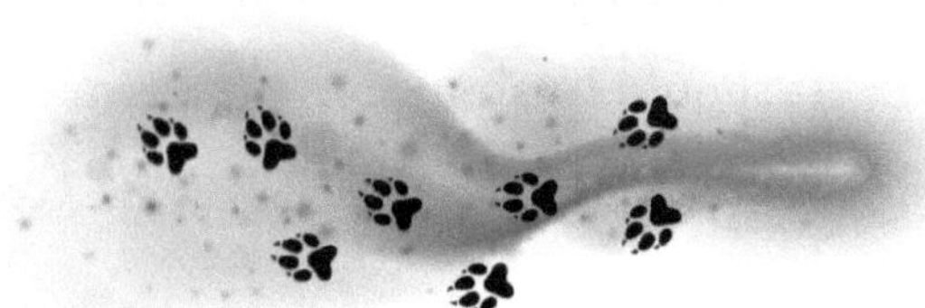

GARNET

I'm anxious and terrified that I can't save James. I have no idea what to do. What if I make it worse? Panic grips me, and I start to freeze up. Then, as if they're reading my mind, my guys send their love and confidence along our bond. It hasn't been that long since I've felt them this way, but it feels like it's been forever.

Tears stream down my face as I soak up their emotions and use them to bolster myself for what I have to do. I can't afford to be scared. I have to clear my mind and focus on healing James. Stopping those magic tendrils from getting to his heart is my number one concern right now.

As the white glow coming from my hands gets brighter, James starts to thrash. "Hold him down, please," I bark at Ry and Luca. I pour my magic into him, begging him to heal, praying that this works and I'm not too late.

The more magic I push into him, the more it seems to hurt him. I'm ready to back off, but Trevan steps forward. "It's working, keep going."

I close my eyes and focus on pushing as much healing magic into James as I can. My legs buckle, but strong arms wrap around me, and a hard chest holds me up. Orym's fresh cedar scent fills my nose. I lean back against him and continue to give everything I have to saving James' life.

After a few more minutes, I know I can't keep this up. I'm getting weak and the world is spinning. "It's okay, Red, you can stop now. It worked," Ry's voice cuts through the pain in my head.

I open my eyes to see that he's right. All that's left of James' injury is a small scar on his calf. The black streaks that had covered his leg and were climbing toward his heart are gone. I did it. With that thought, I collapse and the world goes dark.

I have no idea how long I was out, but I hear voices, and everything feels like it's a dream. "Is she okay?"

"Yes, she's fine. She just needs to rest. Using that much power at once is taxing for any Fae, but more so for one who isn't as experienced. Since she'd never used that particular type of magic before, it was more difficult for her. I'm certain that she will wake when she's recovered, just like James will." I know that voice, but my brain doesn't want to process it.

"If they both don't wake up soon, I'm going to take you outside and enjoy every single punch that it takes to knock you out," Ry says. Oh, shit. Ry is going to kill Trevan if I don't wake up. That's who he's arguing with.

I groan as I fight my way back to the light. The darkness calls to me, making me want to sleep. But I need to save my father from my mate. I slowly open one eye, looking from Ry to Trevan and back before closing it again. "Stop fighting. I'm tired." It comes out whiney, and I hate that, but it works. They both instantly stop arguing and focus on me.

"Are you okay, Red? What can we do for you?" Ry asks. I smile at him being so sweet. It's not like my big, bad wolf. He's usually gruff and hateful, but not with me.

"I'll be fine. How's James?" I ask, finally forcing both eyes open. I'm lying in our bed, with Ry and Trevan standing guard.

"Luca and Orym are watching him," Ry says.

"I hate to ask, but will you carry me out there? I need to see him, but I just don't have the strength right now." I smile at him, knowing that my love can't deny me anything. He scoops me up without another word and carries me to the living room where James is sitting up on the couch, talking to Luca.

"Garnet!" James exclaims. Ry sets me on the couch next to him, where I'm pulled into a huge hug.

"How do you feel?" I ask, trying to check him out.

"I'd wager that I'm feeling better than you are, from the look of it," he answers, not letting go of me. "Thank you. Luca told me what you did. You saved my life."

Before I can respond, Orym brings in a tray with tea and cookies on it. "You both need to drink some tea and eat something. Then we need to talk about Amber and your father."

I wondered how long it would be before one of them brought that up. "We should get started. I feel like that's gonna be a long conversation."

Everyone gathers around. Ry brings a chair in for Trevan, and another for Grammy. When they're all settled in, I start.

"Trevan is my father. He's also the king of the Fae realm. He's here to help us, well, I'm not sure now. He came back with me to help heal James. Now that I've done that, I'm not sure if he'll be staying to fight against Amber or not."

We all turn to look at my father and see what he says. "I cannot stay indefinitely, but I am able to hang around for a few more days and offer my assistance."

"That will have to do. Thank you," I answer. It's not what I wanted to hear, but some help is better than none. And I understand that he has a kingdom to take care of. I just wish I was confident in my ability to take on Amber.

"I'm guessing from how freaked out you guys were when we got back, that Amber escaped." I look at Ry for confirmation. His subtle nod is all I get. "And you were worried that she'd taken me. I understand."

"We found out shortly after you disappeared that it wasn't her." Orym says.

FIVE
REVELATIONS

JAMES

Being healed is great, until we learn that Amber has escaped from the council's custody. I shouldn't be surprised, but I am. Garnet isn't. She appears to have expected it. I have no idea what we're going to do now. According to Ryland, no one knows where Amber is hiding, and her minions have been kidnapping more supernaturals as well as humans.

"I know what she's planning, I just don't know what her timeline looks like," Garnet explains.

"An army of hybrids, we know," Ryland responds. Her eyebrows raise in surprise, but she doesn't comment. "Luca told us that you and he figured it out just before James got hurt."

"It won't work," Trevan says quietly. "Not without your power. So, is she trying to steal your powers, or is she trying to make you complete the transformation for her?"

"She wants to kill me and take my power. I'm not as worried about facing her now that I know how much Fae power I have," Garnet replies.

"You should still be cautious. She managed to escape from the council, and it seems like she's figured out how to bypass the power-blocking cuffs you put on her." I stand up and pace the room.

I start to feel dizzy, but don't want to worry anyone. Instead of mentioning it, I lean against the wall and watch as the conversation continues.

"I understand that, and agree, caution is the way to go. But I'm not scared of her anymore. I think that was the thing that held me back when she was training me. I felt intimidated by her. I'm not anymore. That's all I was saying," Garnet explains.

"I think we need a plan. We can't just chase after her. There has to be a way to find out exactly what her timeline is. Hybrids are rare, but they've been around longer than Delilah. Why wait until now to build that army?" Orym insists. I agree with him, but I'm feeling weak again.

"Orym is right," Ryland says.

Luca takes my place pacing the floor. "But how do we get her to admit everything? We can't get close to her without risking Red. And it's not like she's just gonna send us a letter explaining it all." His frustration is evident. I feel it too, but getting caught up in it won't help anyone.

"We start by catching a witch. Then we send a very specific message back to Amber with that witch. As many of them as she has scouring the woods for wolves, it shouldn't be hard," Ryland explains.

"That's a good point. We encountered a lot of them when we were searching for Garnet. That's actually how we found out that Amber didn't have you," Orym says.

"Okay, let's catch a witch." Garnet winks at me and smirks. I like that she's feeling confident now, but I'm worried that she's a bit too cocky and will put herself in danger.

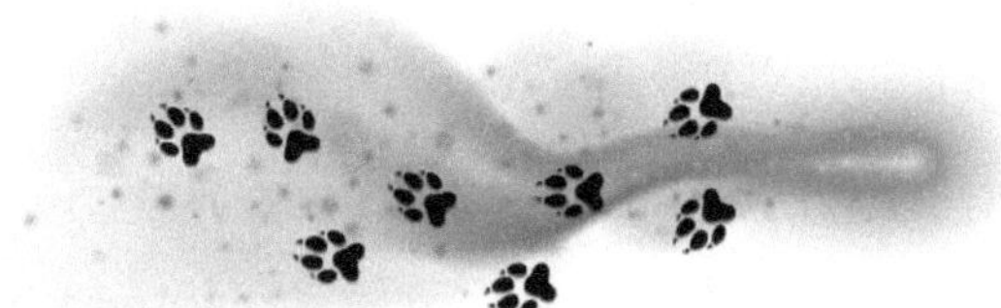

LUCA

Our meeting goes better than I expect, except for Red. Her new attitude is a little disturbing. But if it helps her to control her magic, I'll support it. I wish she was taking the risk more seriously, though.

It doesn't really matter what I think, because I would never call her out for having a new attitude. Probably because I'm still hesitant about the strength of our bond. I know that Red loves me, and I love her. What I'm not sure about is being worthy of her. I couldn't even keep from being captured by Amber's followers.

Then I wasn't able to escape without help from Red's father. I think that was less frustrating when I didn't know who he was. It was one thing for a friend to help me. It's entirely another for it to have been my mate's father. How weak does that make me look?

I can't show weakness here. I have to be the alpha mate that Red deserves. As much as it pains me to think, I have to be more like Ryland. His big, bad wolf energy shows that he can protect Red and the territory. I have to prove that as well.

I'm so caught up in my own thoughts and feelings that I miss half the conversation. I look up to find James wincing in pain. No one else seems to notice. I slide an arm under his and guide him to the kitchen. "Are you okay?" I ask, grabbing a mug and making him a cup of Red's favorite tea.

"I don't know. I just got dizzy and then pain shot from my scar up my leg. Do you think they noticed?" He seems more concerned with the others noticing than with being in pain. I poke my head into the living room. They're still talking and don't seem to have noticed that we're missing yet.

"I don't think so. They're still debating something. Honestly, I got lost in my own thoughts and missed most of what was said," I admit. James nods in understanding. "You seem like you understand what I'm going through. I'm guessing it's because you're not a shifter."

"I get it. You blame yourself for getting captured. I blame myself for getting injured. It is hard feeling like the odd man out. But you have to know that it hurt her when she couldn't find you. She nearly destroyed Midnight when she found out you were being tortured and they wouldn't let her storm the forest to go after Amber." James' words seem strange, but I'm certain he's telling the truth.

"She blamed herself for you getting hurt. And she was terrified that you weren't going to make it." I don't know if my words are comforting to him like his were to me, but I feel like I should tell him. "We kept looking for ways to heal you, even after she disappeared."

"I know. You guys are my family."

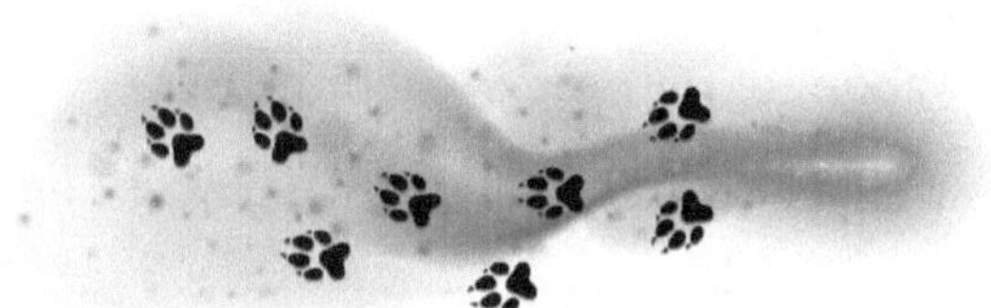

GARNET

While listening to Trevan and Ry argue about the best way to lure Amber out, I notice that Luca and James have disappeared. I shift a little on the couch and see them in the kitchen. I won't interrupt their bonding session, but I make a note to ask them about it later. James still looks a little green, and I'm worried that I didn't completely heal him.

It bothers me that he's less durable than the rest of us. Being human is a vulnerability that Amber can exploit when we go up against her again. If only there was something I could do to protect him more. I'll have to give it some thought and do some research on ways to make him stronger.

There has to be a spell or a potion. Something that will give him more protection. I just have to figure out what it is. I can't focus on that right now, because it looks like my mate and my father are about to start throwing punches.

"Let's take a beat and calm down a little," I offer, stepping between them. "You go into the kitchen and get a cup of tea," I say to Trevan. "And you, step outside for some air." I shove Ry a little to get my point across. I plan to join him outside and try to diffuse the situation. It only takes a glance at Orym for him to realize that I'm going to need his help here.

"Trevan, why don't we get that cup of tea, and you can tell me about the Fae realm?" I know he's only being nice to appease me, but I appreciate the gesture. I make a mental note to tell him that later. I know he struggles with Fae beings because of the ones who killed his family.

It seems that I've been causing trouble for everyone for longer than I realized. I know that the Fae who killed Orym's family did so because they were searching for me, and no one would give me up. Instead, they made the ultimate sacrifice. And now, it's time for me to stand up for everyone who kept me safe as a child. Even if they're gone, they deserve justice. If not for Amber, I wouldn't have been hidden away. I would have grown up with my parents and learned to control my powers as a child.

It's unreal to me that my aunt is the cause of all of my problems. If only she hadn't been in love with my father, she might have let my mother be happy. If she hadn't been jealous of my mother's powers, or if my mother had fought back, things might be different now. But I can't live in the past. I have to focus on defeating Amber. And to do that, I need to get everyone on the same page.

I follow Ry out onto the porch. "That guy really knows how to push my buttons," he growls. I slide behind him and wrap my arms around his waist, pressing my cheek to his back.

"I know he's frustrating, but please, for me, will you just try to get along? He's only going to be here for a couple of days. We need to get a plan in place and set things in motion so this can end. I'm so tired of worrying about Amber." I hate admitting that to anyone, but I also know that Ry will understand.

"I'm sorry. I get that he's your dad, but I just want to punch him so bad," Ry says as he turns in my arms. "I missed you." He drags me closer and presses his lips to mine. I let myself sink into his kiss, melting against him. The only thing that would make this moment better is if I had all four of my guys around me. Ry breaks our kiss and smirks at me. "You know you'll have that later. We have to get all of this planned. Remember? You just told me that we only have Trevan for a few days."

"Oh, shit. Where's he gonna sleep? I can't have sex with my mates if my father is sleeping on our couch." I make a face and Ry laughs at me.

"I think Grammy will let him stay with her. She understands that we need some time alone after you've been gone so long."

"Thank the goddess," I breathe, dropping my head onto his chest. "I hated being away from you guys. It was nice to have James with me, but he was mean and wouldn't have sex with me. I was denied orgasms." I pout a little as I complain to Ry about my time in the Fae realm.

"You poor baby. We'll have to make up for that tonight. The guys and I will give you all the orgasms while James watches. How does that sound?" Ry's voice against my ear makes my core contract.

"That sounds amazing. But we have to go back in there and work out this plan first, don't we?" I ask, disappointed.

He kisses the top of my head and laughs. "Yes, we do. The sooner we get this handled, the sooner you get orgasms. So, let's get moving. I'll try to control my temper and work with your father."

"Thank you. I'm not sure how I feel about him, but I think he can help," I admit. I'd much rather stay out here with Ry than go back to discussing Amber. This problem isn't going to solve itself, though.

I let Ry drag me back inside where we find everyone in the living room waiting for us. "We need to get as much of this sorted as we can. I'll be staying with Grammy while I'm here and would rather not be traipsing through the woods after dark if possible." Trevan's announcement catches me off guard. I wonder if he was listening to Ry's and my conversation outside.

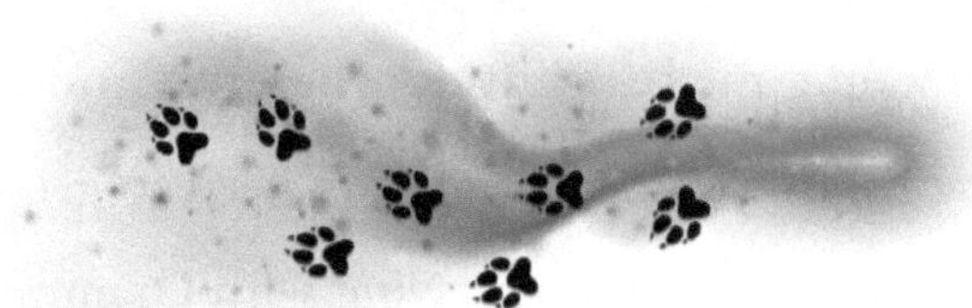

RYLAND

The moment Trevan makes his announcement about staying with Grammy, I know that one of them was listening in on our conversation. I can tell that Red is embarrassed by it, but I don't care. It gets her father out of our way so that we can take care of our girl. She needs our attention, and if I'm being honest, we all need hers.

This situation has everyone on edge. The sooner we get a plan in place, the sooner I can spend some time with my mate.

"We should eat and get a basic plan together. We can work out the details in the morning, then prepare to execute the plan within the next day or so. That way Trevan can still be here to help, without abandoning his people for too long."

Red smiles at me, showing appreciation for me including her father in our plan. I know she's hesitant about him, but I also know that he could be helpful to us. If he wants to be. I can't tell if he means it when he says that he wants to defeat Amber or if he's got something else planned. I'll keep an eye on him and deal with it if I have to.

I make a mental note to discuss it with Orym later. He seems to be the only one besides me who isn't sure about our Fae companion. Between the two of us, we can keep our family safe. I'm sure of it.

"Don't we already have the basic plan figured out? We have to grab one of Amber's witches, then we send our message back to the bitch. We can figure out details tomorrow, after everyone has had a chance to rest," Red says.

"I'll get dinner going, then," Orym insists, heading to the kitchen. I exchange a look with Red, then follow him. I want to talk to him alone and can't do that if she follows me.

"Can we talk for a minute, Orym?" I ask, walking up behind him as he pulls ingredients out of the fridge.

"Sure, Ryland, what's up?" He turns to me and freezes. My expression probably tells him that this isn't a joking matter.

"How do you feel about Trevan?" I keep my voice low, so that Orym has to take a step closer to hear me.

"I'm not sure. I don't want to upset Garnet, because he's her father. But I don't know if he's here to help or if he's got ulterior motives." Orym's words confirm my own concerns.

"We need to keep an eye on him. I agree with you, but I don't think Red, Luca, or James sees it that way. I'm not sure about Grammy. She may have invited him to stay with her for the same reason." Perhaps I should talk to our pack elder and see what her reasoning was.

Orym nods and continues getting dinner prepped. "It's possible. She is very perceptive. I guess we'll see soon."

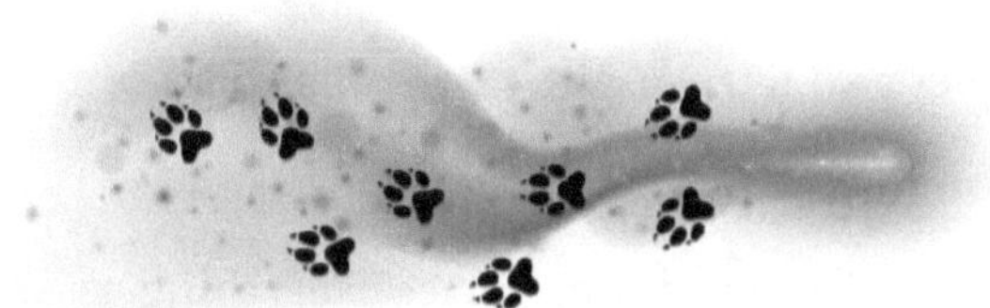

ORYM

My conversation with Ryland puts me on edge. I'd nearly convinced myself that my fears were unwarranted, but if he's got the same concerns, then maybe we're picking up on something the others just don't see. I've never hoped so much to be wrong about someone before in my life. I want Garnet's father to be the man she deserves him to be. I don't want her to deal with another betrayal from her family. It's bad enough that she's going to have to kill her own aunt to stop the chaos that's coming.

Since Ryland and I agree about what needs to be done, I refocus my attention on making dinner for everyone. Tacos are quick and easy, so that's what I make. I wonder if Trevan eats tacos. Oh well, if not, he can make himself a salad with the veggies and lettuce. I'm not going to go out of my way to pander to him.

When the food is done, I place everything on the table. It's not fancy, but everyone will be able to put what they like on their tacos. As soon as we all have plates of food, we settle back in the living room to eat and chat. With the basic plan in place, we don't have to focus on Amber right now.

"So, Trevan, what's it like in the Fae realm?" I ask before taking a bite. I need to interact with him more to tell if he's being sincere.

"Well, you know, it's like here, but with magic," he responds. I glance at Ryland, who seems to understand my annoyance.

"Okay, but some of us have never been there. We'd genuinely like to know," Ryland interjects. That gets our visitor talking. He describes the forest that mirrors our own, except in different colors. Then he tells us about the palace where he lives and the courtyard garden where he trained Garnet.

She, Luca, and James all chime in at different points to explain something different about the unfamiliar realm. I can't help feeling a little jealous that they've all shared this, and I've been left out. One glance at Ryland, and I know he's feeling the same. He's not as good at hiding his emotions as I am.

You might want to relax your expression, alpha. Your jealousy is showing. I nudge him through the bond.

Thanks. I can't help feeling that way. But they don't need to see it. I'm a little surprised that his response is so sincere. We haven't always gotten along so well.

Same here. And you're right; they don't need to see it. We can talk about it later, when they're not around. I offer, though I'm not sure why. Maybe I'm softening a little toward my alpha. He's proven that he takes the position seriously and doesn't let it interfere with caring for our family.

While I listen to Trevan's stories, I realize that I care a lot about these people. My pack. My family.

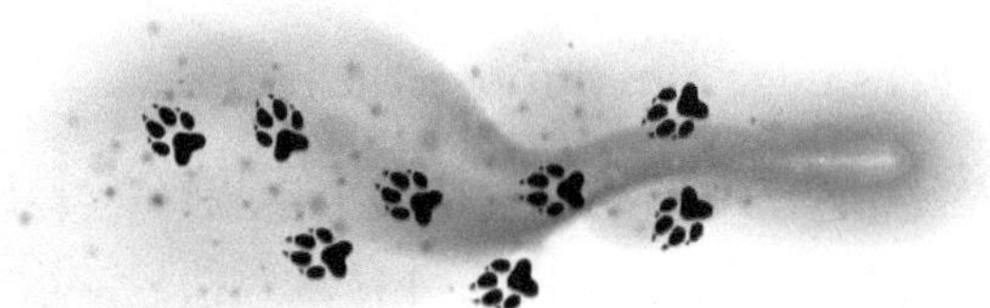

GARNET

I know that Ry and Orym are having a private conversation along the bond, but I have no idea what it's about. It seems odd that they got my father talking, only to ignore him. I decide that it's not worth worrying about. They'll tell me when they're ready.

Trevan's stories make me a little sad for missing out on so much as a child. I want him to be a better man than he is. I know he's only here because we pressured him into it. If he was left on his own, he wouldn't fight Amber. He would hide in his own realm and pretend that none of this was happening. I hold no illusions about my father or his ethical leanings.

I wonder what he has up his sleeve that's making him stay a few days. I'd expected him to go home as soon as we healed James. Yet he found a way to stick around and intwine himself into our plan. I consider Orym and Ry again. Perhaps this is what they're discussing. I'll have to ask later.

For now, I'll be content having dinner with my family and listening to stories of happenings in the Fae realm. He's still talking when we finish eating, and I find myself amused by it. Orym's initial question wasn't enough to get Trevan to open up, but once he did, it's been difficult for anyone to get a word in.

After telling us about the obvious differences between our realm and his, he launched into stories about my mother and their courtship. I want to ask him how Amber fit into all that, but I hesitate to steer the conversation back to her. We're having a pleasant evening, and the last thing I want is to ruin it.

So, I let him talk, without bringing her up. There's always time to ask about that later. After all, it's possible that Amber lied about everything. Maybe he never was interested in her at all, and she was obsessed with him. I don't know, but that thought makes me feel a little better about everything. I'll let myself hold onto that for a bit.

It doesn't really matter how it all happened, anyway. Amber became jealous of my mother and ended up killing her. It's a sad truth that I have to accept. Even if Trevan was romantically involved with Amber before my mother, that doesn't excuse Amber's behavior.

I realize that I haven't been paying attention to Trevan's story because I let my mind wander. "Am I boring you, daughter?" he asks with a smirk.

"No, I was just thinking about something rather unpleasant. Sorry. Your stories are fascinating, really," I insist. I'm not sure if he believes me or not. I still don't want to offend him, if he actually is here to help.

"Sometimes she gets a little distracted, thinking about all the things we're going to do to her later," Luca says, making me blush while pulling attention away from me. I'm not sure if I should be mortified or relieved. On one hand, he just implied to my father and Grammy that we have some kinky stuff going on in the bedroom. On the other, he did get them all to stop staring at me as if I'd done something wrong by not listening.

"Think nothing of it, child. With four mates, I'm sure it's hard not to focus on the depravity that happens in the bedroom." Trevan's response makes my face warm even more. At this point, I'd like to crawl into a hole and hide.

"Now, now. Let's stop talking about Red's sex life. Can't you see that the poor girl is embarrassed. Not that she has anything to be embarrassed about. I'm sure she'll be relieved when we finally leave for the night and she can get some attention from her mates," Grammy says with a wink. I know she thinks she's helping, but it embarrasses me even more. I duck my head and try to hide behind James.

Of course, he's amused by this situation and doesn't let me. "Oh, no. You can't hide from this. It's too amusing," he says, pulling me to his chest.

"You guys are too much. I got distracted. I'm sorry. And no, I wasn't thinking about sex. I was thinking about what Amber told us about how my parents got together. But I wasn't going to bring it up, because I don't want to talk about her again." I hate that I just blurted all that out but feel relieved that it's out there now.

Trevan looks at me for a moment, considering. "What did she tell you?"

"That you were dating her until my mother swooped in and stole you from her," I answer reluctantly.

He laughs. My father actually laughs at that statement. I don't know if that's good or bad, but it catches me off guard.

"What?" I ask. Everyone is staring at us now.

"I did not date Amber. I was never interested in her, though she did throw herself at me several times. I explained to her, on more than one occasion, that I was not romantically interested. There was no spark there, even when she forced herself into my embrace and kissed me. I offended her by pushing her away. Your mother apologized for her sister's behavior, and after we talked, I realized that I was interested in Ruby." Trevan pauses, then continues. "She was kind and sweet. Of course, she was beautiful, too, so that didn't hurt."

"Wait, so you weren't with Amber?" I ask. The relief that washes over me is instant. Sure, he could be lying, but why would he? It's not like we would have treated him any different if he had been with Amber before my mom. But his explanation makes me feel better anyway.

"Not at all. I tried to be her friend after Ruby and I started dating, but it never worked."

SIX
PREPARATIONS

LUCA

Finding out that Amber lied to us doesn't surprise me. I don't believe half of what she told us while she held us hostage anyway. Red seems skeptical of her father and his claims. But having been in his position before, I understand how he felt. Being chased by someone you aren't interested in is challenging.

At least the girl who wanted me wasn't Red's sister. That would have been awkward to say the least. There's something about the earnest way he explains the situation that makes me believe him. And I'm pretty sure there is an old story about how Fae can't lie. But that may just be something they spread around so people would believe them no matter what they said.

Shortly after his revelation, Trevan decides that it's time for him to get out of here. I don't mind, because that will give us some alone time with Red. I've missed her, and I want to take care of her. We have a lot to prepare for, but I think we all need to take some time to reconnect. Focusing on our family will remind us exactly what we're fighting for.

We've all lost so much already, and there's always a chance that we won't be able to defeat Amber. If she wins, then all of this is for nothing. Every supernatural race will be under her control, and there will be no way to defeat her. But that will only happen if she gets Red's powers. So, we won't let that happen.

As much as we need to plan for what's coming, we need to take care of Red. She was away from us for what felt like an eternity, and we all deserve to spend some quality time together. "Why don't we get ready for bed? It's been a long day, and we could use the rest," James offers.

He's been acting kind of distant today, and I wonder if it's just that he's not fully healed yet. It has to be difficult to process having your soul in one realm and your body in another. Then being squashed back together; I just can't imagine what he's going through.

"That's probably a good idea," Ryland agrees, placing his hand on Red's back to encourage her to move toward our bedroom.

She shakes her head and pushes him away. "I won't be able to sleep right now. I'm too wound up from everything Trevan told us about Amber and her lies."

"Then let us take your mind off it," Orym suggests. I know what he's hinting at, because it's exactly what I was thinking myself.

Red freezes and stares at us. "What exactly do you have in mind?" Her seemingly innocent question makes me laugh.

"As if you don't already know," I respond. She glares at me, but it has no heat to it. I step closer to her and cup her face before kissing her gently.

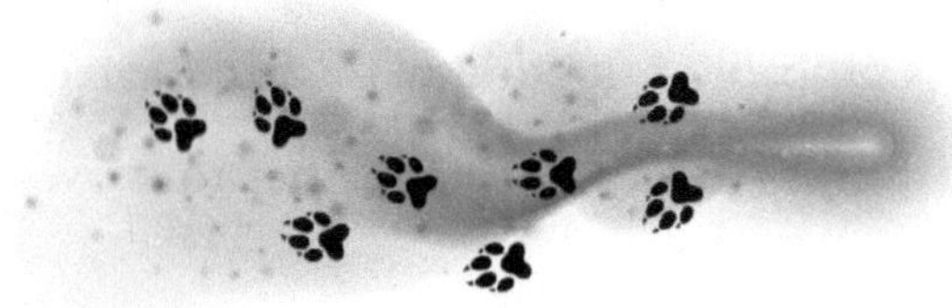

RYLAND

The moment Luca kisses Red, I know that she'll give us a chance to take care of her needs. She wants to work through everything we've learned today, but we all know that she needs to take a break. We need to show her what she's fighting for so that she can refocus on defeating Amber.

I'm used to taking charge, but I take a step back, letting Luca and Orym lead this interaction. James holds back as well, and I wonder if he's feeling off from just being healed or if there's something else going on.

While Luca kisses Red, Orym sandwiches her to him and brushes her hair over her shoulder to kiss her neck. I have to admit, watching this is sexy as hell, and my dick completely agrees. Her soft moans and purrs of pleasure at having their mouths on her drive me crazy. Part of me wants to shove them out of the way and make her scream my name as she comes. But I know that's not how a pack like this works. I have to respect that my mate has other mates, which means that sometimes I have to take a backseat and enjoy the show.

The look on James' face distracts me from watching as their hands roam over our girl's body. It's almost like he's in pain or trying to make a difficult decision. I'm not sure which is happening, but I'd like to find out. I catch his eyes, and nod toward the door, silently asking if he wants to talk. He makes a sour face, then slips outside.

I hate to leave while things in here are heating up, but part of being the territory leader is making sure my charges are safe.

It's strange how much I've matured in such a short time since taking over from Gunnar. This responsibility is nothing like I expected. I take one last glance at the trio before following James outside.

"You wanna tell me what's up with your face?" I ask as soon as the door clicks behind me.

"What are you talking about?" he counters. It isn't surprising that he wants to play games about this. I want to know what his problem is, though, so I'll keep pushing.

"You looked like you were about to throw up when they started making out. That's not your usual response," I explain. I watch his face as he considers what I've said. I take a step closer. "You know that we're family. You can tell me anything."

His expression relays the conflict he doesn't want to discuss. "I've just been thinking about everything today. I almost died. Somehow, Garnet saved me. I don't understand what's going on here. I know she has to fight Amber, but I don't like it. I don't want her to do it. I want to take her and leave. We should go somewhere that Amber can't find us."

"You know that wouldn't work. I'm responsible for these people."

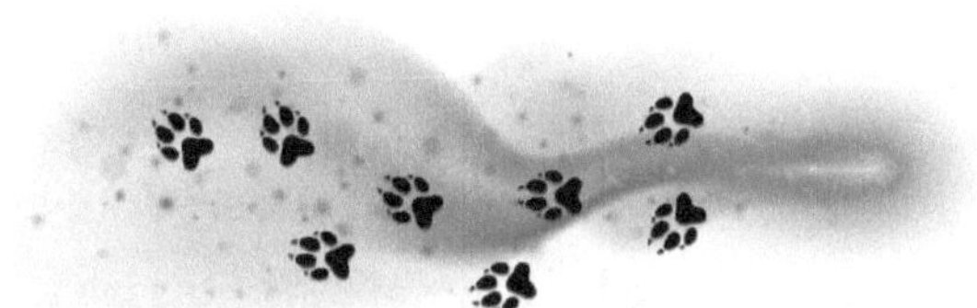

GARNET

Even with Luca's and Orym's hands and mouths on me, I notice the second James and Ry leave the cabin. I reach out through our bond, asking Ry if everything is okay.

We're good. James is still adjusting to being healed. We'll be back in a bit. Enjoy yourself.

It seems odd coming from Ry, because he usually wants to be the center of attention. I have noticed some changes in him since he became the territory leader, though. I'm proud of how he's taken control and matured.

"Are we not distracting enough for you, Red?" Luca asks with a pout.

I smile and shake my head. "Of course you are. I just noticed that we lost a couple of participants, that's all. I was checking in with Ry."

"Everything okay?" Orym asks, kissing my neck.

"Yeah, James just needed some air." I know it's not the truth, but I don't want anyone else to worry. He's been acting off today. I'd thought it was my imagination until Ry took him outside. "Where were we?" I ask, turning to face Orym and pressing my lips to his.

I lose myself to the kiss, letting all my worries and fears go to focus on the love I feel from these two men. I still notice Ry and James' absence, but I don't let it interfere with showing these men how I feel about them. While I'm kissing Orym, Luca presses himself to my back. I slide a hand down his back and grab his ass, pulling him closer so I can feel his erection against my ass.

He growls and pushes harder against me until he's backed the three of us up against the wall. Pressed between him and Orym, I can feel both of their hard cocks. Wetness pools between my legs and I clamp my thighs together. Luca's growl is enough to soak my panties without having his lips on my neck and shoulder and his hands roaming my body while Orym's lips are devouring mine.

I pull Orym's shirt over his head, revealing his chiseled chest. Damn, my men are hot. I've missed this so much. My desire is wound tight and about to burst free. I reach an arm over my head to grab Luca's shirt, but he's already peeled it off. Both men take this chance to pull my shirt over my head, baring me to them. Orym's groan at the sight of my lace bra makes my thighs quiver. He licks his lips and I know exactly where I want his mouth.

Luca unfastens my bra and tosses it away. None of us are too concerned about doing this in the living room, right next to the front door. Any thoughts of someone walking in are eclipsed by hands and a mouth on my breasts. Luca pinches one nipple while Orym sucks the other. My knees buckle, and I'm held up only by the two men sandwiching me between them.

While Orym is licking and sucking on my breasts, Luca slides his hand down the front of my leggings. I gasp, the sensation almost too much for me. He strokes my clit, rubbing the little bundle of nerves just how I like it. Orym kisses me, swallowing my moans of pleasure.

The two of them work together to remove the rest of our clothes and lower me to the floor, where a blanket is spread out. I wonder when that happened. I don't have time to worry about it, because Luca turns me to kiss him as Orym settles between my legs, spreading them open to give him access.

The moment Orym's tongue touches my clit, I come so hard I nearly buck him away from me. If Luca wasn't holding onto me, I would have probably run away. The sensations are overwhelming after going weeks without this kind of touch.

"That's it, Red. Relax and let Orym enjoy you," Luca says as he strokes my hair away from my face. He trails his hand down my neck, drawing a pattern on my collarbone before moving lower to trail over my breasts.

Orym laps at my pussy as if he's starving and it's the best thing he's ever eaten. He growls against it, and I come again. "I can't take it, please. I need you. Both of you," I pant.

"I wanted to taste you too, Red. Are you sure you can't handle more?" Luca asks.

I shake my head, insisting that I can't handle any more sensation there. Luca shrugs and pulls Orym to him, kissing him the same way he'd just been kissing me. I don't know if I'm more shocked or turned on by it. Luca finishes the kiss by licking my release from Orym's chin, then turns back to me. Orym's cheeks turn pink, but Luca looks at me as if he's a lion and I'm his prey.

"That was so fucking hot," I admit, biting my lower lip.

"I thought you'd like that," he replies. "How do you want us?" He gives me the chance to tell them exactly what I want, but I'm not sure.

"I want you both to fuck me. Please, I need it." I'm begging, but I don't care. My men will take care of me, and I don't have to be ashamed of needing them.

"It's okay, Garnet. We've got you," Orym says, moving from between my legs to let Luca take his position. "Just relax and enjoy the orgasms." Luca's thick cock slides into me way too slowly. I try to squirm and move my hips to move him faster, but Orym holds me still. "Let Luca do it, love."

I groan in frustration, but relent, because Orym is stronger than me. They would never force me to do something I don't want, so I let them have their way this time. My breath hitches as my body stretches to accommodate Luca. His thrusts are painstakingly slow, and I know he's doing it to torture me.

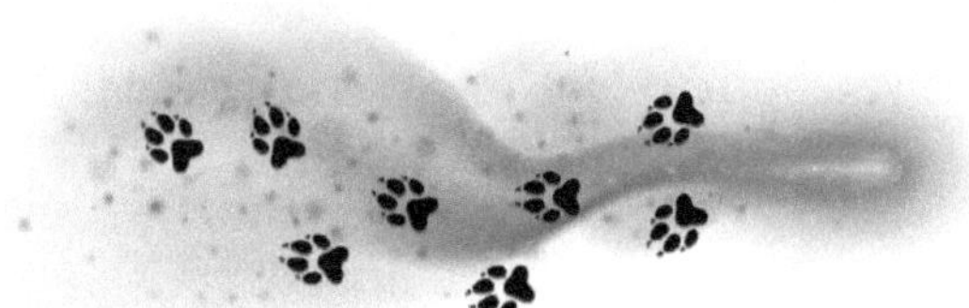

ORYM

I can tell that Garnet isn't happy about Luca's pace, but we need to worship her properly this time. We can do fast and frenzied later. She needs slow and tender as much as we do. I'm annoyed that Ryland and James left, but I can only assume that one of them is dealing with the other's bullshit trying to fix things.

I refocus my attention on Garnet, who is finally letting herself relax into Luca's pace. He thrusts his cock into her over and over, moving so slowly that you'd think he wasn't building up to anything. But the look on his face tells me that he's getting close. I know he wants her to get there first, so I slide a hand between them and flick her clit. Garnet tries to buck her hips and speed Luca up, but he resists that temptation.

With just a few more thrusts, Garnet cries out in pleasure as she comes undone. "Luca!" He follows her over the edge, and I'm even more turned on from watching them.

He collapses on top of her, panting. I shove him over and take his place. "My turn," I insist. Garnet licks her lips and nods. I'm surprised that she didn't ask for both of us to fuck her at the same time, but Luca didn't really give her a choice. I'm not mad at having her to myself for a moment, even if he is in arm's reach or touches her.

I slide my cock along her soaked folds, before slapping it against her clit. She gasps in shock, and I do it again. "You like that," I say, not asking. She nods again. "Use your words, Garnet, or I'm not going to fuck you."

She pouts for a second, then sighs. "Yes, I like it. Please, Orym, fuck me now." I love the way she begs for it. I have no idea how James could have resisted her while they were in the Fae realm. I would not have had that kind of willpower, no matter what the consequences.

I thrust into her slowly, following Luca's lead. Garnet whimpers but doesn't complain. "We want to worship you. Be our goddess and let us tend to your needs." Her expression changes from annoyed to shocked. She hadn't realized that going slow was our way of showing her how much we care about her.

"Fine, worship me. But move faster than this. Please," she insists. I can't argue with her, because I can feel her need wash over me. She's pushing it through our bond, and I can't resist. I slam into her over and over, driving her closer to another orgasm.

Garnet screams in pleasure at getting her way. I smile at her, wondering if she knows just how much we love her. The four of us would do anything to make her happy. I lean down and kiss her as I thrust into her again, hard and fast, just like she wanted.

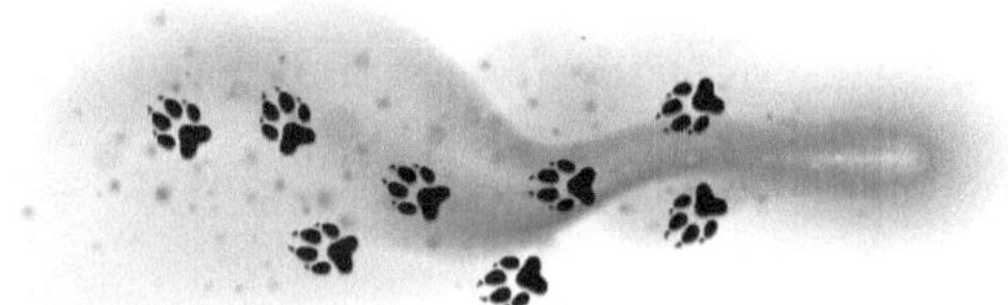

JAMES

"Then what are we going to do? If you won't help me take her away from here, how are we going to make sure that we can defeat Amber? Because she's stronger than we've given her credit for." I'm fighting a losing battle here and I know it. Ryland isn't going to change his mind about this one.

"We have to do whatever we can to help her. Red is the one who has to fight Amber. There's nothing we can do to protect her from this. We can't run away." He's repeating his argument again, and I understand what he's saying, even if I don't like it.

"This situation is not fair. She shouldn't have to fight against her own aunt just to keep her powers," I insist. It's a pointless argument, but I can't stop myself. "Why can't Trevan do more to help?"

"He's already overstepped his bounds as it is. If he does more, he risks starting a war with the witches. There's no reason for that," Ryland says.

I pace back and forth, running my fingers through my hair. "I just can't deal with the thought of losing her."

"I figured that was the root of your problem. We're not going to let anything happen to her. I promise you that. We will all fight by her side, and at the end of this, we will be the victors." His quiet confidence nearly has me convinced that we can do this. I hate the thought that Garnet could be injured or killed though. It's too much for me to bear.

"There must be more we can do. I feel like I'm not enough and there's nothing I can offer in this situation." I hate admitting my shortcomings, but I don't know how else to explain to Ryland how I'm feeling.

"Look, James, we're doing everything we can to help. There's nothing else we can do besides listen, plan, and do what Red needs us to do. She will tell us what's going to help her the most. We just have to trust her."

I lock eyes with Ryland, and something clicks. I realize that he understands what I'm feeling, because he's feeling it too. I nod, and his posture relaxes. I didn't notice that he'd been braced for a fight. As if I was dumb enough to attack him. He's easily twice my size in his human form, and he has a wolf that's even bigger. The thought is laughable.

"Now that we have that sorted, do you think we should head back in and take care of our woman?" he asks, nodding toward the cabin. I had been so caught up in my fears that I blocked out the fact that Luca and Orym are currently fucking our mate.

A sudden wave of jealousy washes over me. "We can't let them have all the fun, now, can we?" I'm desperate to get in there and sink myself inside of the woman I love.

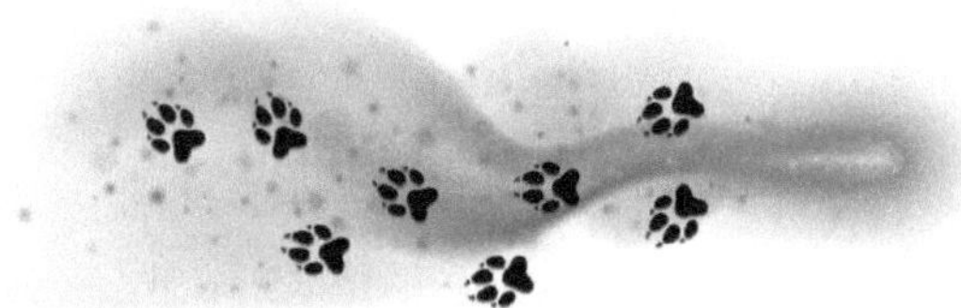

GARNET

Just as I'm coming down from another orgasm, the door opens. I know it's Ry and James, but my head snaps toward them. I lock eyes with Ry and he nods slightly. Everything is okay. I don't have to worry about James or what they talked about.

I feel less anxious with all four of my mates here. Desire builds again as I watch them strip for me. When James and Ry walk across the room to us, Orym and Luca slide out of their way, giving them a chance to be with me. After multiple orgasms, I'm not sure that I can handle more, but the wetness pooling between my legs tells me otherwise.

I reach for Ry because he's closer. He drops to his knees and pulls me up to kiss him. While our lips are locked together, my hand wraps around his hard length. I only stroke him a couple of times before he turns me and breaks our kiss. Before I realize what's happening, Ry lowers me onto James, who is lying on the blanket where I was a moment ago.

James guides his long cock into my tight entrance, pulling me down until he's fully sheathed. I can't stop the moan that escapes my lips at how good he feels. Each of my men is different, and I completely understand why I need them all.

James pauses and looks at me for a long moment. I start to feel self-conscious, but a beat later, he starts to move, bucking his hips and fucking me hard. It's obvious that he doesn't feel the same about worshipping me as Orym and Luca do. It doesn't upset me; this is just a different kind of worship. I don't need them to worship me, anyway. I just need them to love me.

I glance over my shoulder to see Ry stroking himself. "Let me do that," I say. He shakes his head and turns to take something from Luca, who I didn't see leave the room. Ry shakes a bottle of lube at me, and I grin. Leave it to him to be the one who asks to take my ass. I watch as he rubs lube along his length before bringing the bottle over to me.

He gently spreads it across my rosebud, then pushes two fingers into me to prepare me for his cock. With James thrusting up into my pussy, the sensations are almost too much. I shudder and throw my head back. I freeze when Ry lines himself up and starts to push his dick into my ass. "It's okay, love, just relax." His voice in my ear makes me shudder again, but I manage to convince my body to relax a bit. A moment later, he's fully seated inside of me.

James and Ry work together to find a rhythm that keeps me full of either one or the other of them. I let the pressure and sensation wash over me. I'm not trying to control anything right now, just hanging on for dear life. I ride the waves as I climb closer and closer to another orgasm. They thrust into me, over and over, alternating then pushing in together.

I take them with me when I fall over the edge, the three of us coming at the same time. As we untangle, Luca is there with a warm rag to clean us up, and Orym has brought water and snacks. They weren't kidding when they said they were going to worship me. I feel like a goddess with the way these men care for me.

We take our time getting dressed, then decide to watch a movie to take our minds off what's coming tomorrow. I know we'll have to face our fears and insecurities, but I'm glad to have tonight for just us to be together. James picks the movie, and of course, it's a super-hero comedy.

The five of us snuggle on the couch, which has never happened before. Usually, one of the guys sits on the floor. But tonight, it's clear that we all need to be close.

I let my mind wander as the movie plays. I've seen this one a dozen times at least. I could quote every line if I wanted to. So, instead of focusing on the movie, I think about our future, and what I want when this is all over.

We need a bigger cabin, for sure. I know that the guys have been talking about it, and I think we should move forward with building a new one. With more space, would we have kids? Can we even do that? Witches and Fae can, but I don't know about a witch-fae halfling and a wolf shifter. I'll have to do some research to find out. I would love to have a house full of pups with my men, but if it's not possible, I'll have to accept that the Moon Goddess knows what she's doing.

That thought leads me to worrying about James again. He nearly died, because he's human and isn't as durable as the rest of us. Even witches have more natural defenses than humans do. I should talk to him about this. Perhaps he'd be open to letting Dec turn him into a vampire. Then he'd be stronger and more protected. I know it will be a difficult conversation, so I'll have to approach it carefully.

I can't just say, "Hey, James, have you ever considered letting your brother turn you so that you're not so weak?" That would not go over well at all. Because he's not weak. He's just not as strong as a wolf shifter or a vampire. I wish there was a way for me to protect him more. I'll have to keep him close until I come up with a spell, or a charm, or something.

Hopefully I can manage that without him getting suspicious about my motivations.

SEVEN
TIMELINE

RYLAND

During the movie, Red seems distracted. I don't say anything because I'm certain she's not stressing over the conflict with Amber. I'm pretty sure she's focused on James and his distant behavior.

When the movie ends, we all get ready and climb in bed, falling asleep easily. I'm the last to sleep and the first to wake before the sun rises.

I slip out of bed carefully, so I don't wake anyone else. I need a few minutes of peace before we continue planning this war. There's nothing else I can call it. This conflict with Amber has become a war.

I make coffee and sit on the front porch as the sun crests the horizon. I let my mind wander as I enjoy the little bit of solitude I know won't last. Before I'm finished with my cup, the door opens and someone steps out onto the porch.

The moment the door closes, I know it's Red. Her presence always feels different to me. "Did you get coffee?" I ask, not turning to look at her. I gesture to the seat next to me, and she settles in.

"I did. Thanks for making it," she says, then takes a sip. "Are you okay? You were up and gone before I could say anything."

"I'm good. Just looking for a little quiet before the storm. Since I took Gunnar's place, I haven't had much alone time. Things have been pretty much non-stop for a while now. Then you were gone, and we spent days searching for you. It's nice to have a little breather." I look at her now, just to be sure she doesn't think I want her to leave because I said I was enjoying alone time.

Red smiles at me and threads her fingers through mine. "I'm so proud of you for taking this on to protect us. You've grown so much. I might even think you've mellowed out a bit." She chuckles and I growl low. I won't let her think I've gone soft. I'll still rip a man in half if I need to.

I don't argue with her, knowing that she's mostly teasing me. I'll prove myself in battle and take my frustration out on our enemy. Amber's people won't know what hit them. "I hate that you have to do this. If I could fight her myself, I would."

We lock eyes, hers shining with unshed tears. "I know. And if I could keep the four of you out of this, I would. But we have to stick together. We can't defeat her alone. It has to be all of us." Her words confirm what Grammy told us while she was missing. Even if we'd tried to take Amber out, we would have failed without Red to finish it.

The door opens again and I sigh. My reprieve is over sooner than I'd hoped. "Am I interrupting?" Orym asks, closing the door quietly behind him and sitting down by Red.

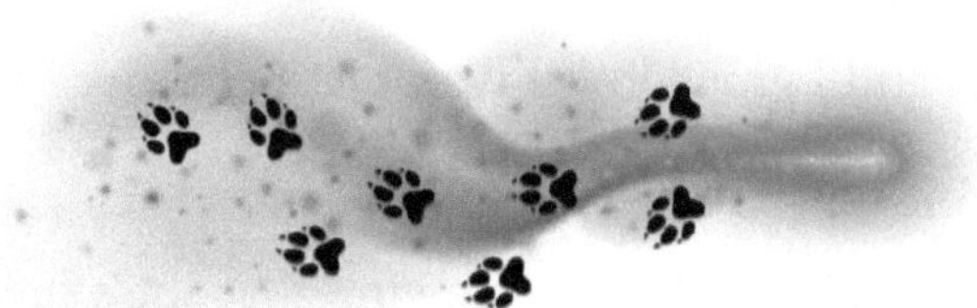

ORYM

Ryland shakes his head at my question. I'm not sure I believe him. They were discussing the upcoming fight, I'm sure, but I don't know what was being said. I won't pry. Everyone deserves to have their privacy. I trust them not to keep secrets.

"We'll finalize our plan today to move on Amber's followers," I say, taking a sip of coffee. I don't know if our plan will work or not, especially with the limited trust I have for Trevan and his efforts to help. Just because he assisted with Garnet's training, that doesn't mean he's on our side.

I'm doing my best to keep my doubts from Garnet. He's her father and deserves a chance to prove me wrong. I hope he does, for her sake.

"As soon as Grammy and Trevan get here, we'll get started. I wonder when they're coming," Garnet says, staring at the tree line near the cabin.

"Probably soon. I know that Grammy gets up with the sun. I feel like your father is probably the same way," Ryland responds. I noticed some chemistry between our elder wolf and the Fae king last night, but I'm not mentioning that either. What they do in the privacy of Grammy's cabin is their business. I shake that thought away, because who wants to imagine their father-in-law screwing the pack grandma? Not me.

"There's no sense in us discussing things until they get here. I didn't mean to stop your conversation," I offer. Part of me hopes they'll return to their topic, and I'll learn what they were talking about.

"It was nothing, really. Just that neither of us wants the other to have to deal with Amber. You didn't interrupt anything," Garnet assures me.

Before I can respond, we hear footsteps coming up the path. "I'm glad to see Grammy was right about how early you all wake. I would have been terribly upset to walk all this way to find you still in bed." Trevan's voice is loud and I wonder if he's using magic to project it to us.

They come through the trees and I notice how closely they're walking. They may have even been holding hands. Interesting, but I'm still not mentioning it.

"We've been up for a while. I'm not sure if Luca and James are or not. But we'll get everyone together and have our meeting. I'm sure you're anxious to get on with all of this," Ryland answers.

"Well, not too anxious. I can't stay indefinitely, so I would appreciate moving things along. But I'm happy to be here as long as I'm needed," Trevan says, glancing at Grammy, who blushes. I knew it. Those two have something going on.

"Let's go inside and I'll get the others," Garnet replies as she stands up. I open the door for everyone and follow them inside.

Luca and James are finishing up setting breakfast on the table. "That smells amazing," I say.

"We can eat, then discuss the plan," Ryland says.

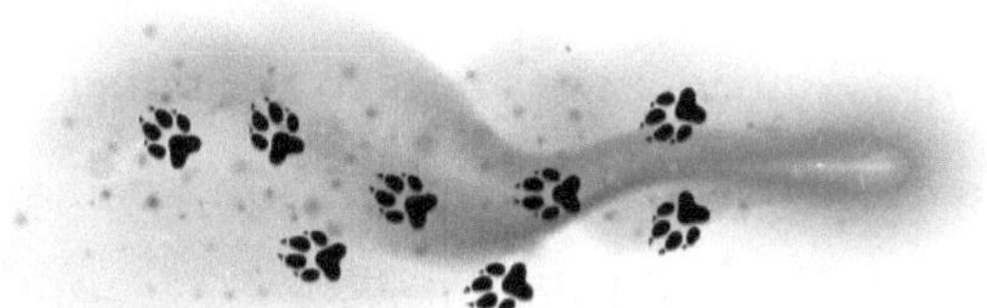

GARNET

It seems odd to me that Grammy and Trevan are acting so comfortable with each other. If I didn't know better, I would think my grandmother-figure had taken a lover. That would be way too weird, though, so I'm pushing that thought away.

We're supposed to be figuring out the details of capturing one of Amber's followers, but instead, we're chatting and having a family breakfast. I'm not upset about it; I would just prefer to get this over with. Just as we finish eating, there's a loud noise like a tree falling outside.

"What the hell?" I ask, jumping up and racing to the door. My guys are right behind me, with Grammy and my father following fast. I throw the door open and my jaw drops at what I see.

My aunt, Amber, stands next to the rather large oak she knocked down to get our attention. "Oh, good, you're home. We need to have a word, dear niece."

I roll my eyes at her and step outside. Everyone follows, even though I motion for them to stay back. "What do you want, Amber? Did you come to surrender?" I know there's no chance of that, but I can't stop myself from asking.

She laughs, clutching her stomach and doubling over as if that's the funniest thing she's ever heard. "Oh, no. I'm not giving up until I have your powers flowing through me. I came to see how you're doing. I haven't heard from you in a while and figured you were hiding while you tremble in fear."

I shake my head at her. "I'm not scared of you. We're ready to end this now."

"It's not quite time yet, dear girl. We need to wait a few days until the Wolf Moon. That is the exact moment when I'll kill you and take your powers. Until then, everything will end in a stalemate, I'm afraid. I can't let you harm any of my people, and your mangy wolves are doing a pretty good job of protecting themselves." She scoffs as she speaks, clearly upset that she's not getting more test subjects.

"Why don't you just let your prisoners go and surrender now? We don't actually have to fight to the death. There's no reason why you can't leave here and live your life."

Amber's expression turns from disgusted to shocked in a moment's notice. When I follow her gaze, I realize that she's just noticed Trevan standing behind me. "You—what are you doing here?"

He steps forward and blocks me from her. "I'm here to help my daughter defeat you. It's about time you paid for the pain you've caused."

She growls at him in response. "The pain I've caused? What about the pain you caused? Treating me like I was less important. Ruby didn't hang the moon. She wasn't even the best witch in our coven. That would be me. But you couldn't recognize that, could you? No, you just had to throw yourself at her feet and become her slave." She shudders in disgust.

"That's not what happened, and you know it. You should try being honest with yourself, Amber. It'll go a long way toward getting you the peace you deserve," he spits back.

Amber takes a step forward and raises her hand in front of her face, palm up. There's some sort of pink powder in her hand, and I realize a moment too late what she's about to do. She exhales and the powder floats along the wind, heading straight for my father. I try to push him out of the way, but I'm not fast enough. He blinks and shakes his head, appearing to be in a trance.

"What did you do to him?" I demand, holding him still as he tries to walk toward her.

"You might as well let him go, dear. He's mine now," Amber insists. Fuck, that had to be some sort of love potion or mind control. We have to stay back so she can't hit us with it too.

Ry and Luca step forward and take Trevan from me, then Orym and James are at my back. Grammy helps get Trevan into the cabin where they can keep him safe and try to break the spell.

"You won't win this, Amber. I will fight you every step of the way. And I know I can defeat you. I've figured out my Fae powers, and I'm gaining better control of my witch powers every day. You will pay for what you've done to my family. It's not a matter of if, but when. You wanna wait until the Wolf Moon, that's fine by me. I'll see you then."

With my declaration, I turn and stroll back toward the cabin, with James and Orym in tow. I hate turning my back on her, because I know she fights dirty, but I'm not really scared of her anymore. I just need time to figure out how to counter her attacks. If I can come up with an antidote to the powder she just used on my father, I'll be able to stop her.

I can't let her take anyone from me. I won't give up the people I love. I refuse to even hand over the father I've never known, no matter how easy it would be. I'm still so conflicted about my feelings for him, that I'm not sure I'd be too upset if he had gone with her. But he would make a powerful ally for her, and that would be disastrous.

So, I turn my back on my aunt, bracing for an attack that never comes. James, Orym, and I walk into the cabin to find Trevan fighting against Luca's hold while Ry ties him to a chair. This will be fun.

"Trevan," I say, trying to get his attention. He's writhing as if he's in pain. I wonder if it's something in the powder that makes him need to be near her.

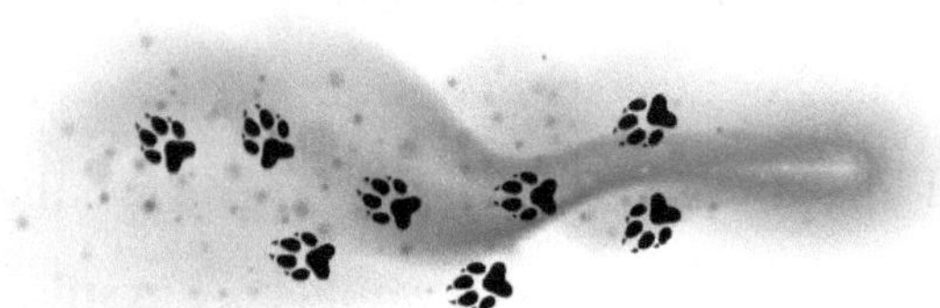

JAMES

"Trevan!" Garnet says her father's name again, but he still doesn't respond. Ryland and Luca finish tying him to the chair so he can't escape. Grammy heads to the kitchen to start making some sort of brew that might break the spell. Her explanations are muttered more than voiced.

The anguish on my mate's face breaks my heart. She falls to her knees in front of the bound man and looks up into his eyes. "Father, please. I need you. Don't leave me." The single tear that slides down her cheek seems to be the one thing that gets Trevan's attention.

"Oh, child. I would never leave you. I had a sudden urge to help Amber. Damned love potion. It only works on people who aren't already in love. So, it didn't make me think that I love her. But it did make me sympathetic to her cause. We must make sure no one gets hit with that again." He shudders as if it was a horrible experience.

"I'm so glad you're back. Maybe Grammy can come up with something to keep that potion from working in the future," Garnet offers.

At the mention of Grammy's name, Trevan turns toward the kitchen. He's trying to get a glimpse of her, and it's pretty obvious that he's concerned about her reaction to what just happened. "Is she okay?"

"Do you and Grammy have something going on?" Garnet whispers to her father. If I wasn't standing so close, I wouldn't be able to hear their conversation.

Trevan's cheeks redden, and he dips his head. "I didn't want you to find out like this. She's the first woman I've cared for since your mother. I hope that you are okay with it. She's concerned that you won't approve."

Garnet throws her arms around her father's shoulders and hugs him. "I definitely approve. But only if you treat her well. She's the only reason I survived my childhood, and I will not have her mistreated. Do you understand me?" Her words are low, but they carry the force of her threat. I'm convinced, as is Trevan, that she means it.

He nods his head. "I would never do anything to hurt her."

"That's good to hear, because we're all rather fond of her," I say, taking a step closer so the others don't hear me. His cheeks turn red again, and it's clear that he didn't realize I could hear their conversation. I am only human, after all.

"Well, we have more information than we did earlier. I don't know how helpful it will be. Is she still out there?" Garnet turns to Ryland and points her question at him. He opens the curtain and shakes his head.

"Looks like she left. She didn't even bother to put the tree back. Bitch," he says, venom dripping from his words.

"I think I can help with that, if you would be so kind as to untie me," Trevan offers with raised eyebrows.

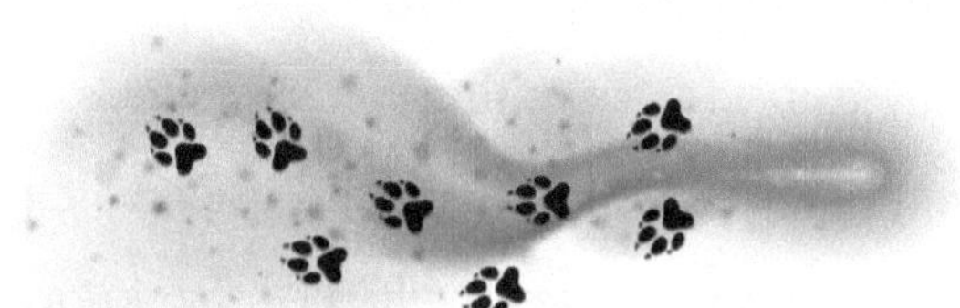

LUCA

"You can put the tree back the way it was?" I'm shocked at his claim, and not sure I believe him. Ryland and I exchange a glance as Orym unties him.

"I am capable of a great many things, boy. As is your mate, if she chooses to use her magic that way," he says.

"I don't even know what magic I would use for that. But I'm interested to learn," Red responds to him.

"Follow me. You can watch and learn," Trevan offers. Red nods and follows him outside. I'm still on edge from Amber's visit, so there's no way I'm letting Red out of my sight.

Ryland, James, and Orym must all feel the same way, because they follow us outside too. We stand behind our mate as her father uses his magic to lift the downed tree and put it back in the ground as if nothing ever happened. I don't believe it will stay. There's no way he could use magic to fix all the roots that had been torn apart when Amber knocked that tree down.

"Good as new. Or old, I guess," Trevan insists. He turns to me as if he can read my skepticism. "Climb it if you don't believe me."

I share a glance with the others, then stroll toward the tree. If it's sturdy, I'll owe him an apology. If the tree doesn't hold me, I'll kick his ass. Either way, I'm okay with it. I shake myself from head to toe as I approach the tree. I'm honestly a little nervous that it's going to come down on top of me. With a deep breath, I reach for a branch and pull myself up. So far, so good.

I continue to climb the tree, anxiously waiting for it to topple over. It doesn't. Instead, it feels solid. This Fae man has actually put the tree back as if Amber had never been here. To say I'm impressed is an understatement. "It feels solid," I call down to the others from high in the tree.

"I can't believe you doubted me, boy," Trevan says back.

"My apologies, Trevan. I didn't think you could repair the roots so easily," I answer, dropping from the tree and rolling.

"That will be a handy skill to have, even after we deal with Amber," Orym says. I nod in agreement. Ryland just stares at the tree, as if he's inspecting it without going near it.

"That was definitely impressive, Trevan. Thank you for repairing the tree for me," he finally says. I wonder what he's thinking, but nothing is floating through the bond.

Red turns toward her father. "It seems pretty straightforward. You lift the tree back into place, then reconnect the roots to the system that's still underground. I won't be able to do it that fast, but I think I can do it."

Her new found confidence makes me smile. I'm certain that anything her father can do, she can too.

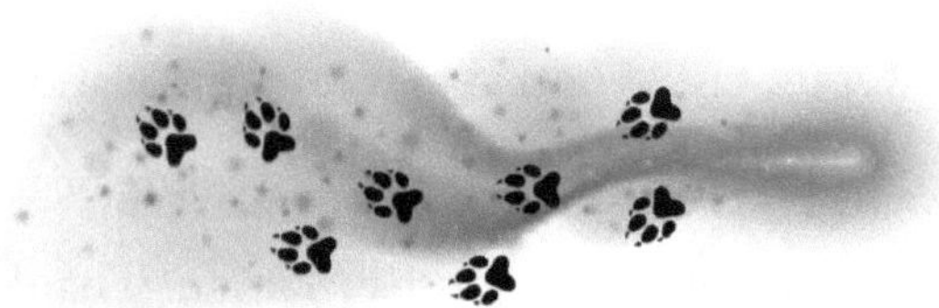

GARNET

New skills are intimidating, but if Trevan can do it, so can I. Of course, I'm not knocking down trees to test that theory. I'll figure it out if and when it becomes relevant. I have bigger things to worry over at the moment. Like the fact that I have less than a week before my aunt comes for me. I meant it when I told her I'm not scared of her anymore. I'm not. But the idea that she's coming after me is intimidating. What if I'm not ready? What if I can't defeat her?

These insecurities hound me until I'm ready to scream. But I can't let my mates, my father, or Grammy know that I'm unsure. I have to project confidence. There is no other option. I must defeat Amber, or everyone I love will suffer.

It helps a little knowing that her love potion won't do much to my guys. I'm still processing Trevan's little bombshell about him and Grammy being an item. I'm not upset by the news, just a little surprised. I don't know much about him, but the little bit I know about Fae tells me that he's either way older than Grammy, or way younger. I guess it's none of my business either way. I still have to keep them both safe.

I'll do what I have to. I know that. I may have doubts about my ability to win, but I have no doubts about my ability to fight. Even if Amber defeats me, I'll take her down with me. It has to be this way. I just wish I understood the Moon Goddess' plan. There had to be a reason she gave me these mates.

"Red?" The way Ry says my name tells me that it's not the first time he's tried to get my attention.

"Sorry, I let my mind wander a bit. What is it?" I ask, playing my distraction off as nothing.

"Are you okay? That news Amber dropped was huge. We have less than a week to figure out how to defeat her," he responds, pulling me into his arms. Orym sandwiches me to him, and I enjoy their warmth.

"I'm fine, really. I was trying to process everything. It's a lot. And not just Amber's news. I don't know how I feel about my father suddenly being interested in the woman who raised me. I'm not mad about it, but it's odd." I decide that a partial truth is better than no truth.

"There's more to it than that, but okay," Orym whispers in my ear. "We trust you. You don't have to tell us everything."

"I hope you realize that we would follow you anywhere." Luca comes up beside me, adding himself to our little group hug. He motions to James, but my human mate is hesitant. I wish it didn't hurt my feelings for him to reject affection like this. "Give him time; he's still healing."

"I know. I'm worried about him, though," I admit. I don't want to worry, and I hate admitting that I am. "He's not as sturdy as we are. I wish there was something we could do to protect him."

My eyes follow James as he walks toward the tree that Trevan healed. A quick glance around tells me that Trevan must have gone back inside with Grammy. Let's hope they're not getting it on in the living room. Or anywhere else. I don't want to think about that at all.

"He just needs time to process. And who knows? Maybe he's struggling with that same thing. You should talk to him," Orym suggests. I know he's right, but I have no idea what to even say. I don't want James to think that I view him as weak. I know he's strong. He's just not supernatural.

"You're right, I should talk to him. If the three of you will excuse me," I say, wiggling my way free of the three sets of arms holding me in place. I walk over to James and watch him for a minute.

"James?" I start, pausing when he doesn't turn to meet my gaze. "Can we talk?"

He nods but doesn't face me. "I know what you're going to say. Don't worry about it. I'll head back to the city this afternoon."

"What?" His words catch me off guard, and I don't know how to respond. "Why would you leave?"

"I don't belong here. I'm not like your other mates. This was a mistake." He finally turns toward me, and I reach for him. He shakes his head and continues. "Garnet, you mean the world to me, but I'm not a wolf. I'm not a witch, or a vampire. I'm just a human. This is never going to work. I shouldn't have let myself be fooled for this long. I'm sorry."

He turns and walks toward the cabin. I spin around to watch him go. "James. Don't do this. If I mean as much to you as you claim, you'll come back here and talk to me."

James pauses at the door of the cabin, then goes inside. What the fuck just happened here? Where did he get the idea that I don't want him? Pain slices through my heart, and I drop to my knees. Tears stream down my face, and I sob into my hands.

I feel the strong arms lift me and hold me against a broad chest. I know from his scent that it's Luca. Neither Ry nor Orym handle tears well. Luca holds me while I purge the pain, while my heart shatters. I wipe my eyes and look around, surprised that my other two wolf shifter mates are gone.

"Where'd they go?" I sniffle with the question.

Luca holds me tight and rubs his hand up and down my back. "It's okay, Red. They went to talk to James. We felt your pain through the bond. None of us were going to interfere, but it was too much."

EIGHT
RECOVERY

ORYM

Ryland and I follow James into the cabin. The searing heat that lanced through my chest as he walked away from Garnet nearly knocked me off my feet. There's no way they had a decent conversation, especially with the way she calls after him as he walked away. Luca runs to her side, and I follow Ryland. Maybe running from her tears is cowardly, but I'd rather face someone I can punch than to watch her cry.

Once inside the cabin, I spare a glance at Grammy and Trevan. Grammy nods at me and grabs the Fae man's hand, dragging him outside. I would guess they'll go back to her place, but at this point, I really don't care. I stalk back to the bedroom where Ryland is facing off with James.

"What did you say to her?" Ryland asks, his hand around James' throat with the human pressed against the wall.

"I told her the truth. This is a mistake. I shouldn't be here. I don't belong. I'm not one of you," James spits. Pain stabs through my chest again, and Ryland rubs the identical spot on his chest. He feels it too. Mate bond rejection is something we've never experienced until now. If James leaves, it could destroy Garnet.

"You think so little of us? We're your pack. You are one of us now. Our mate claimed you. That makes you family, idiot. Stop being a jerk and go apologize to her," Ryland insists.

"Go tell her you didn't mean it," I say. I know he did, though, because I already feel the emptiness where his bond used to be. I rub at my chest.

"I did mean it, though. I shouldn't be here. I'm not enough for her." His voice breaks with his words, and I know that he's feeling the pain too. A damaged mate bond is one thing, but James destroyed this one. I'm not even sure that we could repair this if we could change his mind.

"This will destroy her," I whisper, still rubbing the stabbing pain on my chest. I want to reach in and rip my own heart out to make it stop.

"It's already destroyed me. Please, just let me go. You're all better off this way," he begs. Tears slide down his face. Ryland lets him go, and James walks out. He's leaving, and we're not stopping him.

"We can't let him go," I say to Ryland.

"We don't have a choice. You can't force someone into a mate bond, and you can't keep them there if they don't want to be. All we can do now is comfort Red and hope he changes his mind before it's too late." Ryland's words echo in my head.

I nod and follow him outside where Luca holds Garnet as she cries. James is nowhere to be seen, and I know it's already too late. He's gone, and there's nothing we can do about it.

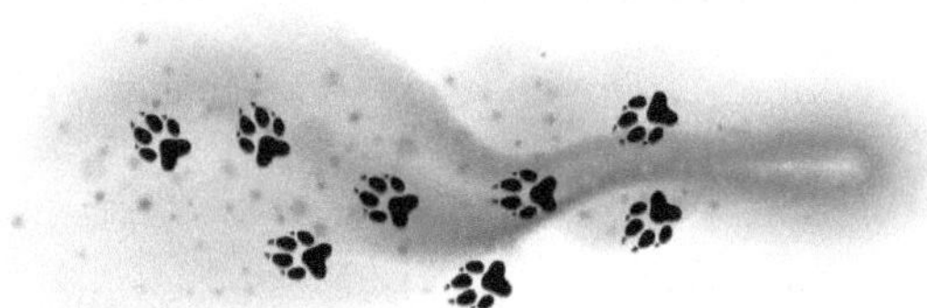

JAMES

Walking away from Garnet is the hardest thing I've ever done. But nothing I said to her was untrue; I know it in my heart. I'm not like her other mates. I don't fit here. A human in a world of magic and shifters will never work. I can't just stay and pretend that everything is okay. I have to give her a chance to survive this fight. And the only chance she has is without me.

I wipe the tears from my eyes as I race down the path toward the edge of the forest. I already let the lease on my apartment go, but I can stay with Dec for now. I'll get things sorted and move on. Somehow. I rub my hand over my heart, where the pain is growing in intensity. I feel as if I might die.

I don't know enough about mate bonds to fully understand what's happening. My body aches, and the further I get from Garnet, the more pain I'm in. If I can't find a way to make it stop, I might not survive.

I must push through. I'm doing this for her good, not mine. For once in my life, I'm not going to be selfish in a relationship. I'll do what I should have done after the first time we kissed. Walking away isn't easy, but I can't go back.

She won't defeat Amber with me by her side. I'll only hinder her ability. I'm the reason her magic went wonky anyway. It's my fault. This is the only way to protect her. If I really love her, I have to leave.

The words echo in my head, and I struggle with the weight of them. I'm hearing my own voice, but it sounds off somehow. I believe the things I'm telling myself, even though it's as if someone else is saying them. I shake that thought away, stopping at the edge of the forest.

The pain is so intense that I'm barely able to remain upright. I have to get out of here before Ryland, Orym, or Luca comes for me. They don't understand. They can't. I'm not enough, and I never will be. All I can do now is leave so that Garnet is better off.

She deserves so much more than I could ever give her. She's worthy of a mate who can protect her; someone who has been touched by magic instead of a weak, worthless human. I'll never be good enough for her.

I continue to berate myself, fighting against the pain, as I climb into one of the SUVs, hotwire it, and head into the city toward Midnight. There's one person in the world who might understand, and that's my brother. I need him now more than ever.

I don't know what caused my sudden realization, but I'm glad that I left when I did. No matter how much it hurts me, I know that Garnet is safer without me. She'll be stronger without me too.

At least that's what I tell myself. I refuse to admit that I'm terrified of dying, or of watching her die. I can't face Amber because I can't defeat her, and I won't watch the people I love fail. My heart can't take that pain.

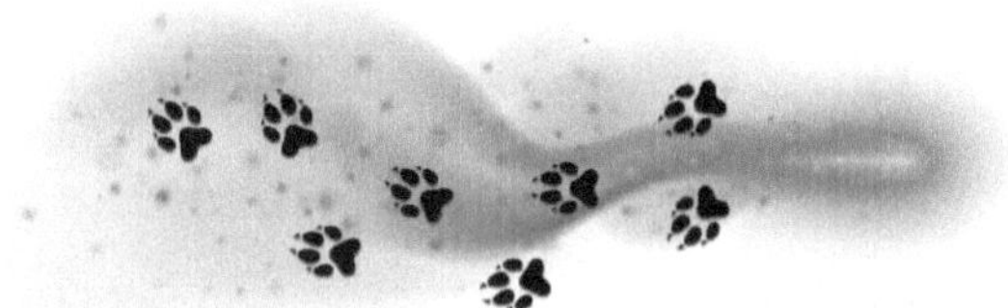

GARNET

The moment James walks away, my heart shatters. Pain lances through me, and I can't even think. His words were painful enough, but his actions tear through our bond. I can't feel him anymore. In the place where he should be is nothing but searing agony.

I collapse on the ground, my magic going crazy along with my emotions. How could he think this is what I want? What could have made him leave me like that? I saved him. And now he's leaving me. Why?

I can't deal with my other mates trying to comfort me. Nothing can heal this wound. I might as well lay here and die for as much as this hurts. I'll never defeat Amber now. Not with a piece of my heart missing. There's no way for us to win this battle. I should just go to her and surrender myself. Then the pain would stop at least.

But I know I can't do that, no matter how compelling the thought is. I have to find a way to fight for what's right. Once Amber is dealt with, then I can die. Unless I'm not strong enough to kill her, and she takes me out instead.

This situation is my biggest fear come to life. I don't know how to go on without James here. Logically, it makes no sense. I should be able to get up and keep moving forward, no matter how badly this hurts. But the mate bond changes everything.

"I can't get her up. She won't respond. Where did Grammy go? We need her," one of the voices near me says. The pain is so bad that I can't even tell which one of my mates is talking. Did Grammy leave? I wonder if that means that Trevan left too. I'm glad they've found each other. They deserve to be happy.

I really should get up. But I can't. I try to force my limbs to move, but they won't. Pain tears through me again, and I know that James has left the forest. The last tether that connected us has torn apart. He's gone, and all that remains are the scars his love left on my soul.

I've been so worried about protecting him, that I never considered how badly he could hurt me. Human or not, what he's done to me is unforgivable. What is wrong with me? How can he just walk away like that?

Even his explanation of why makes no sense. I would never wish for him to leave. I want to keep him safe and near me. But I can't do that now. I have to let him go. Even if it kills me.

I barely register the new voice I hear in my head. *You chased him off. Always putting him in danger and never considering how fragile he was.* The thoughts echo in my head. The voice is familiar, but I don't know who it belongs to. I shrug it off, figuring it's the numbness setting in. I can't afford to care about anything right now.

If I don't get a handle on my emotions, someone is going to get hurt. I feel my magic swirling around me, and I finally tune in to the conversation I'd been ignoring.

"We have to get through to her before she destroys the forest."

"I know, but she's not responding, and her magic is going nuts."

"Red! You need to come back to us. Now. This isn't the way to deal with James and the pain he's caused."

I know that the voices are right. But I can't make it stop. I need the pain to stop. There has to be a way. I just have to figure it out.

That's right. Push the pain down, lock it away. You must be rational now, or you won't survive this. The heartbreak is too much. You should just give yourself to Amber so she can make the pain stop.

The voice is very convincing. I shake my head, pushing my emotions down. I lock the pain away, refusing to acknowledge it. I have to make it stop.

"Garnet, please. Come back to us. We love you."

"Red, you can do this. Get your magic under control and come back to us."

"We're here for you, but you have to breathe. If you don't calm down, you're going to kill everyone."

The anguish in those voices pulls me back. It's not just my bond with James that's broken. They all had bonds with him too. I'm not the only one hurting, and I have to stop acting like I am. That thought alone is the one that pulls me back together. I have to continue to fight, for these men who stayed with me.

With one final devastating cry, I pull my magic back into me, along with my emotions. I sit up and look at my fated mates. Each of them stares back at me with lost expressions. I can see their pain. But mine is tucked away, no longer visible. I'm hiding it just out of reach.

Standing up, I hold up my hands to stop them from pulling me into their arms. "Thank you for making me realize that this isn't the time to fall apart. We need to get to work. There's a lot to figure out before the Wolf Moon comes." I walk back into the cabin without a backward glance.

I don't know how long I'll be able to keep this pain at bay, but for now, I'm okay. I don't feel anything. Not happy, not sad. Nothing. And that's just the way I want it. I hear the door open and close behind me, indicating that Ry, Luca, and Orym all followed me inside. I don't have time to deal with them right now, though. I have to work out a list of spells I can use against Amber. There is no more time to waste on emotions.

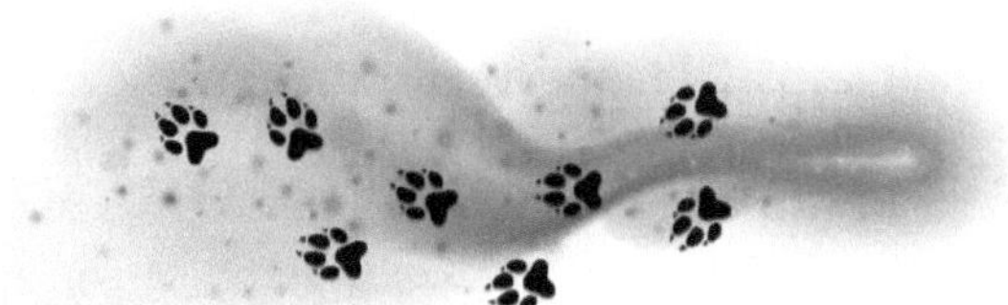

LUCA

I hold Red until her magic pushes me away. It rips me off her and tosses me as if I'm the one who hurt her. I don't know if her magic can tell the difference, or if she just needs space from everyone. I kneel as close to her as I can get without being slapped away again. All I can do is watch as she breaks down even more than she did when she was in my arms.

My heart cracks at her pain. It's bad enough that James destroyed the mate bond that connects him to me, Ryland,

and Orym. But this is too much for Red. She can't take it. With the buildup of magic, I worry that she's going to explode.

James storms out of the cabin and races through the forest. Orym and Ryland step out after him, stopping close to where I kneel. The three of us beg our mate to come back to us. She can't leave us like this. We won't survive without her.

The way Red switches off her emotions is terrifying. One minute she's inconsolable, wailing as her magic swirls around her, keeping us away. The next she's calmer than I've ever seen her. She pulls her magic back into her with an ear-splitting cry and stares at us for a moment. Then she stands up, and walks into the cabin, as if nothing has happened.

I look at Ryland and Orym, unsure of what to do. Ryland shrugs, Orym shakes his head, and both follow her inside. I trail behind, moving a little slower. Part of me wants to go after James and bring him back to her. I know it's pointless now, because he's already destroyed the bond, and our mate. My only solace is that if my heart aches this badly, his pain must be worse.

That shouldn't make me feel better, but it does. Knowing that he's suffering as much as she is, makes me wonder if he won't come back. The pull of the mate bond is strong; maybe it can be repaired. I stare at Red, now perfectly calm and professional, as she searches her spell books and makes lists of supplies and useful spells that she'll need to fight Amber.

Orym and Ryland stare at her too. None of us sure of how to approach her. This situation is too much. Her pain can't be gone, but she looks perfectly at peace. How is that possible?

"I don't understand," I whisper. "How did you turn it all off, Red?"

She looks up at me. "I don't know what you're talking about, Luca. We have work to do. Please, let's just forget about what happened and move forward." It's clear that she doesn't want to talk about it, and I decide not to push. Maybe she's right. We should focus on defeating Amber, then worry about getting her other mate back and fixing this.

I just wish I could be confident about our chances.

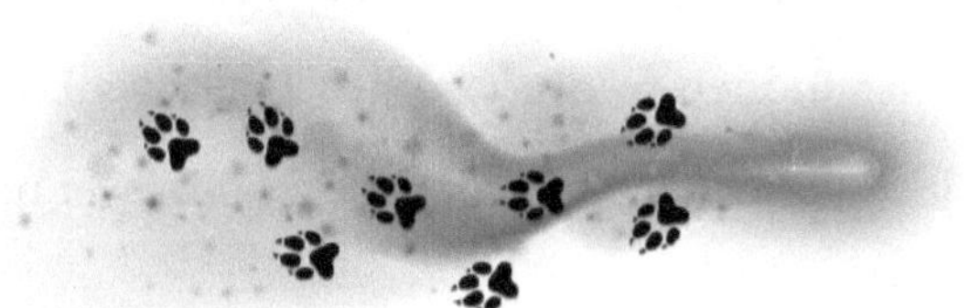

RYLAND

Fuck. This is all going to Hell, and there's nothing I can do to stop it. From the moment James walked away—okay, ran—Red has been destroyed. I don't blame her; I feel the pain of the broken bond too. I know it's stronger for her, and probably for him, than the rest of us. No matter how badly I want to force her to deal with this, I can't.

So, I'm stuck. Standing here while she makes lists about ingredients and spells. While Orym stares at her, just as dumbfounded as I am, Luca tries to figure things out. It takes her two seconds to shut him down. She doesn't want to talk about it, and we all understand that. There has to be a way to fix this.

Something made James leave. But what? What could have gotten to him so quickly? I can't wrap my head around what's happened, or Red's reaction to it. I understood her meltdown, but not her sudden recovery. When James walked away, I expected it to break her. I didn't expect her to get up and move on so quickly.

"Red, it's okay to let yourself feel. You don't have to hold it in for us. We can feel your pain. It's still there, even if you refuse to acknowledge it. Please let us help you," I beg her.

She responds without looking up from the book she's scanning. "Ry, I'm fine. I had a moment, and now I'm better. I don't want to keep repeating myself. If you're not going to let me work, then you need to leave. I'm busy."

I stare at her in disbelief. It's obvious that James leaving has broken something inside of her. There is no way she should be this calm or focused.

We need to keep an eye on her. I say to Luca and Orym along our bond. I purposefully block her from this conversation, because I don't want her to flip out. She's safer here than anywhere else, so I want to keep her here.

I agree. Something happened. Did you see anything, Luca? Orym asks, making sure not to let Red know we're talking along the bond.

Her magic attacked me, throwing me away from her. After that, she got really calm and you guys saw the rest. Luca's explanation doesn't really tell me anything, but it doesn't surprise me either.

I wonder if Grammy or Trevan would have answers for what's happening. I pull my phone out and send a quick text to our elder hybrid to see what she thinks. Until she answers, we'll stay here and watch our mate.

"Are the three of you just going to stand there and stare at me while you talk about me with the bond? Because that's not creepy at all. At least go make yourselves useful and get me something to eat and some tea." Her demand paired with her tone makes Luca jump. He and Orym go to fill her request.

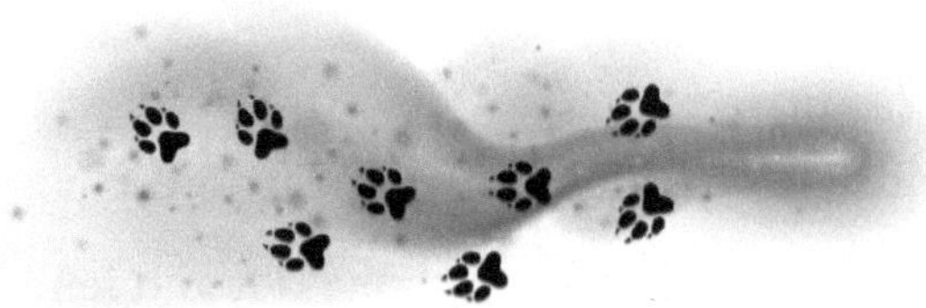

GARNET

I'm a little disturbed by how concerned my guys are. James didn't want to be here, so now he's not. It's not that complicated. There's nothing to dwell on or worry about. If I have lingering feelings related to his abandonment, I'll deal with them after I defeat Amber. I don't have time right now to even consider anything but preparing to face my aunt.

I pull spells from my books, making lists of ingredients and situations where each one will be helpful. I try not to think about the last time I did this, when James helped me. Maybe one of the others will step in and do research with me.

We only have a few days before the deadline Amber gave us. I have to be ready. I can't let my family down. I stare at the book in front of me, suddenly frozen. I can't move and I can't talk. I'm still standing and breathing, though, so I think I'm okay.

"What the fuck just happened?" Luca's voice echoes behind me. I can't turn to face him, and I'm not sure what he's talking about.

"I'm not sure. She was flipping through that book and then this happened. There was nothing I could do to stop it," Ryland says, gesturing to me as if there's something wrong.

Guys, I'm fine. What are you freaking out about? I ask along our bond, but don't get a response. Why am I frozen? Is this one of Amber's tricks?

"I tried to reach her with our bond, but she's not responding. I don't think she can hear us." Orym steps in front of me and stares into my eyes. "Can you hear us?" I blink twice, hoping that my eyelids actually move.

"She blinked. So, she's still in there, just not able to move," he relays to the others.

"No shit. She's covered in ice everywhere but her face. How would she be able to move?" Ry slaps Orym on the back of the head and I try to laugh, but no sound comes out.

I play back the past few moments in my head. Reading spell books and making lists, that's all I was doing. I didn't cast any spells or repeat any incantations. I didn't even read anything with ice involved. Yet here I am, frozen in a mostly intact block of ice that I can't get out of.

Ry pulls his phone out and calls someone. "Something's happened. We need you here now." I can't hear what the other person says in response, but he hangs up the phone and starts to pace.

"Are they coming back?" Orym asks. Clearly, he knows who Ry called. Why can't I figure that out? Things are starting to feel hazy, and I don't remember exactly what I was doing here.

My mates and I are working on something important. I have to go through the books and find spells to—to what? I can't even ask them what I was doing, because my only method of communication right now is blinking. If only I knew Morse code. But would they understand it? I don't know.

"It's okay, Red. Grammy and your father are coming. They'll figure this out," Luca tells me, pressing his warm palm to my icy cheek. I wish I could ask him why they would go to Gunnar for this. How could he possibly know what happened? Grammy has more practical experience, so she might have some idea. But my father is a wolf shifter. What can he possibly do in this situation that will help?

Come to think of it, what exactly am I doing with these books? Did they leave me to research their war with—with who? Fuck. I want to remember what is happening here. *Okay, Garnet, let's focus. You have four mates. Wait, no. I only have three. Luca, Orym, and Ry. But there was someone else, right? Why do I feel like I'm forgetting something important?*

I try to look down at the book in my hands, but I can't see it through the ice that covers my body. Hold on, that's weird too. How am I covered in ice, but I'm not cold? None of this makes any sense. My mates stare at me while we wait for what feels like an eternity. The longer I'm encased in this ice, the more uneasy I feel.

My heart races and I feel like my lungs are closing up. The door opens and Grammy walks in with some man I don't recognize. I thought Luca said my father was coming. I want to ask so many questions right now, but I can't. All I can do is stand here and stare at the strange man who is now inches from my face.

"What happened?" he asks. His eyes are kind, and he looks familiar, but I have no idea who he is. Where the hell is my father? Does Gunnar really not care enough about his defective daughter to come help us?

"We were hoping you could tell us that," Ry says, putting his hand on the man's shoulder. Why are my mates treating this man like he's someone they know? And where the fuck is Gunnar? I'm going crazy with my questions that just keep building up in my mind. I need to be out of this ice so I can figure out what the fuck is going on here.

"She's getting upset. We need to get her out of there, now. Trevan, is there anything you can do?" Grammy steps closer, realizing that I'm getting desperate for help.

"Let me try this," the man says, turning to me. "Hold on, daughter, I'm going to get you out of there."

Daughter?! What in the hell is this man talking about? I can't be his daughter, can I? Thoughts swirl around my brain as I try to process this new information. I get flashes of memories, too.

NINE
DIVISIONS

JAMES

When I get to the edge of the forest, I realize that I have no way out of here. I haven't needed a car in months, so I had my brother take mine to keep it maintained. And since I stole one of the pack's SUVs earlier, they have them guarded. Fuck. Can this day get any worse? I shake my head and start walking toward the city.

After a few minutes, I pull out my phone and dial Dec. When he answers, I wonder if someone has already told him what's going on.

"What happened?" he starts.

"I need a ride. Can you come get me? I'm walking toward the city now," I say, ignoring his question.

"Of course, I'll come get you. But why are you walking? What happened? Is everything okay?" he assaults me with questions that I have no intention of answering. At least not right now.

"Just come get me, and we can talk about it. Please." I won't answer his questions, so he relents. Once I know he's on his way, I hang up and continue walking. I'll meet him halfway if I can. I just can't stay here any longer.

I keep rubbing at the pain in my chest as I stumble down the dirt road that connects the edge of the city with the forest community. It's a pretty well-kept secret, even if it seems obvious that it exists. I wouldn't have even known this place existed if my brother wasn't a vampire who controls a quarter of the city we live in.

All of this supernatural stuff is insane. Vampires and wolf shifters control the city, but most humans have no idea that they exist. And that there's a community of wolf shifters and one of witches living in the forest right beside them. That's not even considering the Fae community. I have no idea how to get there, so I'm not sure if they count as neighbors or not.

The further I get from Garnet, the worse I feel. I'm sweating and shivering, hot and cold at the same time. Maybe I'm getting sick. I'll have to get checked out after Dec picks me up. What was I thinking getting involved with this mess?

Relief washes over me as I see my car speeding toward me. I step into the grass on the side of the road and wait for my brother to stop. He streaks past me, and for a moment I worry that he didn't see me. A few minutes later, the car pulls up behind me and stops.

"Get in," he orders, stepping out of the car for a second before dropping back in. I rush to the passenger side and climb in before he puts it in drive and races down the dirt road.

"What's the big rush?" I ask, puzzled at this new development.

"We've been under attacks from witches for the past few days. I figured you needed backup and that's why you were calling. We have to get back fast to protect Delilah," he explains.

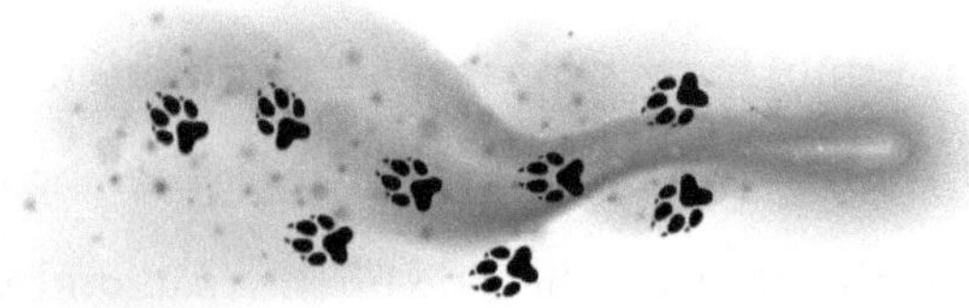

LUCA

Trevan gets close to Red, checking out the ice that encompasses her entire body, except her face. I have no idea how she's even still breathing. The ice is holding her in place, and preventing her from speaking.

"I think this is a magical malfunction. I'm not sure what I can do to reverse it." He turns his back to her and faces the rest of us. "Tell me what happened before this, and I'll see what I can come up with."

We explain about James breaking the bond and her reaction, then how it changed. The whole time, I watch her face. Red's expression doesn't change much because of the ice, but I can see the pain in her eyes.

"So, if she's blocking the pain in order to move past it, could that be what's frozen her?" I ask, my eyes locked with hers.

Trevan nods. "That is a possibility. I'll see if I can thaw her a little, but I doubt I can make the ice go away if it's there because she doesn't want to deal with her emotions. There may only be one way to remove it."

"We'll do whatever we have to in order to save her," Ryland insists. I'm worried that it won't be up to us to do anything to save her, and that she'll make the wrong decision. What happens if she decides that losing James is too much to bear and she doesn't fight?

"Dear one, I need you to help me. Use your magic to warm your head. We'll start where the ice is the thinnest and work our way down. Okay?" Trevan speaks to Red, but her eyes are full of questions, as if she has no idea who this man is or what he's talking about.

"What if she can't?" I say, considering my thoughts out loud. "What if she's blocking the pain so fully that she doesn't remember things that she should?"

"You think she could have given herself amnesia?" Orym asks, stepping closer. I shrug. It's just a thought, but I felt compelled to say it to everyone.

"That could have catastrophic repercussions. Let's do what we can and deal with this one step at a time." Worry creases his brow as he focuses on melting the ice that surrounds Red's head.

"What can we do to help?" Ryland takes a step closer then stops, not wanting to get in the way. I'm wondering the same thing, because we don't have magic, and I need to do something to help.

"Just give me space to thaw her out. Have blankets and towels ready, just in case she can't get to her magic right away. I fear this is worse than I expected." His somber response kicks us into motion. Ryland heads to the bathroom and grabs towels, Orym gathers every blanket in the cabin, and I move to the fireplace to start a fire.

We will thaw her out one way or another. I hope.

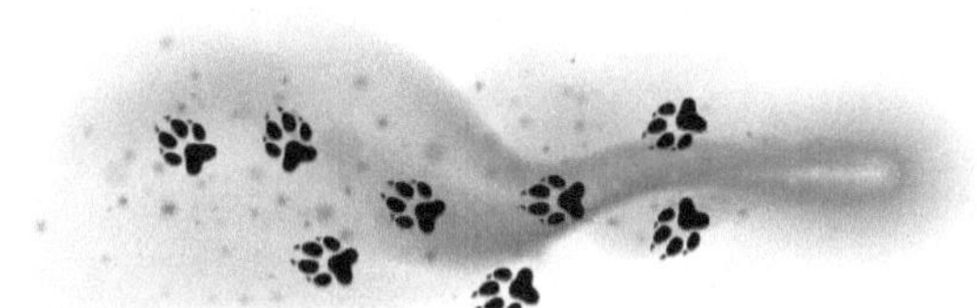

GARNET

Did he say I have magic? Everything gets hazy, and I'm even more confused than I was a little while ago. I still don't feel cold, but is that connected to what he's saying? If I have magic, and I did this, I should be able to make it stop. How does a broken wolf shifter have magic, though? None of this makes sense. This guy is going to have a lot of explaining to do when I get out of this mess.

I close my eyes and think warm thoughts. I'm not sure I believe his claims that I have magic or that I did this to myself. And even if I did, I have no idea how to fix it. After a few minutes of trying to melt the ice, I give up. This guy is insane if he thinks I can create or melt ice. I hope I get the chance to tell him just that.

How dare he come in here and tell my family that I have powers? What is he trying to do? Anger ripples up my spine, and I embrace the feeling. More than anything, I want to find out what happened to cause this, and I want to corner this man who seems to have answers. He may even know why I can't shift. Maybe he has a way to break the curse.

"Step back, she's starting to glow," the man says, gesturing for everyone to get away from me. My body warms and tingles, as if I'm sitting on the bank near the waterfall in the sunshine. Everything goes dark, then a bright red light takes over the darkness. I squeeze my eyes shut tightly to block it out.

The light grows more intense, and I cover my eyes with my hands. Wait, how did that happen? He must have found a way to melt the ice. When the light finally subsides, I lower my hands slowly. I'm not sure when I hit the floor, but everything hurts now.

There's a sharp pain in my chest, and I rub at it as I try to stand up. My legs won't hold me, so I drop back down onto the floor. Ry wraps a towel around me, then Orym follows with a blanket. Luca brings me a cup of my favorite tea.

"Are you hungry? Do you need anything else?" Luca asks. I can feel his concern along our bond, but I don't understand the intensity of it. He's worried about more than just that block of ice.

I shake my head, not trusting my voice yet. I'm wet, and should be cold, but I'm still not. I glance around the room and realize that the fire is probably why I'm not chilled.

"Will you let us help you get into dry clothes?" Ry asks. He's hesitant and I don't understand why. Normally, they'd all take any opportunity to get me naked without reservations. I nod, and Orym scoops me up from the floor. Once we're in the bedroom, Ry peels my wet clothes off of me, and Orym dries me with another towel while Luca digs out some comfy clothes for me to put on.

Dry and dressed, I feel a little more myself. "What is going on here?" I finally find my voice to ask.

"What do you mean, Red?" Luca asks. I hate that it feels like they're keeping something from me. I sigh, exasperated.

"Why are you all looking at me like I've grown a second head? And who is the guy with Grammy? I thought you said my father was coming. Where's Gunnar?" I blurt it all out at once, and they gape at me. What the fuck is going on here?

"You don't remember anything that's happened recently?" Ry asks, taking my hand and easing me onto the bed.

"Of course I do. The four of us are fated mates, and—"

"The four of us? What about James?" Orym cuts me off with his question.

"James? Dec's brother? What does he have to do with this?" I feel like maybe I have forgotten something important. But I don't want to admit that, because they all look worried enough as it is. I continue to rub at the pain in my chest. For some reason, when Orym mentions James, it gets worse.

"Oh, shit. This is worse than we thought." Luca and Ry exchange a look, then Luca rushes toward the living room.

"Would one of you please explain what the fuck is going on here? Apparently, I'm lost and don't understand things. I need answers. Now," I growl.

Both men hold their hands up in surrender. I glare at them, but neither responds to my question. Fury bubbles inside me, and I clench my fists as I stand up.

Ry and Orym pull me away from the bed as flames appear, cocooning my hands and running up my arms. The pain in my heart is forgotten as fear takes over. I'm on fire, and I have no idea how, or why it's not burning me.

"Keep her away from the furniture," the strange man says as he walks into our bedroom. Who is this guy? "You're going to need to take a deep breath. Once you're calm, the flames will subside. We need that to happen before you burn the cabin down."

With my jaw clenched, I do as he instructs, shocked when things happen exactly as he said they would. The flames coating my arms rescind, and I stare at my hands as if they're some alien substance that might attack me at any moment.

I fight the tears that threaten to fall. "Will someone please explain what is happening here? I'm losing my mind." I drop carefully to the floor, hoping the flames don't come back. Wrapping my arms around myself, I stare up at the people surrounding me.

Grammy sits down next to me and pulls me into her arms.

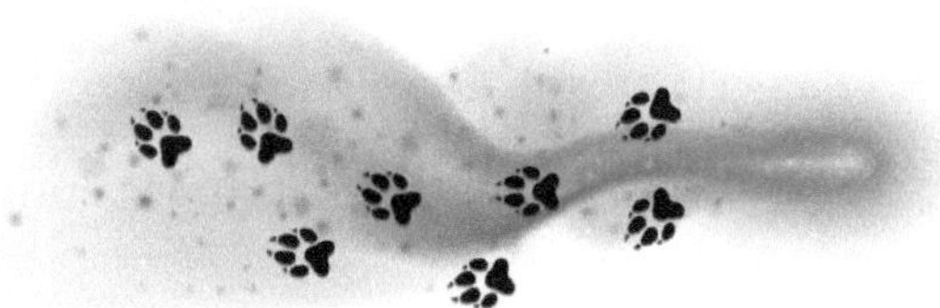

RYLAND

Watching Red cry as Grammy holds her nearly breaks my heart. I don't understand why she suddenly has memory loss, but we need to fix this so that we can defeat Amber. With our deadline approaching faster than we'd expected, we have no time to waste.

"What can we do?" I ask Trevan, expecting him to have some idea of what's going on.

"Luca filled me in on what she seems to have forgotten or blocked out. I fear that James breaking the mate bond has damaged her emotionally and she's managed to block out any memory that involves him." Trevan's explanation makes sense, but I don't like it.

"That doesn't answer the question, Fae. Can you fix her?" Orym demands, stepping closer and intimidating our guest. I move between them and ease Orym back.

"We can't blame Trevan for this. It's not his fault. We have to figure this out together. If you can't refrain from violence, take a walk." I give the order with a little extra alpha influence to be sure that Orym will listen. He's nearly as strong as I am, and sometimes we butt heads.

Instead of arguing with me, Orym closes his eyes and takes a deep breath. "I'm sorry. James walking away hasn't just affected Garnet. I feel it too."

I pull him in for a hug. "Same here. We can't let that get to us, though." A thought occurs to me, and I turn to Trevan without letting Orym go. "Could this be something that Amber did to James? Making him believe that Red wanted him to leave and that we were all better off without him?"

Trevan tilts his head to the side, considering. "I suppose that's possible. She could have been using the love potion as a distraction for the real attack. That would also explain why it was so easy to break through that magic."

Knowing what happened isn't going to fix Red, but it will help us to figure out our next steps. "Is there a way to bring her memories back?" Luca kneels on the floor next to Grammy and Red. He pulls them both into his arms and holds them protectively.

"If she breaks through this block on her emotions, her memories may return. I don't know of a way to force the issue," Trevan explains. We all look expectantly at Red. Will she agree to this? Does she even know how to lower the barrier she put up to hold back her emotions?

"Let's start by explaining a few things, and see how she reacts," I offer, turning to Red. "Red, does that sound okay to you?" When she nods, I start explaining how after she bonded with me, she and James accidentally sealed their bond. Luca jumps in and explains about me challenging Gunnar with her encouragement. By the time we're finished telling her our story, she looks horrified.

"I'm not sure I want to remember any of that. It all sounds terrifying."

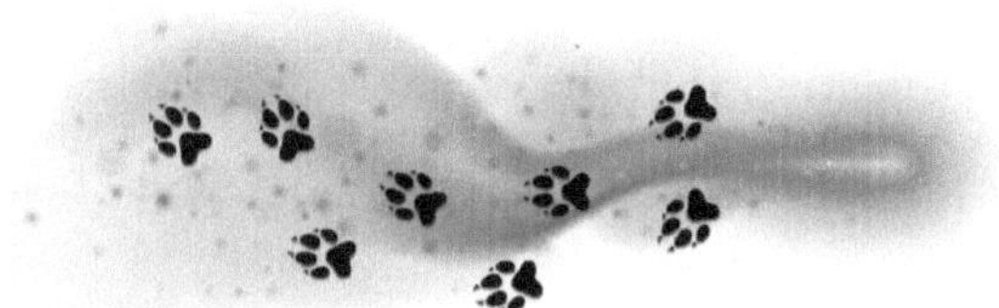

OYRM

"It may sound scary, but I guarantee that facing Amber without knowing all of it would be way worse," I suggest. The look Garnet gives me is uncertain. I understand why she feels this way, and I want more than anything to fix it. I just don't know how.

"If facing the emotional turmoil created by James leaving is the only way to fix Red's memories, shouldn't we be discussing that?" Luca asks, releasing Garnet when she tries to stand and step away from him.

"I don't remember being mated to James, so I don't know how I would possibly be able to do that. Can't we just move forward with the plan to fight Amber? It sounded like we were making progress there before all of this mess happened." Her insistent tone tugs at my heart. I want to pull her into my arms and kiss her until all of this goes away. It won't help, so I don't try.

She starts to pace, still avoiding talking about James and facing her feelings. "We just need a plan of attack, and we can go after her first. If I can defeat her quickly, then we can move on with our lives."

"That's an interesting plan, but what if this emotional block fucks with your magic again?" Ryland offers. "I'm not being mean, just asking the obvious question here."

Garnet growls at him, then pouts and returns to pacing. "Well, we can't force you to talk about James or to feel the things you don't want to. But you need to consider what could happen if you don't. If we're in the middle of a fight with Amber, and your magic backfires, you could get injured or worse." At my statement, she stops and stares at me.

"Amber has already made it clear that she plans to kill you so she can take your powers. We have to stop her. Which means we need you at one hundred percent. So, what can we do to help you consider what we're asking?" Luca takes a step closer before she turns and glares at him.

"I don't want to think about James. I don't want to hurt. How do I make that any more clear to you?" She rubs at her chest again, and I'm certain that's the broken bond manifesting itself physically.

"What's that?" I ask, gesturing to where her hand rubs at her sternum.

"Just a pain that doesn't wanna go away. I'm sure it's nothing," she insists, continuing to rub at it. I share a look with Ryland and Luca, then continue.

"Do you want to know what that pain is? Because I can tell you," I say, reaching a hand out to her. I want her to let us help her with this, but she isn't willing to cooperate. I know that Ryland wants to force her to feel, and Luca wants to beg her. That leaves me to use reasoning and understanding to get through to her.

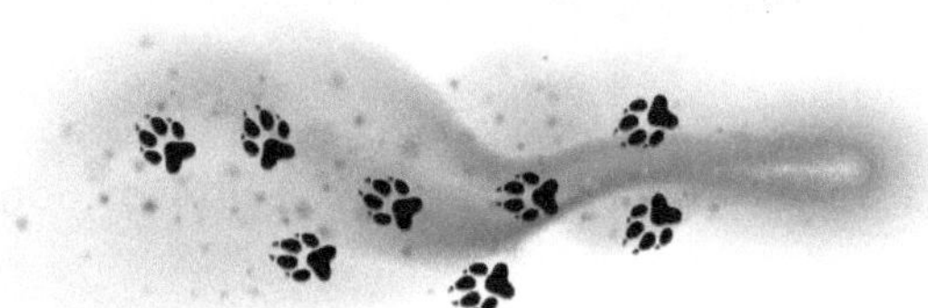

GARNET

I stare at Orym's outstretched hand. "I'm scared. Of course, I know the pain has to be from this broken bond you keep talking about. I don't want to face it. As bad as this hurts, I don't want it to get worse. Please. I can't."

The admission costs me, because now they know that I'm not as invincible as I was pretending to be. I can tell from Orym's face that he already knew that I'm scared. I gingerly place my hand in his and let him pull me into his arms.

I bury my face in his chest and focus on our connection. His strength helps to reign in my fear and bolster me. "You won't be doing it alone. We'll face it together. You just have to agree. Ryland, Luca, and I aren't going anywhere," Orym tells me.

"As long as you all promise not to leave me." I can't fight them. I give in, feeling overwhelmed and sad. I know it's going to get worse before it gets better, and I am not looking forward to that.

"We're right here with you, Red," Ry reassures me.

I turn to the man they claim is my father. "I'm sorry I don't remember you. I trust my mates, and they say you're my father and you can help. I don't really understand any of this. Will you help us?"

Trevan smiles at me. "My darling daughter, I would do anything to help you. We should probably take this out into the clearing, though. Just in case your magic goes a little haywire." His suggestion scares me a little, but I nod. Outside would be better than risking hurting someone or ruining our home.

Once we're all outside in the clearing, far enough away from the cabin to be safe, we all look to Trevan again. "Now you just have to focus on James and open yourself to remembering. It may work better if you three make a circle around her, holding hands." He waits for us to do as he instructs.

"Very good. Now, dear one, place your hands on top of their joined ones. Good, very good. Yes, this could work. Don't fight the emotions; let them wash over you. With them should come the memories."

I close my eyes and take a few deep breaths. I hear my mates do the same, though I'm not sure if they're staring at me or if they've closed their eyes. Against my eyelids, I see a variety of bright colors come and go. I hold tightly to their hands as the pain lances through my chest. I start to fight it, then remember that if I want this to work, I can't. I have to accept it and acknowledge it.

The pain stabs me again, and I hear a sharp intake of breath. My mates feel it too. I wonder if I should let go of their hands so that they don't suffer too, but I can't. I need their strength, even if it's selfish.

As the pain courses through me, I see flashes of memory. "It's working," I whisper. More flashes of memory come with every intense slice of pain in my chest. I feel as if I'm breathing through sand, and my heart is pounding so hard it might explode.

Throbbing starts at the base of my neck and pulses up through my head. At this rate, I'm not sure if I will survive this pain, or the memories it's returning to me. I see everything.

Ry's challenge of Gunnar and his subsequent takeover of the territory. Then James' injury and our time in the Fae realm.

Time skips around, and I see my first kiss with James, then the moment I learned that I'm not a wolf shifter after all. Just when I think it's all too much and I can't take it, the images stop.

The pain intensifies, and I can feel my heart being ripped into pieces. At that moment, I hear James' words. I see the pain in his eyes as he tells me that he's leaving. When he insists that I'm better off without him, my heart shatters. Again. I remember everything now, including how I managed to push my feelings down and lock them away.

I could do it again, but that won't help anyone. So, I don't. Instead, I focus on the love that I felt for James before he destroyed the bond. I use that feeling to help me stay strong through this agony. When I look into his eyes, I hear that voice again. At first, I thought it was my voice. But it's not.

It wasn't my voice. Wait, was James hearing that voice too? Is that why he destroyed my heart? Tears streaming down my face, I open my eyes and look at the men surrounding me. "I know what happened. I don't know how she did it, but Amber is behind this. She wants to weaken me. Ripping this bond away will do that. It has done that. We need to find James and fix this."

Luca, Ry, and Orym stare at me. It takes me a minute to figure out why. There are flames circling my left arm, and a ring of water around my right arm. Vines wrap around my right leg, and what looks like a small tornado rings my left leg. I've never seen anything like it.

"Are you okay?" Ry asks, clearly worried about my magic manifesting that way.

"It's not hurting me. I remember everything." I reach for my magic and all four elements disappear from my limbs. "I can control it again. I'm sorry for scaring you all. I couldn't deal with James leaving, and I blocked it all out. It won't happen again."

"You have to lean on us when things go wrong, Red," Luca scolds me like I'm a misbehaving child. I grin at him.

"I know. You're right. Don't get used to hearing that."

TEN
WAITING

LUCA

I know that Red is okay when she tells me not to get used to hearing that I'm right. I drag her into my arms and kiss her. Red's arms wrap around my neck and I think she's holding on, but in reality, she's reaching for Orym and Ryland. It catches me off guard but doesn't upset me. She needs all of us, James included.

Now that we know this was all Amber's doing, even if we don't understand how, we can find a way to fix it. "So, what do we say to James to get him to come back?" I ask as Ryland kisses Red.

I turn toward Trevan, realizing that it should be awkward for us to be making out with his daughter in front of him. It's not, but it should be. He doesn't seem to notice, deep in conversation with Grammy. They keep it in hushed tones, but it's impossible to miss the connection there. I would have picked up on it sooner or later. Luckily, they're not hiding it anymore.

Orym clears his throat, and the Fae man finally looks at us. "Oh, that was directed at me. I didn't realize." Trevan's cheeks go pink and he takes a step away from the elder wolf. "I believe that speaking with him about this matter may be enough. Perhaps if he knows the truth, he will decide to return."

"I don't know if that will repair the bond, though," Grammy adds. That was what I was worried about. If we want Red at her best, she needs the bond connections with all four of us. We need James in order to win this. I just hope it's not too late.

"So, we have to figure out where he'd go," Ryland says, holding Red to his side.

"There's only one place," Orym insists. "He let his apartment go, so he would have called his brother."

"We need to talk to Dec." I pull out my phone and dial, then wait a couple of rings for him to answer. When he doesn't, I leave a short voicemail asking him to call back. "No answer. I wonder if that means James is with him and doesn't want to talk to us."

"Or something is wrong and they can't answer," Red says, fear marring her features. I hate that she's worried about James, and that Amber caused all of this. I want to rip the bitch's heart out for what she's done to the people I love. Since I can't do that, I have to make do with helping Red prepare to take her out.

And that means finding James. "We could head to Midnight and see if he's there. If nothing else, Delilah will talk to you, Red." I can't come up with a better idea, but I'm not sure this one will work. I'm hoping that they won't throw us out the moment we get there. We don't know what James has told them, though.

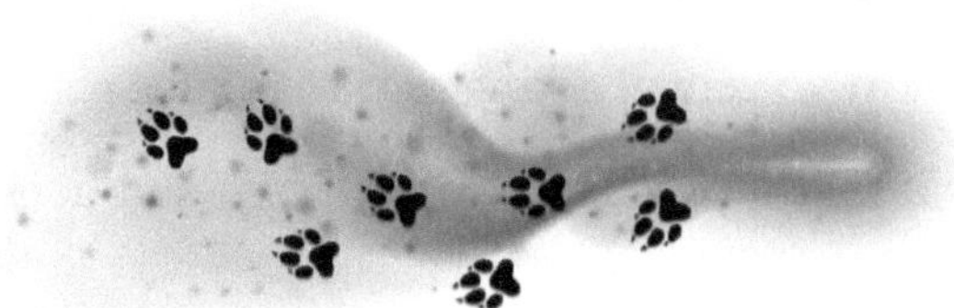

RYLAND

Luca's idea isn't bad, but things may not be as complicated as he expects. The crew at Midnight have always been our allies, especially since Kayden was one of us until Gunnar tossed him out. There's no reason to think that they won't welcome us.

"Let's get moving, then. It's been a couple of weeks since we've spoken with them. There may be more going on than we know," I offer, nudging everyone toward the path that will take us to the SUV. I'm pretty good at tracking, and can tell that this is the way James came.

We pile into the SUV, leaving Grammy and Trevan behind. They promise to call if James comes back or if anything happens. I put the car in drive and head toward the city. My thoughts are swirling inside my head. There are a lot of reasons for Dec not to answer.

I glance over my shoulder to Orym. "Call Vik and see if he answers. Luca, try Eli." I keep our speed steady as they dial and hang up a moment later.

"Vik didn't answer," Orym says.

"Eli neither," Luca adds.

"That tells me it's got to be something bigger than our little family drama." I look at Red in the passenger seat. "Don't worry, love, we'll get this all straightened out."

She nods at me, and I can see the unshed tears in her eyes. I want to take her pain and fear away, but I can't. It's killing me. Knowing that no one at Midnight is answering their phones, I speed up and make a bee line for the club. It's early enough that they shouldn't be open yet, but everyone should be awake. I doubt they go to bed in the middle of the afternoon, anyway.

We pull up to the club, and I immediately recognize the problem. "Amber's got witches attacking them. That's why they didn't answer. They're a little busy."

"We have to help them," Red insists. I nod. I would have suggested it myself, but I was busy trying to find a place to park where the witches won't see us coming.

"Sneaking up is our best option. But how do we do that? They've got the building surrounded," Orym says as I turn the corner and park at a convenience store.

"If we use the back alley, I can try to cloak us by combining my witch magic with my Fae magic," Red suggests. It's not something she's ever done, and I don't know if it will work, but it's the best chance we have.

"Do you think you can do it?" I ask, turning to look at her.

She shrugs. "I think it's the only chance we have. I'll try for camouflage, to make us blend in with our surroundings. Trevan thinks I have all of these powers for a reason. Let's see if I can use that for my needs."

I kiss her hard, then climb out of the SUV.

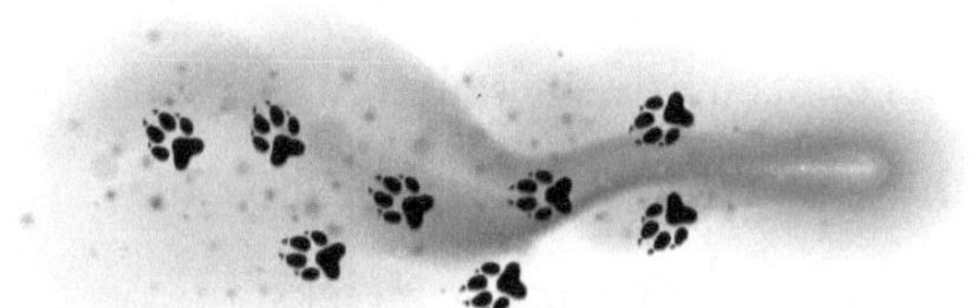

GARNET

I've never tried to combine different magics before and have no idea if this will work. No. It has to work. James is in danger, as are our friends. They're powerful, sure, but there are a lot of witches attacking here and there's no way they can take them all out.

I, on the other hand, have a chance. As a last resort, I can use the spell I worked on before. It basically turns me into a bomb that will target specific types of supernatural. I can sense that the people attacking Midnight are witches, so I can make sure it takes them out. I just can't guarantee it won't blow up the bar while I'm at it.

"Give me a second, then we'll move," I say as I close my eyes and focus on what I'm trying to do. Trevan told me it's as simple as telling my magic what I want. I'm going to test that now. I concentrate on making a shield that will surround us and hide us from view. It will look like the alley while protecting us from stray magic attacks.

"Okay, stay close and move quickly," I command. It's not my place to tell them what to do, but Ry lets me anyway. Probably because I'm supposed to protect them, and they love me. Both are good motivators.

I'm determined to protect them while we're out in the open. More than that, I'm focused on making sure we get to the building undetected. We move as a unit, staying as close as possible while still able to run. I feel a few spells bounce off the shield, but it holds. The moment the foreign magic hits, I stumble.

Ry scoops me up and keeps running. "Don't lose focus. Keep the bubble up. It's working," he whispers in my ear as he runs. Once we make it to the door, I realize that we never considered how to get inside.

As if they were waiting for us, the door swings open at our approach, and Dec motions for us to hurry. "Get in here, come on."

When the door closes, Ry sets me on my feet. "How did you see us?" I ask, curious about his ability to see through my magic.

"I didn't. I watched their attacks bouncing off of some invisible force, and figured it had to be either reinforcements or a sneak attack."

His explanation makes sense. "But what made you decide to welcome us in?" Orym asks, equally skeptical about Dec's story.

"I did. I can still sense Garnet, and I told him it was you." James steps out of the shadows and my heart leaps. I can't speak, locking eyes with his.

"We need to talk to you, but that can wait until we deal with these witches," Ry says to James, speaking for me because he knows I can't. James nods in response before turning and walking away. His lack of emotion pisses me off even if part of me understands it.

He's doing what I did and blocking the pain out. As much as I want to talk to him, I know it has to wait. My heart aches as he walks away from me again.

"I think I can take them all out, but I might damage the building," I offer. "I don't want to destroy your home."

"They're doing a pretty good job of that already," Dec says, gesturing to where magic has knocked down bricks and shattered windows. This place is usually pretty well protected, but it looks like these attacks have been going on for a while.

"How long have they been out there?" Luca asks.

"Two or three days now. We're running on very little sleep and we're low on supplies. I was barely able to make it out to pick James up." He pauses and looks at me. "He still won't tell me what happened. I hope you can work it out." His concern for me in the midst of his brother's refusal to explain touches me.

"I hope so too," I respond. "But we have to focus on defeating these witches right now, and worry about that later." I know what I need to do, I'm just not sure that I can do it without James. He was the one who helped me control my magic enough to make this work the first time. Before I had his help, I almost killed Delilah with it.

I make my decision and refuse to back down. "I'm going out there. I can stop them without anyone else getting hurt."

Ry, Luca, and Orym shake their heads. "You can't go out there alone." It's James' voice that echoes in my ears though.

I turn to face him, realizing that he hadn't gone very far after all.

"I have to. Your brother and his family don't deserve to suffer just because my nutjob aunt decided that she wants to make a hybrid army, and she thinks that she needs Delilah's blood to do it. I've got this," I respond, finally feeling confident that I do have this under control.

"At least let me go with you. I think I know what you're planning, and you'll need me to keep you grounded so you don't destroy the entire block," James says, his voice softer now.

My heart races at the thought of being close to him again. I want this more than I want to breathe, but I know it's not going to last. He's not offering to come back to me. He's offering to help me defeat his brother's enemies, who just happen to be mine as well. But I'm selfish and I'll take whatever I can get from him.

I nod. "Okay, but you have to stay close so I can protect you from their attacks." It's another ploy to be near him, and I'm sure he knows it. But he agrees without argument, and he takes my hand as we move toward the door.

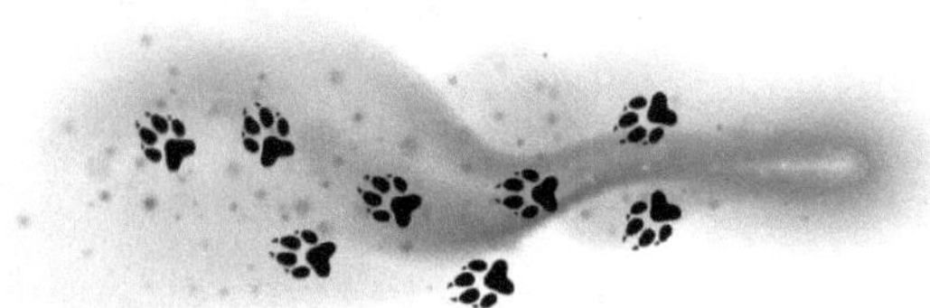

ORYM

I don't want to let Garnet go out there, much less with only James as her support. But there's no other option, and I know she can do this. There's just something about asking your mate to detonate herself like a bomb that seems strange to me. I can't even be mad that James wants to be the one who goes with her. He's been her rock when it comes to all things magic.

That's not to say that Ryland, Luca, and I haven't tried. James just took charge of that part as a way to bond with her, since we've all known her longer. I think that's why we didn't fight too hard to be included. They needed something just between the two of them.

But with him breaking the bond, I don't know if I'll ever be able to trust him again. I understand that it was Amber's fault. I just can't get past the pain he put Garnet in. And the rest of us only felt a fraction of it. I'll never figure out how Garnet is able to push past that pain and let him help her so easily.

From the look on her face, it may not be so easy for her either. I feel her uncertainty along our bond. Something is missing and her soul is reaching out to find it. Absentmindedly, I rub my chest in the same spot that she does. Then I glance around and realize that all five of us are doing it at the same time. James realizes and stops, his cheeks turning red.

Ryland insists on discussing Garnet's plan before he agrees to let them go outside. He steps in front of the door to stop them. Of course, she's pissed about it, but we all understand his concern. He wants to be sure that James won't leave her side, no matter what happens.

"Ry, please. We don't need to talk this to death. Just let me go out there and blow these witches up," Garnet insists. Her frustration is clear, but he's not backing down.

Ryland shakes his head. "Not until I'm sure *he* isn't going to abandon you when you need him."

James steps closer to Ryland. "I get why you can't trust me now, but I'm not going to leave her. I'll stay with her until this is done. I love her just like you do."

My alpha growls. "No, you don't. If you loved her like I do, you wouldn't have destroyed her heart by leaving. Now we have to put the pieces back together that you tore apart. So, don't try to tell me that you love her the same as we do."

Pain scrunches James' features. Dec grabs Ryland's arm and pulls him away from them. "We need to let them do this. You all can work out your issues once Midnight is safe."

Garnet nods and pulls James out the door without hesitation. I hope they can do this.

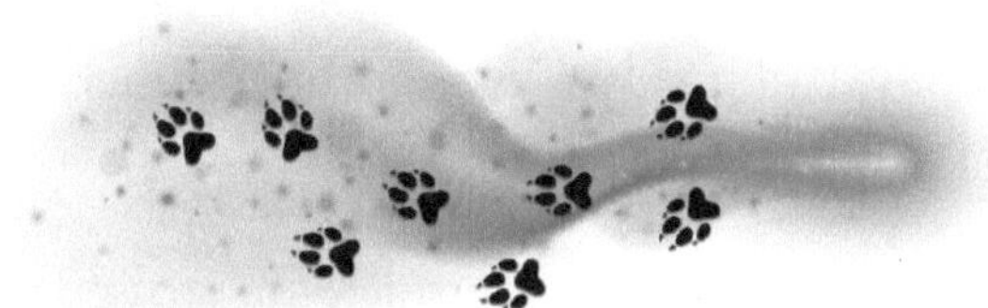

JAMES

Ryland's mistrust and harsh words hurt me. Not nearly as much as I've hurt Garnet, so I understand his point. I deserve so much worse. I never want to hurt her; I just can't get past my feelings of inferiority. How can a mere human compete with alpha wolves and other supernatural creatures?

Garnet grips my hand as we walk out into the alley. I'm not sure exactly where she's planning to do this, but I know we shouldn't be this close to the building. It's not safe for anyone to be this close, even if she's figured out how to control the blast.

"Where are we going?" I ask, tugging on her hand to slow her down a little.

"We have to get them to follow us. I need more room. I don't want to destroy Midnight. May not have a choice, though." Her response is clipped as she shoots magical attacks at different groups of witches as we pass.

I notice that she's keeping a shield up around us too. That doesn't stop me from flinching when a blast of blue energy hits it right in front of my face. I'm a little gun-shy since that last fight where I got hit in the leg and nearly died.

"It's okay. They aren't strong enough to get through my shield. It's Fae powered, not witch magic." She smirks at me and keeps moving, dragging me along with her.

"You figured out how to combine them? That's fantastic. I know you were frustrated when Trevan suggested it before." Her face scrunches for a minute, then relaxes. I hit a nerve, discussing our time in the Fae realm. I shouldn't be here with her right now. It should be one of the others.

"I'm sorry," I say, trying to pull my hand from hers. "I shouldn't have come with you."

She stops in the middle of the alley, refusing to let go of my hand. "Why? What did I do to make you think you aren't enough?"

"You didn't do anything. It's me. I'm just a human. I can't protect you, or myself. There's nothing I can do to help you win this battle with Amber."

"Then why did you volunteer to come with me for this?" She stares at me, forcing me to consider my actions.

"Because you need someone to help you focus," I say, not understanding what she's trying to tell me.

"And you felt like you were the best person to help me focus?" She's leading this conversation somewhere and I'm not sure I like it.

"Yeah. We've done this maneuver so many times, and I was always the one who helped you concentrate and focus." I feel like I'm defending myself against something, but I can't figure out what.

"If you are the best person to help me focus, then that means you're not useless or less than just because you're human. Now you have to admit that those thoughts may not have been your own."

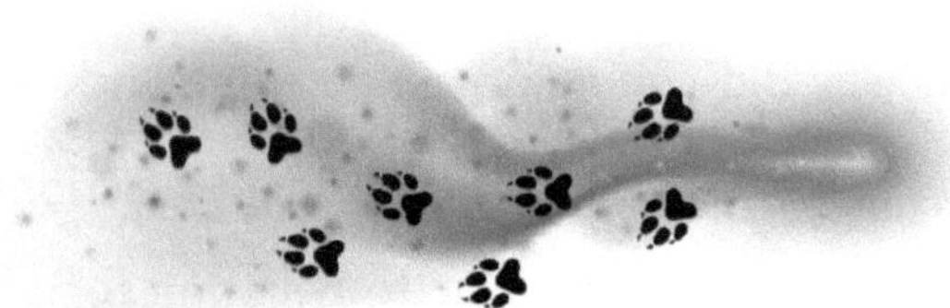

GARNET

This is clearly not the time or place for us to have this out, but here we are. I don't want to fight with James, because I'm not sure I can stop him from running off if he decides to. The thought of losing him again hurts, and I don't know if I'll be able to walk away this time.

"What do you mean, they weren't my thoughts?" he asks, confusion crinkling his brow.

"I mean, Amber got in our heads. She needed to push us apart to weaken me. It wasn't just you. She got to me as well. But they wouldn't let her win." I gesture back to the door we came out of.

"So, you never thought I was less because I'm human?" he asks. I wish he hadn't, but I can't ignore the question hanging between us.

"I've never thought you were less. I have, however, tried to come up with ways to protect you because you're human. Not because you're less capable or less strong, but because you don't have the same natural defenses as the rest of us."

"But that's what I'm talking about. That's what makes me less," he insists. I shake my head.

"We really don't have time for this right now," I say, shooting purple magic at one of the witches who's trying to sneak up behind us. "I need to detonate and take these bitches out. Can we come back to this conversation after?"

I don't care if he says yes or no; we will discuss this later. I will make sure of it. I can't let it go, not when I know he still loves me. I have no idea if our bond can be repaired or not, but I don't care. I want James to be part of my family, and I'm not giving up on him yet.

"Sure, sorry," he offers and dips his head. I want to scream at how submissive he's being right now, but there's no time to react. I have to focus on what's happening right now, or our people are goners.

We lead the witches out into the street in front of Midnight, where four more groups ambush us. I pretend to be shocked, but really, I'm thrilled. They've clumped up better than I could have planned. It should be easy to detonate myself and take them all out. I just have to focus.

As the witches surround us, I can feel James' nerves, even without a mate bond. "It's okay; this is all going according to plan. Just act scared," I whisper to him, not letting go of his hand.

"That'll be pretty easy," he responds with a slight chuckle. "You need to focus and stay grounded."

I nod at his recommendation. I will do what I have to, then we'll get back to our conversation. I take a deep breath and close my eyes. I hear his gasp and know that I must be starting to glow. "Close your eyes, James." I don't look at him, keeping my eyes closed tightly and focusing on the point where our hands meet.

He was right; it had to be him to come with me. No one else could make me feel this grounded or focused. I hate admitting that, but at least I didn't say it out loud. I feel the magic swell around me, growing and pulsing with its desire to be set free.

James gasps again as the magic pulses. One more deep breath, then I push the blast out around us, targeting each group of witches that surrounds us. I don't want to kill them, but I can't hold the magic back. I open my eyes to see puddles of muck where each witch had been standing.

Shock takes hold, and I'm weighted down with so much guilt for the lives my magic has taken. My breath hitches and I start to collapse. Strong arms hold me tightly to a broad chest. James. James is here with me. Tears stream down my cheeks.

"Garnet, look at me," he encourages. I shake my head. I can't look at him. If I do, I'll see the disappointment and fear in his eyes. There's no way he could still love me after what I've just done.

James turns me to face him and lifts my chin, so our eyes meet. "You did what you had to in order to protect all of us. It's not your fault that your magic did more than knock them out. I know you weren't trying to kill anyone. This is Amber's fault, not yours."

I want to believe him, but I'm not sure that I can. How could my magic do this if it wasn't my intention? I shake my head again and he stops me, one hand on either side of my face, forcing me to look at him. Our eyes meet, and my heart jumps in my chest. James presses his lips to mine, kissing me so tenderly, so sweetly, that I can almost forget the gaping hole in my heart from where our bond used to be.

My arms wrap around him on their own, and he deepens the kiss, sliding his tongue between my lips to tangle with mine. I wish I could be strong enough to push him away. But I'm weak and I let myself drown in his affection.

His hands move from my face to my body, and he holds me to him. I can feel his erection against my stomach. I want nothing more than for him to rip my clothes off and fuck me right here in the middle of the street. But I know that he won't. He won't even keep kissing me. I know I'm right when he pulls away a moment later.

"You did it," he whispers, pressing his forehead to mine.

"I did, but at what cost?" I ask, closing my eyes as more tears fall. I feel so alone now.

ELEVEN
CONTROL

RYLAND

Red's emotions are all over the place. She's clearly upset about something but is also relieved that our enemies are stopped for now. I start to race out the door and comfort her. A hand grips my shoulder, stopping me before I can make it.

"Give them a minute. They need it," Dec says quietly. I nod, knowing that he's right. Leaving her alone with James while she's already feeling vulnerable pains me. Yes, they need to talk. Does that mean she should do it alone? I don't know.

Instead of running out the door to her side, I watch from the window, feeling like a creeper. "This hurts him as much as it does her. He refuses to talk about whatever happened. It's not my business, but I'm here if there's anything I can do to help." Dec's offer makes little difference in the grand scheme of things.

"Can you make him stop being an idiot? Maybe teach him not to act on thoughts that aren't his own. If he had just talked to us about it first, we would have figured out that Amber was manipulating him sooner." My response is not kind, but I'm not concerned. If I hurt Dec's feelings, he can punch me.

He nods. "I figured it was something like that. He doesn't seem to be himself. I feel like he's hiding the truth from me."

"James almost died from a magical attack when we were trying to rescue Amber's captives after she got caught," Luca whispers as if saying the words aloud will make them worse somehow.

“What?” Dec roars. “Why didn’t anyone tell me?”

“You guys made it pretty clear that you were handling vampire business, and we were supposed to take care of our own shit,” Orym answers. “We were doing what you told us to. You can’t get pissed at that.”

“I thought someone called you. Even with the demand that we leave you out of it, I was certain that one of my guys said they’d told you. I’m sorry, Dec,” I apologize, knowing that it means very little at this point.

“Let’s just move on. There’s no point in us fighting over this. What’s done is done, and no number of arguments will change the past.” The way he says it makes me think that maybe he did brush off the message when it came through. He’s right, it doesn’t matter now.

I continue to stare out the window as Red stares at her hands and James tries to talk to her. I can’t tell if she’s responding to him or just standing there. I would rather be out there with her than in here watching this as it unfolds. She looks so lost, as if someone has just kicked her puppy and stolen her ice cream cone.

“She’s going to struggle with what she did here today. We’re going to have to help her through it,” Orym insists. I completely agree with him.

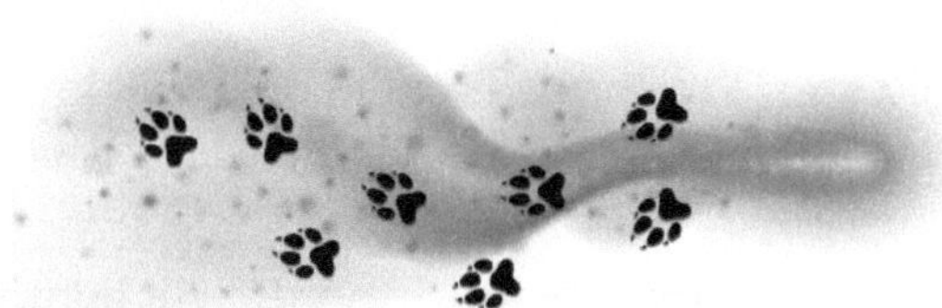

ORYM

After a few minutes, I expect Garnet to come back inside, but she doesn't. She just stands there, staring at her hands. James seems to be talking to her. She's not answering him. I hate that he destroyed our bond, so I can't ask him if she's okay. Clearly, she's not. "I get that they need to talk. I'm not opposed to that, but she's in shock and isn't talking. We should bring her in to take care of her."

I don't wait for Dec to agree, walking out the door before he can stop me. I jog toward the two of them, avoiding the puddles that used to be witches. I know that Garnet is upset about killing them, and that's thrown her into shock.

"James, clearly, she's in shock. Stop talking at her and help me get her inside. We need to make sure she's okay before you two try to fix this." I snap the order at him before scooping her up and turning back to the building. I don't stop to see if he's following me or not. I press a kiss to the top of her head as I wait for someone to open the door and let us back inside.

The door finally swings open, and Dec ushers us inside. "Take her to the elevator. We'll get her checked out upstairs."

He turns to his brother and slaps him in the back of the head. "Get your head straight. Your mate needs you to check her out. Make sure it's just shock and she didn't hurt herself." I don't stay to hear James' response, carrying Garnet to the elevator with Ryland and Luca close behind.

"Red? Can you hear me?" Ryland asks when we step onto the elevator. She nods her head but doesn't say anything.

"Are you okay?" Luca gently turns her to face him. She shakes her head this time, but still doesn't say a word.

"That's pretty obvious, Luca. She's not okay at all." Ryland's growl echoes in the small space and Red flinches.

"That's enough, you two. Let's get her upstairs where we can see if she's injured. Then maybe she can tell us how to help her. Even if it's through the bond where no one else can hear," I offer, giving her a little squeeze.

A single tear slides down her cheek when I say the word bond, and I wonder if this reaction is being so close to James with the damaged bond. If there's a way to fix it, we need to find it fast. Grammy and Trevan were both certain it wasn't too late, but I just don't know. If the bond can be repaired, will we ever be able to trust him again? Or will the pain he's inflicted on Garnet be too much to forgive?

I wish I had the answers. Delilah is waiting for us when the elevator opens into their penthouse home. "Bring her in here and put her on my bed."

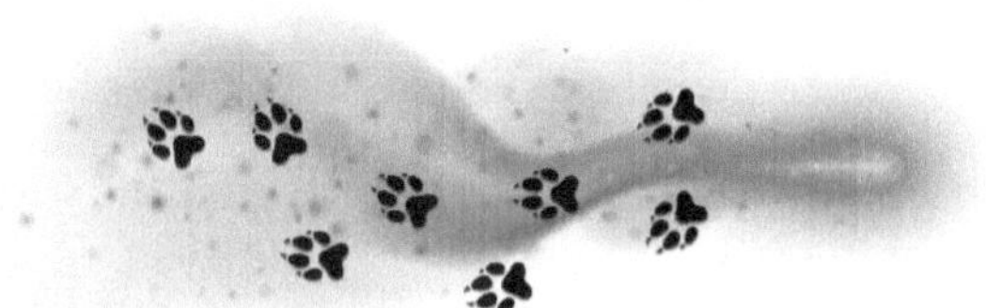

GARNET

I killed people. I took their lives. And I would do it again if I had to. The fact that I'm not more upset about the outcome is upsetting. The whole situation freezes me, stealing my voice. I hear everything James says to me. His apologies for the pain he's causing me are meaningless right now.

Orym carries me up to the penthouse while Ry and Luca try to get me to talk to them. I couldn't speak if I wanted to. I'm not even sure that I would if I could. Maybe it's better if I stay quiet. I can't hurt them if I don't talk. If they have no idea what's going through my mind, there's no way for me to lose them.

Part of me feels like I'm going to lose them all in the end anyway. There's no real point in any of this. Amber will continue to kill wolves, vamps, and humans until someone stops her. The only way to defeat her will involve killing her. Everything forces more death. There is no way to win this without death.

I want to go back to the way things were before all of this. If I could travel back in time, I would choose the moment I realized who my mates were. That was the scariest realization of my life, at least up to that point. I miss that simplicity. There was no fear of death or killing. Just a consideration of how things will work with four mates. I choke back a laugh at that thought. There was a time in my life that my biggest concern was how to deal with having four mates. How did I get from there to fighting to save three different races of people from a wicked witch?

"Are you okay?" Luca asks again when I strangle the laugh that tries to escape my lips.

I lock eyes with him and try to talk through the bond, since my voice doesn't want to cooperate. *Not really, but I'm trying.* I can't tell at first if he hears me or not. Has this issue with

James damaged my bond with all my mates? Maybe I'm just closing myself off to protect them from my pain. Either way, it's not fair and I need to fix it.

My heartache is eased and intensified by being this close to James. I don't know if I can take much more of being this close without being able to touch him. I can't stop the pull toward him, but I am fighting against it. I won't be the one to give in. Even if all of this is Amber's fault, he went along with it. He didn't fight for me. And that's hard to forgive. I'm not sure I'd be able to trust him if he apologized and tried to make things right.

He doesn't seem too interested in that anyway, so it doesn't matter. When we were alone outside, he kept telling me that he was sorry for hurting me, but it was the only way. Those words echo in my head as he takes on his EMT persona and examines me for injuries. He won't find any. I know I'm not hurt physically. It'll make the others feel better, though, so I don't argue.

They all hover around me as the examination proceeds. I let my mind wander so I'm not focused on James' hands on my skin. "Garnet," he says loudly. The exasperation in his voice tells me that he's been trying to get my attention.

"What?" I manage to force the word out, breathless and gravelly.

"I asked if anything hurts," he responds with a flinch. I should be concerned that he acts scared of me, but I'm not. After all, he did just watch me kill a bunch of witches outside. How difficult would it be for me to do the same to him?

"No, nothing hurts. I'm fine," I insist. My voice carries no emotion, flat and lifeless, just like the rest of me. It's not fair to feel this way, especially with three other mates who aren't rejecting me. But the pain of this damaged bond is miserable. The only thing making it bearable right now is being here with James touching me. I wonder if he feels the same. I would ask, but I refuse to admit that he's hurting me.

He turns to Ry, his back toward me. "No physical injuries. I can't tell about mental. I know that did something to her. I'm sorry I can't tell you more."

"If you hadn't destroyed the mate bond, maybe you'd know what's wrong with her," Luca accuses. As amusing as it is to have him call James out, it still hurts me to be reminded of the damaged bond. I wonder if it means anything that it's not fully gone.

"I never meant to hurt her. If you guys would just let me explain, then maybe you won't hate me so much for what I had to do." I'm shocked that James is begging them to hear him out.

"We already know that Amber made you do it. But why? That's what we'd like to know. Why would you go along with Amber and do what she wants?" Ry asks him, taking a step forward. James backs away from me, refusing to face off with Ry. I don't blame him. My sexy alpha mate looks intimidating right now.

"Because it wasn't just Amber. It was everything. I don't have magic like the rest of you. I barely survived being attacked. I can't put Garnet at risk like that again. I won't. Just because Amber tapped a nerve that was already raw, it doesn't mean I wasn't already having those thoughts myself. She just nudged me toward sharing them." James wipes the back of his hand across his eyes.

"I don't understand," Orym says. "You're family. It doesn't matter to us that you're human."

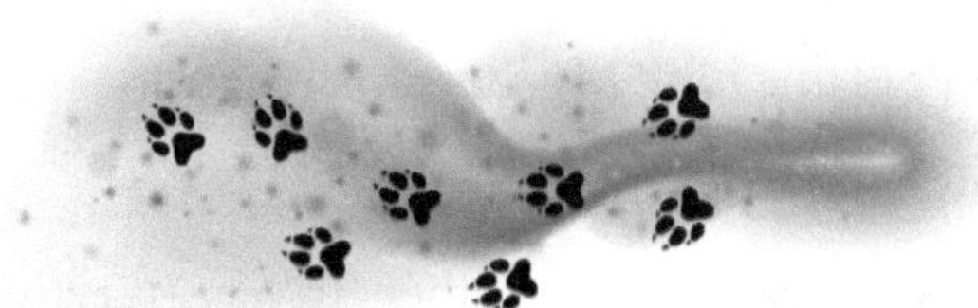

JAMES

"Being human doesn't make you less important to our cause," Orym completes his thought. As much as I want to argue with him, I can see that he believes his words. I just wish I could. I miss Garnet, and the connection with the others. I would love to have it back, but I've already screwed it up.

"I don't know how to make this better. I really think you're all safer without me around. You can't convince me otherwise," I insist, moving toward the door. I have to get out of here. I can't keep fighting about this with everyone. I can tell that my brother is on their side, too.

I expect someone to stop me, but they don't. As soon as I step into the elevator to go down to the club, Dec's hand holds the door open. Here comes another lecture from my big brother. The doors close and the metal box starts to descend, but he doesn't speak.

"Look, I know what you're going to say," I start, not able to stand the silence any longer.

He cocks an eyebrow at me. "Oh, you do? Then tell me little brother, what am I going to say?" His arms cross his chest and he pins me with his glare.

"I've fucked up and I need to fix it. I'm running away instead of facing things head on. Stop being a coward and grovel to the woman you love."

I meet his gaze and he starts to laugh. "What the fuck is so funny?" I ask.

"You. You're hilarious. Yeah, I should say all of that to you, but you already know it. So, I'll say this instead: it's not a good idea to fight with the woman you love. You should be fighting for her, not against her." He holds up a hand when I try to object. "I understand your insecurities, but none of that matters to her. You were chosen as her mate for a reason.

There's a purpose for you to fulfill. You can't do that if you're not by her side. Consider that."

I pause, letting his words sink in. Maybe he's right. "But I'm just a human. I can't compete with the supernatural."

"Yeah, you're human. But you don't have to be. Little brother, you have choices. There are options. I'm not recommending anything, just explaining. If I were you, I would talk it over with your girl before you make any rash decisions, though. That is, if she still wants to be your girl."

The elevator doors open and Dec walks off, hitting the penthouse button as he exits. It's apparent he wants to send me back up to talk to Garnet. I want to, but I'm scared. And what options is he talking about? I'm human, what else could I be?

I consider his words as the elevator moves back up to the penthouse. As the doors open, realization dawns. My brother just offered to turn me.

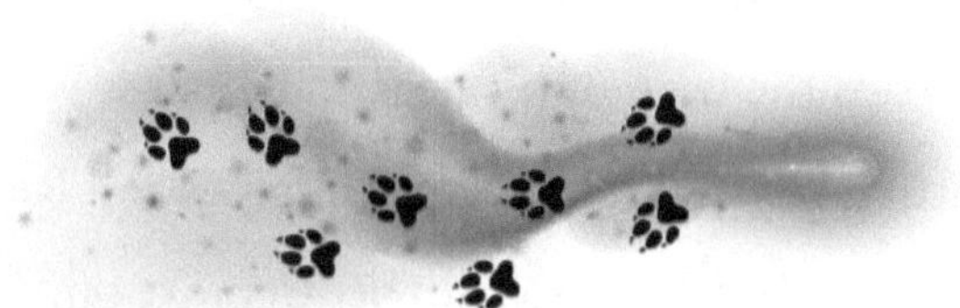

LUCA

I want to chase after James and punch him for making Red cry again. Tears fall as soon as he's out of the room. I know that her pain is worse than what we're able to feel along the bond. I wish she'd share more with me. I can take it and she won't have to hurt so badly.

Unfortunately, it doesn't work that way unless she wants to share it. I'm so annoyed with James that I nearly miss Orym comforting Red. Ryland and I exchange a glance and he nods toward the hall. I follow him out, wondering what he has on his mind.

"What's up?" I ask, trying to calm my nerves at this situation and how it's unfolding.

"We have to get her out of here. Being this close to James is hurting her, especially since he won't really talk to her." Ryland rubs the back of his neck as he talks. We both know that putting physical space between James and Red will cause her more pain but will also help her to move on.

"I agree. But I think we should kick his ass before we go. He's being stupid," I offer. Ryland nods, agreeing with me. For a moment, I think he's going to approve of my idea.

"As much as I'd like to, that's not the answer. We have to let James figure this out on his own. It's not up to us to force him into something that he may not want. Maybe in time, the goddess will ease their pain and remove the mate bond. Or he'll come to his senses and fix things with Red. It's not up to us," he explains. I know he's right, but it doesn't make my desire for blood any less.

"We should get back to planning our attack against Amber. I don't like letting him get away with this, but I'll do what you ask, Alpha." As much as I hate bowing to anyone, this doesn't feel like I'm being forced to do what Ryland says. He explains himself and I can see his point. Arguing would only lead to him commanding me to follow orders. I don't want that, so I'll concede before it comes to that.

"You know I hate it when you call me that," he says, punching my shoulder. I laugh and hit him back.

"But it's your title," I insist. He's nothing like Gunnar, not expecting the same utter reverence we were forced to show to our last leader. Honestly, he's not what I expected when Red announced that they were mated. I guess it just goes to show how first impressions can be completely wrong.

He rolls his eyes and turns back to the room Red is in. "Shut up, you asshole. Let's get our girl and go home." I follow him back inside where Orym is still holding Red and rubbing her back.

"Is she feeling any better?" I ask, knowing the answer before Orym shakes his head.

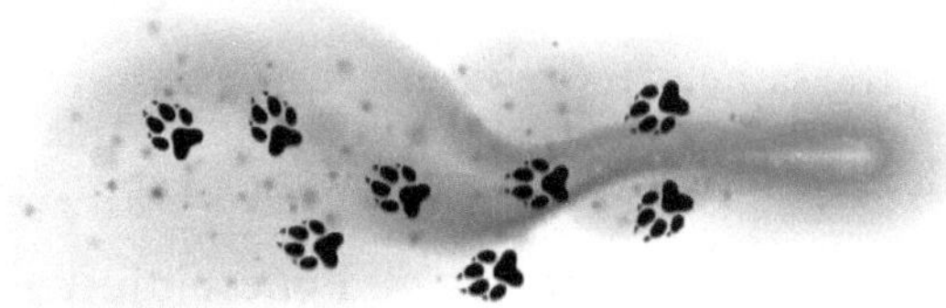

GARNET

I let Orym comfort me while Ry and Luca leave to talk. I'm sure that Ry wants to get out of here. He's never been comfortable asking for help, especially from these vampires. I feel like they're my family, so it doesn't bother me. I wish that James would talk to me, but I know that it won't matter. If he is convinced that he's not good enough to be by my side, there's nothing I can do to change that.

Ry and Luca come back into the room, and I make a decision. "We should go. James isn't willing to talk, so there's no point in us bothering anyone here," I say, pulling out of Orym's arms.

"If that's what you want," Ry says. I'm shocked that he can keep the smirk off his face.

"As if that's not what the two of you were in the hall talking about," Orym chides. I laugh, and they all stare at me. It really wasn't that funny, but I can't stop myself. For some reason, the whole thing is hilarious, and laughter keeps bubbling out of me.

It only lasts for a minute before the door opens and everything goes quiet again. James stands in the doorway and all eyes focus on him. "Can we talk?" he asks without stepping into the room.

I start to shake my head, but something in his expression stops me. "Okay. Family, or just us?" I need to know if he'll say what he wants to in front of the others or not.

"As long as no one is gonna hit me, I'm okay with it being a family talk. Everyone deserves to know what I'm thinking," he answers.

I stand and walk past him into the living room. I don't want to have this talk here, but there aren't many options.

I decide that Delilah's bedroom is not the place to have our heart-to-heart. We risk other people listening or joining our conversation here.

I turn to my wolf mates, raising an eyebrow. "We're not going to attack him unless he hurts you," Ry says in his most authoritative alpha voice.

"There you go. Now talk," I order, taking a seat on the huge couch.

"I'm sorry I hurt you. I meant what I said. You're safer without me. As a human, anyway," he starts. My eyes go wide, and I wait for him to continue. "If I were more, then maybe I'd be more helpful."

"Wait, what exactly are you talking about here?" Luca asks, dropping to the couch beside me and taking my hand.

"Are you saying you want to be a vampire?" Orym interrupts, not letting James answer Luca's question.

"I don't know what I want. I just know that I can't be with you as a human. I'm not strong enough to protect you, or myself. If you want me to come back with you, I have to be more." His explanation is a little thin, leaving a lot to the imagination.

"I need you to spell this out for me. Exactly what are you talking about doing?" I force the words from my mouth, which is suddenly dry. I had considered discussing this with James before, but I never thought for a second that he would agree to being turned.

"Dec says there are options. I don't know what those are other than being turned to a vampire. It's not something I've ever wanted, but it would make me stronger. I would heal faster and have other abilities. Knowing that, it's hard to argue against it." James paces the floor as he talks. I can tell that he's trying to decide if this is something he wants to do.

I don't want to force him into anything. My heart races as he talks through this option. "Obviously, if I did this, I would ask Dec to turn me. It would take a little while to fully control everything. I understand that. But I think it might be the only way."

"You don't have to do anything you don't want to do," I insist. I won't let him make this decision if he's hesitant at all. I hold up a hand to stop Luca from whatever he was about to say. "No one is going to force you into anything. We will, however, support your decision." I hope that doesn't sound too flippant. I hate the idea of sounding like I don't care. I need this to be his choice. Otherwise, he may hate me for it later.

"I need to know what you all think about it. This isn't an easy choice to make, and I don't want to ruin what we have more by making the wrong decision." The pain in his voice nearly makes me cry. I want to hold him and ease his mind.

Instead, I meet his gaze and try to comfort him with words. "When you got hurt, I wanted to talk to you about letting Dec change you. But you were unconscious, and when we met in the Fae realm, there wasn't time. I was busy training and preparing to save you."

He nods at my explanation, then turns to Luca. "I think it's a bad idea," Luca says. "But I will respect your decision either way."

Orym looks up. "It couldn't hurt."

"I agree with Luca. It's a bad idea, especially this close to the battle." Ry offers. "That said, I'm behind you if that's what you want."

I slap my hands on my thighs. "Well, it looks like we're all on the same page here. So, it's up to you. What do you want?"

James stares at me for a minute before answering. "To fix our bond; to be worthy of you; to be more than just a human."

"Then I guess we should talk to your brother," I say. The look on his face tells me that he's not as sure of his decision as he seemed.

TWELVE
BROTHERLY LOVE

JAMES

I've made my decision; I should feel better about this. But somehow, it's not as easy to reconcile as I'd hoped. It's the right thing to do. It has to be.

Some unseen force brought me to Garnet and made me fall in love with her. If it then rips me away from her because I'm human, that's not fair. But should I have to change myself completely to be with the woman I love?

I'm struggling with my choice, and definitely hiding it poorly. I can tell from the faces that stare at me as we finish our conversation. "Then I guess we should talk to your brother," Garnet says.

I nod, then shake my head. "James, you don't have to do this. No one will judge you either way. It's completely your decision," she quickly amends.

"It's not that. I should talk to Dec alone. I don't want him to think you guys are forcing me into this. You're not. This is my decision. Just—wait for me here, okay?" I hold out a hand and she takes it easily. I'm surprised that there's no hesitation. Instead, what I see in her eyes is the pain I've caused her by listening to Amber's voice echoing my own thoughts.

"Are you sure you don't need moral support?" Orym asks. It's the first time one of them has spoken to me in a way that made me feel like they're on my side. I nod and turn toward the elevator. I don't know where Dec went off to, but I'll find him. I lean down and kiss Garnet's cheek before leaving.

I argue with myself the whole way down to the club. I have to do this—I can't do this. Back and forth, I go. I don't know if it's my own hesitation or Amber's spell trying to force me to stay away from Garnet. It doesn't matter. I've made my decision.

I find my brother in the stockroom, grabbing liquor bottles to stock the bar. "Dec, can we talk?" I ask, taking a couple of bottles from him and following as he goes to the bar.

"In private?" he responds, understanding that this is bigger than a casual conversation. He nods toward the stockroom, and I follow him back. I'm surprised to find that there is a small private room in the back where we can talk uninterrupted. "What's up?"

"I need you to turn me," I blurt out, not bothering to preface it.

"What? Why? No," he questions, shaking his head.

"It's the only way I'll be able to be with Garnet. Please. This is my choice," I insist, gripping his shoulders and forcing him to look in my eyes so he can tell I'm serious.

"Are you sure? Your reaction to me being turned wasn't exactly accepting. Have you discussed this with her?"

"I'm sure. I'm sorry I was so hateful when you were turned. Having you is better than not."

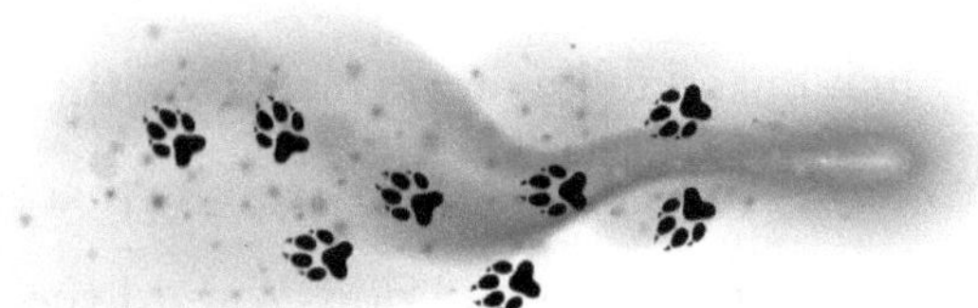

LUCA

I can't help following James down to the bar to eavesdrop on his conversation with Dec. I'm careful not to let him see me as I sneak into the stockroom where I just watched them enter. How is it empty?

I hear a loud 'What?' and realize that there's a secret room in here. I quietly pad to the wall and place my ear on it. Dec is not happy about James' decision. That doesn't surprise me.

What does shock me is the admission that James was less than supportive of his brother's choices. He's always seemed like the type to understand and love his family anyway, even if he doesn't agree with them.

I shake my head, focusing on what I'm hearing through the door.

"I don't know, James. What you're asking me to do is...well, it's a lot." Dec sounds pretty upset about being asked to turn his brother. I bet he won't do it. So much for James coming home with us.

"Dec, you have to do this for me. Or I'll just go ask one of the others. I bet Vik would understand the situation and help me out. Or Eli. Even Delilah," James begs.

"You wouldn't," Dec insists. Oh, but I would put money on that being exactly what he does if his brother doesn't cooperate. I get distracted imagining Dec's reaction to James asking someone else to change him.

I barely jump out of the way as the hidden door swings open. "What the fuck are you doing? Did you follow me down here?" James accuses the second he sees me.

"Yeah. I'm sorry, I just wanted to make sure that this was what you wanted." I turn to Dec. "You know that if you don't help him, he'll find someone else who will. Then he'll be vulnerable because he won't have someone to turn to for help with the transition."

"Why do you even care? You and Ryland are against this anyway," James huffs. I nod, agreeing with him.

"That's why we're against it. We care about you. Look, I don't want you to do this, but if your mind is made up, there's nothing I can say or do to change it." I glance at Dec again. "But if I can help to convince your brother to help you, I will."

Dec looks back and forth between us as if considering my words. "You think this is a bad idea, but you want to convince me to do it anyway?"

"Basically," I answer. He sighs in exasperation and throws up his hands. I know at that moment that he'll agree, and James will get what he wants.

"Well?" James asks, staring at his brother.

"Fine, I'll do it. But we have to prepare first. I won't do it until I'm sure you're ready," Dec says before walking away in a huff.

"He seems thrilled," I offer, grinning at James.

James rolls his eyes. "Definitely. Thanks for your help. It means a lot."

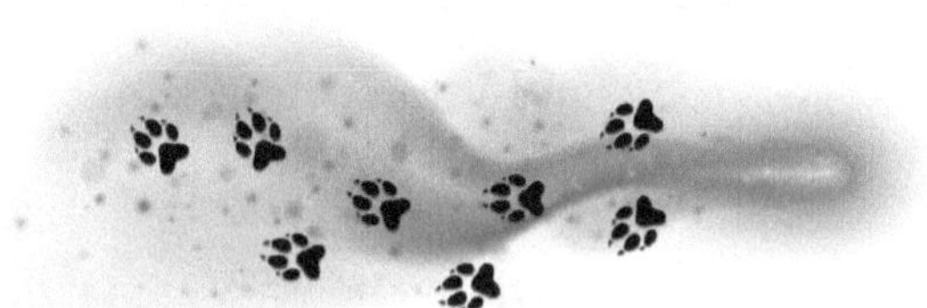

GARNET

I feel helpless when James walks away. Then Luca follows him, and I'm concerned that he'll try to talk James out of his decision. I don't know if that would hurt me or make me feel better about everything. Yeah, this was originally my idea, but I hate the thought that I somehow backed James into a corner and made him think this was the only way he could be with me.

All of this happened because I'm worried about him getting hurt. Apparently, I'm not the only one who's been bothered by it. I should be happy that he came to the same conclusion that I did, but I'm not. I'm terrified. What if he does this and resents me for it later?

What if Dec refuses to help him? There are so many things that could go wrong, and I don't want to focus on them. I need to do something besides sit here and wait. I hop off the couch and start to pace. Orym and Ry watch me, exchanging sly glances that they think I don't notice.

"He'll be fine. Dec will take care of it. He has to, right?" Orym's complete faith in James' brother amazes me. We have no reason to believe that Dec will help James with this. Of course, we have no reason to think he won't. None of us really know Dec that well.

"I hope so. I don't want James to do this and regret it, though," I admit. Ry walks over to me and pulls me into his arms.

"That's why I'm against it. I don't think it's what he wants. I think that he believes it's the only way, and it's not," he says. The elevator doors open and we turn to see Dec stomping into the room.

"Did you tell him that he has to be turned to be with you?" The vampire growls the words at me, and my wolf mates growl back at him. I hold up my hands for them to stand down as I step away from Ry. I don't need him to protect me here.

"I did not. Honestly, I was considering talking to him about it because of how he nearly died from a magic attack. But I didn't say anything. He came to us with this idea. Ry and Luca tried to talk him out of it. Orym and I told him we'll support his choice. None of us told him to do it." My words come out strong, but my heart flutters.

This man could kill me in a moment, and there's nothing my mates could do to stop him. Sure, there would be repercussions, but I would already be dead, so what does it matter? I can feel the rage rolling off him in waves.

"What the fuck is wrong with him, then? If you aren't forcing this, why does he think it's the only way?" Dec's rage is building, and I wish that Delilah hadn't left us alone up here. She does have a nightclub to run, though, so I can see why she wouldn't want to babysit when there are more productive things she could be doing.

"Back off my mate, Dec. This isn't her fault," Ry growls again. I press a hand to his chest and shove him back. He barely moves but understands what I'm telling him. I give him a look, causing both of my mates to sit down on the couch.

"Don't worry about them. I can handle myself here. I didn't put this idea in his head, even if I had considered suggesting it. You can believe me or not. I don't think you'll change his mind. You should know as well as I do; your brother is pretty stubborn. We came here to bring him home with us. All of this is Amber's fault. I just want my mate back where he belongs." It feels weak admitting that James hurt me, but there's no other way to make Dec see what I'm trying to tell him.

He sighs and takes a couple of steps closer before reaching out and dragging me into a hug. Orym and Ry growl, but he glares at them. This isn't a romantic gesture. He's simply offering me comfort because our mutual loved one has hurt me.

"It's not like that, and you both know it. My sister needs comfort, and I'm going to give it to her," he insists, hugging me tighter. "Look, Red, if this is what James wants, and you're okay with it; then I'll do it. But not today. I need to know for sure that he's considered what this means."

I nod against his chest. "I completely agree. Thank you."

"You could make him wait until after the confrontation with Amber. The Wolf Moon isn't too far away. That would give him time to think about it and be sure. And you could add the caveat that you'll only do it if he comes back home with us instead of abandoning Red when she needs him." Ry's suggestion makes sense, and I wonder if it's a viable compromise.

Dec releases me and takes a step back. "That's perfect." Just as he's about to say more, the elevator doors open again. This time, Luca and James walk in.

"Did you seriously come up here to get them to talk me out of this?" James accuses his brother. I can't stop the laugh that bubbles up, and everyone stares at me.

"James, your brother has a compromise for you. Just hear him out," I say between giggles. I don't know why I'm laughing, but I can't stop.

Dec clears his throat and suddenly whatever was funny isn't anymore. "I will turn you, but not until after the Wolf Moon. And only if you go home with your mate and stand by her side for what's coming."

"That defeats the whole purpose, Dec. I need to be stronger now, so that I can help her."

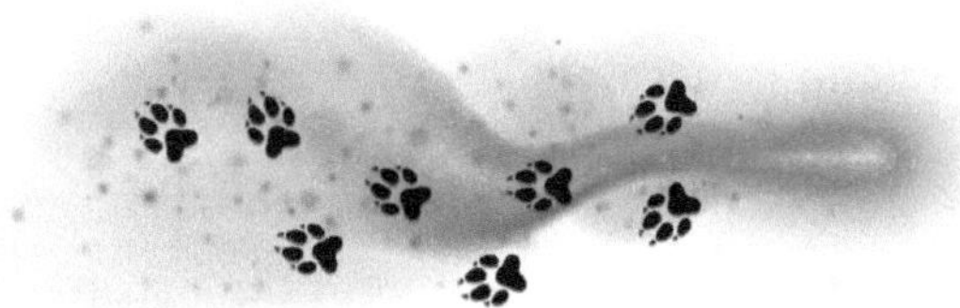

RYLAND

For a minute, no one makes a sound. I think James is about to punch Dec, but he doesn't. Instead, Dec pulls his brother in for a hug. "I understand your concern, little brother, but I won't do it. And none of the others will either. If this is truly what you want, then you'll have to wait until after Amber is dealt with. Red told me about the deadline, and she agrees that this is the best compromise."

The pain written on James' face is palpable. So much so that I wonder if our bond is back. I can nearly feel what he's feeling. That's when I realize how much I missed that connection. We're more than just Red's mates, we're family.

"If there's no way to talk you into doing it now, then I guess I have no choice but to wait," James concedes.

"And to go home with us," Red reminds him of that part of the deal. He has to come home, and wait until after the Wolf Moon, or Dec won't turn him.

I understand why he wants to be changed. I just wish he could see his value as more than having super powers or not. Not that wolf shifting is a super power, but that seems to be his opinion. Personally, I don't think we're that different. I was born with the ability to become a wolf to defend and protect my pack. He studied to become an EMT to save people when they get injured. We're basically the same guy.

The look on his face when Red tells him that he has to come home with us is priceless. He'd purposefully blocked that part out, apparently. "Wait, what?" he asks.

We all laugh this time, taking our cue from Red's reaction to James nearly catching her hugging his brother. "It was part of the deal. Take it or leave it. Your family needs you." Dec stares at him. “Yes, we’re family, but they need you right now. Red can’t fight Amber without you, so go.”

James stiffens, but doesn’t argue. “Fine. I’ll go, even though I think this is a huge mistake.” He turns to the rest of us. “I’m guessing that’s why you came here? To take me back.” When I nod, he starts toward the elevator.

“I guess we’re going now. We’ll keep you updated,” I say to Dec before following James onto the elevator. Orym, Luca, and Red rush to catch up to us. The ride downstairs is silent and I could cut the tension with a knife. It’s obvious that James is pissed, but he’s not trying to fight about it.

I exchange a glance with Orym and Luca, silently letting them know that I wanted James in the back seat sandwiched between them on the ride back. I don’t want to give him a chance to run off again. I know that I can’t stop him once we’re home, but maybe by then he’ll be calmer.

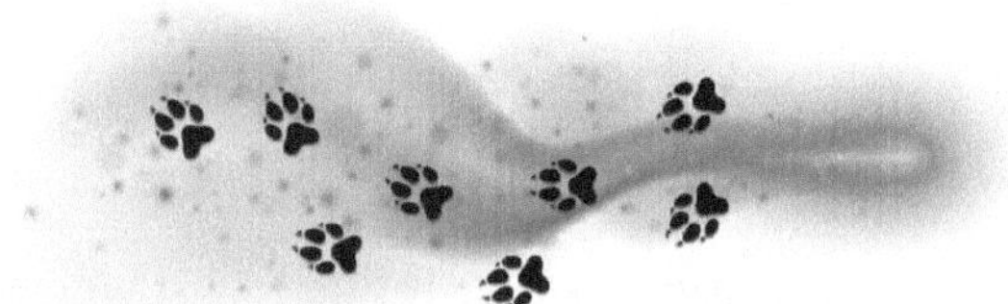

ORYM

The ride home is quick and uncomfortably quiet. James sits between myself and Luca, glaring at each of us for not trusting him. I understand, but I'm with Ryland. He agreed to come home, he should stick with that. There's no sense in taking chances.

As soon as we get to the forest, I sense Garnet's fear. She's scared that James will take off again, and this time we won't find him. They need to talk this out on their own, without the rest of us involved. His issue is with her anyway. If he can't trust her enough to love him for who he is, that's a James problem.

We walk back to the cabin, stopping to talk to most of the wolves we meet along the way. I'm relieved to hear that there haven't been any more attacks or sightings of Amber since we left. I split off to check on the shifters who are going through training. Learning to fight is important, especially when we're about to go up against a coven of witches who want us all dead.

The outdoor training course is filled with wolves in various spots. They're working together to make it across obstacles, and I'm impressed with their teamwork. "We've paired off for most of the course, sir." The wolf who speaks is one of the few Ryland trusts to handle training.

"That's perfect, Aaron. How are the younger ones taking to it?" I'm not expecting them to fight, but I want the small ones to be able to defend themselves if necessary.

"Everyone is working hard to master all the expected skills. The little ones are struggling, but this is all new to them. They do great with the climbing and running away parts, not so much with the fighting methods parts. But we're all working on it."

I'm pleased with the update, and relieved that the entire territory is taking this threat seriously. "Stick with the pairs for everything. Make sure that little ones are paired with older ones for travel and trail runs. And be sure that they know to stick together. Bigger groups are preferred, but no one walks through the woods alone. Understood?"

He nods his agreement before running off to share what I've said with the others. In all fairness, the order should have come from Ryland as our alpha, but they all know he's selected me as his second. I walk the entire length of the training course before leisurely walking back toward home. I'm breaking my own directive and I know it, but I'm not worried about myself. I'm worried about everyone else.

I can't bear to lose anyone else. We've all lost too much already. I walk up to the cabin to find Luca and Ryland standing outside talking to Trevan and Grammy. Garnet and James must have gone inside. I exchange a glance with Ryland and understand exactly what's going on. They're trying to encourage them repairing the bond.

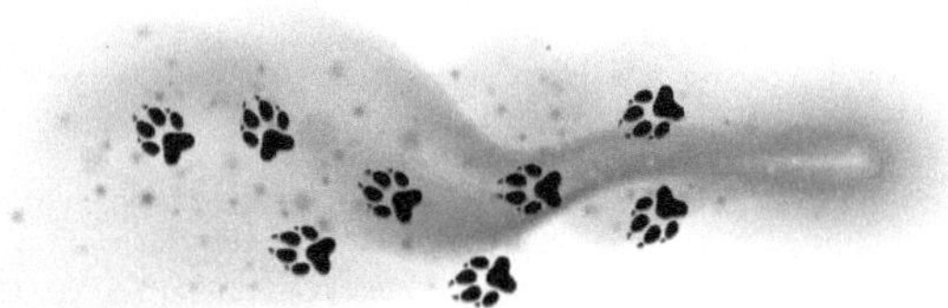

GARNET

"I know this is awkward, but I really would just like to spend some time with you, if that's okay," I offer, holding a hand out to James. He's been pacing the floor in the bedroom since we got to the cabin and we were basically shoved in here to fix our bond.

I don't think it's fair to force things, so I won't do it. If James is interested, he'll make the first move. Otherwise, we'll just talk or cuddle. Or sit on opposite sides of the room until the others think it's been long enough.

"It is awkward. Do they really think that putting us in a room together will just fix the bond? Or are they expecting us to have sex?" he snarls, clearly not happy with the situation.

"I'm quite certain they expect us to go at each other—whether that means sex or fighting." I stare at him, still holding my hand out. "But I'm not going to push you for either. I just want to talk. Can we do that?" I ask, maintaining eye contact with him until he shifts uncomfortably.

"Fine." He stomps over and sits on the bed, as far away from me as possible. "What do you want to talk about?"

"We could start with what I did to make you think you weren't enough," I offer, turning to face him as he turns away. He refuses to look at me. For a moment, I think I can feel his guilt, but that can't be. Our bond is destroyed and there's no way I can still feel his emotions, right?

"You didn't do anything. It was me. I think I'm not enough—no, I know I'm not. I don't understand why you all want to argue about it. If you hadn't, then Dec would have changed me and we'd be having a completely different conversation right now." His quiet insistence is frustrating. I need to find a way to get through to him.

I let my thoughts wander for a minute, trying to come up with something that will get him to really listen to what I'm saying. While I'm being quiet, I can hear his breath. What were calm intakes becoming more ragged. I glance at him again, and I see he's holding back tears. "I'm sorry. I didn't mean to upset you. But you hurt me. No, that's not fair. You destroyed me, and I'm not sure I'll ever be the same again. I deserve an explanation. Honestly, I deserve groveling and begging my forgiveness."

I keep my eyes trained on his while I speak, waiting for a reaction. He just stares at me, as if he wasn't expecting any of this.

"Garnet," he starts. Then he stops talking and stares at me longer before turning away again. I want to make him look at me at least, but I can't. I won't force anything from him. I've made that abundantly clear. All of this is his choice. If he doesn't want me, he needs to tell me.

Before I can voice those thoughts, he stands and goes to the window. "I never meant to hurt you. It was the last thing I wanted. I know it's hard to believe, but I love you. That sounds so insignificant. Love isn't even a big enough word to explain how I feel about you. I don't know that I'll ever be able to. I left to protect you."

He turns to face me and continues. "It's stupid and ridiculous, but it's true. Even if Amber was partially responsible, it's the truth. She may have taken my insecurities and twisted them around her little finger to get me to do what she wanted; what I thought I needed to do. But they were my thoughts and concerns first. She didn't plant them in my head. I promise you that. I spent my entire time in the Fae realm wondering what more I could do to be enough for you."

I stand and walk toward him, stopping when he starts to back away. I hold up my hands in surrender. Tears streak down my face, falling because I'm so disconnected from my mate. "I don't think you fully understand this mate bond. We're connected. I knew you were feeling insecure, but I didn't realize it was this bad. I need you by my side. Not just to defeat Amber, but to be happy. I can't do either without you, James. And I agree—I love you, even if those words are too small to properly express the way I feel for you."

His eyes meet mine and we stand there, staring at each other. He starts to cry as well, and I feel a familiar tingle. Perhaps our bond isn't fully broken after all. I latch onto that feeling, willing it to grow and heal, as if the tethers of the bond are a physical string that can be patched until it's good as new.

I watch James' expression change as I work my internal magic, unsure if it's doing anything until his face tells me that he feels it too. "How did you do that?" he asks, shocked.

"I didn't. We did. You opened yourself up to me, and I did the same to you. It's not fully healed, but this is definitely a start." I wish that it was an instant fix, because I hate this uncertainty that I feel. I want to know that James is mine and I'm his. There's still a part of me that has doubts because he ran away. No matter his reasons why, that's what he did.

"I'm sorry that I hurt you. I know now that it was wrong. I should have talked to you about how I was feeling instead of pushing you away," he offers, taking a tentative step toward me. I'm careful not to move a muscle. I wait for him to approach, to reassure. I've done what I can.

THIRTEEN
VINCENT

ORYM

Giving Garnet and James space is difficult. I can feel her fear and anxiety through the bond. After a few minutes, I start to feel James along the bond again. I know that doesn't mean everything will be magically fixed, but it's a start.

Ryland's phone rings and he steps away to answer it. "Yeah. Fuck. We'll be right there." He slips it back in his pocket and turns to us. "We have to go to the training center. Now."

"What about Red and James? Should we get them?" Luca asks. Ryland shakes his head.

"They've found Vincent and it's bad. I don't want her to know yet." That is bad. I understand why Ryland doesn't want to tell her right now. She's more concerned with repairing the bond with James, and that's what she needs to focus on.

"I'll let her know we have to check on the trainees," I offer, opening the mental link. *Garnet? Ryland, Luca, and I are going to check on the trainees while you and James talk. If you need us, just call and we'll come back.*

We start heading toward the training center when she responds. *Is everything okay?*

Yeah, it's just awkward standing outside while you two are in there. We didn't want to add pressure to the situation. It's not exactly a lie, but hopefully she doesn't figure out that I'm not being completely honest.

Okay, stay safe. Her response is quick, and I know she's distracted by what's going on with James.

"Garnet knows we're leaving, but I told her it's because we feel awkward standing outside right now," I explain to the others. They nod, understanding that if she asks, they need to go along with my story.

"What happened to Vincent?" Luca asks as we get further from the cabin.

Ryland shakes his head. "I have no idea. Mark said they found him, and it's bad. That was it. I told him we'd be right there. So, we'll find out in a minute." None of us bother to shift, because while this is urgent, it's not an emergency.

The training center seems deserted, and I realize that Mark must have sent the kids away when they brought Vincent in. We enter the building, and the smell of death surrounds us. It takes everything in me not to start gagging. The air tastes the way it smells, blood, charred flesh, and something I can't quite place.

No one says a word as we walk over to where they have him laid on a table. Shock rips through me at what I see when I'm close enough.

I'm not even sure how they know it's Vincent. This creature is mangled beyond repair. With our increased healing, this shouldn't be possible. The man in front of us is broken, with bones jutting out of his flesh. He's been set on fire, more than once from the look of it. And large chunks of skin, muscle, and tendon are missing from different places along his body.

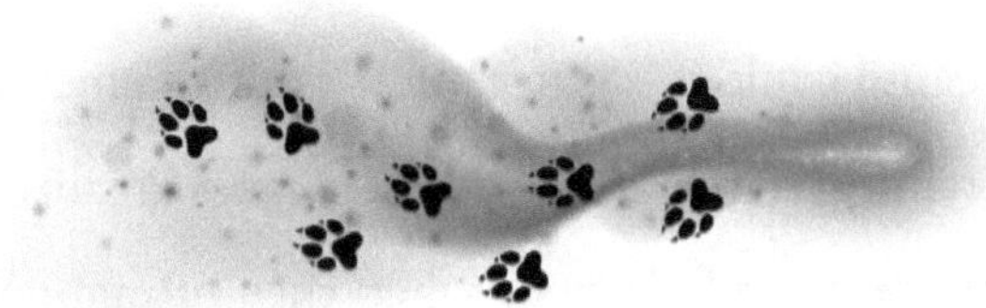

JAMES

I don't know how to do this. Can I let myself stay here? Can I allow Garnet to depend on me when I know I'm only going to fail her again? It's not fair to anyone involved, but I can't turn away from her again. Now that our connection is back, I can feel how badly I've hurt her, and I never want to do that again.

I take another step toward her, noticing that she's not reaching for me. The bond between us confuses me. I don't know how to interpret her emotions, especially when I'm certain I can feel the other guys as well. It's hard enough to deal with my own feelings and thoughts, much less four other people's. Does she regret bringing me back here with her?

What I regret is nearly losing you in the first place. I hear her voice in my head, and it startles me. I know it's part of the magic that connects us, but it still catches me off guard, even more than her emotions seeping into me.

"Are you reading my mind?" I ask, feeling bothered by the intrusion. I know it's ridiculous to get upset about it, but I can't stop myself. The only reason I agreed to come back here was that Dec refuses to turn me until after Garnet deals with Amber.

"I'm sorry, you were projecting. I'll try not to comment if I hear anything else," she offers, taking a step backward.

Disappointment and hurt assault me through the bond, along with frustration and anger. I know the latter are the other guys' reactions to Garnet's emotions. I hate hurting her, but I can't deal with other people in my head right now. Learning that part of this happened because of Amber's influence is hard enough. I don't want to start doing things because it's what someone else wants.

"Look, Garnet, I'm sorry. I'm feeling overwhelmed and frustrated about everything. I don't want to put you in danger, and I feel like that's all I'm doing here. I can't take the idea that you could lose this battle with Amber, and it would be my fault," I admit. I want to reach for her again, but I know she's not ready. I don't think that I'm ready. Knowing doesn't make it less painful, though.

"I understand. And I promise, we won't push you for anything you're not ready for or don't want. But you will not be the reason if I fail here. That will be all my fault. I need you by my side. All four of you make me stronger. You give me a reason to fight," she insists. Part of me understands her point and wants to do whatever I can to help her. The rest of me still feels the aftermath of whatever spell that Amber used to push me toward leaving.

I know that she just preyed on my insecurities, but that doesn't make it easier to accept.

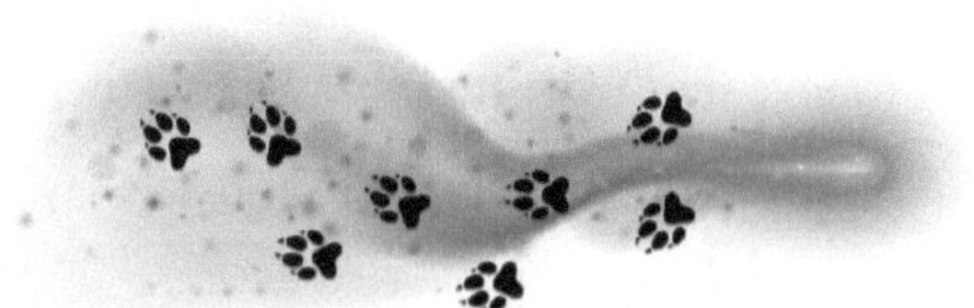

GARNET

James' rejection stings. So much so that I can't keep my hurt and disappointment from flowing along the bond. He's not shielding his emotions from us, or his thoughts. I promised not to use that against him, so I won't. I know I'm not the only one who feels the other's responses to my emotions. I can see it on James' face.

I understand fear. I'm terrified that I'm going to fuck all of this up and leave them alone. Since James nearly broke our mate bond, I know that the pain of me dying would drive them all mad. I can't let that happen.

"I can't make you help me fight Amber, any more than I can make you love me. Those have to be your choices. No one can make those for you. What I will say is that I hope you decide to be part of this family again. I hope you want to help; that you want to love me. We were brought together for a reason. Just think about it. I'll leave you be for now," I say, turning and walking out the bedroom door.

For a moment, I think he might follow me. Then I hear the bathroom door slam and the shower kick on. So much for that. I'd hoped that my little speech would be encouraging and inspiring. It doesn't look like it helped much at all. Instead of cementing our bond back in place, we're spending time in separate rooms, frustrated, hurt, and angry.

I can't take these walls right now, so I step outside. I want to scream, but I know people will be scared if I do. Of course, if I make a sound-proof bubble, I can scream as much as I want. I step out into the clearing next to the cabin and focus. I must clear my mind for this to work. Once I've calmed my mind, I set to making the clear bubble around myself that will allow me to scream to my heart's content without startling anyone.

I wonder for a moment if the bubble will interfere with the mate bond, but I shove that thought away. I need this more than I need to be concerned about a hiccup in our bond. With the bubble set in place, I take a deep breath, then let out a blood curdling scream.

I scream and yell, letting myself vent my frustration in this safe space, until I'm spent. Dropping to the ground, I sit cross-legged and start to meditate, not letting the bubble fall. I need a few minutes to recharge after expending that much energy and magic. But I don't feel like moving, so this is the next best thing.

I close my eyes and clear my mind again, this time focusing on my breathing. I have no idea how long I sat like that, with my eyes closed, just breathing in and out. I feel calmer than I have in a long time. A gasp from outside the bubble and my concentration fails. I open my eyes to see James standing in front of me, staring.

"What?" I ask, looking around as the bubble disintegrates.

"You were surrounded by different colored lights. Fire, water, earth, and air were circling around you, and I wasn't sure if you were alive or not. What was that?" he asks in awe.

"I needed a quiet place to think," I say, not wanting to admit that I'd needed to scream for a bit. If he doesn't know, then he doesn't need to right now.

"I've never seen you do that kind of magic before." The statement isn't accusatory, but more curious.

"I've never tried it before. It was easier than I expected. As long as I stay focused, my magic is pretty easy to reach and use. I'm hoping that it stays that way when I go to fight Amber," I admit, then instantly wish I hadn't.

I don't want to feed his insecurities or make him think that he's the reason I could fail at this. It's not on him. This is my fight; it's my war. I have to win. I can't let Amber defeat me. And I can't admit how scared I really am. To anyone. I keep that particular emotion locked down so that none of my mates can feel it.

I can't afford for any of them to realize that I might not be ready for what's coming. We have less than a week to get ready. It's not enough time, no matter how powerful I am. I'm facing the fact that I'm going to have to kill my aunt before she can kill me.

Given that I haven't known her for that long, it won't be as hard as if I'd grown up with her as a part of my family. Then again, I don't like to kill, even in self-defense. I would rather find a way to defeat her without that kind of violence involved.

I've tried everything to come up with a way to do just that. There isn't one. The only option is death. It's just a matter of which one of us will die. I hope it's not me.

James waves a hand in front of my face and says my name. "Garnet." From his tone, I can tell that he's said it a few times already, while I was lost in my thoughts.

"Sorry, I got distracted. What did you say?" I feel my cheeks heat as he stares at me.

"I asked if you were really ready to face Amber. She wants to kill you and take your powers. Why can't we just run away?" James steps closer to me, and I realize that he's about to reach for me. Could this be the breakthrough I wanted?

"I have no choice but to be ready. I can't run. Even if I did, she'd find me. Of course, that would be after she killed everyone I've ever cared about."

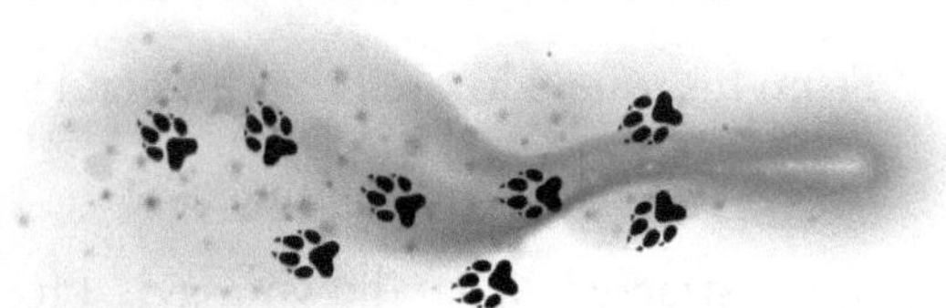

LUCA

Vincent's injuries are so much worse than I expected when we walked into the training center. I can see why Mark sent the young ones home. They didn't need to see this. I wish I hadn't seen it. I don't know that I'll ever get this image out of my head. Just when I think I've seen the worst of his injuries, my eye catches something else.

His body is broken, he's covered with open wounds that are seeping blood and pus. And as if that's not enough, he has bones sticking out nearly everywhere. But that's not the thing that makes me feel sick. I can see the magic bubbling under what little unbroken skin there is left. It's as if the magic is crawling around inside of him, looking for a way out.

Before anyone can say anything, Vincent starts to shake and writhe. "What's going on?" I ask. Mark looks at me and shrugs.

"This is new. We've been trying to treat his wounds the best we can. Obviously, we should get Grammy, but none of us wanted her to see him this way." I nod at his reasoning. I don't want Grammy to see this either.

"You made the right choice," Ryland tells him. "It looks like he's trying to shift. But he's barely alive, and not conscious. It has to be the magic forcing it."

I lean closer as he thrashes, noticing something strange. "Ryland, Orym, look at this," I say, holding Vincent's head still and pulling his upper lip away from his teeth. "These don't look like wolf fangs."

"Fuck. Amber gave him the mutation potion. I wonder if that's what broke him," Orym says quietly.

"It's possible, but there's no way for us to know for sure without asking Amber. Since we can't do that, we need to prepare for what needs to happen next. There's no way we can save him, especially if he has magic inside preventing him from getting any real rest." It takes a moment for Ryland's words to sink in, and then I realize that he's talking about killing Vincent.

"You can't mean—" Orym stops himself short of saying the words out loud.

Ryland nods somberly. "I'll do what I must. It's my responsibility as territory alpha. I can't let one of my wolves suffer like this. I would expect any of you to do the same for me in this situation."

Knowing that it's what any of us would want doesn't make it any easier to make this decision. And understanding that it's the right thing to do won't ease the pain I see on my alpha's face.

"We're here with you, Ryland. We'll do whatever you need us to," I offer. I know that he won't let either of us do this for him, but that won't stop me from offering to help.

"Good, because I'll need you both to hold him down. I'm going to make it as painless as possible," he says.

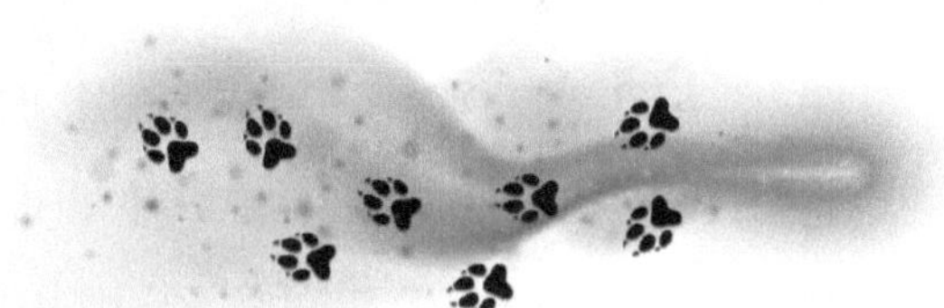

RYLAND

Logically, my decision makes sense. It's the right thing to do, even if I'm not sure I can actually follow through. These are my people; this is my responsibility.

I ask Luca and Orym to hold him still while I step away to grab a hunting knife. I breathe a sigh of relief knowing that Red won't have to see this. She grew up thinking this man was her brother, and even though they hated each other, I know that she loved him too.

Pushing those thoughts away, I grip the knife tighter and turn back to Vincent. Or rather, what's left of him. Orym and Luca look uncomfortable, and somehow that eases my mind a little. I'm not doing this alone. My pack is with me. I step up to the table where they're holding his arms and legs down.

He's still thrashing, but they're using blankets to hold him in place, since we'd rather not get stabbed with jagged bones covered in magic goo. I nod to Mark, and he grips Vincent's head. Once he has one hand on the top of his head, and the other on his chin, I take a deep breath.

I plunge the hunting knife into Vincent's head at the temple. With it fully inserted, I twist a little, and Vincent stops moving. "We'll bury him before anyone sees what happened," Mark offers. I nod, stepping away from the body.

Doing the right thing shouldn't feel this bad. I force myself to take one last look at Vincent before Mark and a couple of other shifters cover him up. I'll never get this image out of my head. I close my eyes for a moment and watch myself stabbing into his brain. This one will be hard to keep from Red.

As much as I want to protect her from this, I know that I can't. We'll have to tell her before she sees it through the bond. There's no way we can actively block her forever. And even if we could, it's not fair to her. I just want to spare her the gory details.

Almost as soon as I have the thought, the training center door slams open and Red rushes in. "Where is he?" she asks before her eyes lock on the corpse laying on the table, currently being wrapped up by Mark, Dave, and Steve. Red shoves them out of the way and uncovers Vincent. Tears flow down her face. "What happened to him?"

She looks from him to me, then Luca, then Orym. "Did Amber do this to him?"

"Most of it, yeah," I say, taking her hand and pulling her away from him. "But, Red, I killed him. He was suffering, and it had to be done."

She freezes in my arms. "You didn't even give me a chance to heal him."

"There was nothing left to heal, Red. He was too far gone."

She glares at me.

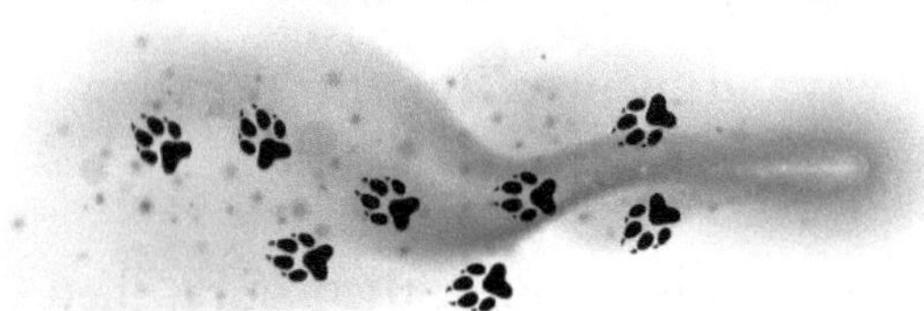

GARNET

"You can't know that. I could have healed him," I insist. It doesn't matter that I know this isn't something Ry would do lightly. I believe I could have saved him.

"Amber gave him the potion, Red," Luca offers. I whip my head around and stare at him.

"What?"

"The hybrid potion. She gave it to him. And he reacted badly; just look at his injuries. There's no way a wolf shifter should ever be injured this badly. His natural healing would have taken over at some point. But it didn't. What does that tell you?" Orym steps in to explain.

"That bitch," I cry. "I will kill her." The vow leaves my lips before I even realize that I've said it. An hour ago, I was trying to figure out how to end this without violence. Now, I want to do to Amber exactly what she did to Vincent. He may not have actually been my brother, but we grew up thinking that was the case.

My four mates stare at me. I won't apologize for what I said. Or for racing down here with James struggling to keep up. I spent my life training with wolves, after all. The moment I felt something off with Luca, I knew I had to get down here. I wasn't expecting this.

I feel as if salt has been poured into the cracks of my heart. It was just starting to heal from James destroying it. But losing Vincent burns. It makes me crave revenge, even more than I did when she kidnapped Luca.

If he hadn't escaped, I would have killed her then, or died trying. But now, this feels like she's just rubbing it in that she can do what she wants to anyone. And I will not stand for that. I can't.

"Red, take a breath. We can't go off half-cocked or she'll have the upper hand," Ry warns. I shake my head at him.

"I'm not going to chase her down right now. But I will kill her. On the evening of the Wolf Moon, when she plans to kill me. Let her think she's gotten away with this for now. She doesn't think I'm strong enough to take her on, much less to kill her." I hate how much I enjoy the thought of torturing Amber. I want to snuff out her life like she did to every single one of her captives who've been killed so far.

I want her to feel that moment of panic just before it happens. I can almost feel the darkness creeping into my soul, and I welcome it.

"Garnet? We should let them take care of the body. You don't want Grammy to see this," James suggests, finally stepping close enough to touch me. I want to push him away; to punish him for rejecting me. But I don't. Instead, I let him drag me into his arms and hold me while I cry against his chest.

I don't watch as the three guys wrap Vincent up and take his body away. I need to tell Grammy what happened, but I can't do it right now. "Let me tell her," James offers, passing me to Orym. "I'll handle it and be back as soon as I can." He kisses the top of my head and is gone before I can say anything to stop him.

Orym holds me tightly, as if that will keep me together. I feel broken inside—it's a feeling I'm getting used to, and I don't like it. Everything that's happened to us plays over in my head, and the more I relive, the angrier I get. It doesn't matter that I'm broken. My mates can put me back together again.

I have to fight this; I can't give in to the sadness. I won't let Amber win. We've lost too much to give up now. There have been way too many sacrifices in this war. It's time we turn the tables.

"We need to go home. I have spells to prepare, and magic to practice," I say, wiping my eyes and stepping out of Orym's embrace.

"Shouldn't we wait for James?" Luca asks, gesturing toward Grammy's cabin.

"He'll be with her for a while. She won't be surprised, but she won't take the news well," I offer. I've known that woman my entire life. I am certain that I can gauge her reaction to this situation. She's going to be as pissed as I am. But she'll need time to process first.

"Trevan is with her, though," Ry reminds me. I nod, but I still think James is using this as an excuse for space. Who knows? Maybe Grammy will talk some sense into him while he's there comforting her.

"James will be back when he's done. We can't worry about that now. I have to get things ready. Time is running out," I insist, walking toward the door. I know that they'll follow me, if for no other reason than they don't want me walking around alone in the forest. My aunt is out to get me, after all.

The walk back to the cabin is quiet. I'm not sure how long it took, or even if anyone tried to talk to me. I'm caught up in going over my spell books in my mind while trying not to trip over tree roots. I race through the door to the cabin and head straight for my books. It's strange how this has encouraged me instead of discouraging me.

I can't let myself think about the fact that Ry was the one who took care of it, either. It had to be done, and he handled his responsibility. Part of me resents him for not letting me try to heal Vincent, but I have to let that go. I can't let that be a way for Amber to get to me. I won't let her manipulate me the way she did James.

FOURTEEN
HYBRIDS GONE WRONG

LUCA

Finding Vincent that way hurt us all. As much as we want Red to take some time off and process what she saw, we can't afford it. So, while James is telling Grammy what happened, the rest of us are babysitting Red to make sure she doesn't race off into the forest to hunt Amber down.

"We've been at this for a while. Do you want to take a break?" I ask. The growl she responds with tells me that she's not.

I know she's still pissed about what happened to me while I was captured, and this only compounds her feelings. Now that she knows how the wolves are reacting to the potion Amber is using to attempt hybrid creation, she won't stop until she finds a way to reverse it.

I don't want anyone to suffer, either, but I'm not sure we can do anything about it besides trying to rescue who we can. Of course, I can't convince her of that. Orym and Ryland busy themselves in the kitchen while I do my best to help Red figure out what spells might actually work when combined with her Fae powers. James is better at this stuff, but he's still at Grammy's.

"What about this one?" I ask, showing her the page I'm reading. It looks like a cleansing spell, and I wonder if it could clean the poison from the blood.

Red takes the book from me and reads the page a few times. She turns to her notebook and starts scribbling furiously.

When she begins muttering to herself, I slip into the kitchen for a minute to check on the others.

"Dinner is almost done. Is she at a point where she'll pause long enough to eat?" Orym asks as I pop my head into the room.

"I think so. If she's not, you guys will have to convince her. We've found some useful things, but she needs a break," I explain. I haven't been able to get her to stop, even for a moment.

"I'll handle it. Orym, you and Luca get things set up on the table. I'll get Red to take a break," Ryland insists, strolling into the living room. I want to follow him and watch her tear him apart, but I won't.

"You said you guys found some useful spells? So, you think we have a chance, then," Orym says as we carry the salad and spaghetti to the table. I set the table while he goes back for the garlic bread.

"I think so. We may have found a way to stop the potion's effects. I don't know if it will reverse the damage or not. But she might have been right about being able to save Vincent," I say quietly.

"Let's avoid telling her that, okay? Ryland already feels guilty about having to make that decision and then follow through on it. He did the right thing, and we need to back him up on it."

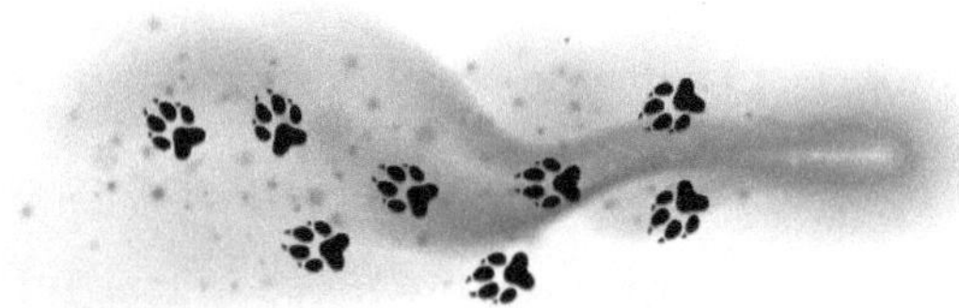

RYLAND

The moment I step into the living room, I know she's going to fight me on this. And I don't blame her. "Red? Food is ready. You need to take a break and get something to eat."

She looks up at me and snarls. If she was a wolf, I would have said she was about to shift. "I'm busy." She turns back to her books, intending to ignore me.

"Red, you know what's going to happen if you don't listen to me. I don't want to be a dick and destroy your books. But I will if you don't cooperate." I know the threat is a dirty trick, but she doesn't know that I have no intention of actually doing it. I hope the threat will be enough.

"Ry, I don't have time for this. I'm preparing to fight for my life here. Just leave me to it," she says, exasperation clear in her voice. I walk over to her, taking the books from her hands and putting them on the table behind me.

She tries to pull away from me, but I box her in, backing her up against the wall. There's nowhere for her to go, and we both know that she can't overpower me. Her eyes slowly raise to meet my gaze, and I see the tears she's fighting.

"It's okay to take a minute to grieve. He was your brother, even if you weren't actually related. It hurts, I know. Even more that I was the one to do it. And that I didn't think to let you try to save him." I pause, then continue, "Red, you have to know that it wasn't intentional. I never would have done that on purpose. I know how badly my decision hurt you. But he was suffering, and I couldn't leave him that way." I pull her into my arms and hug her tightly.

"I know, Ry, and I'm trying so hard not to hold that against you. It just hurts, and I can't handle it right now. I need to stay focused so I don't fall apart. Everything is too much—between what happened to Vincent and James not wanting to be here—I have to keep moving or I'll collapse," she admits against my chest.

It hurts me to see her like this. I understand her need to do something, but I can't let her wear herself down, either. "I understand, but you have to eat. You can't just run on adrenaline and anger until you fall over because you haven't taken care of yourself."

She starts to object, but I stop her. "I know, and it's fine. But you have to let us take care of you. Starting with dinner. You're going to sit at the table and eat with us like a family. James will be here in just a couple of minutes. He texted me that Trevan is taking care of Grammy, and he's having Mark and Steve walk back with him. No one goes anywhere alone."

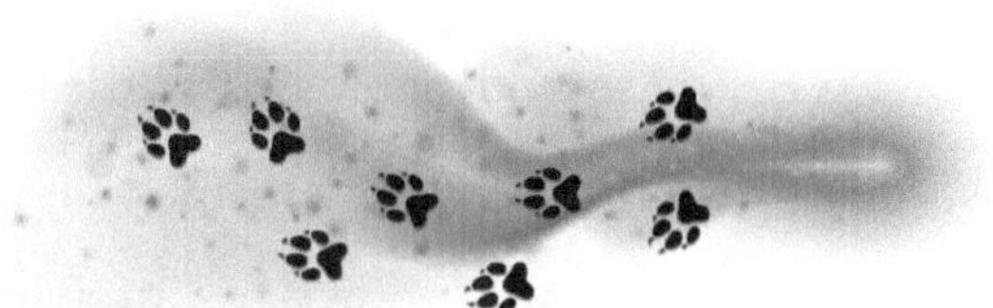

GARNET

I finally relent and let Ry lead me to the table to eat. I don't want to, but he makes a good point about running myself down. I know he's right, even if I won't admit it. And I feel as if I've made more headway in the last two hours than I have in the last two weeks. I realize it's not true, because over the last two weeks, I learned how to utilize my Fae powers and combine them with spells and other witch abilities.

Knowing that I may have a way to prevent someone else from ending up like Vincent makes me feel better, though. If only I'd had a chance to save my brother. I can't stop myself from thinking of him that way, no matter what biology says. Just because he was an asshole, that doesn't mean I stopped loving him when I found out we weren't actually related.

Maybe Ry is right; I should give myself a little time to grieve this loss, then figure out how to use that pain to make me stronger. I consider that as I sit down. If I do take his advice, then I'll have to figure out how to forgive James, too. It won't be easy, but it's not fair to hold Amber's manipulation against him.

Fuck. None of this is going to be easy. Even knowing that ahead of time isn't helpful. I could die facing off with Amber. Arguably, she's a much more skilled witch than me. I have more raw power, but less control. I could actually hurt everyone I'm trying to save if I'm not careful. Which means I need to get my emotional shit in order so that I can focus on controlling my magic.

I don't like the idea of it, but it's what has to be done. I've made my decision by the time James walks in the cabin. "Grammy didn't take it well, but Trevan is comforting her. I think she'll be okay," he says. He strolls over to me and drags me out of my chair, pressing his lips to mine.

I freeze for a moment, then let myself relax into his kiss. This is all I've wanted since he told me that he had to leave. As he kisses me, I feel our bond snap back into place. It feels as if it never left. I guess it must not have been broken after all. When he finally breaks the kiss, we're both panting to catch our breath. "I'm not complaining, but what was that for?" I ask, looking at him in shock.

I wasn't expecting him to act this way, and I have no idea what prompted it. Our conversation earlier led me to believe he wanted space and time to figure things out.

"Grammy had some things to say to me about my behavior. I thought about it on my way back, and she's right. I was an ass. Please forgive me. I don't want to be anywhere but by your side," James says. I can feel the other guys staring at us.

"We can talk about this in private, if you'd like," I offer. He shakes his head.

"This affects them as much as it does us. They deserve to know that I can't handle my own intrusive thoughts, and that I let Amber manipulate me into leaving. She played on my insecurities, and it's not an excuse. Only an explanation. I take full responsibility for my actions. I am going to call Dec and see if I can convince him to turn me sooner. But I know that my place is here, with you. If you'll still have me," he explains nervously.

I pull him into my arms and hug him tightly. Somehow, this day is turning out pretty good, even if it's a little sad. "Of course, I'll still have you. I love all of you, and need you to be with me through this. I also need to take a bit of time to process everything. I don't want to be alone for that, though."

"What did you have in mind?" Orym asks, wrapping his arms around me and James. It's exactly what I need, even if I didn't realize before.

"I hate to admit when Ry's right about something, but I need to grieve Vincent. I'd like to take some time this evening to do that. If that's okay with you all. I need a clear head to face Amber, and I'm not sure I can get there on my own," I admit.

Luca joins our group hug next. "We can watch Vincent's favorite movie and tell stories about him. And if you need to cry, you have so many shoulders to choose from."

I nod, realizing that Luca's idea is perfect. "Thank you." I look over at Ry, who seems hesitant to join us. "Ry? Is that something you can do with me?"

His eyes meet mine, and I see the tears he's holding back. My heart breaks for the decision he had to make, and the guilt he must feel over it. Luca and I each hold out a hand for Ry to come to us, and he moves slowly toward us. When he's close enough, Luca grabs him and engulfs him in the group hug. "We'll get through this together. You did what you had to, and there's no shame in that. Guilt will be there, no matter what we say or do. We don't blame you for what happened." I'm shocked at how mature Luca sounds. He's usually the least serious one here.

We stay like that for another moment, then my stomach growls. Everyone laughs at the timing of it. "Sorry, I guess I'm hungry after all. It smells so good."

We sit down to eat, chatting and keeping the conversation light. I can't help wondering if this is the last time we'll get to do this before I have to face my aunt.

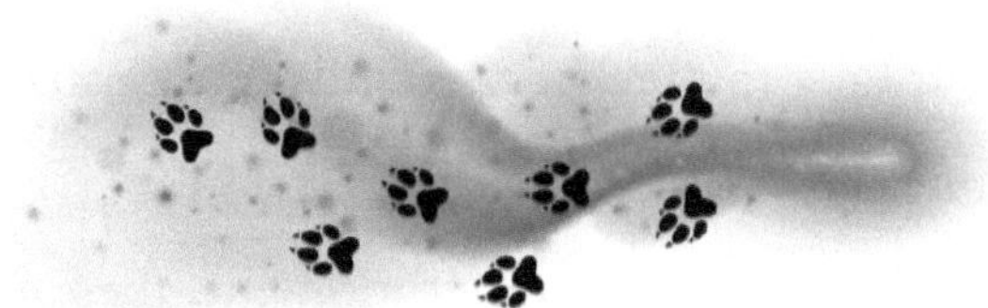

ORYM

Once dinner is done and we've cleaned up, the five of us settle in the living room to watch Vincent's favorite movie. I would rather watch almost anything than this over-the-top spy movie, but I understand Garnet's insistence. This was the one that Vincent was obsessed with when they were growing up. He fancied himself a ladies' man like the lead actor.

Instead of complaining, I settle in and snuggle with Garnet until she decides that she needs attention from one of the others. She doesn't say a word through the movie, but her silent tears tell me that she's not as okay as she wanted us to believe.

I'm glad that she's taking this time to grieve for her brother, even if he wasn't actually related to her. It's natural to feel emotional about a loss like this, especially since not too long ago, she believed that he was her brother. I still think she should have taken time to mourn Gunnar, too, but she insists that she doesn't need to.

I won't push her, but I will be right here to support her in any way I can, even if that means watching a movie I don't enjoy. Having my arms wrapped around the woman I love is enough to make it worthwhile for me. When she rests her head on my shoulder, I rub my hand up and down her back slowly, letting her know that I'm here for her.

A few minutes later, she shifts and snuggles up to Luca. I don't expect her to need the rest of us, since he's been her best friend for as long as I can remember. I shouldn't feel jealous of their relationship, because I know that she's as much mine as she is his, but I do. I wish that she could confide in me the way she does him.

Maybe after a while, we'll get there. But for now, I tell myself to be happy that her best friend can be there for her when she needs him. When a knock sounds against the door, I jump to answer it, so that no one else has to miss the movie. They all seem more interested in it than I am.

I open the door a little and see Trevan and Grammy outside. I step outside, ushering Grammy in. "They're watching Vincent's favorite movie. Garnet needed some time to reflect." She nods at me as she enters and heads straight for the couch.

I step outside with Trevan. "What's going on? We didn't expect you guys tonight."

He gives me an apologetic look. "They've found some more hybrid attempts. Grammy thought that you all should know. I wanted to wait until tomorrow."

"Oh, shit. How bad is it?" I ask, hoping that this news doesn't ruin Garnet's plans for tonight.

"It's worse than the other one," he admits. "I can't get that image out of my head. I know Ryland will want to know."

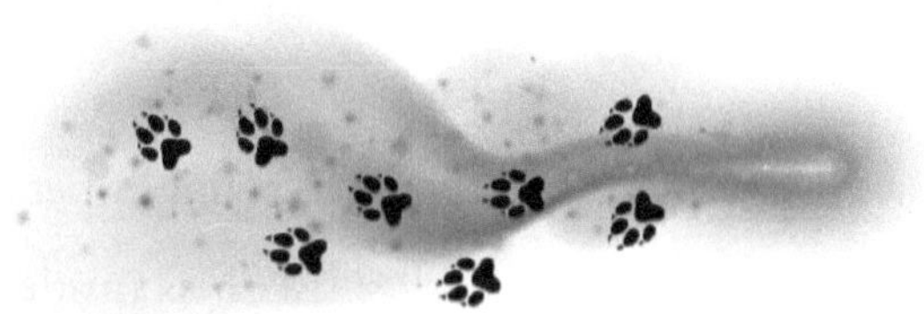

JAMES

When Orym asks for Ryland and me to meet him outside, we exchange a glance, then head out the door. Luca is taking care of Garnet, and Grammy is here now too. As soon as we're out the door, I know it's bad.

"What happened?" Ryland asks before I have a chance.

"You should come with me. It's bad, but you have to know," Trevan answers.

"We're leaving without telling Garnet?" I ask, gesturing to the cabin, where the woman we love is mourning the loss of her brother.

"I'll let her know we have to run a quick errand," Ryland says. We follow Trevan to the training center, and it's eerily familiar. It feels like we just did this. Because we did. With Vincent.

The smell is worse when the door swings open and two of the shifters who were here earlier usher us inside. Without a word, I know what we're about to see. Bile rises in my throat, and I want to run away from the scene ahead of us. I won't, because I have to prove I'm here to stay this time.

If I run again, they may not stop me. And if I'm being honest, there's nowhere else I want to be besides here. So, I follow Ryland to the table where another poor being lays, suffering from Amber's torture. I keep my focus on the wolf shifters with me, not the ones on the tables around us. I can't handle looking at what Amber did to them.

"Why is she doing this to these people?" I ask, staring at Ryland instead of looking around.

"She wants to create an army and take out all the other supernaturals," he answers, without looking at me. Unlike me, he refuses to avoid staring at the misshapen and disfigured people who've suffered far too much.

"That's her end game? To eradicate species by creating a new one? That woman is a monster," I insist. "I can't wait until Garnet takes her out."

"I hope she can," Orym says. "Because Trevan was right; this is worse than Vincent." I glance at him and see tears filling his eyes. These are people both men knew. They probably grew up as a part of this pack, and now their friends have to witness this tragedy. All because one errant witch decided to play god.

"We can't let her win. Garnet has to defeat her. There's no other way," I declare. Suddenly I feel even more stupid for letting Amber manipulate me into leaving. I realize that she was trying to weaken Garnet, which means I have to stay by her side no matter what.

"Well, at least one good thing came from all of this," Orym whispers to me with a knowing look. Even if I didn't mean to, I let him hear that thought. I'm not upset about it. If anything, I'm determined to see this through because of what Amber has done to these people.

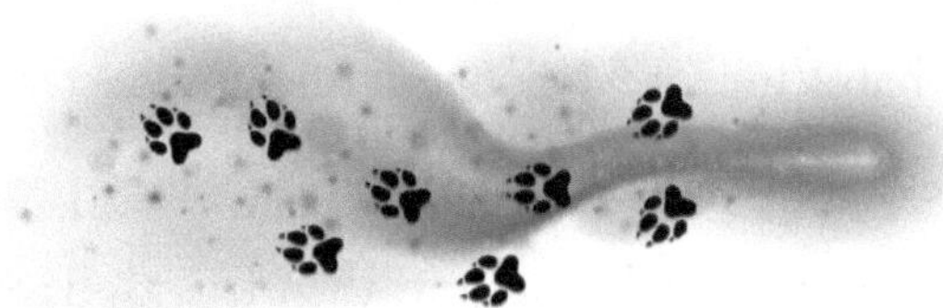

GARNET

I curl up in Luca's lap, letting myself doze off while the movie plays and Grammy rubs my back. I'm certain that Ry's *little errand* has something to do with Amber and possibly what happened to Vincent. But I don't feel up to asking about it, since I probably don't want the answer anyway.

I let myself drift off, trying to hold onto memories of Vincent when we were kids and things were easier between us. After a few minutes, I find myself in the training center, staring at the reason Ry, Orym, and James left. The only reason I know this is really happening is that they're all gathered around the three figures laid out on tables.

These three look so much worse than Vincent. One resembles a puddle of somewhat human parts. Another is more or less the same, but with fur. And the third—I turn away, unable to handle what's left of whoever that was.

A wave of nausea washes over me, and even though I know this is a vision, I'm sure I'll be sick. I try to leave the training center, but I'm stuck. I close my eyes and focus on Luca, trying to pull myself back to him.

Instead, he materializes next to me. "What the fuck just happened?" he asks, looking around in shock.

"That's not what I wanted to do. I'm sorry," I respond, closing my eyes again. Since I can't leave this room, I turn away from the mangled bodies. I'm glad that we're not really here, so I can't smell this. I won't ever forget what Amber did to Vincent, or the way it smelled. This has to be worse.

"Red, are you okay? This is hard to look at," Luca admits.

I nod. "I don't know how we're here, though. And I can't seem to send us back." I feel as if I'm failing at everything right now. I need to figure this out. Luca and I need to get back to our bodies.

"Just breathe. You can do this. Take my hand, and we'll walk outside," he offers. I almost tell him that I can't leave, but something in his voice gives me hope. I do as he asks, and he leads me out the doors. I'm shocked that it works.

"How did you know that would work?" I ask, staring at him in disbelief. Before he can respond, movement catches my eye. I hold up a hand for him to wait, even though no one here can see or hear us. I follow the movement and see Trevan standing at the edge of the woods.

"What are you doing here, Briar?" Amber asks.

"I hate to break it to you, Amber, but that's not my real name," he answers.

She looks surprised, and I wonder what prompted him to give her a false name in the first place. "You lied to me? I didn't think Fae could do that," she accuses.

"Well, I didn't lie. Your sister did, and I just went along with it. You never even asked me if what she told you was true. You were too busy trying to convince me that I should leave her for you," he counters. That makes sense, even if it's a little strange.

"Then what is your name?" she asks with a snarl. He laughs and shakes his head.

"I'm not dumb enough to give you my true name. Even if I can't lie, there's nothing forcing me to answer your questions.

And in just a few days, my daughter will deal with you anyway." His confidence in me is astounding. I don't know what makes him think I can defeat Amber.

He barely knows me, and I haven't exactly got full control over my powers—witch or Fae. Maybe it's that he understands how determined I am to finish this and protect the people I love. I can feel his pain at losing my mother, so perhaps he can sense my emotions too. For a second, I swear he looks right at me, but that's not possible, right?

Luca and I aren't actually here. We're projecting somehow, but maybe he can see it because of the connection to my Fae magic. I exchange a glance with Luca. "Did you see that?"

"He looked right at you and winked. He knows we're here," Luca answers. Good, it wasn't just me. With everything that keeps happening, I feel as if I'm losing my mind half the time.

"Do you think he can hear us as well?" I turn back to where my father was standing a moment ago, but he's gone. "Oh, shit, did she take him?"

Luca shrugs and then jumps when a figure pops up next to him. "The two of you should not be hanging out here like this. You're lucky that Amber didn't see you," my father says.

"First of all, how can you see us? Second, how do we get back?" I toss the questions at him and wait expectantly for his response. I can feel panic rising in my chest as if my body were here with me.

"Oh, child. I can see you because our magics are connected. As for returning, you need to calm your mind. Then you'll be able to will yourself and your tag-along back into your bodies." He smiles at me as he speaks, and his tone is soothing. He can obviously sense my panic.

"That sounds easy enough. Now if I could figure out how to do it, that would be great," I respond, trying to smile back at him. I take a deep breath, close my eyes, and feel Luca take my hand.

When I open my eyes again, I'm sitting on Luca's lap on the couch. I give him a shake, and he comes to as well. "Oh, thank the goddess," I cry, hugging him tightly.

"That was interesting," he answers, kissing my forehead. "We're okay now." I know he's right, but I'm still feeling overwhelmed.

FIFTEEN
OUT OF OPTIONS

RYLAND

When Trevan bursts into the training center, I know something is wrong. I barely get turned to face him when he starts shouting. “We need to go, now. My daughter is in danger.”

"What are you talking about?" I ask.

"She was here. I think she's gone back to the cabin, but we need to make sure," he explains. I'm still lost, not understanding what he's saying.

"Who was here? I'm gonna need more info, Trevan," I insist.

"Amber was here, but Garnet was too." His explanation still doesn't make sense. How was Red here without us knowing?

"Red was here? Where did she go? How was she here without us knowing?" Orym asks. It's a relief that he's as confused as I am.

"She was using soul projection. I'm pretty sure she had no idea what happened. Luca was with her. They caught Amber sneaking into the camp," Trevan explains further.

I turn to the guys who have been standing guard here. "Go see if you can find Amber. We need to keep her away from Red until we're ready for the confrontation." Once they take off, I race toward the cabin, hoping that Orym and James follow. I can't stop to wait for them; there isn't time.

I throw the door open and rush inside, my body refusing to relax until I see Red in Luca's arms. "Are you hurt?" I ask, pulling her from him and wrapping her in my embrace.

"I'm fine. It wasn't something I meant to do, but I didn't know how to stop it or control it. I'm guessing Trevan told you we were there. Amber is sneaking around the camp; your guys need to be careful," she responds. I can't believe that my mate is in so much danger but is more concerned with everyone else. She amazes me.

"My guys will be careful. Don't worry about that. We have to keep Amber away from you until the Wolf Moon. Unless you think you can defeat her before then." Red shakes her head, and I understand her hesitation.

"Where are Orym and James?" she asks, and I see the fear cross her features.

"They were right behind me," I insist, turning toward the door. They should have been here by now. Something must have happened.

Luca walks out the door, and we follow. "They must have been ambushed; that's the only explanation. We need to find them." He starts toward the other end of our encampment, but I stop him.

"Wait. We can't just go running off like this. If Amber is trying to get intel or worse, we have to play this safe. We need a plan," I insist. He stops and turns to face me.

"Then plan quick, because I'm going to find them. I won't take a chance of losing someone important to us," he says.

"I'll see if I can reach them through the bond," Red offers quietly.

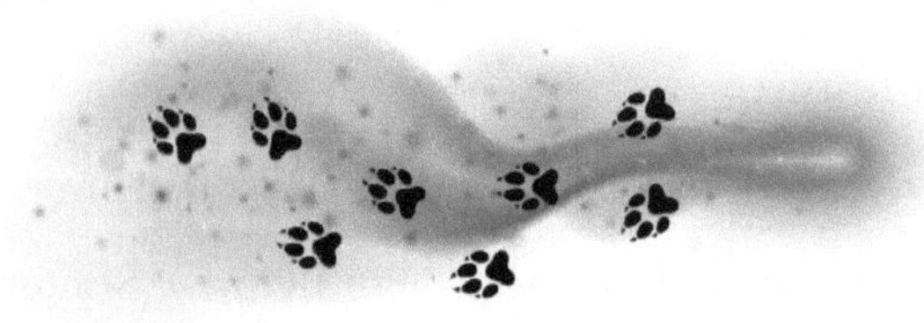

ORYM

When we start to follow Ryland back toward home, James stops me. "I think I just saw her over there," he says as he points toward the trees.

"Who?" I ask, wondering if he means Garnet is out here instead of at home where she's supposed to be.

"Amber," he answers before darting off. I can't just let him take off by himself, it's not safe.

"Fuck," I mutter, then race off after him. I understand his desire to capture Amber, but I wish he'd at least waited for me to call for back up.

Just as he disappears into the trees ahead of me, I hear Garnet's voice in my head. *Orym, James? Where are you two? Is everything okay?*

Should I tell her? I have to; I can't lie to her about it. *James thinks he saw Amber. We're chasing the trail now.* I explain where we are so Ryland, Luca, and Garnet can catch up to us. I don't want to face Amber alone, even if that makes me a coward.

Noises nearby stop me in my tracks. I frantically look around to see where it's coming from. Once I settle on a direction, I turn toward the commotion, hoping that James isn't involved. It doesn't sound good. I peek around a tree and see that he's surrounded by a group of people. So much for James not being involved. I shift closer to the tree and watch, hoping that the others get here before this escalates any further.

We have a problem, I say along the bond. *James is surrounded and there are too many for me to be able to take them all out by myself. Hurry!*

"Where's your witch, *human*?" one of them snarls. The more I learn about Amber's followers, the less I stress over doing what needs to be done to deal with them. I don't enjoy killing anyone, but it's a little easier when they're as awful as these assholes.

We're almost there. Ryland responds instead of Garnet. It catches me off guard for a moment and I jump. The group surrounding James looks toward me, and I wonder if they know I'm here. I freeze, expecting to be dragged out of the brush any minute.

"Did you hear that?" another of them asks. They're starting to panic and I feel as if we're running out of time. What are they planning to do with James?

"What do you want with Garnet?" James asks without looking at my hiding spot. I'm certain he's trying to draw their attention back to him because he knows I'm here.

"Amber wants us to bring her to our camp. Honestly, her obsession with your witch is ridiculous. Amber acts like she's the devil or something." From her tone, I imagine the one speaking rolls her eyes as she talks. It's clear she doesn't think much of Amber or her vendetta against Garnet.

Good, we're learning things. This could be helpful when Garnet faces her aunt.

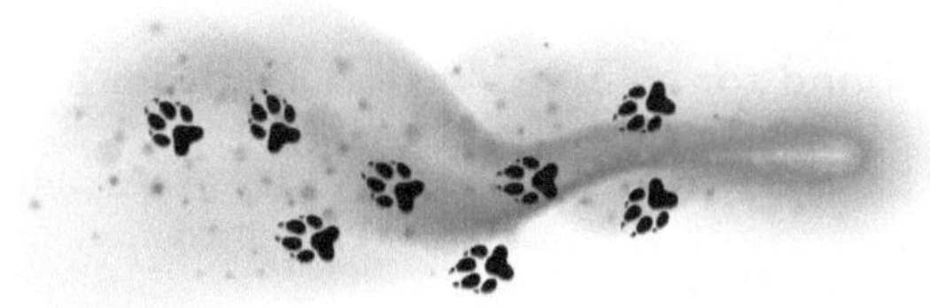

GARNET

I sense James' fear when we approach the area Orym said they were in. I don't understand why James didn't call out to me along our bond, but maybe he was worried the witches could track that communication. Or maybe he didn't think about it. He's been resistant to our reconnection, and I wish I knew why. He claims that he's trying to protect me. Is there more to it than that? I don't know.

Ry holds up a hand for us to stop just as I see Orym tucked behind a tree. *We don't want to alert them to our presence.* Ry's words echo in my mind. This is an intense situation, and we need to be careful so that we don't trigger the witches to attack before we can get James out of there.

We carefully make our way to the small group of trees near Orym's hiding spot as soon as he motions for us. I'm glad we have the bond for communication, because that means less chance that the witches will hear us than if we had to actually speak to each other.

James, we're here. Try to stall them until we can get into position. Ry's quiet command is implied in the tone he uses. I wonder if he thinks James is one of his wolves who will just obey. It's risky to treat him that way, since he's been really sensitive about being human.

"If you think Amber's lost it, maybe you shouldn't be following her orders," James says to the witches. I wonder what they said to make him think they don't agree with Amber.

"It's not like we have a choice. She's insane and super powerful. And she'll be even more powerful once she kills the half-breed and takes her powers. I'm not about to go against that. Now tell us where she is, before we decide that you're not so helpful after all, *human.*" The way she sneers as she says human makes me want to rip out her throat.

I don't realize that my internal growl wasn't so internal after all until James dives at one of the witches who's started to walk over here. "Fuck," Ry's voice rings in my ears, even though he didn't say the expletive loudly.

Things get chaotic as everyone is attacking everyone else. My wolf mates fight against the witches to both protect me and to save James. I do my best to protect my mates, but splitting my shield between the five of us when we aren't sticking together is hard. At some point, Ry shifts and starts attacking with his claws and teeth.

Magic is tossed around so much that it's hard to see. "I can't tell where they went," Orym shouts.

"We need to get out of here and regroup. Is everyone accounted for?" Since Ry is in wolf form, I take point. I wonder if it will upset him, then decide that I don't care. I will make my demands and push my mates if that's what it takes to keep them safe here.

"I'm right here," Orym says. "I can't see the others."

I take a deep breath and push a blast of air out to clear the smoke-like magic that surrounds us. "That should help," I offer as our field of vision clears. "I don't see the witches."

Orym shakes his head. "Me neither, but there's Luca. Where did Ryland and James go?" He starts walking across the small clearing toward Luca, who's leaning over someone on the ground.

"Is that James?" My heart starts to race and my throat constricts as I dash over to Luca. I'm scared to look, but I have to know. The body he's leaning over is mangled, but it's not James. I breathe a sigh of relief, letting out the breath I'd been holding.

"Red! You're okay. Wait, you are okay, right?" Luca turns his attention to me.

"I'm fine. Are you okay?" I ask, then as soon as he nods, I continue, "Where are Ry and James?" Luca points toward the trees, but before I can race off after them, a shuffling noise catches my ear.

James stumbles into the clearing, half dragging a barely conscious Ry. "He's hurt. Someone come help me. This guy is heavy." He drops to his knees and eases Ry to the ground. "I don't know what they hit him with."

I rush over, with Luca and Orym on my heels. They lift Ry easily, and I look him over to see what's wrong. Blood drips from his hairline, and he has a knot. They must have hit him on the head with something heavy. "We should head back to the cabin." I turn to James. "Are you okay?"

He nods. "I'm fine. A few scratches, but nothing like what he took." I want to push the issue and check him over, but I also don't want to force him to do something he's not comfortable with. I'll have to trust that he's telling me the truth.

Ry groans and my attention is pulled away from James. It's obvious that if we don't get Ry taken care of soon, it's going to be bad. "Try to stay awake, Ry. We're taking you back to the cabin where I can heal you." He stills at my words, but I can see him trying to hold his eyes open. I look at Orym and Luca. "Hurry; we'll be right behind you."

They start running toward the cabin, carrying Ry between them. James lets me take his hand as we walk behind them. We're moving quickly, but not running. I'm not sure if James is exhausted or actually injured. I know he said he was fine, but I have a bad feeling about this. It's probably because Ry is hurt, and I'm scared.

James squeezes my hand and urges me to move faster. “I’m sorry we got ambushed. I shouldn’t have tried to track Amber on my own.”

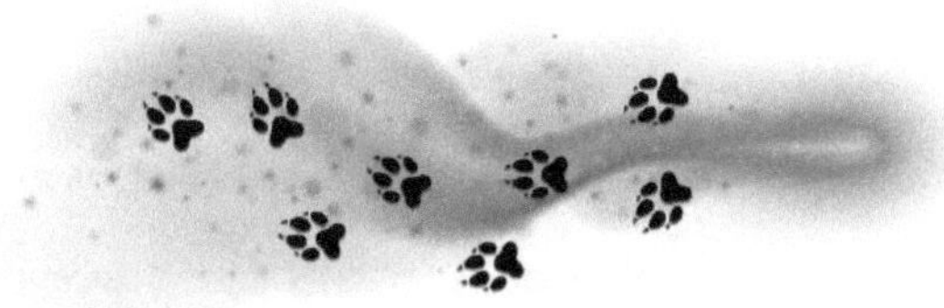

JAMES

The admission costs me. I know that it wasn’t smart to follow Amber into the forest, especially after she held all of us at her cabin without much backup. I should have known better. I have no idea why I was so obsessed with finding her right then. I wonder if she still has some kind of hold on me.

I can't tell Garnet that I got stabbed, either. Ryland is hurt worse than I am, and that's where her focus should be. Besides, it's not that bad. I'm sure it'll heal in a few days as long as I keep it clean and covered.

I keep her hand in mine as we walk because that's the only way I know that I can be sure she won't start poking and prodding at me to check for injuries. I don't want to worry her, so I decide that this is what I have to do.

We get to the cabin shortly after Luca and Orym arrive with Ryland. Garnet drags me inside, where they have him laid out on the floor. I head to the kitchen and start gathering herbs and other ingredients she'll need to make a salve for him.

When she kneels next to him and starts checking all of his injuries, I slip into the bathroom to check my own. I slip my flannel off and peel my t-shirt over my head. It's soaked with blood, so I toss it in the trash. I'll have to remember to get rid of it so the others don't get concerned.

The cut on my side oozes blood, but it doesn't look too bad. I could probably use a few stitches, but I don't have time for that. Besides, I'm an EMT, I can take care of this myself. I grab gauze and tape from under the sink and get to work cleaning myself up. I secure six layers of gauze over the wound and tape it down tightly. It's sore, so I take some ibuprofen and grab a clean shirt before heading back into the living room.

"Where'd you take off to?" Luca asks when I squat beside him.

"Bathroom. I was just tending to my scrapes." It's not an outright lie, and I prove it by showing him the shallow scratches on my arm. "How's Ryland?" I change the subject pretty easily, since everyone is more worried about the territory alpha, who is lying on the floor nearly unconscious.

"She's working on him. He's got a nasty head injury, and lots of cuts and bruises. What happened, exactly?" Orym looks up from Ryland to meet my eyes.

"They ran off when visibility got bad. He and I chased them, and they ambushed us. He took the brunt of it since he was more of a threat, according to them. I am only human, after all." I hate to admit that their words had any effect on me, but I can't lie to myself. Their disdain hurt.

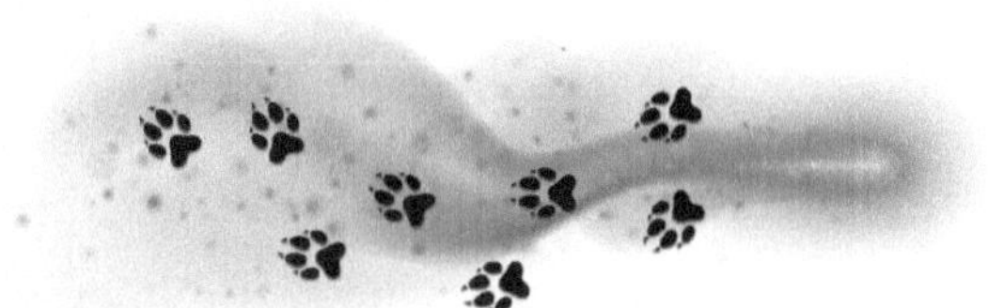

LUCA

It seems odd that James disappeared for a few minutes when we got home, but in the chaos of Red inspecting Ryland's injuries, I can't focus on that. Maybe he's just overwhelmed by what happened and needed a minute. I don't know.

I'll worry about whatever is going on with him after we're sure Ryland is okay. His wounds look better now that we've cleaned him up a bit. Red is concentrating on his head, which is still bleeding and swollen. Orym and I are dressing his arms and torso. James jumps right in, although he's moving slower than usual.

He's probably got some pretty bad bruises and is sore from the fight. I know he's pretty salty about the witches treating him as less than because he's human. That has to hurt, especially since he's been pretty sensitive about it lately. We'll have to make sure that we check in with him soon.

"Hold him still. This is going to hurt," Red demands as her hands start to glow. James winces, and I know it's because he remembers how her magic healing feels. She waits until James, Orym, and I have Ryland pinned to the floor, then starts letting her magic flow.

It takes longer than I expected, but after a while, she motions for us to let him go. "He'll sleep for a while, but he should be fine." Her attention turns to James. "I can heal you, too, if you want."

He shakes his head. "I'm okay, really. Just a few scratches. Nothing that you need to bother with." She doesn't push him, but I can tell that she wants to. I know her better than anyone else does. Red will worry herself to death over James being distant and pulling away, once she's sure that Ryland is okay.

"It's no bother, James. I can use my magic to heal your cuts," Red insists. When she stands up, she sways a bit and collapses. I barely move fast enough to catch her before she hits the floor.

"She used too much magic at once. Let's get Ryland and her into bed so they can rest," I say, readjusting Red in my arms and taking her to the bedroom. She doesn't feel warm and has no injuries herself. It's clear she's just exhausted from using her magic so much.

She tries to protest when I tuck her in, but I shake my head. "You rest. If James needs healed, it can wait until you're rested."

Orym and James bring Ryland in and put him to bed next to her. That seems to relax her a bit as she settles into his side and closes her eyes. The three of us stand there for a minute, just watching them sleep.

"They're going to be okay, right?" James asks. Concern fills his tone, and I feel the need to reassure him.

"Yeah, they will. After some rest," I insist. He looks relieved, which is exactly how I feel right now.

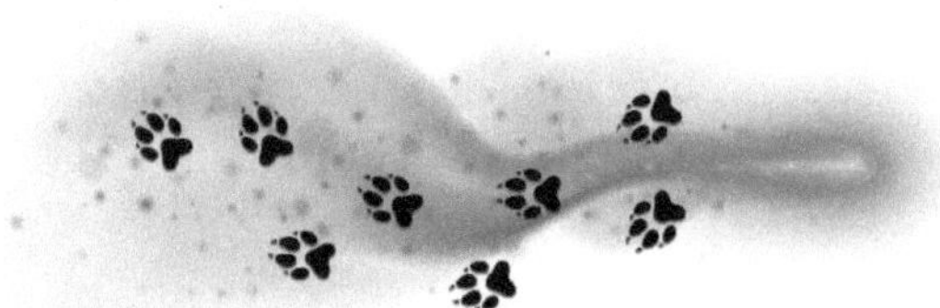

GARNET

After a few hours of sleep, I wake up to find myself alone in the bedroom with Ry. It's dark outside, and I wonder where everyone went. Not wanting to disturb Ry, I slip out of bed carefully and head into the living room.

Orym and Luca are curled up together on the couch, asleep. James is sprawled out in the chair with his feet on the table. I walk over to give him shit about having his feet on the furniture. Before I get a word out, I see the large puddle of maroon spreading out in the chair around him. “Fuck, I knew he was hurt worse than he let on,” I mutter, dropping to my knees to check him out.

I need more light, I think, then watch the room illuminate. It’s as if my magic hears my plea and automatically lights up the room. Luca growls, turning away from the light. Orym jumps up as if someone hit him. “What’s going on?”

“James is hurt, and he hid it from us. It’s bad. I don’t know if I can heal him. Will you call Dec and see if he can come now?” I respond, not taking my eyes off the stab wound I just found. It’s not bleeding fast, but it’s steady. I can tell that James cleaned and dressed it. He must not have realized that it was this bad. Why else would he have insisted that he was fine when I offered to heal him?

Orym nods and steps outside to make the call. I feel Luca’s hands on my shoulders as I pour my healing magic into James, praying that it will work. My vision goes hazy, and Luca pulls me away from James. “Red, it’s not working. You can’t kill yourself to save him if the magic isn’t working.”

“Dec is on his way. He claims that he’s not sure what he can do to help, but at least he’s coming. I don’t think he took James’ request to be turned very seriously,” Orym announces as he comes back inside.

"Is that how you're planning to handle this?" Luca asks, astonished.

"If it comes to that, I don't think we have much choice," I respond. I suspect that James asked Dec to turn him as a spontaneous thing, and that he didn't give it much thought. But right now, that may be the only way I can keep James in my life. If that's the case, I'll do whatever it takes to convince Dec to make his brother a vampire.

"What if he won't do it?" I don't like Luca questioning me like this, but I understand his concern. I can't exactly force Dec to change James.

"Then I guess James will die, and we'll all suffer from the pain of a broken bond again. But at least his brother will have the chance to say goodbye," I snap. I drag myself up from the couch and start to pace.

I don't want to think about what will happen if Dec refuses to turn James. I kneel beside my mate again, noticing how pale he is. He's lost too much blood, and I know that I can't heal him. There's no point in trying again. I know it won't work, but I do it anyway.

I'm not sure how long I sit there, pulsing my magic into James and cursing because it's not working, before a pair of strong arms pulls me away. "No, I have to keep trying," I insist weakly. I know if I don't stop, I'll pass out, but I need to save him.

"Red, it's okay. Dec is here. Let him take a look," Luca says from behind me. I realize he's the one who pulled me away. I want to struggle against his hold, but I don't have the energy for it. I relax into his arms and watch as he sits on the couch with me on his lap.

Orym and Dec speak in hushed tones as Dec checks over his brother. I can't tell if Orym is trying to talk him into turning James or not. I jump when Dec shifts his attention to me. "And you've tried your magic to heal him?"

I nod, "I did. Twice. But it didn't do anything. I'm not sure what happened to him. Maybe if I'd known sooner, I could have helped."

"So, he hid the wound from you?" Dec doesn't seem surprised.

"He told us that he just had scratches," Orym insists. "Are you going to change him?"

"I don't know. This isn't an easy decision. Especially with the way he reacted when I first became a vamp. I know it's not what he wants, even though he asked for it. He wants to be worthy of you, and thinks this is the only way. He's wrong." Dec makes the statement with no hesitation.

"I agree completely. I'm the one who's not worthy of him. I wish he could see that. I've tried, Dec, I really have. But I can't lose him; not like this. Please." I'll beg if I have to. I will get down on my hands and knees, then I'll promise this vampire anything he wants if he'll just save my mate.

"What do I do if he hates me for it? This isn't like borrowing his car without asking or taking his favorite shirt. This is a lot bigger than that. Can you deal with the fallout if he hates you for it too?" Dec asks, staring into my eyes. I see the unshed tears in his eyes that match mine.

"I will take full responsibility for the entire situation. If he hates me, at least he'll be alive to hate me. I won't let him blame you at all," I insist. I clasp my hands in front of my chest and let my tears fall. "Just please don't let him die. Turn him so he can survive this. Please, Dec."

SIXTEEN
ADJUSTING

ORYM

"I just don't know," Dec says again. While I understand his frustration and uncertainty, a decision has to be made. Now.

"Look, I get that this is tough. But you have to decide, right now, if you're going to let your brother die. Or if you're going to risk pissing him off by saving his life. None of us can make that decision for you. James' life is in your hands," I say, pulling Garnet off the floor and into my arms.

"It's not fair, I know. Please, Dec," she begs again.

James' brother glances from Luca, to me, to Garnet, and back again. I don't envy him this decision. I'm not sure that I could do it if I were in his place, either. When his expression softens, I know that he's come to a conclusion.

"I don't think he's going to be okay with this. But you're right. If I let him die, I'll never forgive myself. At least if he hates me, that means he's alive," Dec says, leaning over James' unconscious body.

Before any of us can react, he drags James up and bites into his neck. A minute or so later, he drops his limp brother back into the chair and opens James' mouth. Then Dec bites into his own wrist and forces it between James' lips. "Come on, brother, drink," he says quietly.

It feels like forever as we wait to see if this is going to work. I sit on the couch with Garnet on my lap and Luca as close to us as he can get without joining her. She grips my arm and his hand tightly while we wait.

"How long does this usually take?" Luca asks, unable to hide his curiosity.

Dec glares at him. "I don't know. I've only ever turned one other person, and that was a bit chaotic. Also, she was actually conscious when I fed her my blood. He's not even drinking." He pulls his wrist away from James' mouth and inspects his bite mark. We notice that it's nearly healed already.

"Then we wait," Garnet says. "Thank you, Dec. I promise you that James won't blame you for this."

"I guess we'll see when he wakes up," the vampire responds. I wonder if he's going to stay until James comes to. It's a dumb question; of course he is. None of us know how to deal with a newly turned vamp. Dec will have to teach him how to control his thirst, otherwise he could kill us all.

Oh, shit. We never even considered how we would get blood for him. I guess I wasn't the only one who expected James to change his mind and stay human. With Ryland out of commission, it'll be my responsibility to make sure James doesn't hurt any of the wolves after his transition. At least until my alpha is healed and able to handle things.

"We're gonna need blood for him."

"It's on the way."

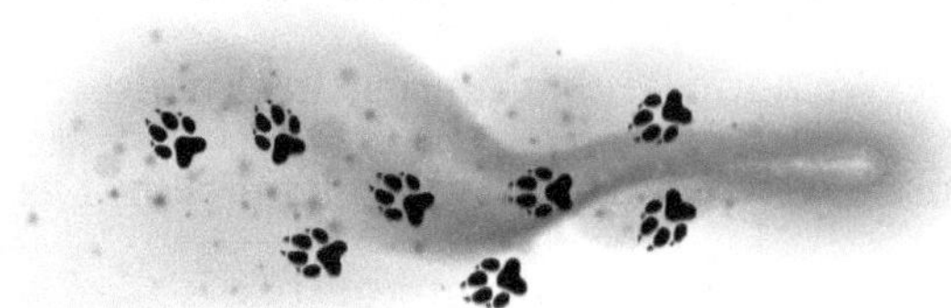

JAMES

Darkness envelops me, swaddling me in its comforting embrace. Wow, that was poetic. I wonder where that thought came from. I try to open my eyes, but I can't. All I see is black, and I can't escape it. Before I can panic, I force myself to think back. What happened just before it all went dark?

I remember putting Garnet and Ryland to bed, then coming out to the living room and collapsing in the chair. My side hurts, but it's fine. I've done everything I can to make sure it doesn't get infected. I just need to sleep for a bit. That's it! I closed my eyes and I'm sleeping now. This is just a weird dream from whatever magic was used in that fight earlier.

It doesn't feel like that's true, though. I vaguely sense my brother is nearby. How would I know that? And why would Declan be here? Did something happen? Fuck, I need to wake up. I have to protect Garnet.

I try again to force my eyes to open, but they won't. A sharp pain pierces my throat, and I feel as if my life force is being drained. Just when despair makes me want to give up, I hear Dec's voice. "Come on, brother, drink." My lips are forced apart and something warm with a metallic taste trickles down my throat. What is he making me drink?

Swallowing is the only option, though I can't even feel myself moving. Everything goes quiet, and I think I've died. This is nothing like the Fae realm, or anything else I could have imagined death being like. That's when the burning starts.

My body feels as if it's been set ablaze. I'm on fire, and somehow, it's started inside my veins. I feel myself buck and thrash as the sensation spreads from my center outward. This is so much worse than the pain I was in before Garnet healed me. What is happening to me?

The pain intensifies until I scream, unable to hold back any longer. My eyes finally open, and I see faces surrounding me as I lay on the floor. Garnet, Orym, Dec, and Luca hover over me. No, that's not right. Dec and Luca are holding me down, while Orym holds Garnet back. Did I try to hurt her? Am I being controlled by Amber again?

"Fuck, this hurts," I rasp.

"It's okay, brother. Take a breath." I obey the command instantly. Dec shoves a straw into my mouth. "Now drink."

Again, I do as I'm asked without hesitation. Oh, this is that same metallic flavor from before. What kind of potion am I drinking? And why did it taste strange before, but delicious now? My thoughts are foggy as I try to figure out what's going on here.

"Okay, let's help him sit up. Keep her back until I'm sure he's not going to attack," Dec says.

"Why would I attack Garnet?" I ask, staring up at my brother.

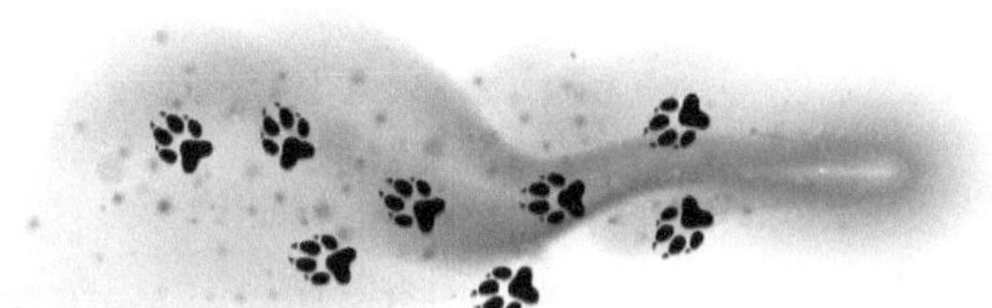

GARNET

"Because, James, you're a vampire now." Dec's quiet answer echoes in the silence of the room. My mind replays James thrashing and screaming in pain before his eyes finally snapped open. I understand the concern for my safety. My wolf mates are better able to protect themselves from a newly turned vamp. As a witch, I don't have as much that I can use. My Fae side, however, should be able to fend for herself.

I won't correct Dec, though. He's done enough for us today to earn my respect and reverence. I'll cooperate with whatever he asks of me. I owe him for saving my mate. As soon as James finishes drinking the blood bag, his panic lessens. I can feel him along the bond, stronger than ever.

Of course, he's scared and confused. I expected that, since he wasn't able to agree to this. And I'm sure he's going to be angry, because he didn't have time to prepare.

"I'm a what?" James asks, looking from Dec to me and back again. "I thought you weren't going to do this until after the Wolf Moon."

His anger is palpable, just like his confusion. He's conflicted and unsure of how to feel. "You lied to us about being hurt today. By the time I found out, you'd nearly bled to death in that chair." I spit the words at him as Orym keeps me from moving closer.

"So, you did this to me? We had a plan and you just go change it to suit yourself?" His accusation cuts me. He's acting as if this is something I've orchestrated to manipulate and control him. Surely, he doesn't really think those things about me.

"James, this wasn't her fault. It was my decision. She called me to come see if there was anything else we could do to save you. This was the only way. You were so close to death already. I did what I had to, brother. If you're going to blame someone, it should be me." Dec's forceful declaration is exactly the opposite of what we'd discussed, and it catches me off guard.

I shake my head. "No. That's not true. Dec didn't want to turn you. I pushed him into it. But not as a manipulation. It was the only way to save you."

"Maybe you should have just let me die, then," James snarls. Tears slide down my face. I know that he's not done processing what's happened, and none of this should be held against him, but his words hurt.

"James, you don't mean that. Stop taking this out on her. If you're mad at me, let's work this out," Dec insists. I understand that he's trying to bear the brunt of my decision, but I can't let him. Can I?

"Why would you suddenly be okay with turning me when you were so against it? This makes no sense. I was fine when I sat down. I wasn't hurt that badly," he insists.

I push away from Orym and stomp toward James as he stands up. "You almost bled to death in that chair!" I point at the chair for emphasis. "If I hadn't found you when I did, you would have died. So, obviously, your wound was worse than you thought. Or you lied to me. Which is it?" I can't stop the fury from rolling over me.

As happy as I am that he's alive, I want to punch him in the face. And I just might, if he doesn't stop being a dick.

"I can't deal with this right now. I have to go," he says and starts for the door. Dec blocks his path.

"If you need some space, you'll have to come home with me. There's no other option. I can't turn you and let you run off. It's too dangerous," he explains.

"I'm sorry, James, but if you leave, I'm following you. Where you go, I go." When he shakes his head, I take a step closer. "You are one of my fated mates. I'm not about to let you run away again. It was stupid of me to let it happen the first time."

"I don't want to break our bond. I just need some time to adjust. This isn't an easy transition." He looks at me and licks his lips. "And honestly, Garnet, you smell delicious." I know that I should be scared, since he is a vampire now, and could easily kill me. But I'm not. Instead, I'm so turned on that I know my panties are soaked.

Luca and Orym's groans through the bond tell me that they noticed too. I won't apologize for the things that get me going, but I do realize that now is not the time. "Fine, I'll let you have some space. If you stay with Dec, and if he brings you back as soon as possible. And you have to keep our bond open so I know that you're okay."

He sighs. "Yes, mother." Before I can close the distance between us and slug him, Dec slaps him in the back of the head.

"Show your woman some respect, little brother. She was willing to do anything to save you. The least you can do is let her stay connected so she knows you're safe." Dec turns to me. "I won't let anything happen to him. And I'll make sure he's back after the sun goes down. Eli will need time to get him an implant and make sure it's working properly before he can go out in the sun."

"Then you two need to leave now. The sun will be up soon," I insist, practically shoving them out the door. I can't take the idea that they could get stuck outside while James isn't protected.

"I can't let him get close enough to hug or kiss you. I hope you understand. It's not safe yet. But I'll take good care of him," Dec explains, dragging James out the door with him.

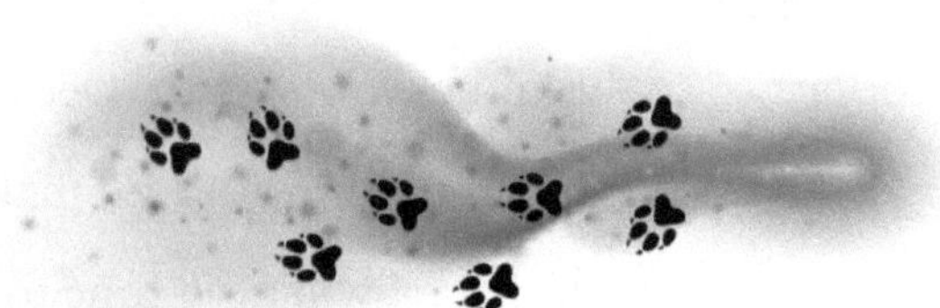

LUCA

I take a step forward and block Red from James' reach. He doesn't seem to be trying to get to her, but until Dec can get him out the door, I have to make sure she's safe. "Should we get them an escort?" Orym asks.

Dec turns back to us, still holding his brother's arm. "I've got him. It'll be quicker if I just take him without endangering anyone else. You have my word, he'll be fine."

When the door closes, I turn and wrap my arms around Red. She drops her head to my shoulder and lets me hold onto her for a while. Orym walks over and sandwiches her between us. The three of us stay like that until Red hears Ryland starting to stir.

"I need to check on him. Hopefully he's okay. I don't know how much more I can take today," she whispers. Orym and I follow her back to the bedroom where Ryland is trying to sit up.

"What hit me?" he asks, dropping back onto the pillow.

"One of the witches, apparently. James said they attacked you because he wasn't as much of a threat," I explain, helping Ryland sit up against the headboard.

"Where is James?" he asks, looking around. "He got stabbed. Did you get him patched up?" Red, Orym, and I exchange a glance.

"That would have been nice info to have before everything went south," Orym responds.

Red sits on the bed next to Ryland. "He's okay now, but we had to call Dec to turn him. James almost died."

"He's a vamp now? Wow, I didn't think he'd actually do it," Ryland says, wiping his hands down his face.

"It wasn't his choice. By the time Red found him, he was too far gone for her magic to help. Orym got Dec to come, and Red talked him into turning James. When he woke up, he wasn't very happy about it," I explain.

"He went back to Midnight with Dec for the day. He needs a UV implant so he can go into the sunlight, and Dec will help him with his cravings. We will probably need another fridge for blood storage, though," Red insists.

Ryland nods, agreeing with her. I know that he'll do whatever she wants, the same as the rest of us. Red is our top priority, keeping her happy makes us happy.

"Do we know when he'll be back?" Ryland asks. "I feel like I got hit by a truck. I don't know if I can deal with everything right now."

"He should be back tonight, after the sun sets. You don't have to deal with anything. I've got the wolves handled. I can arrange for a small fridge to be brought in if that's what you want. Let me help while you recover," Orym says, stepping forward to lay a hand on Ryland's shoulder.

Our alpha nods at him. "Thank you. I'm going to need more rest."

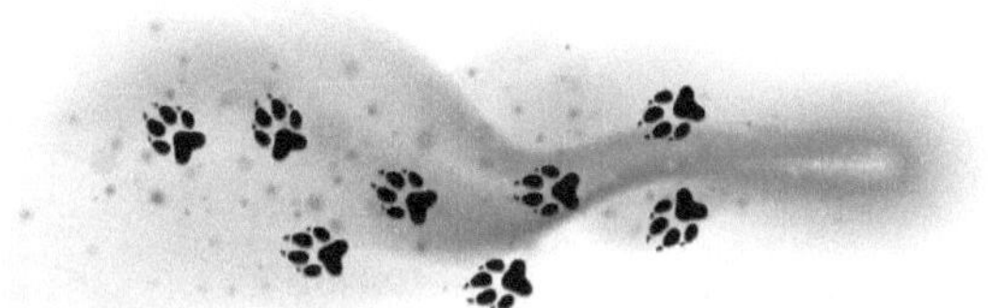

RYLAND

Waking up to learn that James didn't tell anyone about his injury and now he's a vamp is definitely going to take a minute to process. "I don't understand why he would lie about being hurt," I say.

Red shakes her head. "I don't know, but he did. He insisted that he only had scratches on his arms and wouldn't let me check him out. He was adamant that we take care of you first. I used too much magic at once, and nearly knocked myself out.

When I came to, I checked on him, and he was almost gone." She grimaces and continues. "We'll have to replace that chair. It's covered in his blood."

"My chair? Seriously? The guy couldn't bleed out on the floor? Fuck." I'm not really worried about the chair, just trying to figure out what to say to my mate so that she isn't making that face.

She slaps my arm and laughs. Good, it worked. "We can get a new chair. We can't get a new James."

I cock an eyebrow. "Are you sure? I saw some hot guys the last time we went to Midnight. I bet we could find a replacement pretty easily."

"Ry!" she squeals and slaps me again. I laugh and tug her toward me for a kiss. Of course, she knows I'm teasing. I would never try to replace one of her mates.

"I'm glad Dec was able to help. I'm sorry I wasn't there for you when you needed me. Getting beat up by a group of witches wasn't on my to-do list for yesterday," I say in her ear. Red rests her head on my chest and I feel my heartbeat pick up.

I love being this close to her and hearing her laughter. When this is all over, I'm going to make sure that she laughs every day. I wish that I could end this fight now, but it's not my place to take Amber out. I understand that the universe has a plan, and I'm going to do my part. No matter how hard it is.

"You need to rest. I'll get you some tea and food," she says, trying to pull away from me. I wrap my arms tighter around her and shake my head.

"Nope. I need you to stay right here. You need rest and care too. Luca, do you mind getting us something to eat while Orym checks in with our security teams?" It's not an order, but I still don't expect either of them to tell me no.

"Of course, Ryland. We'll take care of everything," Luca says, ushering Orym out of the room.

"How did I get so lucky?" I ask after they leave.

"What do you mean?" Red answers my question with one of her own.

"Our family is pretty awesome. We take care of each other and do what needs to be done without letting ego or pride get in the way. I love that."

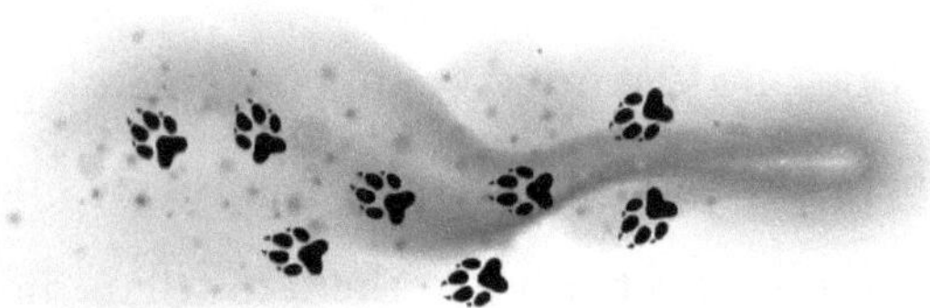

GARNET

Ry's words bolster me in a way I didn't know I needed. I thought I was prepared for James' anger. What I wasn't prepared for was his hunger. How did I not think about vampires drinking blood? Even after Declan gave him a lecture about being certain this was what he wanted, and thinking that I knew what it would entail, I still managed to screw it up.

"Thank you for making sure everyone has what they need. I know that you don't have to take care of this for me. It should be my responsibility. I'm the one who insisted he be turned. Now I'm making everyone do extra work, and James is pissed at me," I admit, nuzzling against Ry's chest.

He's not going to let me have a pity party. I know him well enough to realize that. But he does let me snuggle for a minute before he tears into me. "So, you've decided that all of this is your fault, huh? Well, then. I guess it's pointless to remind you that your mates are grown men who are perfectly capable of making up their own minds. And even more ridiculous to tell you that the four of us love you, otherwise, we wouldn't get so annoyed when you say something stupid."

"But, Ry, this is my fault. I'm the one who asked Orym to call Dec. I begged Dec to turn James instead of letting him die. And it's my aunt who's after me, forcing you four to try to protect me. All of that makes it my fault," I argue.

He shakes his head and shifts so he's sitting up straighter. "You're lucky I'm not feeling well enough to storm out of here. This poor me bullshit is on my last nerve. I can only imagine how Luca and Orym feel, since I'm sure it was worse before I woke up."

I lift my head, putting some space between us. His harsh words sting, and I wonder if he's trying to upset me. "Why are you saying this?"

"Because it's true. You constantly take the blame for things that aren't your fault, and I'm sick of it. I know it's what you think you're supposed to do because of how Gunnar raised you. But he's gone, and I'm the territory alpha now. You're not even a wolf, so you shouldn't care about all that. I appreciate you taking responsibility for your mistakes, but this is not one of them." His tone is icy, and his words burn.

"You don't think I'm to blame for any of this? Amber is my aunt. She wants my powers. The Moon Goddess linked the four of you to me. That puts me in the center of everything. Of course, it's my fault." I know it's not smart to keep arguing, but I can't stop myself. I need him to see my point and agree that I'm right.

He refuses, though, and keeps arguing. "Red! Stop that right now. You are no more responsible for any of that than you are for the sun coming up this morning. You cannot take the blame for things other people do anymore. Do you understand me? I won't have it." His veiled threat constricts my chest, and I struggle to draw in a breath.

"What are you saying?" I whisper the question.

"I'm saying that if you insist on trying to force us to blame you, there will be consequences." He leaves it at that, and I'm not sure what he means exactly. I don't know if I want to find out, either.

"Fine. Then tell me, who am I supposed to blame?" I spit back, part of me scared that he'll decide I'm giving him too much attitude and he'll make me leave.

"Whoever is actually responsible. I understand that James' situation is difficult, but it's not your fault. It's his. If he had just told you that he'd been injured, then the wound could have been treated before it got to the point where turning him was the only way to keep him from dying. Hell, his brother can share the blame. It's not like you forced Dec to change him. He had a choice. So, please, stop blaming yourself." Ry's tone is softer now, more pleading than hurtful. I realize that he's trying to get me to see his side, and I do, even if I still blame myself.

"What if I still feel responsible, even after you've made a pretty convincing argument?" I counter, making sure to leave the edge off my tone as well. If he's trying to discuss this, it won't do any good for me to keep snapping at him.

Before he can respond, Luca comes in with a tray. "I have tea, sandwiches, and carrots. Orym insisted that I give you a veggie option, even though I wanted to bring you chips. He's worried that we're not eating healthy enough lately." Luca rolls his eyes for a second, then realizes that we were in the middle of something. "Oh, I'm totally interrupting. Sorry. I'll just leave this here." He places the tray on the bed and starts to back away.

"Wait," Ry stops him with one word. Luca raises his eyebrows and freezes. "I need backup. She's arguing with me, and I want her to stop."

"Oh. What are we arguing about?" Luca strolls back and hands each of us a cup of tea before setting the sandwich plates in front of us and moving the tray so he can sit.

"Red thinks everything is her fault," Ry growls.

"Well, she's right," Luca says with a grin. I can't stop the laugh that barks out.

"What? How is she responsible for other people's actions?" Ry snarls at Luca. For a moment, I'm worried that they'll fight.

"It is all her fault. She controls everyone, right? So, she's the one who makes us do all the stupid things that we shouldn't," Luca says.

That asshole.

Seventeen
Making Up

JAMES

My throat burns the entire way to the SUV my brother shoves me into. Once we're locked inside, he thrusts another bag of blood into my hands. "Drink it. Now." I grimace against the order, even though I'm certain this is the one thing that will quench my aching throat.

"I mean it, James. Drink it, then we'll talk about what happened back there," he orders again as the vehicle starts. He puts it in gear and heads back toward the city.

I sigh and do as I'm told. After all, I'm a vampire now. This is my new life. One I asked for but never expected to get. How did we get here? I find myself anxious to hear what Declan has to say. I wish that I hadn't reacted the way I did toward Garnet. I'm sure this isn't what she wanted for us. When the bag is empty, I turn back to my brother, who is brooding as he maneuvers the SUV through the city streets toward Midnight.

"Okay, let me have it. I'm ready," I insist. I'm pretty sure I know what's coming, but I owe him the ability to say it.

"You shouldn't have lied about your injuries. What if she hadn't checked on you? Then what?" He looks over at me before turning his attention back to the road. "Then you'd be dead, you idiot. Do you know how badly that would have destroyed her? Not just her, either."

"It's not like I wanted to die. I didn't think the stab wound was that bad. I cleaned it and dressed it. The bleeding had nearly stopped, until we had to move Ryland and Garnet to the bed so they could rest." That was what did it. Helping to carry them is what re-opened my wound and caused me to bleed. I can't argue with Dec; he's right. I shouldn't have hidden my injury. It was my fault.

"You're lucky you have a woman who's willing to beg for your life. She would have given me anything to save you. I should kick your ass for putting the two of us in that position. I know this isn't what you really want, but you have to make a decision here. Either you're going to learn to control the hunger and be a good vamp, or I'm going to have to lock you up when we get to Midnight." Dec keeps his tone light, but I know he's serious.

"I'm trying, okay? This isn't an easy adjustment to make. When I went to sleep, I was human; then I woke up something else. Can I have a minute to freak out before I have to decide how the rest of my life is going to go?" I can't tell him that I'm terrified I'll hurt Garnet, or that she'll decide she doesn't want me now, because I'm a monster. I wanted to taste her, to drink her in until there was nothing left.

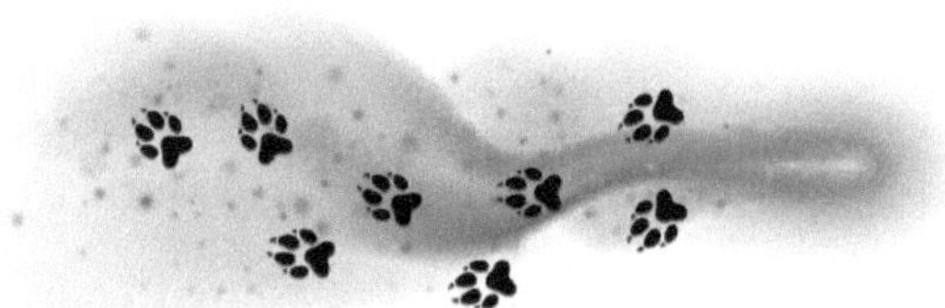

LUCA

"What?" I ask, looking at the shocked and annoyed faces staring back at me. "It's ridiculous to think that Red controls everything and is the cause of all our misery. But telling her that isn't going to prove my point."

Ryland is annoyed, and I understand. I need him to consider for a minute that he's going about this the wrong way. He'll get further with Red by listening and sympathizing than with growling and shouting orders.

"I know what you're doing, and I kind of hate you for it," she snarls at me.

"Because you know I'm right." I wink at her.

Ryland sighs. "Fine. You wanna blame yourself, go ahead. Just stop trying to make us blame you, too. Because we don't."

Who knew James being turned into a vamp would cause a rift in our little family? Oh, yeah, that would be me. But hey, nobody wanted to listen to me. I meant it when I told James I would respect his decision, and I will. Even if it wasn't exactly his decision. He's still family.

"Why don't we relax for a while, and try to figure out how to show James that we accept him in his new form? If he was feeling insecure before, I bet it's worse now. That's probably why he lashed out before Dec took him away. It can't be easy waking up to find out you're a vampire now," I suggest.

Red looks at me and smirks. "Look at you, being all sensitive and shit."

"I'm sensitive," I counter. She smacks my arm, but takes a drink of her tea and starts to eat her sandwich. Relief washes over me. She needs to eat and rest, but I couldn't figure out how to force her into it. I guess all I had to do was drop some knowledge on her.

"I think that's a great idea. We should figure out what we need to do to make James feel welcome. We'll start with ensuring that there's plenty of blood for him and a place to store it. Then we'll have a family meeting when he gets back," Ryland orders, finishing off his sandwich and laying back against the headboard.

"You two should rest. Orym and I will take care of things. Don't worry," I say, taking the tray and heading back to the kitchen. I hate being away from Red, but she's exhausted.

Oyrm meets me as I set the tray on the counter. "Did they eat?"

I nod. "They're resting again. We need to get things together for James. There are things we didn't discuss before."

"I've already spoken with Eli. He has a team bringing a small refrigerator and a delivery of blood. And I've set up twice weekly deliveries to make sure he has plenty of blood to drink," Orym explains.

"You've been busy," I say.

He laughs. "It wasn't nearly as stressful as you and Ryland trying to convince Garnet that this isn't her fault."

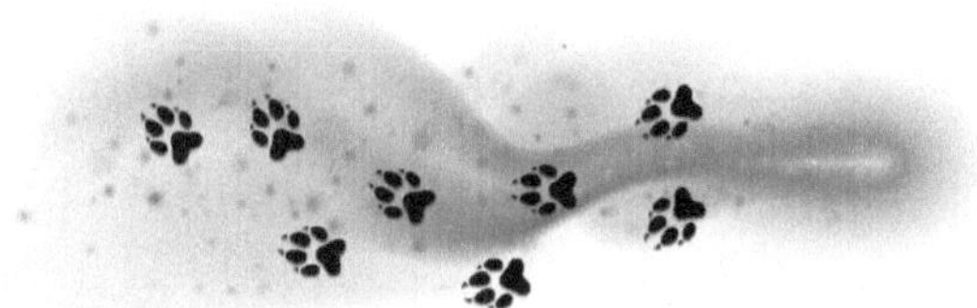

GARNET

After sleeping for a few more hours, I wake with the sun shining in my face. I'm surprised to see Ry still sleeping, but he went through a lot yesterday. I check to make sure he's okay before I climb out of bed and head for the shower. I feel grimy and can't take it anymore.

I don't bother to lock the door, because there's no reason to. If Amber really wanted in here, a lock wouldn't stop her. As for my mates, I wouldn't object to them joining me. I don't pose the invitation, though, because I know that none of them would take me up on it right now. And if they did, it wouldn't be so we could have shower sex.

I strip down and step into the spray of hot water, standing there with my eyes closed for a moment. The warmth of the stream heats my body. I hadn't even realized that I was cold until the heat starts to rise inside of me. Surrendering to the sensation, I sigh and lean against the wall for support.

Exhaustion still threatens to drop me to the floor, but I refuse to give in. I let myself sleep long enough, and I have to build up my tolerance to using my magic without rest. I'll never defeat Amber if I don't.

If I stand still too much longer, I'm going to fall asleep again, and I don't want that. I force my eyes open and wash myself. Once my body is clean, I feel more awake and start on my hair. I take my time rinsing the conditioner out and combing through the tangles. By the time I'm finished, the water is getting cold.

I shiver as I turn it off and wrap one towel around my body and a second one around my hair. My vision goes dark and suddenly I'm in the forest again. It's dark, and I'm watching those same witches around the fire. I thought these visions had stopped when we realized it was Amber coming after me.

Looks like I was wrong. This time, I'm determined to pay attention and learn everything I can about their ritual. I'm seeing this for a reason. It has to mean something. But what?

The figures are in dark cloaks with hoods pulled up to hide their faces. This time the light from the fire is reflecting off the cloaks enough that I can tell they're red. I can't quite make out what they're chanting, but this time that part doesn't seem as important as the symbols they're drawing in the dirt and the air. How are they drawing in the air like that? It has to be some sort of magic, but I've never seen witches use that.

Could these figures be Fae instead of witches? Have I been looking at this completely wrong the whole time? That would explain so much. If these people are Fae, they could be speaking a completely different language that I've never heard before. That's why I can't understand what they're chanting.

It's also why they can see me. I know that I'm not really here, and they shouldn't be able to see me. But when I did this before, at the training center, my father could see me and interact with me. I wonder if that's why these people could see me before.

"Excuse me," I whisper. I hate to interrupt the ritual because I have no idea what they're doing, but I need to know if I'm right.

They all freeze and their heads turn toward me. The hoods remain in place, but I hear a voice answer quietly. "You aren't supposed to be here. How are you here?"

"I don't really know. I was hoping you could tell me. Are you Fae?" It's insensitive and rude, but I ask anyway.

"We are the Fae elders. You must have our blood or you wouldn't be able to find this place. It's hidden from all but our direct relations. Who are you?" one of them asks.

"My name is Garnet. I'm Trevan's daughter," I say with more confidence than I feel. I hope it's the right choice to tell them who I really am.

"Ah, the half-blood child has found her way. We were beginning to think you'd never make it," another says.

"Wait, you knew about me?" I ask, curiosity shoving fear to the side.

"We tried to talk to you before when you were here, but you got scared and ran away," a third one explains.

"I was terrified the first few times I came here. Then I met my father and learned about my powers. I guess that was how I finally figured out you're Fae and I didn't have to be afraid," I respond.

"Some would argue that you should be more afraid because of who we are. I, for one, am relieved that you would not agree," the first who spoke says.

"You know who I am now. Who are each of you?" I ask, feeling bolder now.

"We are friends. That is all we can tell you right now. We must get back to our ritual. The Wolf Moon approaches, and you're going to need all the help you can get." They turn back toward the fire, letting me know our conversation is done.

"I don't know how to get home," I admit. The one who spoke first walks around the circle and takes my hands in theirs.

"Keep this with you. It will help protect you and ensure that you can return to us when you need to. We can't intervene much, but we're doing what we can. You must defeat her, otherwise, our people will be in grave danger." Their words emphasize exactly what I already knew. When they let go of my hands, I look down to see a beautiful moonstone pendant set in silver. The threads of silver surround the stone, appearing like a tree of life.

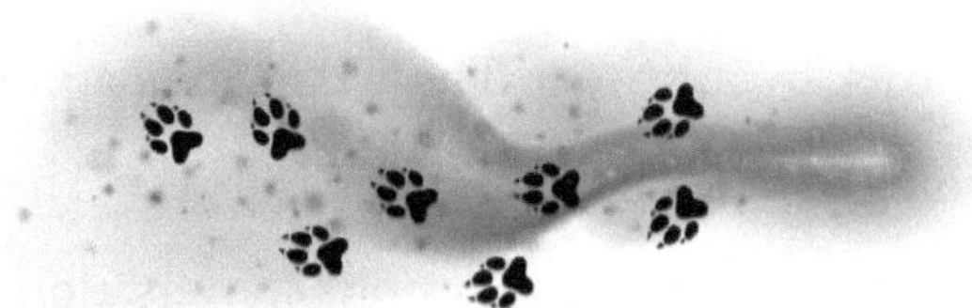

RYLAND

I wake up alone. Hearing the shower, I figure that's where Red is. I give her some time to herself. I know that she's processing things and might appreciate some space. But when she doesn't come out of the bathroom after the water has been off for a while, I get concerned. Pain lances through me as I stand and walk the few steps to the bathroom door. If it's locked, I'll have to call for Orym or Luca to help me. I'm still too weak to break it down myself.

I find the door unlocked, and Red lying on the floor next to it. She's wrapped in a towel and shivering. It's cold in here, even with the steam from her shower lingering. Before I can even call to Luca or Orym along the bond, they're crouched next to me.

"She doesn't look hurt. I don't know what happened. She took a shower, but the water's been off for a while," I say.

Luca looks between us. "Orym, help Ryland back to bed. I'll get Red. I think I know what's happened here. Hopefully she'll wake up soon." He scoops her up and carries her back to bed. I let Orym help me stand up and walk into the bedroom.

"Will you get her dressed so she stays warm?" I ask. Orym nods and starts gathering clothes for Red. Then I look at Luca. "What do you think happened?"

"I think she projected again. When Vincent was found, she did it accidentally, and took me with her. I suspect it's happened again. I just hope she can figure out how to get back. Last time, Trevan had to push us." Luca's explanation does little to quell the nerves rising inside of me. I'm worried that this is one of Amber's tricks.

"Should we call him to see if there's anything he can do to help?" I don't know what else to try, since I'm not familiar with this particular power of hers.

Orym carefully dresses Red in comfy clothes before tucking her into the bed. I need a shower too, but I won't leave her like this, even if I know she won't be alone. He pulls out his phone and types a message. A responding ding indicates that his text was answered quickly.

"Trevan says he's on his way, and he's bringing Grammy. Maybe they can figure out what's happened to Garnet. Should I text James and let him know what's going on?" Orym tucks the phone back into his pocket without waiting for my response.

I shake my head. "We should let him concentrate on whatever Dec has him doing right now. He needs to control his vamp urges so that he can live here with us. Otherwise, I'm not sure what we'll have to do. We can't have him racing back to see her and end up killing innocent wolves because he got hungry."

I don't like that thought, but it's the truth. James is dangerous right now.

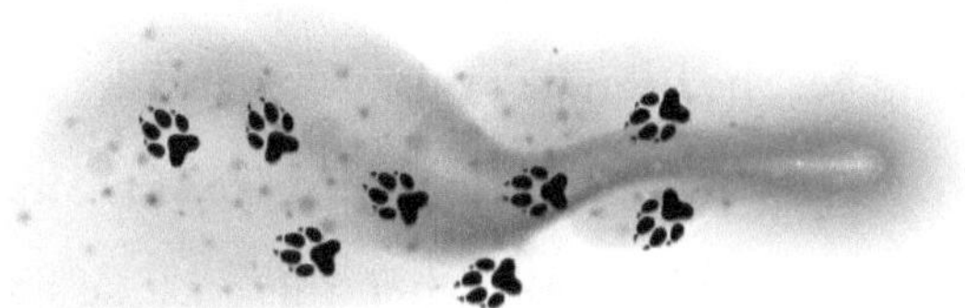

ORYM

I don't feel good about leaving James out of the loop with what's happening. I do understand Ryland's opinion. James isn't much good to us if he can't learn to control his vamp urges. And we all know that sometimes that's harder to get the hang of than people would like.

I'm still surprised that Dec thinks James will be okay to come back tonight. All we can do is wait and see. Trevan and Grammy don't bother to knock when they arrive, and I wonder how they got here so quickly.

"I'm sorry, love, those portals are a bit tricky to get used to. But it really was the safest way to get here." I overhear Trevan apologizing to Grammy, and their speed makes sense.

Luca opens the bedroom door and ushers them inside. "How long has she been like this?" Trevan asks.

Before we can answer, Garnet starts to stir. She groans and I worry that she hit her head when this episode started. When she opens her eyes, they're completely white. She climbs from the bed and grabs a marker from the dresser.

"Not this shit again," Ryland says with a sigh. "It took seven coats of paint to cover that the last time."

We watch as she starts to draw symbols on the walls. Trevan steps up behind her and examines them. "You won't want to paint over these. Are they the same thing she drew last time?" he asks.

"Yeah. They look the same. I'm guessing you know what they mean?" I can't help questioning him. We need to know what we're dealing with.

"You shouldn't have covered them the last time. But you couldn't have known what they meant. It's okay." He pauses, then continues. "They're protection runes. These specific ones were created by our Fae elders. You said this has happened before? Tell me about it."

"She appeared to be sleepwalking and started writing on the wall, just like this. But she didn't remember doing it." Luca paused and exchanged a look with Grammy. "She's been doing it off and on for the better part of a year. We didn't know they were for protection, so I covered them up every time. I'm sorry."

"Apologies are useless here. We have to concentrate of keeping my daughter safe and making sure she can defeat Amber. Where is her other mate? She needs all of you," Trevan says, looking around the room frantically.

"There was an incident. He's with his brother, learning how to be a vampire," I explain carefully.

I expect shock or confusion, but Trevan nods as if I've said James is at the market. "Perfect. Things are progressing exactly as they're meant to, then. I'm sure she'll be relieved when he gets back."

"Why does it feel like you know things that you aren't sharing?" Ryland glares at him.

"Probably because I know things that I'm unable to share with you. That would be my best guess."

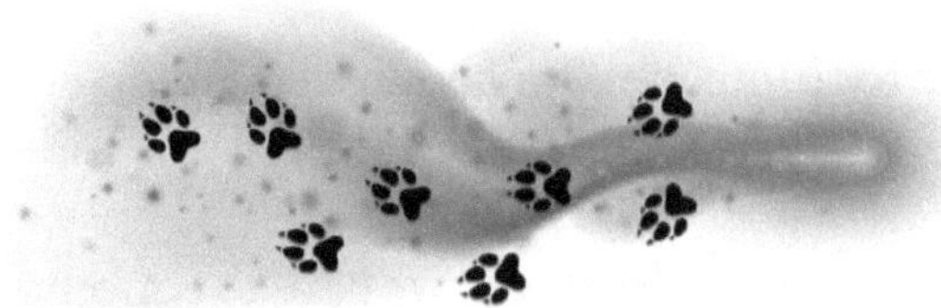

GARNET

I shake off the vision and open my eyes to find myself writing on the walls again. Fuck. Ry is gonna be pissed. I thought this stuff was behind us. I turn to see him staring at me. "I'm so sorry, Ry. I'll take care of it, I promise."

He reaches a hand out for me, and I go to him. "You won't. We're going to leave them, just like we should have the first time. I'm sorry that I didn't understand you were trying to protect us."

"Wait, those are protection symbols?" I'm so confused. I glance around the room and realize that my father and Grammy are here. "What's happened? Is James okay?" My heart races and I feel my chest constricting.

"Your mates were concerned about you because you went into a vision. When we arrived, you started doing this," Trevan gestures to the symbols on the walls. "And I explained that these were for protection and should not be removed or covered up."

"I met the Fae elders. Kind of. I have no idea who they are, but I saw and talked to them. They claim to be trying to help me. I don't know if I can trust them, but one of them gave me this." I hold up the moonstone pendant.

My father looks impressed. "That is a lovely boon, for sure, daughter. Indeed, they must be trying to ensure your victory against Amber. This should give you an edge."

"I don't understand anything that's going on," I say as Ry pulls me into his arms and sets me on his lap.

"Obviously, these Fae elders decided they needed to talk to you, and they pulled you into some sort of alternate dimension. Then they somehow told you how to help protect us with these symbols. Once James gets back, we'll have to start talking about exactly how we want to approach this fight with Amber," Orym explains quietly.

Luca looks at me, obviously feeling guilty about something. "I'm sorry, Red. I kept getting rid of the symbols when you drew them at Gunnar's house. I'm sure you felt like you were going crazy. If I had known they were for protection, I wouldn't have done it."

Grammy steps over and grabs his arm. "Don't blame yourself, boy. That was my fault. I asked you to cover them because I wasn't sure what they were. I didn't want Gunnar to get upset because she was writing on the walls. It was stupid. I should have found someone who could tell me what we were dealing with when it happened at Midnight."

"What? This happened at Midnight? I didn't dream that?" I'd let myself believe that night was a crazy dream. I pushed away the tense moments with Luca, and the vision I'd so clearly remembered. And now I learn that all of it was true. I had nearly convinced myself that none of it had actually happened.

"Well, I think we should leave the past where it is and move forward. I'm certain we've all learned a valuable lesson here. If you're not sure what something says, you should consult an expert." Trevan gestures at himself and grins. I can't help laughing at how ridiculous he's being.

"And just how were we supposed to know these were Fae protection runes?" I ask, squinting my eyes at him.

"Well, that is a good point. I guess there's no way you could have known. But now you do," he responds. I roll my eyes at him.

We have a few hours before James is set to return. I wonder how he's doing, but don't want to bother him to find out. Hopefully Dec will be in touch if there are any setbacks.

"I need to get out of this room for a while," Ry says, sliding me off his lap and pushing to stand. I jump up at his side and wrap an arm around his waist. I don't know how weak he's still feeling, but he doesn't look like he's back at a hundred percent yet.

"We should go sit outside for a while. The sunlight will do you some good," Grammy suggests. I agree with her, and I'd like some of that sun myself. Orym and Luca take Ry from me and help him to the porch with Trevan leading the way.

I don't mind being left alone with Grammy, though I wonder if she maneuvered it this way on purpose. "You're going to be fine, child. I promise. You can do this. With your mates by your side, you'll be unstoppable."

Her words touch me. "How can you have so much confidence in me?" I ask, moving toward the door.

"Because I've watched you grow up. I'm the one who's been here every day to see how you've matured and changed. You've really come into your powers, and I know you'll be able to defeat Amber." Her support bolsters my own confidence a bit.

"I hope you're right. We only have one chance at this, and I'm so scared I'm going to fail. I don't want anyone to suffer because I couldn't figure out how to fight against her. I know that I have to be ready to kill her before she can kill me, but I really wish there was a non-violent way to end this." I wonder if I should admit my fears out loud, but Grammy raised me. She has a right to know what I'm thinking.

"Fear is not the enemy, Red. Embrace the fear. Use it to make you more cautious. But don't let it rule you. Don't ever give in to the fear. Fight against it. You are more powerful than she is," Grammy insists.

She follows me out the door onto the porch where Luca, Orym, Ry, and my father are chatting in the sunlight. "I won't give up, Grammy. I have too much to fight for."

Grammy pulls me into a huge hug, holding me there.

EIGHTEEN
CALM BEFORE THE STORM

LUCA

Guilt eats at me for removing the protection symbols every time Red drew them. It doesn't matter that Grammy told me to, or that I did it to keep her from getting in trouble with Gunnar. I should have found a way to learn what they were before I touched them.

“I think we should let James know what’s going on. If these symbols are protecting us from Amber, then he should probably be surrounded by them too,” I say to Ryland, Orym, and Trevan. Glancing around, I see that Grammy and Red have come outside too but aren’t quite close enough to hear our conversation.

“I agree, but he has to be able to be around people and control his urges. I’ve heard that’s hard for new vamps,” Orym replies.

Trevan looks at us for a moment before he speaks. “There is a magical option. It’s a spell that can be tattooed on the skin and prevents vampires from being able to feed off a being without permission. If you warn your packs that it’s coming, I can do it from here and cover everyone.”

“How is that possible?” I ask, but Ryland already has his phone out, starting the text chain. Within a few minutes, everyone will be aware of the new ‘ink’ coming their way.

“You’re going to take away James’ ability to prove he can control himself. Why would you do that?” Red steps closer and glares at her father.

"To protect you all, of course," he responds.

"Leave me out of your spell. I trust him, and I don't want a mark that will prevent him from feeding on me if he needs to." Her words echo between us, and I understand her irritation.

"I agree. Protect the packs, but I don't need it. James won't hurt us. We're his family," I say, knowing it may not be the smartest decision I've ever made. If we were in a situation where I was not able to agree to him feeding from me, and the result would be him being harmed, I don't want that.

"You'd risk your lives just to keep from hurting his feelings?" Orym asks. I'm not sure I can explain my reasoning in a way he can understand.

Luckily, I don't have to. Ryland holds up a hand. "I don't want the mark either. If we get into a situation where James needs to feed and we somehow can't give consent, I want him to be able to take what he needs. I agree with Red and Luca; he won't hurt us." He turns to Orym. "It's your decision, but you know if the roles were reversed, he'd agree with us."

"It's not like he has some sort of wolf protection. I get it. He trusts us with his life, we should do the same. I don't want the mark either. But the rest of the packs need it," Orym insists.

"Of course," Trevan agrees.

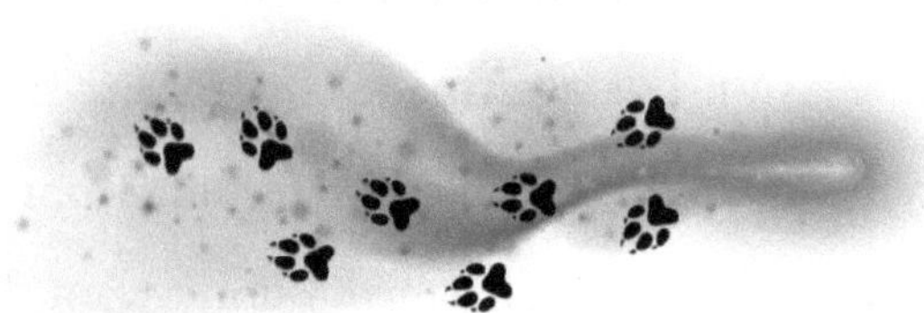

RYLAND

With the protection tattoo spell in the works, I call Dec. James needs to be here, because he needs to be part of what's going on.

"What's wrong?" he asks the second he answers my call.

"Can you bring James back now? We have deliveries on the way that will take care of his needs, and my people are protected. He needs to be here for this. We've learned things and are preparing for Amber." I don't waste time explaining everything on the phone. If he wants to know, he's welcome to stay while we discuss it with James.

"Eli is finishing up the implant now. We'll have to test it, but as long as it's positioned correctly, I should be able to have him there in an hour. Is there any reason for me to bring back up? You said your people are protected; does that mean from him, or from Amber? You know new vamps don't have the best control," Dec explains.

"Red's father is Fae. He's casting a spell that will keep James from feeding on the packs without consent. He won't be able to hurt anyone here." I purposefully leave out the part that his pack won't be getting the mark, because it's not Dec's business. We'll tell James when he gets here, and if he shares with his brother, that's his decision.

"That's fantastic. He's been worried about hurting someone because he can't control his thirst. I'll bring some bags with us, even if you have deliveries set up. I'm sure Eli will put a rush on those when he finds out that we're headed back out there. I'll text when we're on our way." He hangs up the call without another word.

"James should be back within a couple of hours. We need to make sure the packs are protected as soon as possible. I trust him, but Dec said he's struggling with control. I don't want him worried about hurting one of the littles," I bark at Trevan.

I need to run. Red, please stay here. I'll take Luca or Orym with me, but I need to know that you're safe. She nods and threads her fingers through Luca's. I understand her silent signal. I need Orym's reassurance right now, and I should make sure he's good with his decision to not have the protective mark. Especially since he was against James being turned in the first place.

I lock eyes with Orym and jerk my head toward the forest. We take off running, waiting until we're into the trees to shift. I welcome the pain of my body rearranging itself to set my wolf free. Once we're shifted, my senses are heightened. Smells are more intense, colors are brighter, and I can run faster.

Are you sure you don't want the protection tattoo? I ask along the bond, glad that we don't have to shift back to have this conversation.

I'm sure. It took me a bit to understand, but I do now.

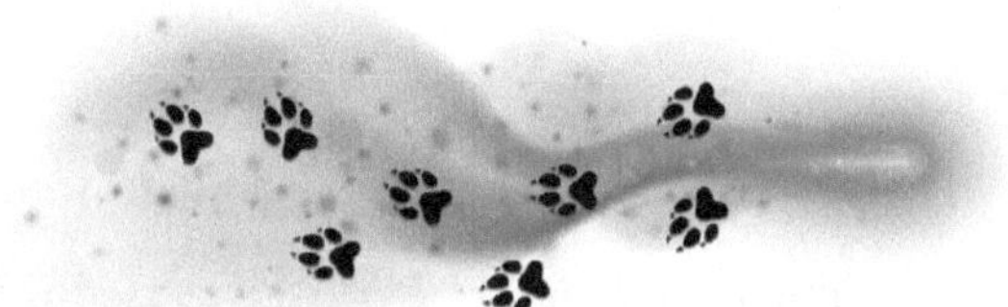

GARNET

The forest is quiet now, too quiet. I don't trust the peace that seems to be surrounding us. When Ry said he needed to run, I bristled. I know he saw, because he immediately offered to take Luca or Orym with him. If they're not here when James gets back, I'd rather have Luca here than Orym.

I need Luca to prove to James that he supports this. We all need to show James that we love him and trust him. Honestly, I was shocked when Luca agreed with me and said he didn't need the mark. This situation isn't easy, but we'll get through it together. I just have to trust my mates and they have to trust me.

"I need to meditate for a bit. Would you like to join me, or just stand guard like a growly alpha?" I ask Luca with a smirk. I already know his answer, but it's way more fun to tease him about it.

"Growly alpha, of course. I mean, I do it so well," he quips back at me. I love that we can be ourselves again. We've been through so much lately, that I started to worry I'd lose this.

I fist my hand in his shirt and pull him to me for a hard kiss. His arms wrap around my waist and he drags me against him. I don't even care this time that my father and Grammy are watching. Luca is my mate, and this is perfectly natural. Life is too short to worry about what other people think.

"Keep telling yourself that you're not a cuddly teddy bear," I tease, pulling away from him. I walk over by our picnic table where there's a small patch of grass under the shade of a tree. I settle in to meditate, and as I close my eyes, I sense Luca standing guard. I know that even if Amber attacks right now, I'll be safe. Luca won't let anything happen to me. I have no problem putting my life in his hands.

I focus on my breathing. In, out. Slow and steady. I feel my magic pulse inside of me and wonder if this is something new. *Don't fight your magic, daughter. Let it ebb and flow. It will guide your meditation and protect you from harm while you're in there.*

I should feel annoyed that Trevan invades my meditation, but instead, I'm relieved for the instruction. I let myself relax, doing exactly as he suggests. My magic flows around me inside my mind, a rainbow of colors and textures, swirling and dancing. It's hypnotizing, and relaxing is easier than I'd anticipated.

For this meditation, I want to commune with the Moon Goddess for guidance. I need to know that I'm following her desires. If I'm somehow meant to be her champion, I must know what she expects. With my magic surrounding me, I reach out to her, asking for anything she can give me. A sign, a conversation, clear instructions of some sort.

The only change I notice is my magic moving faster. There's no response from the goddess I'm trying to reach. I start to feel disappointed, but I realize that she can't be everywhere. This must not be the right time to talk to her. Time is the one thing I don't have, though.

"I know you're busy, being a goddess and all, but I won't have another chance to talk to you. Please, just let me know that we're on the right track. I need to know how far you want me to go to defeat my aunt." I hate feeling like I'm being ignored, even if I know that I can't expect a literal goddess to drop everything to talk to me.

I force myself to accept that I'm not going to get an answer. My magic starts to swirl in front of me, creating an oval that looks like the portals Trevan has made for us. A bright white light comes from the center of the oval, and I shield my eyes for a moment.

Someone steps through the opening, glowing in a way that makes it hard to see her face. Her dress is a pale silver that seems to be the source of the glow. The brightness starts to fade a bit, but her head is haloed by a circle of that same bright light. I bow my head in respect, knowing that this is the Moon Goddess.

"My dear child, did you think I would refuse to guide you on this journey?" she asks, reaching out to lift my chin with a finger. I don't feel her touch, but my eyes meet hers.

"I just figured you were busy and this wasn't a good time," I say, feeling the stupidity of the excuse. I should have trusted her to appear when I needed her.

"You must rely on the strength of your mates and your powers to defeat Amber. I understand that she is your aunt, and that makes this difficult for you. There will be no other option but to take her life. If you don't, she will continue to hunt you. And you will be the only one who can kill her. I fear if you hesitate when the chance arises, all will be lost." Her words send a shiver up my spine. This is exactly what I feared.

Knowing that I have to kill Amber isn't a new feeling, but I'd hoped that something would change. "I want to separate her from her magic. But that won't be enough?"

Sadness fills the goddess' eyes as she looks at me. "No, child. There is no way to do that without killing her. And if you did somehow find a way, that would leave her the ability to reverse it and take your magic as her own. There is no other way. Amber must die so that you and your mates can protect all the innocents."

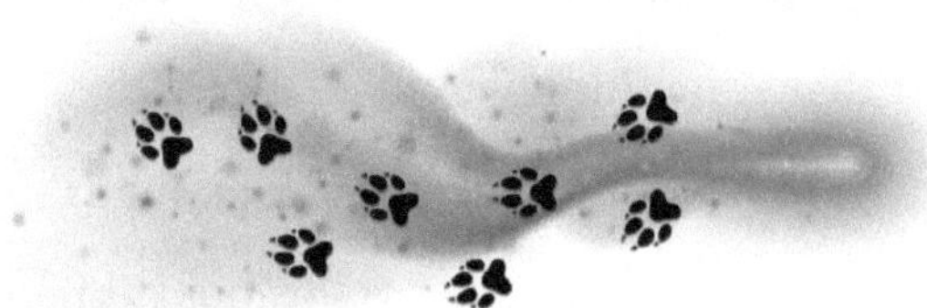

ORYM

I appreciate that Ryland checks on me but wonder why he thinks he can't trust my decision. I don't want to fight my alpha on this. We have better things to do than argue about something that's pointless.

We've been gone a while. Should we head back? I ask along the bond. We run along the marked trails, racing between the trees and giving our wolves freedom to do as they like.

Probably. James will be back soon. We should be there to explain things to him. That's all I need to hear for me to turn around and run back toward our home. I know that once this is all over, we'll be building a new cabin to give us more room, but I enjoy how crowded our small home is. The closeness of it comforts me.

And there I go, thinking about things that aren't important in this moment. Right now, we have to be focused on the fight with Amber. Nothing else matters if we can't defeat her. I know that the guys and I think she has to die, but Garnet doesn't want to do that. I hope that we can find a solution that will give her peace. I hate thinking that she'll have to do something that goes against her heart.

Ryland slows as we get close to the cabin, and I follow his lead. I wonder if he's sensing something that I haven't yet. When he starts to shift back to human, I do the same. "Is everything okay?" I ask, stopping him from walking away.

"I think so. Red's not answering on the bond, but that doesn't mean there's a problem. I don't want our wolves to interrupt if she's meditating. You know how delicate that process is," he answers. I nod, and we walk through the trees into the clearing.

Sure enough, Garnet is sitting on the ground under a tree with her eyes closed and her magic swirling around her. Luca watches with wide eyes and a goofy grin. I can't help thinking that's the way all four of us look at her when she doesn't know.

Ryland and I walk quietly over and stand next to him. *She's been doing this since you guys left. She doesn't seem upset anymore, so I haven't bothered her.* Concern washes over me for a moment at his mention of her being upset. What could have upset her while she's meditating?

I'll stay here to help guard her, if you want to talk to Trevan about the spell. I make the offer and Ryland nods before walking away. I know he's concerned about protecting the innocent people in our territory. Even if we trust James, this spell will protect them from any vampire feeding without permission. That's a huge advantage, when we may end up fighting vamps that are being controlled by Amber.

My heart aches knowing that we aren't done with this fight yet. I want to move on with our happily ever after.

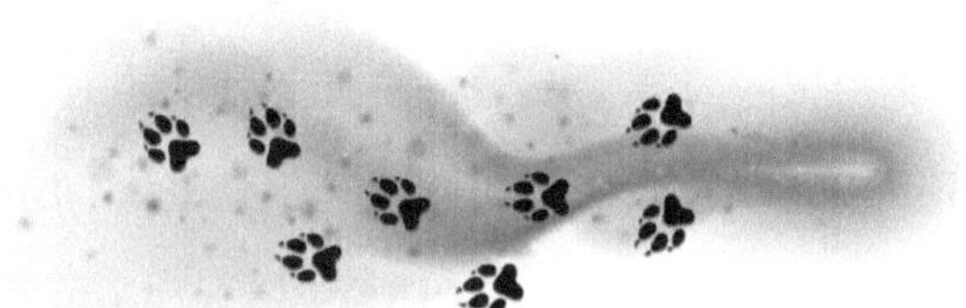

JAMES

I wake from the implant surgery feeling famished. "Why am I so thirsty?" I ask Eli as he removes the IV from my arm.

"Because you're a new vamp, and your body is getting used to the craving. You'll get the hang of it. Trust yourself," he says. I wonder if he means it, since they've kept Delilah away from me the whole time I've been here. If there was nothing to worry about, wouldn't she be safe with me?

"So, what now?"

"Well, now we take you home. We tested the UV implant while you were knocked out, and it works perfectly."

"Eli, I can't go home yet. I have no control over these cravings," I argue, grabbing his arm and forcing him to look at me.

"You'll be fine. The Fae has taken steps to protect anyone you might hurt. And my guys are delivering your supplies right now. By the time we get there, you'll be all set up. If you can't trust yourself, then trust me." I know that my brother trusts this vampire with his life, and I should too. I'm just not sure that they understand how reckless I feel right now.

Within minutes, Dec and I are in the SUV and heading back to the forest. I feel like I'm heading toward my doom. I appreciate their faith in me, but I'm terrified that I'm about to do something I'll spend an eternity regretting.

As we walk through the forest toward the cabin, I see wolf shifters watching us. They don't look scared, and I realize I'm not feeling the urge to attack any of them. This is strange, since I've felt that urge continuously since I woke as a vamp.

"What did Trevan do?" I ask, following my brother toward my home.

"I'm not sure. Why?" he replies, turning to look at me. "Are you feeling okay?"

"I'm good. It's just strange how none of these people smell the way they did last night." The revelation feels strange to say, considering how badly I wanted to drain them all a mere twelve hours ago.

"They said there was nothing to worry about. I'm glad they were right," he says. We continue through the paths until we reach the clearing where Ryland's cabin stands. I feel a tug inside of me and wonder what that's all about.

Since I haven't had the urge to kill anyone, I step into the clearing to find everyone waiting for me. It feels strange to be the center of attention. Almost as if they're waiting to see what I'll do, like I'm an experiment. My eyes are instantly drawn to Garnet's, and I freeze.

All I want is to go to her, but I'm scared. What if I hurt her? I can't take that chance. I'll keep myself away from all of them as much as I can. "Eli's men delivered a new fridge and a few days' supply of blood for you," she says.

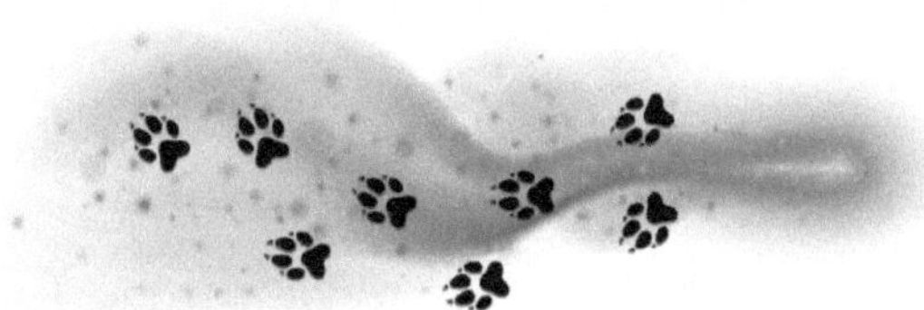

GARNET

I hate how much distance is between us right now, but I sense his hesitation. I hold myself back for a moment, not wanting to make him uncomfortable.

"That's great. Thank you." His response is polite and reserved. It almost feels like when our bond was damaged.

"Fuck it," I mutter and race toward him, not giving James a chance to do anything but catch me when I jump into his arms. I kiss him deeply, my tongue delving into his mouth and exploring. I gasp when it scrapes along his new fangs, but not from fear. I'm excited for him to bite me, even if I won't admit that to anyone.

His arms tighten around me, and I hum in response. It's only been a day, but I missed him. I ease back from the kiss and look at him. I can't explain why, but he looks a little different. It's like his features are sharper somehow.

"I know, it's weird. But I'm mostly still me," he whispers, hugging me tightly to him and pressing his nose against my neck. "Why do you still smell as amazing as you did yesterday, but no one else does?"

"Because I don't need a spell to protect me from you," I answer. "None of our family took it. We trust you. You won't hurt us."

His arms release me as if I've burned him and he jumps backward ten feet before I fall on my ass. "Fuck, James, what was that?" Ry steps forward and helps me up while staring at my new vampire mate.

"I thought everyone was protected from me," he responds.

"Everyone who needs to be is," Ry answers. "We don't need it, because you won't hurt us. The four of us are the only ones not covered by the spell. Because we don't need it."

I can feel the confidence Ry is exuding, as well as James' fear. "I know you're worried about it. But honestly, James, you don't have to be. We trust you and we know that you'd never hurt us." I wish he could believe my words, even though I understand why he can't.

The tears in his eyes nearly break my heart. I want to hold him and reassure him, but every time I step closer, he backs away. I don't know what we can do to convince him that it's safe for him to be here. He takes a deep breath, then steps closer. "I'm terrified that I'll hurt one of you, or worse. But I'll try. I need your assurance that you'll stop me if I do something to harm you."

"We'll find a way to restrain you," Ry says calmly. "But we won't need to."

Luca and Orym move closer now, and the four of us approach James. He stands still, hesitating, processing, waiting to see what happens next.

"See? This isn't so bad, is it?" Orym asks.

"I'm actually feeling calmer with the four of you so close. I'd expected the thirst to take over. What is going on?" James is as confused as the rest of us. We all look at Dec.

"It's part of the mate bond. You'll keep him centered and grounded. I would think it should work the same way with your magic. The five mates together will be stronger than on their own," he explains.

That explains a lot of things that both Trevan and the Moon Goddess have said. The five of us need to stick together. And I'm certain we can do that. For the first time in a while, I finally feel like we could defeat Amber and save everyone.

Confidence feels good, and I'm determined to hold onto this feeling for as long as I can. Ry clears his throat, though, and I know that it's time to tell James what he's missed.

"What is it?" James asks, realizing that the mood just changed.

"Those symbols Red drew on the wall before?" Ry starts, and James nods. "Those were for protection. She drew them again today, but Trevan was here, and he explained that they're Fae magic. We have to leave them up, and the five of us need to be here for the protection to work."

"Oh. Wow, that's crazy. How did you discover the symbols? I thought you didn't know you were half Fae until after you'd been drawing those for a while." James' statement and question draw me back into the conversation.

"The Fae elders were trying to communicate with me, but I didn't realize it until last night. I actually talked to them. They didn't mention the symbols, but if my father says that's what they are, then I believe him," I explain.

"So, that's just another piece of the puzzle falling into place. I'm realizing that you were right when you said we each have something to offer and a part to play in this. And I'm sorry it took me so long," James says, pulling me back into his arms.

I sigh against his chest and let him hold me for a minute. "As much as I want to stay here with you guys like this all day, we have a lot to do. And we're running out of time. The Wolf Moon is tomorrow."

I watch their faces as they process what I've just said. We all knew it was close, but I'm not sure anyone was aware of just how close. I'm ready to get this over with, and can't wait to face off with Amber, now that I've spoken with the Moon Goddess and have my mates with me.

Everything is falling into place, and I'm not afraid anymore. Even knowing that I'll have to kill Amber, I'm ready to do what I have to. There are innocent lives on the line, and they're depending on us to save them. I won't let them down. We will win this and save as many lives as we can in the process.

NINETEEN
WOLF MOON

RYLAND

After a restless night and a day that's far too calm, we're as ready as we can be for Amber's attack. I would feel better about it if I knew where it was supposed to happen, but we can't know that. Orym suggests an early dinner, and I insist that it be something light. We can't risk being in a food coma when Amber makes her move.

The family eats in silence, knowing that what's coming is going to be rough. There's no way to know how many lives will be lost. I've sent the families with children away for the day. They'll return tomorrow as long as I let them know it's safe. Otherwise, they'll wait for Kayden to reach out.

When we finish eating, Trevan and Grammy show up. "I'm sorry, daughter, but I must go home now. This is your battle, and I've remained here longer than I should have."

They embrace, and I see the tears she's fighting. I know that Red feels conflicted about her father. She's not sure if she should be sad or relieved that he's leaving. In the Fae realm, he'll be safe from Amber, but it's hard to let someone you care about leave.

If we could win this without her, I would insist that she go with him. Instead, we all hug Grammy when she announces that she's returning with Trevan. "You'll always have a place here," I tell her before letting go.

"I know, Ryland, but there's not much here for me now. My son and grandson are dead. Red has you boys, and I think I could be happy with Trevan." Her sad smile shows that she's not as ready to say goodbye as she wants us to believe.

They walk across the clearing, and Trevan starts to create a portal. Before his magic has a chance to take hold, a blast of blue light hits him in the back. Both he and Grammy are thrown forward as the magic seems to detonate.

"What the fuck?" Luca asks, rushing to jump in front of Red.

She pushes against him, racing toward her father. I stay by her side, unable to let her do this alone. I know what we're going to see before we reach them. Grammy's eyes are open, but unseeing. Blood pours from her head where it banged against the trunk of a tree.

Trevan is lying face down, but he's not moving. Red drops to her knees next to him. She turns him over and gasps, covering her face with both hands. His skull is crushed and he's nearly unrecognizable. And like Grammy, he's dead.

Red's head falls back and she screams at the sky. Her magic swirls around, surrounding us. It's a violent storm that mirrors her emotions. I feel James, Luca, and Orym join us in the center of it, even though I can't see them. This loss just might cripple our mate. Amber has to die. Today.

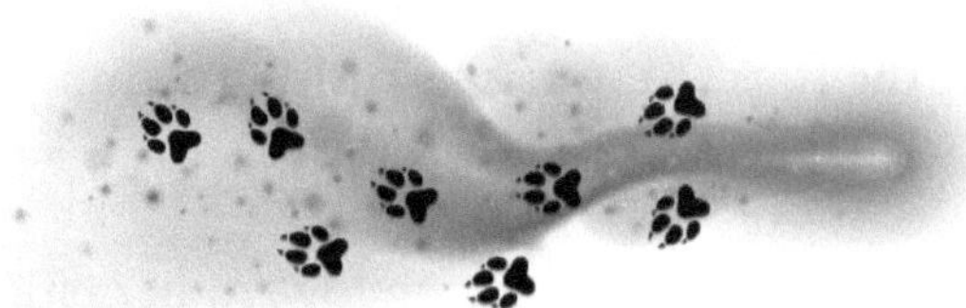

ORYM

Garnet's pain tears through me, joining my own. Grammy was the one constant through all of our lives. She was the territory matriarch, and we all love her dearly. Watching her die breaks my heart. I can't imagine what it does to Garnet. Of course, with our bond, I don't have to imagine it. I feel it. She's not holding back anymore.

Her emotions pour into me, and I feel her devastation. We should have been prepared for this. We should have known that Amber would attack when we were least expecting it. The sun is setting, and Garnet is still screaming. Her magic swirls around us—it didn't hurt rushing through it to get to her. Even if it had, Luca, James, and I would have done it.

Garnet needs us right now, and we will not let her do this alone. I feel my wolf tugging at me. He wants to break free and tear someone in half over this. I can't see the enemy, though. I can't see anything right now, because of the multi-colored magic surrounding us. I'm not sure if it's a shield or a tornado.

It doesn't matter, because I don't have time to think about it. Her magic swirls around us, then slams out away from the center, taking down everything in its path. Trees are uprooted and fall. The cabin shakes, and I wonder if it will remain standing when she's done. I've never seen Garnet do this much with her magic and still be conscious.

She looks stronger than ever, though, dragging herself to her feet and looking around as if she's searching for something. "This way," she growls, marching off into the forest with us jogging to keep up.

"Red, wait," Ryland says, trying to keep her from walking into a trap. She doesn't even slow down, forcing him to keep pace with her.

We step into the trees and hear rustling. A moment later, Garnet holds out an arm and I hear choking sounds as a body is dragged toward us. "You killed my father. And Grammy. Give me one good reason not to end you."

Her words are cold, and before the witch even has a chance to respond, Garnet twists her hand. The crunch of that witch's neck snapping will stay with me forever. I shudder at how easily she took this person's life. I understand the desire for revenge, but I never expected Garnet to give in to it.

I refuse to think less of her, though. She's doing what she has to, and I will support her any way I can. "We can't stay here," Ryland says, trying to usher us back to the cabin.

"We have to. Amber's coming," Garnet responds, her voice even colder than when she spoke to the witch who murdered her family.

"All the more reason to get back where we have cover," he argues.

"I don't need cover. I need her to die," Garnet replies, turning away from him.

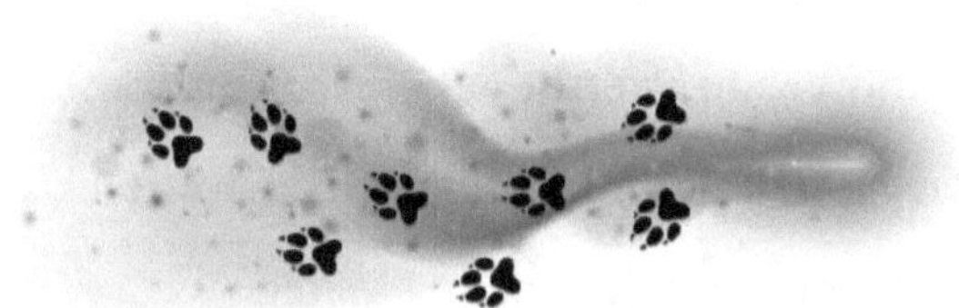

GARNET

When I caught the witch who killed Trevan and Grammy, I went cold. I snapped her neck without a second thought. Now I let the numbness spread through me. I'm not sure I can do this, but I have to. Amber has to die, or we're all doomed. If being numb is the only way to make sure I win, that's what I'll do.

I understand that Ry wants an advantage, but there's no way to get one. Amber sent this woman to kill whoever she could, so that Amber could get to me easier. It could easily have been one of my mates who'd been blown up. And I will not give her a chance to do that again.

I'm not sure how, but I can sense her. I know that she's coming closer, and that she's not alone. I won't let my mates try to shield me or protect me. I'll be the one doing that for them. Almost as an afterthought, I create a dome shaped shield around us. It will alert me if anyone tries to attack and will keep anything magic from hitting my mates.

"She's close," I whisper. Then I turn in the direction I feel her and yell, "Amber! I know you're there. Show yourself."

Her laughter echoes through the trees, and for a moment, I think I've mistaken the direction she's coming from. I turn to see magic hit my shield. It's not Amber's, though. How can I tell that? It's almost as if my power is growing with every step I take. That's not possible, is it? I would ask my father, but I can't. That reminder sends a pain through my heart, and I double over for a moment.

Maybe I should just give up. I've lost so much already. It's going to hurt so badly when I watch my mates die because I'm not strong enough to protect them. The words are in my head, in my voice, but they aren't my words. I see what Amber is trying to do, and I refuse to let it happen. I shake her words away, pushing those doubts aside.

"She's trying to get in our heads. Don't listen to anything she says, even if it sounds like your own voice," I warn my mates. We have to stay strong or she'll win. I can't let that happen. There's too much at stake. Trevan and Grammy didn't give their lives for me to give up now.

I can't help thinking we should have had an army of our own, but it was safer for Ry to send everyone away. I know there are still wolves guarding the village, but most of them are somewhere else, safe with their families. And that's my comfort. If I fail here, it will take her longer to find them. Hopefully she won't.

No. She won't find them, because I'm not going to let her win this. I will defeat her. *Do you hear me, Amber? I will take you out.*

I hear her laugh echo through the trees again, and I know that she can hear me. "Are you scared, Amber? Is that why you're staying so far away?" I don't yell this time, instead, I lower my voice to nearly a whisper. I want her to strain to hear me. I need her to come closer.

"Do you really think your false bravado will defeat me?" she asks, and I know that she's taken the bait. Amber is closer now, and I know exactly which direction she's moving in. As long as I can keep her moving toward us, I'll be able to attack her before she can reach us.

"It can't hurt. Besides, who says it's false? I have every reason to feel confident in my ability to defeat you. I have more power than you do. And you'll never get my power, so there's no way you can win."

A wave of freezing cold washes over us, and I wonder how she got past my shield. Then I realize that I let myself get distracted when I started taunting her. I dropped the shield. *Fuck.* I curse in my head.

Another laugh echoes. "You can't even hold a simple spell while you have a conversation. Tell me again why I should be so scared of you," she taunts me. I mentally kick myself and put my shield back in place.

Then I warm our bubble up enough so that no one ends up with frostbite. "Are you okay?" Luca asks quietly.

I nod. "Are you sure we shouldn't move into the clearing?" Orym asks next.

"I'm sure," I reply. I don't wait for anyone else to distract me further. I start walking toward the direction Amber is coming from. "Come on."

I don't look back to see if they're following; I know they are. They want to take Amber down as much as I do. The moment I have a visual on her, I throw a lightning bolt. It hits next to her feet and she jumps. "Didn't see that one coming, did you?" I ask with a chuckle.

"How did you do that?" she answers my question with a question of her own.

"I'm half Fae, remember?" I shouldn't justify her words with any response, but I do. I need to catch her off guard, and I think this is the only way.

I don't expect her to fight fair, so I'm not surprised when her minions surround us. They can't get past my dome with their magical attacks, so I think we're safe. I know it won't last, and I have to maintain concentration or we'll be vulnerable again.

What I failed to consider was that the witches would attack with physical weapons. When arrows start to fly, I realize that my magical shield isn't going to protect us from that. "Guys, watch out," I warn as I feel another arrow fly past my face.

The tide is turning, and I'm worried.

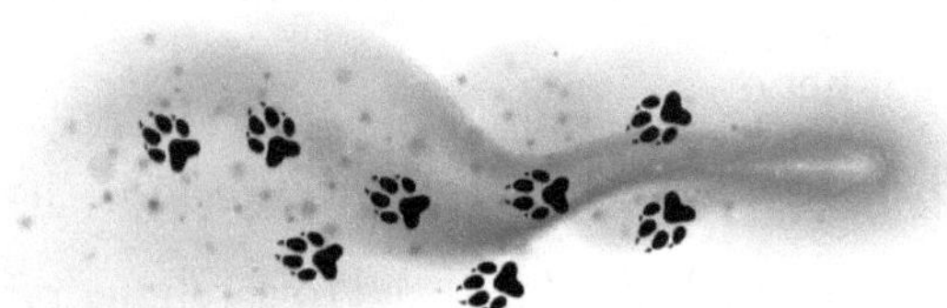

JAMES

When the arrows start to fly past us, my fangs snap into place. There's no magic protecting Amber or her followers from me. Perhaps I can use this blood lust to my advantage. I can smell the witches who surround us. All I need is for one of them to get too close. As far as we know, Amber isn't aware of my change. As long as that's true, we have an advantage. But how do I use it to defeat her?

I'm only going to get one shot here, then they'll know to stay away from me. I can't reach Amber, so it'll have to be one of her followers. It's too bad I don't know who her favorite is. That's who I'd like to go after.

I watch as magic hits near me. Good; Garnet has a shield around us. I'll probably have to step out of it in order to grab this witch, but with my increased speed, that shouldn't be a problem. I'll grab the witch and zip back in the shield before I drain every drop of her essence from her body and throw it at Amber's feet.

I hate the dark urges that course through me, but I understand now why my family trusts me. I don't have those urges toward them. And I'd expected to. Sure, they all smell delicious, and I would love a taste, but I don't have the desire to drain them. Since that's what I was so scared of, I'm feeling much more relaxed now.

Take your time, James. Let her think you're getting tired and you're still a weak human. That's it. Oh, yes, let's trip and stumble. Perfect. I have her attention now. I wait a moment, then dash over and snatch the witch, racing back into the protective bubble. Her scream is cut short by my fangs flashing in her eyes before they sink into her neck.

The metallic tang of her blood coats my tongue and I swallow greedily, sucking her life force out along with her blood. I drink every drop, licking my lips when I finish.

I glance over to see Garnet watching me with lust in her eyes. Who knew my girl is so kinky? I wouldn't have expected her to be the type who likes to watch. My dick twitches as she stares at me. I lick my lips again, making sure to send her an image of exactly what I want to do to her later. She shivers and her cheeks turn pink before she finally looks away.

I raise the body in my arms over my head and throw it at Amber. The dead witch lands at her feet, just as I'd intended. Horror crosses her face for a moment before she masks her reaction. Just as I suspected; she didn't know that I'd been turned.

Part of me feels guilty for killing a woman, but a much darker part enjoyed every second of it.

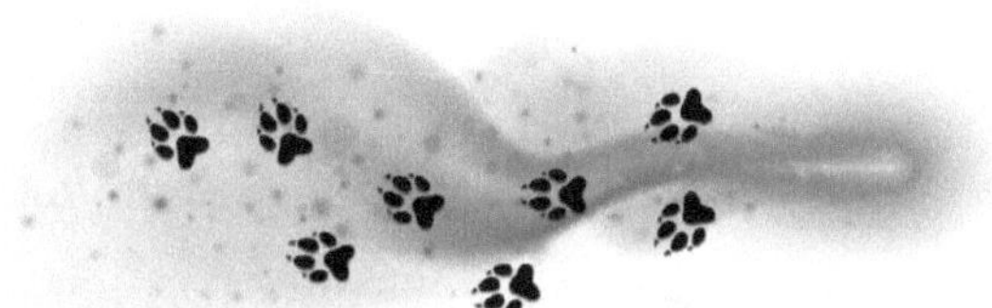

LUCA

I'm not sure which is more disturbing, watching James drain a witch as if he was dying of thirst, or Red's reaction to it. I know she's turned on, and he likes it.

I'll worry about that later, since this bitch is still shooting arrows at me. I've managed to dodge most of them, but a couple have scraped along my arm and leg. Shoving Orym out of the way caused one of those injuries, but I wouldn't have it any other way.

My wolf wants to break free and tear these witches apart. I know that we're supposed to stay close to help boost Red's power, but this is rough. I feel like I'm watching the fight instead of participating in it.

As if I willed it, the witches start closing in on us. If they get a little closer, I'll be able to fight one with my fists, or my claws. *Are we okay to shift, Red? Or do you need us in human form?*

Do whatever you need to in order to survive. Just stay close to me. Her response makes my wolf happy. I wait until one of the witches is close enough to grab, then let the shift happen. My bones crack and reshape until I'm pouncing on the exact witch who's been shooting at me. My teeth rip into her throat, and she's dead faster than I'd hoped.

Am I a monster because I wanted to drag that out? I want Amber and her followers to suffer. I want them to know pain, the same way they've made us feel pain since all of this started.

Once that witch is dealt with, I look around to see that Orym and Ryland have shifted too. Each wolf is tearing into a witch. This is almost too easy. There has to be a catch. Something is coming.

A howl sounds in the distance, and we all turn toward it. "Oh, did you think I would only bring witches to this fight?" Amber's laugh echoes, and she keeps talking. "Silly girl. I brought my new pets. Now, they aren't very pretty, but they are very effective."

A wolf standing upright on its hind legs steps into the clearing. Wait, that's not a wolf. What the fuck is that?

A hybrid. It has to be. "Be careful. We don't know what those things can do," Ryland's voice carries to me, and I realize that he's shifted back. Orym and I are still in wolf form, and I'm glad. I feel like my animal gives me an advantage here.

The beast in front of me attacks, knocking me onto my back and trying to rip out my throat. Something throws it off me, and I manage to get out of the way. I see James dash off. Vampire speed comes in handy.

The beast zips back to me, moving as fast as James did. Now that I can see it clearly, I'm kind of disgusted. It's deformed and looks miserable.

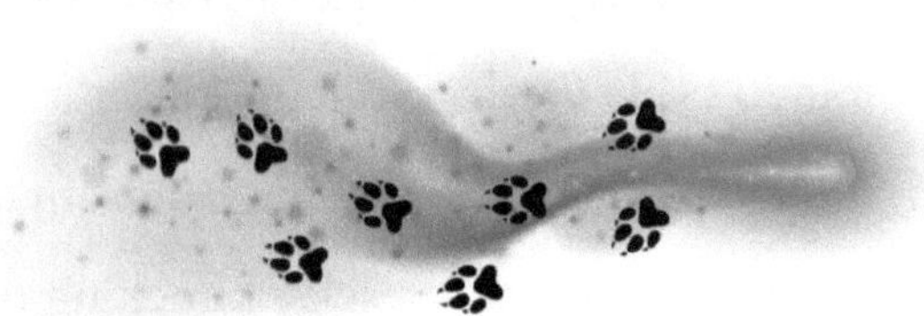

GARNET

When Amber sends in the hybrids, I worry that we're not going to be able to handle this. There are only a dozen or so of them, but that's still more than the five of us. It's especially daunting with Amber and the witches still tossing magic attacks at us while the hybrids pounce. I know it's all designed to distract us so my aunt can get in to position.

Before I realize what's happening, we're backed up against a copse of birch trees that are growing too close together for us to easily climb through. Fuck, how did I not see her maneuvering us into this trap?

With the trees at my back, I watch Ry and Orym take one hybrid down while Luca and James kill another. I zap a third one with lightning. I can't believe Amber managed to trap us like this. I'm pissed at myself for falling for it. She had to have baited us into thinking we were winning so that she could push us this direction.

A yellow glow surrounds us as Amber's witches surround us with a barrier. "Don't touch it," I warn, realizing that it's meant to keep us in while Amber gets into place. Even knowing this is our final stand off doesn't prepare me for this.

I know that she has to perform some ritual in order to kill me and steal my powers, but I never found out exactly what that would look like. I guess I'm about to find out.

"We can't give up now," Ry insists.

"I'm not giving up; I just don't know what to do now. I have no idea how we can get out of this," I admit. It does feel like defeat, but I can't admit that.

"What's wrong, niece? Nothing overly confident to say now? Hmm," Amber taunts. I am shocked that I let this cocky bitch best me. There has to be something I can do to get out of this.

"I honestly have nothing to say to you," I respond. I'd rather ignore her, but I've seen what she does when that happens. I can't afford to risk one of my mates that way.

Amber laughs and walks closer. "That's fine. I'll talk. Then you'll die, and I'll have your powers." She walks closer and my guys circle me protectively. I tighten the magic dome around us, trying to figure out a way to make it physical so that she can't get inside.

She grabs Luca's arm and holds up a syringe. "Now, unless you want to watch your mate turn into one of those," she gestures toward the disfigured hybrids surrounding us, "you'll cooperate and do as you're told."

I can't risk Luca, and she knows it. "Put the syringe away, and I'll come with you. They'll stay here and won't cause any trouble." *Don't fight. This is the only way. Remember that I love you all.*

"That's just as I thought. You're too soft, niece. That's why you'll never defeat me," Amber chides as she puts the syringe back into her pocket and shoves Luca away from her.

I can tell that my mates are confused by what I'm doing. If there was any other way, I would try it. But there's nothing else I can do. Amber can't hurt my mates. Of course, once I'm dead, she'll torture and murder them all. But what choice do I have? I can't let her turn Luca or any of the others into one of those horrible monsters.

Red, you can't do this. If she gets your powers, we're all dead anyway. We have to fight. Ry's voice in my head is laced with terror.

Garnet, please. We can defeat her if we all fight together. James practically begs me not to give up. I don't respond to either of them. I can't.

Red, I love you. I trust you completely, and hope that you have a plan. But if you don't, you know that they're right. Giving up isn't the answer here. Sweet Luca, if only you knew what I'm thinking right now.

I will do whatever you want, Garnet, even if I disagree. Besides, if you're gone, I don't want to live anyway. Orym's silent plea nearly breaks me. Tears stream down my face as I follow Amber to the small clearing where her people have set up for the ritual.

The moon is nearly overhead now, and it's almost time. If she'd fought any longer, Amber would have missed her window. Amber grabs my arm and pulls me close to her. "I don't trust you. So, I'll make this quick," she snarls.

I wrap my arms around my waist, holding myself tightly. I need another minute or two, that's all. She shoves me away and

I drop to my knees, still holding my stomach. I let the tears fall without objection. This is the moment that I've been working for. The moment where two of us start the ritual, and only one can survive.

I already know exactly what's going to happen, but I'm still terrified of the outcome. What if—? I tune out my mates as they continue to try talking me into fighting. I glance over to them, making sure to lock eyes with each of them for a moment. I want to beg them to trust me, but I can't. I need everyone to think I've given up, otherwise there's no chance for this to work.

"Aren't you even going to beg for your life? For the lives of your mates? This is anti-climactic," Amber huffs. I want to laugh at her annoyance, but I concentrate on keeping the tears falling.

The second she turns her back, I jump to my feet, pulling the syringe from my sleeve and plunging it into her neck. "I don't have to beg for our lives, because we're not the ones who are dying today," I say, pushing the hybrid solution into her.

Amber's eyes go wide, she opens and closes her mouth like a fish, then starts to convulse. I blast magic at the hybrids and witches who are guarding my guys, setting them free. They race over to me, watching as my aunt twitches. She falls to the ground and thrashes. Her body starts to change, and I hit her with all of my magic.

She freezes mid-transformation, her flesh melting from her bones, and her bones turning to ash. It's finally over. We've won. The moon shines brightly above us, and I realize that I did it just in time.

EPILOGUE

ONE YEAR LATER

ORYM

Waking up next to my mates and knowing that the danger has passed is a wonderful thing. Being awakened in the middle of the night by screaming because Garnet is having another nightmare? Not so much. With everything we've been through, I know it's going to take some time for everyone to be okay. Hell, James still has nightmares, too, but he refuses to acknowledge them.

It feels like we were so focused on dealing with Amber that our lives got pushed to the wayside. Now that she's gone, and our new cabin is finished, we get to go back to figuring out who we are. Or who we want to be.

Each of us has started to follow our interests. James starts medical school in two weeks. We're all proud of him for that decision. Luca is working with Dec now, learning about woodworking. Ryland is of course, leading the territory. I've been spending time with Eli, indulging my interest in technology.

As for Garnet, she's been spending time in our world and the Fae realm, helping their new leader get settled. She's mastered her powers and is considering starting a school for witches. With Amber gone, there haven't been any uprisings or problems.

I put the final touches on our new security system, then step back and admire my work. Eli slaps a hand on my shoulder. "Good job! Now let's see if it works." He types something on his phone, and I hear footsteps outside. The monitors light up with activity, as Eli's men 'attack' the house.

"FULL LOCKDOWN MODE INITIATED," the automated voice announces. Steel clanks as the security doors slide over the windows and doors, locking us inside and whoever is trying to harm us out.

"It works!" I get a little excited about my first major project. After all, I installed this one myself without Eli's supervision. He insisted on being here when I finished, and I know he'll double check everything. "I can't tell you how much I appreciate your help with all of this."

"You did all the work. It's not easy to learn about this stuff, especially when you live in the forest and have no real sources to work with." Eli's right, I worked really hard to get where I am. But I didn't do it alone.

"Orym! Let me in before the ice cream melts!"

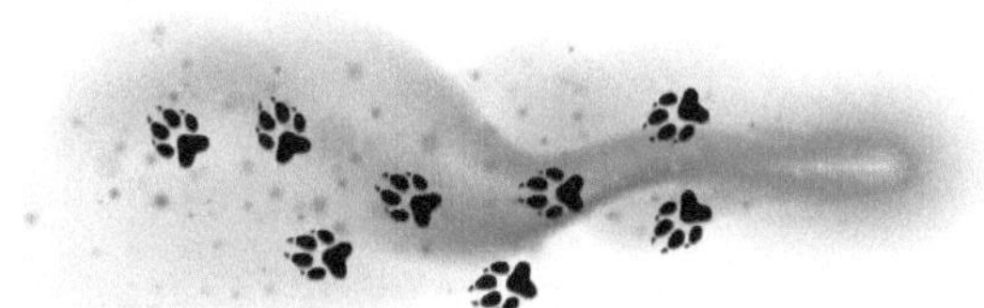

JAMES

I knew the security system test was today, but Garnet was out of her favorite ice cream. I should have waited until later to run to the city and pick it up. But I had pre-admissions testing to do and figured it would be easier doing it all at once.

Now I'm standing outside, trying to figure out how to get into the house while Orym and Eli have a laugh at me. Okay, they're probably not laughing at me, but they're taking forever to let me in.

"FULL LOCKDOWN MODE CANCELED," an automated voice announces. I bet the neighbors will love that from three cabins down.

The steel doors retract slowly, and I dash inside, tucking the ice cream into the freezer before it melts all over. I grab a blood bag while I'm standing there. "That was close. Thanks." I turn to see Orym and Eli walking out of the security room off the living room. "So, we're all set? What if something happens to you? None of us knows how to use the system."

"We'll go over the basics after dinner tonight. Each of you will learn how to arm and disarm the system, as well as how to bring it out of lockdown," Orym says.

"Sounds good. Where is everyone else?" When I left this morning, they were all in various stages of waking and getting ready for their days. Unfortunately, medical school will mean early mornings and late nights for a while. But it will be worth it to have a doctor in the territory.

And with Vik teaching Ryland about running businesses, none of us will actually need to work outside of here. Other than a few wolves supervising the restaurant we bought. But that won't be a huge deal.

I can't believe I've been a vampire for a year now, and I've somehow managed not to lose control and hurt someone unintentionally. I was so terrified that I would, and relieved when I learned about the protection spell for the wolves. It's nice to know that if I kill someone, it will be because I decided to, not because I couldn't stop myself.

"Luca is out back with your brother. They're working on something," Eli responds. "Ryland had a meeting with Vik at Midnight. I'm not sure where Garnet ran off to."

Orym and I exchange a glance. Apparently, he didn't think Eli was paying attention to what's been going on here. I nod and walk out back to see what Luca is doing.

I find him standing over blueprints with my brother hovering nearby. "What's all this?" I call to them.

"We're making a surprise for Red," Luca responds without looking up.

"Good thing she's not here with me, then," I shoot back. Of course, he knew she wasn't. We can sense her, and we'll know if she's in danger, wherever she is.

"I sent her to hang out with Delilah for a while. They were going shopping for decorations."

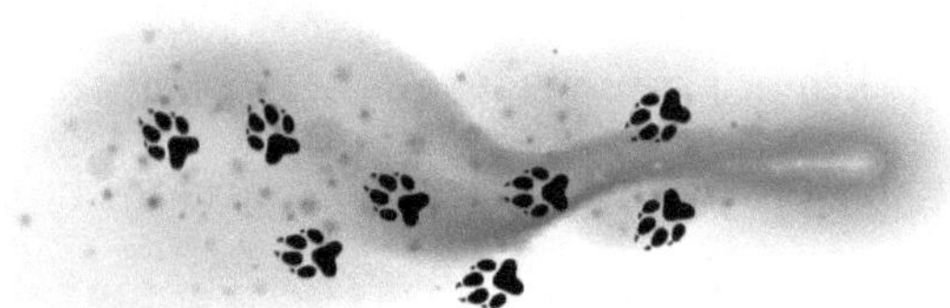

GARNET

Having a day out with Delilah has been amazing. With everything being so busy lately, I haven't seen her much. "What about this one?" she asks, holding up a teal throw blanket. I run my hand over the material.

"Yes! That's perfect." I add it to the list and we keep moving. My list is so long already; I can't imagine any of my guys approving of all this, even if the new cabin is four times the size of the one I destroyed.

Guilt washes over me again at that thought. I destroyed our old home. A year ago today. And yet, no one got mad at me. I'm not sure why that seems strange to me, but it does. And being given carte blanche to decorate the new house is even stranger. I would have expected my guys to be at least a little bit more interested in how the rooms are put together.

"Garnet," Delilah says, grabbing my arm. I grin at her, realizing that she's been trying to get my attention while I'm wallowing in my emotions.

"Sorry," I offer.

"Eli called. He says they're done with the system set up and testing. So, we can go home whenever you're ready. We'll just drop off the list and someone will deliver the items later." It's clear that Delilah doesn't worry about money. I mean, her mates are the wealthiest in the area.

I look at my list again, wondering if I can take a few things off without offending her. We've been shopping all morning, and the list of purchases is very long. I'm not sure we can afford all of it.

"I need to go through my list again before I'm ready," I say quietly.

"No, you don't. Dec was very clear. His sister-in-law gets what she wants to decorate the new house. No limits, no restrictions. Didn't you wonder why no one argued with you picking everything out? He very clearly laid down the law to your mates. And he's insisting that he pays for all of it. Don't fight him on this. You won't win," she warns.

"I had no idea Declan was planning to pay for everything. I can't let him do that," I insist.

Delilah shakes her head. "You don't have a choice. He's going to do it no matter what. You should at least get what you want out of it. And it's not going to hurt us. Just because it was his idea, that doesn't mean I don't fully support it."

I throw my arms around her and hug tightly. "Okay, you win. I won't argue. Let's finish up and head back. We still have to pick towels. That's the only thing we haven't looked at."

Half an hour later, Delilah and I have settled on the perfect towels and turned in my list to the store manager. Someone will gather the items we've selected, and they'll be delivered in a few hours. And Declan will pay for all of it. I can't help feeling a little guilty about that too.

Delilah is right, though. It won't do any good to argue with the vampire who controls a quarter of the city. Hell, this store might even be owned by him. If not, there's a chance that it belongs to Vik or Kayden. Eli tends to stay away from department stores, preferring his tech to housewares.

On our way back to the new house, Delilah and I talk about my selections and where some things will go. We fall into companionable silence after a few minutes and arrive home quickly.

I'm surprised to see delivery trucks already here and unloading. "How did they move so quickly?"

Delilah just laughs as she climbs out of the SUV. I follow her, still trying to figure out how they managed all of this so fast. I also wonder how upset my guys will be when they see everything I got. At least all the blankets are soft, and the pillows are fluffy. Maybe that will help.

"Did you buy out the entire store?" Ry asks, jogging down the steps to meet us. He scoops me up and kisses me hard, turning in a circle.

I slap his arm when he pulls away. "No, we didn't buy out the entire store. I left the ugly stuff there."

He laughs and passes me to Orym. "Hey, you." I kiss him and hug him tightly. These guys act like they haven't seen me in days, but it's only been a few hours.

Not willing to be left out, James drags me out of Orym's arms and kisses me breathless. A girl could get used to this. When he breaks the kiss, I expect Luca to be there waiting. He's not, and I have to hide my disappointment.

"He's working on a surprise for you. Try not to be too upset that he didn't drop everything and head out here to greet you," James whispers in my ear.

"A surprise? What is it?" I ask, not even concerned that James seems to have read my mind. There have been some strange developments with our bond and certain abilities lately. I try not to plan surprises for my mates, because I have lost the ability to keep secrets.

"You'll find out when he's finished with it. Let's go inside and you can show us how much of my brother's money you spent," James answers, turning me back toward the house. I know he's teasing, but I feel a pang of guilt at the cost of everything.

We walk up the steps to the covered wrap-around porch. I show them the patio chairs, tables, and couch I selected, along with the additional set of pillows that can be swapped out. "One set for spring and summer, and another for fall and winter. These will keep us cool, and these will be warmer."

I'm certain that I went overboard, but Delilah pushed me into making sure we had everything we could possibly need.

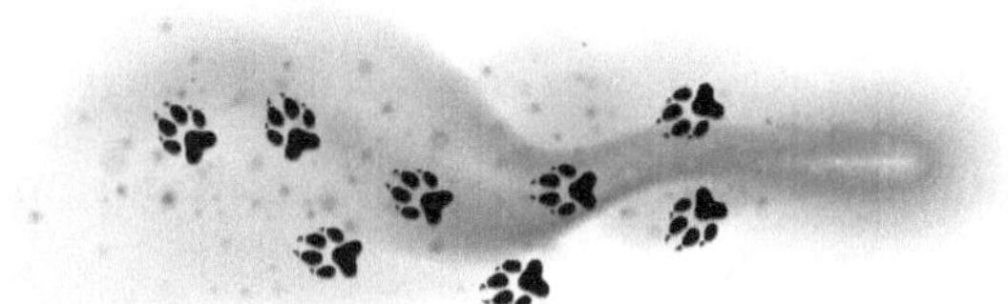

LUCA

Dec and I finish building the swing and hang it on the back porch, then head back to the gazebo. The swing was a last-minute addition to my plan, but I know that Red has always wanted one. The gazebo is a replacement for the picnic table that didn't survive the fight with Amber.

Red has been feeling guilty for destroying the house and everything around it, so we all decided that we'd do something special for her to ease her mind. The porch swing will easily hold all five of us, and I was able to get Delilah to order cushions to match what Red got for the front porch.

The gazebo is large enough that we can have most of the territory over and everyone can sit under it. Dec and I built cozy furniture to go under it. We finish setting it up and I head inside to grab everyone for the big reveal.

I know that Red got back a little while ago, and she was disappointed I didn't greet her. I had to finish this, but I was disappointed too. Now I'm excited to see what she thinks of my surprise.

"Red! Where are you?" I call as I run into the house. She jumps when I yell, and I see that she was closer than I'd expected. "Sorry. I got excited." I laugh and hold my arms out for her to hug me. Red runs and jumps into my arms, kissing me until I nearly forget why I came inside.

When she breaks the kiss, she asks, "So, what's this about a surprise?"

I laugh again. "That's why I came to get you. But I want to show everyone at the same time, okay?"

She rolls her eyes, but waits until I get everyone together and follows me outside. "This is half your surprise," I say, gesturing to the swing.

"Luca! It's beautiful! And the cushions match the set out front. How?" She's amazed and I'm relieved. I'd been worried that she wouldn't like it.

Delilah nudges me and laughs. "I told you she'd appreciate that."

"Here's the rest of it," I say, grabbing her by the shoulders and turning her to look out into the back yard.

"Oh, Luca!" she says, then runs down the back steps to check out the gazebo. The deep red flowers of the Clematis vines contrast against the white pine we used for the structure. I can't tell if she loves it or hates it from her reaction.

"Well?" I ask, following her down to stand next to it.

"How did you guys do this in one day? This wasn't here yesterday. It's amazing," she gushes. Relief washes over me. I was so worried that she'd hate it. I'd prepared myself for having to tear the whole thing down.

"Dec helped me. And of course, he has a crew for this kind of thing. But I did most of the carving myself."

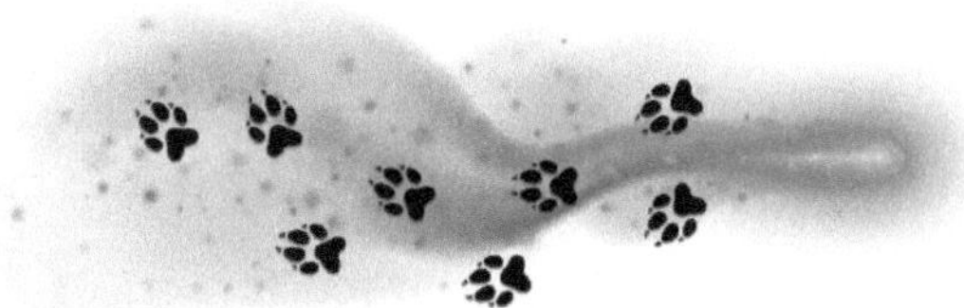

RYLAND

With Luca's surprise, Red decides we have to eat outside tonight. No one minds, and we all work on dinner together. The kitchen is full and chaotic, with Vik and Kayden showing up just before we're ready to eat. The ten of us gather under the new gazebo, eating and chatting. Laughter echoes through the forest, and for once, no one is worrying about what's coming for us next.

Tonight will be our first night in the new house. We've been staying at Luca's cabin because it's the closest to the new one. I'd hardly call this a cabin, though. Sure, it looks like one, but it's two stories tall and has a basement.

The first floor has the kitchen, pantry, security room, living room, spare bedroom, and a bathroom. The top floor is our master suite. It's the largest bedroom/bathroom combination I've ever seen, and I can't wait to make full use of it.

We'll have family time first, because Red is still concerned about everything. She's trying to take care of everyone and ensure that Declan knows how much we appreciate all of their help. What she doesn't know is that he only paid for the furnishings and décor because he insisted on it. The poor girl has no clue what kind of accounts I have access to now that I'm the territory alpha.

Just because Gunnar chose to force the entire territory to live as meagerly as possible, that doesn't mean we don't have resources. I wasn't aware of most of them until Eli stepped in and helped Orym research Gunnar's computer. And we didn't bother with that until six months ago, when we were starting to rebuild the cabin.

I wonder how Red will take the news that we have almost as much money as the family that controls the city. I can't wait to show her the bank statements. Tomorrow morning. Not tonight. Tonight is for family.

I realize that's what we've become. Delilah and her mates, along with the five of us, have become a chosen family. I sit back and watch as they joke around and enjoy what we've built here. Life couldn't get any better than it is right now.

Goddess knows we all sacrificed enough to get here, and we won't soon forget those who gave their lives in the fight. That's what makes me even more determined that we'll make something happy here.

I've invited the previous members of the council to meet next week to discuss forming a new council with extra layers of security. I want to prevent what we went through last year from ever happening again. Who knows if our family will grow in the future? But if it does, I want to be sure the territory is protected for generations to come.

We break ground on Red's magic school next week, and things will be even more hectic. I'm determined to enjoy what I can while I have the opportunity. Our lives are full now.

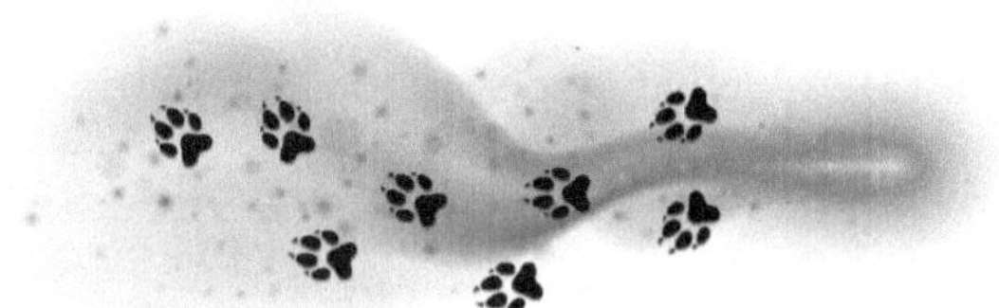

GARNET

Once Delilah and her mates leave, Ry finally lets me go upstairs and see the master suite. These guys have been so secretive about the whole thing. I don't know what to expect. What I do know is that our lives are about to get crazy.

Each of us has our own project that will take up a large chunk of time. We're going to have to work hard to make time for our family. I know we can do it; I just hope everyone is on board.

Luca covers my eyes as James leads me up the stairs to the second level. Ry and Orym rushed ahead of us to 'get things ready' and I'm honestly a little nervous what that means. Am I walking into a sex dungeon that has whips and chains on the walls? Since this is the one room I haven't been allowed inside, it was difficult to pick out decorations.

I suspect that Delilah had seen it, though, because she made suggestions. I guess I'm about to find out. I take a deep breath as they lead me across the threshold.

"Okay, open your eyes," Ry says, and Luca's hand falls away. The room is spectacular. The walls are a pale teal and will go perfectly with the throw Delilah suggested. The dressers and bed are hand carved wood, and I can tell that Luca worked with Declan to build them.

"It's perfect!" I exclaim, turning around and taking in every inch of the room. I walk over to one of the windows and look outside. I can see the back yard and into the forest from here. One of my guys clears his throat, and I turn around.

Standing in front of me are four gorgeous men, completely naked. "That escalated quickly," I tease, looking my fill. Each of their cocks responds to my attention, even if I'm not touching them yet. Seeing the way they look at me has me soaked.

I want to rip my clothes off and jump on all of them. But I also want our first night in the new house to be memorable. So, I decide to move painstakingly slow, taking one step toward them and stopping. I lick my lips and Ry groans. I can tell that they're barely holding themselves back. "What's wrong, boys?" I teas again. Part of me hopes they'll decide they've had enough torture and will take control.

I ease out of my jeans, folding them carefully and placing them on an oversized chair by the window. Luca growls, and I know that I'm testing them too much. I can't help it; I'm having fun with it. It's been so long since we've felt safe, and I'm going to enjoy it.

I slowly peel the rest of my clothes off and take my time folding them and stacking everything on the chair. Just as I finish, strong arms wrap around me from behind and I fly across the room, landing on the bed. I squeal and giggle.

My four mates stalk toward me, eyes filled with lust. The way they get into position around me convinces me that they planned this out to the most minute detail. James sprawls next to me on his back. Luca grabs my legs, Orym grips under my arms, and they lift me on top of James. Ry stands back and watches, as if he's orchestrating the whole situation.

It seems like they all enjoy taking turns watching, but tonight I want all four of them. I'll have to make sure he's involved if he doesn't do it himself. Orym hands Luca a small bottle, and the lube is cold as he rubs it on my ass to prepare me for James. I manage to catch a glimpse of Luca stroking James as he spreads lube on my vampire's cock. They ease me down onto James as Luca positions himself above me. He waits until I've taken James all the way before Luca starts to slide into me.

I moan with pleasure at how full I feel as they stretch me. Reaching for Orym with one hand, I motion for Ry to join us with the other. When I have their hard dicks in my hands, I finally feel complete. James and Luca set a punishing pace as they fuck me hard and fast.

I stroke Ry and Orym, slipping one into my mouth, then the other, until they're panting as hard as I am. Luca and James change pace, one thrusting in as the other pulls almost all the way out, then alternating. They start moving so slowly, I want to beg them for more. But my mouth is busy with two cocks thrusting inside at the same time now. Thrusts increase in speed until I feel like I'm being battered from all sides, in the best way.

With all four of my men inside of me, it doesn't take long for me to come. I cry out with my release, setting them all off at once. I can't swallow fast enough and end up with cum dripping down my face. I feel James throb inside my ass as he finds his release. Luca slams into me, filling me at the same time.

I'm sated and happy and could fall asleep right now. Before I have the chance, someone carries me into the master bath, and turns on the shower.

The five of us fit in the oversized shower easily. Ry washes my hair while Orym cleans my body. I let them care for me this way, then I take my time washing every inch of each of them. Once we're clean and dried off, Luca carries me to the bed and tucks me in. Ry, Orym, James, and Luca crawl into bed with me.

I fall asleep satisfied and hopeful for the future. We've learned so much over the past year and a half. I know that we can get through anything as long as we stick together.

What Next?

If you enjoyed this book, please consider writing a review. Indie authors, even those with indie publishers, can only thrive if word of their books gets out into the world. Reviews matter. They don't have to be overly detailed, just a sentence or two about what you enjoyed.

Thanks for reading!

ABOUT THE AUTHOR

M.P. Starkweather is a wife, mother, author, poet, casual online gamer, self-proclaimed fan-girl, and full-time nerd. She writes free-form poetry, paranormal romance, sci-fi romance, reverse harem romance, and is branching out into contemporary romance. In her free time, she enjoys writing, reading, Dungeons & Dragons, table top games with her husband and friends, and playing with her son. M.P. also enjoys tv, movies, and music across various genres.

To get the most up-to-date information about her latest releases and book signings, check out www.mpstarkweather.

com or follow her on your favorite social media site.

ALSO BY M.P. STARKWEATHER

Anthology – Contemporary RH

Blemished Beauty Anthology

Femme Fatale Freakshow – Shared World – PNR RH

Taking It Off

Standalones - Contemporary RH OV

Cold Princes

Knot My Valentine

The Pack Next Door – Contemporary RH OV series

Princess or Knot

Fiancée or Knot

www.ingramcontent.com/pod-product-compliance
Lightning Source LLC
Chambersburg PA
CBHW030018060826
49398CB00031B/140

* 9 7 8 1 9 6 5 3 5 1 1 3 0 *